PRAISE FOR THE WORK OF MARK MCGINN

I really liked ***Presumed Guilty***. It was a great page-turner, where McGinn drew me in well and made sure I really wanted to know how the legal case would turn out (had Sasha's ex done it or not? where would the verdict fall, regardless?). The character of Sasha Stace is fascinating. Very human - she makes mistakes, has doubts and is affected by her past. She is a character that is easy to follow and empathise with. Overall I found ***Presumed Guilty*** to be a really engaging read that was a pleasant surprise: a top quality Kiwi legal thriller. I'll definitely be going back to read the other Sasha Stace books.

—CRAIG SISTERSON,
Founder and Judge of NZ Ngaio Marsh Crime Awards

Sasha is a memorable, well-rounded character who has an admirable moral core, despite many pressures thrust on her with her new case. The plot is pacey, and the courtroom scenes are particularly engaging. This was a page-turner with plenty of twists and turns that I devoured to the end. It was refreshing to have a novel of this calibre set in New Zealand – I thoroughly enjoyed the local settings. ***Presumed Guilty*** is definitely to be recommended.

—KAREN MCMILLAN,
author of *The Paris of the West.*

McGinn's private investigator novel, ***Deceit***, is dark, gritty and intense and his style is taut and atmospheric. ***Deceit*** delivers action, suspense and an insider's look into politics, law and life 'Down Under'. It's most highly recommended.

—JACK MAGNUS,
Readers' Favorite

A resident of Sydney, Clay Tempero, (**Deceit**) introduced in McGinn's *Trust No One* (2013), would be right at home anywhere as a PI who doggedly pursues a case while wrestling with his own demons or rocky past. McGinn knows his way around the legal system and genre conventions. He also has a facility for the odd turn of phrase: cocaine usage is described as 'vacuuming with straws'.

—*KIRKUS REVIEW* 2014

Really enjoyed **Trust No one**. Felt as though I was in Sydney, and the plot and characters are really absorbing and convincing. It passed my 'want to stay up late and keep reading test' and looking forward to reading more by this author and in this series.

—J JOHNSTON 2020

Trust No one is an intriguing mystery set against the backdrop of Sydney. Sharp and witty dialogue, and memorable characters.

—*ROCKING GREAT READS*, 2015

Perfect Cover is a suspenseful, alarming, spine chilling horror, thriller short story (book). Very well written. Never a dull moment from start to finish. Make another great scary movie or TV series. Very easy for me to give the short story (book) 5 stars.

—TONY PARSONS MSW (Washburn)

A nice balance of court room drama and conflict outside the court, **Best Served Cold** has lots of really interesting characters. The story reminded me of the "Underbelly" series. Great to see Christchurch, New Zealand as the setting.

—*ROCKING GREAT READS*, 2015

Best Served Cold has a great plot and cast of characters. A tightly written story that gripped me all the way to a terrific ending.

—PAUL THOMPSON,
journalist and editor, *Fairfax Media*

HOME TRUTHS

MARK MCGINN

STORY GRID
A STORY GRID EDITION: 0004
STORY GRID PUBLISHING LLC

Story Grid Publishing LLC

223 Egremont Plain Road

PMB 191

Egremont, MA 01230

Edited by Rachelle Ramirez

Cover Artwork by John Coulthart

Cover Design by Natalie C. Sousa

Interior Design by Natalie C. Sousa

First Story Grid Publishing Paperback Edition August 2021

For Information About Special Discounts for Bulk Purchases,

Please visit www.storygridpublishing.com

ISBN: 978-1-64501-070-8

Ebook: 978-1-64501-140-8

Although this is a work of fiction, many fellow Cantabrians, and others, still live in the hope of insurance justice after experiencing devastating earthquakes in 2011. Ten years on, this story is dedicated to those who died with those hopes vanquished as well as those still in insurance battles, who, more than anyone, understand the maxim, justice delayed is justice denied.

ACKNOWLEDGMENTS

Thanks to all at Story Grid Publishing and in particular Shawn Coyne, author of *The Story Grid: What Good Editors Know,* who also trained me in this analytical approach to editing and writing.

I also want to acknowledge and thank US editors, Rachelle Ramirez, Leslie Watts, Anne Hawley, Celeste Sharpe, and my New Zealand editor since I began writing, Anna Rogers. This story would not be in its present form without their invaluable input and support. To Rachelle, a special thank you for her superb editorial questions, guidance, and great humor, which were sources of additional encouragement.

My thanks also to Nathan Blackwell a New Zealand cop turned crime writer who helped with answering my questions and to the late Peter Temple, one of Australia's greatest crime writers whose work inspired me to write this story.

Last, but by no means least, I am always grateful to Ena for her love, support, and robust willingness to question something in a manuscript in the service of clear writing.

HOME TRUTHS

FRIDAY, 6 JULY 2012
23.30 HOURS

Without crime, I'm out of a job, which is why I don't hate offenders. Some come close, though, like ex-cop and fraudster Rachel Trix. If I had a hate list, she'd be on it. She's the reason my letter of resignation sits in my desk drawer, but she's also the reason why I haven't given it to DI Fergus Dowling.

"We'll get her," he says, at least three times a week. "Someone will give her up."

His prediction is the only thing I can recall the boss being optimistic about.

I'm at my desk, several floors up at Christchurch Central, the biggest and busiest police station in the city. Although with a near empty squad room, no one would notice that. Ever since the Port Hills fault line erupted through the middle of the city, hundreds of aftershocks keep reminding us of the devastation. They give other detectives reason to wheedle more civilized hours into their roster, going out for coffee and sandwiches while avoiding the most damaged station in the city as often as they can.

I'm triaging new inquiry files for the allocation of staff

when Dowling's voice punctures my concentration. He's in his glass fishbowl office, staring at the wall.

"Are you certain?" he asks the caller. "Say something that assures us this is genuine."

He listens, nods to himself then faces me.

I mouth the name Trix, realizing a single syllable may not be easy to read.

He holds up a thumb.

I walk to the windows facing Hereford Street. Outside, steady rain glows in the ghost town streetlights. The city's central business district is a red zone, cordoned and inaccessible to everyone except authorized personnel in emergencies and health services. The army bolsters our ability to enforce the zone and reduce crime in the area.

From behind me, the sound of clapping hands. Dowling says, "Right. Got her."

He exits his office looking more alive than he has in the last week, two weeks, even. He puts his blue suit coat on like he's going somewhere.

"Credible intel on Trix," he says, gray eyebrows riding up.

"Not another piss-take?" I ask.

A head shake. "More detailed."

"Who?"

"Won't say." His face says this doesn't matter.

I frown and drop my chin.

"Hang on, Solly. This was a woman. Not some Friday night pisshead with nothing better to do than laugh with his mates at our expense. From the voice, I'm picking a mature woman, maybe forties, no discernible accent."

I look up and ask, "What makes it credible?"

"The person knows someone who knows Trix. After three

weeks, Trix believes the heat's off but she won't risk the airport. She's leaving by water."

"Coming from where?"

"The informant says west of the city, eastbound. Early hours."

I say, "She used to live in Governor's Bay."

He nods. "The territory of her escape route is her comfort zone. She's clever. Given she would anticipate our awareness of it, she might consider the northern beaches, which means we need to seal off the motorway and Marshland Road before she reaches the various beach towns up the coast."

"I agree."

"Which do you want?" he asks.

"Me?"

He draws his head back. "Have I missed something? You've had a hangdog expression ever since she skipped bail."

"Been a long day, boss," I say, looking at my watch, unable to meet his gray-blue eyes.

"And?"

I rub my forehead, summoning the will to effect eye contact. "Well, obviously I want her behind bars. Right?"

He stares at me.

I say, "But this is a job for uniforms."

"I don't get it," he says. "I thought you'd be on fire for this. You'll have uniform support."

"Domestic issues, boss. A difficult matter to deal with. I..."

He interrupts, "You know I'm not unsympathetic about that stuff, especially after what I've been through. But I need your knowledge of her and your determination on this. We can put something to rest here."

What Dowling means is this is my shot at redemption.

As the officer responsible for her prosecution file, various people looked at me sideways when Trix got bail on the robbery charge. Some think a judge sympathetic to her plea was less relevant than my preparation for court. Hence the resignation letter in my desk drawer.

"Okay," I say. "What's her ETD? Do we know?"

He slaps me on the arm. "Around one a.m. she'll be traveling down Blenheim Road in a Chev Blazer, black. I suggest you station yourself on Moorhouse. I'll find someone else for the beaches north of the city.

"Will EAGLE support us?"

"Of course. I'll get a uniform sergeant to organize blocks and spikes at both points and keep the boss informed."

What else can I say?

Dowling looks around, rakes his hands through thick gray hair. "I thought Nick Jarvis was on tonight?"

"He's getting a coffee."

"No problem. Take him. He's as keen as you are to lock her up."

The boss remembers everything. Nick arrested Trix when she first went off the rails.

He says, "Take 239." He's referring to the unmarked police vehicle. "In park seven. I'll call the boss, invite her to come to the comms center. That's where I'll be."

SATURDAY, 7 JULY 2012
00.30 HOURS

I stop and park the unmarked near our broken city's woodland recreation area known as Hagley Park. We're close to the middle of the city. Detective Nick Jarvis and I wait for Trix, unsure whether she will take our route or choose the northern beaches.

Nick, curious and normally talkative, hasn't spoken in ages. I realize I'm jiggling a leg, looking at the speaker in the car, willing it to give us some news, a development.

Nick breaks the silence. "I shoulda checked the box for Glocks."

Trix once owned a homemade gun, which surprised us. It didn't fit her acquired skill at the time—ripping off the elderly.

"Well..." I say, drawing out the word, "minimal prep time here. But in the unlikely event we'll need weapons, we can get them from the uniform cars."

"So, if this is a straightforward interception, why do we need the chopper?"

"Bit of luck," I say. "EAGLE can tell us to go home, that she's gone north."

The car jolts like we've hit an unseen hole in the road

followed by a gentle movement of the car wheels backward and forward. Except, it's not the wheels, but the ground underneath them. We glance at each other, neither of us saying anything. The aftershocks are still commonplace.

When we've stopped moving for a few seconds, I say, "I'm okay about extra precautions. Trix understands where we sniff, what we do."

He nods.

"Without Inspector Dowling's tip, we could still be looking. If she comes our way, car yard alley will be ideal. Only one intersection to block."

He doesn't respond. The orange glow of streetlights above us settles on his face. He's picking at his nails and biting his lips.

"Good to go, Nick?"

"Yes, boss." He drops his head. "Sorry about the firearms."

"Take the lesson," I say, words often delivered to me by Dowling. "We'll have other options."

"Thanks, boss," he says, a tone of gratitude. "When are we going to carry routinely? Not carrying is crazy. We've had all the training."

His frustration bounces around the car's interior.

"I don't like politics any more than you," I say. "I don't think it will help this time 'round. Trix is more cunning than violent. Before I locked her up last time, she got my password, other things too. Like bugging my phone."

He appears thoughtful. "Every move you make, every step you take."

"Sting's got a lot to answer for," I say, wondering how long we will sit here and wait for action.

The windscreen is streaky with rain, and while few cars

and no people are about, I flick the wipers for a clearer view for oncoming traffic. Not checking the car for weapons would be nothing in comparison to missing a Chev Blazer coming our way.

I flip the wipers again and add, "My point is, mistakes are easy to make. As a cop, you're either right or wrong. Accept that, and move on. In my experience, dwelling on what-ifs isn't productive." I turn and face him. "Speaking of productivity, any repairs done at your place yet?"

He shakes his head, looks disconsolate. "My apartment's still unlivable. Back with Mum and Dad. They're on their second quake assessment. I helped them challenge the first one."

"You'll be racing me to the bottom of the list."

"What list is that, boss?"

"Customers marked, 'difficult complainer.' People placed in a black insurance maze, no help to escape. How are your folks getting through a second winter without repairs?"

He rubs a finger over a crack in the surface of the console between us. It resembles a knife wound. "Giving all the assistance I can, without invalidating the policy—sealant around window gaps, minor patch-ups. Got rid of the last of the liquefaction on the weekend."

"After seventeen months?"

"Aftershocks threw up more sludge and I'm the only capable laborer in the street. Plus, I helped a dozen neighbors. Huge lots, some of them. The whole street's buggered."

I pat his knee. "Fantastic work. I'm sure your efforts are much appreciated."

He slides a hand over where I touched him, glances at me, says nothing. Shit, has he taken something from that?

"What's your situation, boss?"

"As I said before, complain, and you race others to the bottom of a long list."

"How's your partner coping with all the quake problems?"

"Sorry, Nick. I shouldn't start a personal conversation. Let's keep it business." He looks unsure how to respond. "Okay?"

"Sure, boss. No problem."

Fergus Dowling's cigarette voice rattles through the speaker: "DI Dowling to CHC. Over."

I reach for the handset. "Copy, boss."

"Sitrep, Solly," he says.

"Zero activity. Maybe she's taking the alternative northern route?"

"Bit soon to tell. What's your exact location and personnel?"

"Detective Jarvis is with me as you suggested, boss." Nick's wide smile returns. "We are at Lincoln and Moorhouse. I can confirm arrival of the canine unit. Will EAGLE support us?"

Silence.

Eventually, Dowling says, "Auckland reports EAGLE's been diverted to a higher priority job. You and Jarvis proceed to the interception point where you'll take control."

"Any unmarked backup behind the offender?"

"I'll see what I can do but resources are stretched."

Challenging Dowling about the chopper's diversion and resourcing in front of Nick wouldn't be right. I accelerate away.

Nick says, "You okay with this, boss?"

"My guess is Commander Hockley's all over our inspector, chewing his ear about budget overruns. She's ambitious, looking for more silver on her shoulders."

"You reckon we should continue?"

I respond to the doubt in his tone and say, "What's the bet

some bloody window peeper gets the chopper ahead of a fugitive ex-cop? However, if she comes our way, we'll manage."

We drive across the Moorhouse and Fitzgerald intersection and move toward the tire-puncturing spikes uniforms laid across car-yard alley. This stretch of the road on both sides is full of cars for sale. Bulky orange barriers used post-quakes still dominate the landscape. Beyond the spikes, two uniform vehicles straddle the middle of three possible routes ahead for Trix, making six cars in all, each with two cops.

"Excellent setup here," I say. "Once she's in the trap, we flick on the red and blue everywhere, light the place up like Christmas. With uniforms behind her, Trix can't reverse out."

"Rain's not helpful," he says, frowning.

"I agree, but with no opportunity for her to flee, it shouldn't be a safety factor."

I stop the car. The weather and absent chopper are not our only problems. One of the car yards, right on the intersection, is no longer covered by used vehicles for sale. Only the low-slung chains across the lot's frontage remain. "Where've all the cars gone?" I ask.

Nick asks, "Can we add cars and spikes across the frontage?"

"No time to get them here from home base without Trix noticing the urgent action. Go to the uniform senior, sign for a Glock." I point to the block wall on the west side of the empty lot. "You'll be stationed over there on the southwest corner, Nick, in case she abandons her car and runs through."

Nick exits the car, wraps himself in his arms, and hunches against the weather, looking old as his warm breath steams into the night.

Dowling radios again. "Solly, your rear backup is gone, T-boned en route. No injuries, a small mercy."

"Copy, boss." I think about repositioning one of the two blocking cars inside the vacant car lot. Although, if Trix notices only one car ahead of her instead of two, we appear less formidable and she might decide to charge, crash, and run. So, I leave them.

Nick returns and straps his holster on. He puts a worried face through the gap in the open car door. "Boss, if you knew before we started where we've got to, would we still be here?"

The pulse in my temple thuds. He might be right. I'm the one in the control tower. I could call this off, lose a criminal fugitive, waste the overtime involved, and possibly cause problems for Dowling with Hockley. "Can't do this job in the rear-view mirror. We're expected to cope with what the brass calls 'unfolding situations.'"

"Yes, boss," he says, unconvinced.

"Not everything's against us, Nick. She's not expecting us to be here. With no other traffic around, we can fully commit our manpower to Trix. Who'd be mad enough to be out on a winter night at this time, eh?" I force a smile.

I hear the call sign from a uniform's car. "She's heading your way, boss."

"ETA?"

"Less than two minutes."

Everyone in the team reacts. Nick strides off to the block wall. Other officers take positions, ready to whisk spikes away from in front of our vehicles and pursue Trix if she abandons and runs. I exit the car and wait for the Chev to approach. It stops at a red, plate number, PUTIS. I estimate three hundred yards of travel to the road block. If she spots the trap and attempts to flee on foot, we'll have the dog unit behind her.

Green light. The Chev approaches but the tinted windows offer no view inside the vehicle.

I lean into our car, grab the handset, and radio the cars blocking her way ahead. "Give her fifty yards of travel before you flash her."

Trix doesn't reduce speed. She accelerates down the centerline of the road. At the empty car lot on Lancaster Street, she veers right, a sudden movement like the total collapse of all the vehicle's steering mechanisms. The Chev mounts the pavement and crashes explosively through the chain, violently ripping it from the pole securing it. Nick's out from the safety of the block wall, gun barrel vertical, face of pure terror.

I scream, "Jump, Nick!"

He dives back to the wall but the Chev slams into him. The force of the collision lifts him above the roof, and he lands behind the Chev.

I sprint toward him. The Chevrolet brakes hard, red lights like rats' eyes in the dark. Nick, prostrate on the cold ground, is five yards from the left rear of the vehicle. I crouch and imagine life leaking from his limp body.

"Fire!" I yell to the cops behind me. "*Fire!*"

But I'm between my team and the Chev's fat wheels.

The engine roars. Red lights change to white. No more than twenty feet away, she angles the car at me. I dive left and roll. The vehicle reverses over Nick's head, causing a sickening sound of breaking bones, like eggshells being crushed.

Bullets ping off the nearby concrete, and the reverse lights vanish. Trix, a shadow in a cap, reaches to the passenger side and leans out with a long-barreled firearm aimed at my head. So close now. How can she miss?

SATURDAY, 7 JULY 2012
02.30 HOURS

I pace in an overheated interview room, waiting for the two Professional Conduct cops. They want my account of how a straightforward interception turned to complete shit and the death of one of our own.

I drop into a gray plastic chair and my pull sleeves to the elbow, my forearms electrified with tension. I stare at last month's *Ten One* police mag, unable to take anything in. I keep it because page five shows a posed picture of me inside one of our fleet. The caption: "Detective Jonah Solomon's first day as sergeant." The subtext could've been: "Equal opportunities failure. Māori takes ten times longer than anyone else to be promoted."

My head protests a hangover, not from booze but lack of water. I gulp from an overused bottle, the plastic well past the shrivel and death stage.

An inspector in a brown suit enters the room, squinting like a pest control manager on the hunt. With large earlobes and a patch of white in his rusty hair, he resembles a spaniel. His offsider is a fat detective whose round face is so pockmarked he looks more like a golf ball.

They introduce themselves and bring the recording system to life. Before they speak, I tell them I'm responsible for stationing Nick Jarvis where he was murdered.

The spaniel holds up his left hand, well-tended nails and a gold band on his ring finger. "I see no Police Association rep with you. And you're also entitled to take a break for…"

"I've been on shift for seventeen hours, Inspector. My written statement's in front of you, prepared with local delegate oversight. I can't add to it as far as what happened in Lancaster Street, and while I want to go to bed at some stage, I also want this over."

"We're interested in the leadup to the murder. How you and Jarvis came to be on the case."

"You know about Trix's history?"

The golf ball opens a manila folder and mumbles.

I say, "You need to speak up, son. I'm already bone tired without you sending me to sleep."

The two investigators glance at each other. The golf ball says, "I'm the same rank as you, Detective Sergeant Solomon."

"How enlightening. I realize this is not personal, and you'll give me the usual crap about doing your job, but no matter what you say in this situation, you guys are the enemy. Right?"

The spaniel says, "I don't think your comment is appropriate, Detective Sergeant. Do you?"

"You can assume an affirmative. Sorry for offending your sensibilities, Inspector."

The golf ball speaks again. "Trix did half of her three-year term of imprisonment for fraud and was paroled. You were the arresting officer. Correct?"

"I was. You guys know she's skipped bail on another charge since being let out of jail. Right?"

The spaniel says, "We're trying to gain an understanding of how the various players are connected."

"I lost one of my colleagues tonight. Maybe I'm the one who's a little oversensitive, but there are no players or game here I can see."

The golf ball says, "It appears it took the best part of a year after the fraud complaints were made before Trix was arrested. Is that right?"

"When you're dealing with elderly victims, nothing unusual there. Some of those old folk never saw justice done."

Neither man reacts.

I add, "When Trix was off the meth, she was smart, a capable cop. It wasn't until she was in prison I discovered she accessed my PC and inserted a listening device inside my phone. When we thought we had traction, we ended up losing ground. We're not dealing with some criminal dunce here. She was about to be promoted when I locked her up."

The inspector raises a file, assumes a studious expression. "While on parole, in fact, two months after Trix was released, you arrested her for robbery?"

"The Bank Secure job."

The golf ball frowns. "Says here it was a cash van, not a bank."

I knuckle both eye sockets, feeling the grit. "Is this a reading and comprehension exercise, gentlemen? I did say I was tired. Didn't I?"

The spaniel says, "We're all tired at some stage. In my experience, an efficient answering of questions speeds up a tiresome process."

"Bank Secure was the name of the transporting company," I say. "Trix was a co-offender. Nick Jarvis arrested her under my direction. And yes, she got bail despite our strong opposition. As I said, she hasn't honored it and should never be free."

"So, during your inquiry, she deceived you for a long time, conned the parole board into thinking she was a good citizen, did only half her sentence, got bail. How did you feel about her?"

"Best mates. Why wouldn't we be?"

"Who's overseen getting her back into custody?"

"Nick."

"Under your direction?"

"Correct."

The inspector leans back in his chair, joins his hands behind his head. "Missing for two months?"

"The greater part of seven weeks. I'm sure I don't have to say returning her to jail hasn't been our only case. Sir."

The golf ball smirks. "Although you tracked her down in the end. Right?"

"No. I understand you know we responded to an anonymous tip DI Dowling passed on."

"We've spoken to Dowling," says the spaniel.

A moment of silence, no doubt designed to let me know he's not going to tell me anything Dowling said.

The spaniel continues, "Are you able to supply the prosecution file you prepared for court when you opposed bail for Trix?"

"Happy to. What's your line of inquiry here?"

He cocks his head to one side, an intelligent dog trying to understand a human. "We've been told you directed several changes to the operation you planned. Is that correct?"

My pulse increases. "Not quite how I'd put it, sir."

The golf ball takes a turn. "How would you describe the

departures from the operational plan, Detective Sergeant Solomon?" When he finishes his question, he draws his lips so tight, they could be a vicious cut on his head, number two iron.

Before I answer, the spaniel asks, "You believe in coincidences, Jonah?"

"They can happen. I understand the term 'if the planets align.'"

"Was it a coincidence you lost your rear support on route to the scene of the interception?"

"The remote control of Christchurch drivers isn't one of my strengths." The heat in my chest and neck rises. "Can I ask again, what's your line of inquiry?"

"Was it a coincidence your vehicle had no firearms box?"

"An omission we realized after we left the station. I corrected it at the scene."

"Who was responsible for the mistake?"

Nick's fearful face, his attempted dive to safety, the sound of crushing bone—it all flashes for me. "As the senior officer, I was."

"Was it a coincidence you put yourself between the escaping Chevrolet and the clear line of sight your team had?"

"No. Not a coincidence."

"No?"

"No."

The cocked head expression again. "Please explain, Jonah."

"I ran to Nick, a man I placed in danger, to offer what little comfort I could as his brain released its contents on the ground. Inspector, do you have any idea what it's like when a promising team member dies in your arms?"

There is a long moment of silence I decide to break. "Didn't think so."

The spaniel says, "What about the offender's firearm? No one we've spoken to saw a weapon. Are you saying her misfire was a lucky coincidence for you?"

My left shoulder, sensitive to any form of emotional tension, cries for relief, and other muscles grip bones and tendons. I can stay and take this on the chin, enter their good books, or stand for those who aren't here to answer this shitty line of questioning. "You're overlooking Nick was deliberately targ—"

"Are you suggesting his killer knew where you were going to station him?"

"Trix intended to kill us both. And I've asked you twice about your line of inquiry and you continue to ignore me." I stand, the chair toppling behind me. "Not only do you ignore me, but you also appear to be insinuating I, or someone in here, helped a cop killer escape."

The spaniel splutters, "We're only doing our—"

"And I did my job and it cost a fine, young man his life. So rather than tell you prof con artists to piss off, I'll be polite and take your advice about representation."

SATURDAY, 7 JULY 2012
03.40 HOURS

I ease my old Lexus over the treacherous patches of black frost built over our cracked drive. The main fissure up the center provides a birth canal to hardy weeds and brown needle-like grasses. The earthquake assessment claimed the cracks were pre-existing damage from tree roots along the side of the drive—merely one documented insurance lie among the millions across the city. Many of these assessors are ex-cops, for whom the quakes have meant a welcome release from crosswords, lunchtime TV soaps, and irritable partners. Supplementing their pension by delivering Earthquake Insure's rote lines is more alluring than marital bliss.

My sister Eve's insomnia is alive. Silhouetted against the kitchen light like a thin statue, her alabaster face peers into the dark. In our teenage years, struggling to rebuild our lives, she scared me with this persona. Over time I got used to the walking cadaver glide down a hallway dividing our house, but the younger me would duck into a room, trying not to be seen, watching and curious. I was never sure whether her ghost-like behavior was for my benefit or the result of what happened to us long ago.

This weather-board house, where we were raised as kids, no longer feels like home. It's not only the gut-wrenching devastation of the February 2011 quakes. I extinguish the butt of my Camel on a stone in the rock garden and climb the four gray-mottled steps to a porch with a kitchen door on one side, laundry on the other. I put my ear to the laundry door to hear Pugwash snoring. I'm happy my arrival hasn't disturbed him. Otherwise he'd expect me to play. He comes and goes through his magnetic controlled dog door.

The kitchen smells of burnt toast. "More insomnia or something else?" I ask Eve.

She doesn't answer. Instead, I get the pinched look and crossed arms, nonverbals that tell me I'm in the shit.

"I fancy pancakes before I turn in," I say, pretending her disappointment in me is unnoticed. The truth is, Eve is so well-practiced in this form of communication I am inured to it. "What about you?" I ask.

Again, no response. My back to her, I walk toward the fridge, knowing her drill bit of melancholy will attempt to penetrate some part of my body and extract a final ounce of empathy.

"Not eaten anything decent in a while," I say, patting my stomach.

The small voice behind me. "Why did you hide it?"

"Hide what?"

It comes to me, the reminder about why I needed to be home earlier. I saunter to the account holder on the timber-topped sideboard, feigning nonchalance. I wipe the dust off Owen's little wooden stand. Older than me, it still serves as the repository for unpaid bills. Yesterday, several items were tucked into this convenience, including a letter to Eve about

Owen from the Corrections Department. We both received one.

I try a reassuring smile. It doesn't work.

"Why did you hide the letter from me? You think I'm a child?"

I hold up my palms. "Do we need to do this at... 3:35 in the morning? Been a long day. A very bad day."

I think about the god-awful life I could lead as a bank security officer, standing with the minimum wage in my pocket. I'd watch surly punters come and go, leering at me like I'm the ex-school dunce, only a small step up from the kid collecting supermarket trolleys in the parking lot. But some of my former colleagues took another route. The blokes got the docs to sign them off with an early retirement package so they could make and sell gourmet pies. That's more my ticket.

"Well, it's kept me awake," she says.

"I didn't mention it because you always need me to have a solution for every problem before it makes its presence known. What time have I had to think about it? Had a bit on. Right?"

She squints at me, deepening the lines around her eyes, and begins her endless pulling of blonde hair between finger and thumb. "I'm not important enough to give it priority. Is that it?"

I bury my face in my hands, start massaging my forehead. When I raise my head, she pulls the prison correspondence from the inside of her turquoise top.

"Compassionate parole," she says with a sour look. "Where's our compassion, Solly? Compassion for me."

"Only another board hearing, Eve. They have to tell us."

"What will you do?"

"Have another squiz at the letter. Little has changed from

the one three years ago and the one before that. We don't have to do anything."

I open the fridge. No eggs. Why hasn't she bought eggs in the grocery delivery, one of the few jobs she has? "Jesus Christ, how come we've got no eggs?" Eve's margarine is prominent on the top shelf. I hate the stuff. "And no butter!"

I turn and give her my well-practiced face of disappointment, the older sibling's attempt at parental disgust. It will be a close likeness to the one I get from Fergus Dowling tomorrow, an expression delivered often enough to alter my neurology.

"Did you put them on the list?" she asks, tone accusatory.

"Come on, Eve. Can you help me out here a little? These are staple items. Yes?"

"Okay, okay. But you should've noticed before now."

She starts washing dishes—a spoon, knife, toast plate, and a brown porridge bowl with a scum line around the top. "That bloody letter threw me."

"So, you think that's relevant to whether you've ordered the grocery delivery? I put things on the list that we don't normally have in the house." I pause for a response, but it doesn't arrive. "What was it the doctor said? I'm offering you a quality of life and care you won't receive anywhere else."

"You could eat the dinner I cooked you last night."

I've lost my appetite and stride toward the bathroom. Down the hall, her call follows me like bad surveillance. "My bike pants need replacing."

Yesterday's damp and crumpled towel is where I left it on the floor. At the thought of her moping around the house all day, I kick it, and my right quad protests with a spasm.

∞

Hot shower taken, I return to the kitchen. Eve stares at the black TV screen, her palms flat on the dining table. Her face is the benchmark for comatose. The radio is on and Fergus Dowling's voice fills the air."Police are appealing for witnesses after this brutal killing. Anyone seeing a black Chevrolet Blazer, license plate PUTIS, or any persons acting suspiciously in the vicinity of Christchurch stadium, or in and around Lancaster Street, are urged to contact 0800-CRIMEWATCH."

An image of Nick's body in the morgue appears behind my eyes and I see myself flee the prelim investigation interview. "Eve," I say. "We both knew this day for Owen would come. Few people die in prison. I'll sort something where you won't be involved."

Eve continues in her trance.

"What are your plans for today?" I ask.

No response.

I clap my hands and her shoulders respond with a ripple. It's now a well-practiced technique.

"Would you pick up some new bike pants for me? Please?"

I'm tired of enabling her failure to be more self-sufficient, her refusal to try new things and build a better life for herself. I don't want to comply, and instead, change the subject."Owen understands why you don't visit."

She lifts yesterday's newspaper and wrist-flicks it to underline she's pissed off."That's a no, is it? And your excuse?"

I pick up the letter she's placed face down. "If I kept my mouth shut..."

She stands, chin raised, offers her full face."That may well be true, Solly. But he was no father to us. He was a hothead, a liar, and an alcoholic."

I raise my hands as a stop sign. "All said many times before, Eve. It hasn't helped."

"Pants?"

"I'll try and make the time."

"It's the store by the supermarket—convenient for you. Yes?"

I'm tempted to remind her she only knows about the store because I told her ten years ago, the lapse of time since she last left the house. I refrain and head for bed. Daylight arrives before I submit to sleep.

FRIDAY, 27 JULY 2012
19.00 HOURS

F for fail, my score for three weeks in a row, the time by which Fergus Dowling reckoned Trix would be back in custody.

I spend the day trying to figure out why I'm lightheaded, overheated and keep clearing my throat. It occurs to me I should try and stop smoking but Dowling suggested it was stress-related. Twice I bump into people's desks like an out-of-control robot.

Now Dowling sits in the passenger seat while I drive us to what Earthquake Insure calls a "celebration of success" function. "Tell me again, why we're attending this piss up so soon after Nick's funeral."

Dowling lets silence hang before he answers. "Bit of advice, son. Stop beating yourself up. He could've been anywhere, and she'd have targeted him."

"It isn't just Nick, though. Is it? If EAGLE was available that night, Trix wouldn't be on the loose. Professional Conduct is stirring everyone up, but no one's learning anything. We shoulda had more cars. Instead, we're scrambling for statements, having them checked, rechecked, looking for faults in our procedures and behavior, finding blame, apportioning blame. None of that brings Nick back. If any of it made any difference in bringing Trix to justice, we could all move on. Bloody internal inquiries are an employment scheme for people who don't know the first thing about policing with inadequate resources."

I stop, late to react at a red, causing Dowling to lurch.

"Christ, Solly, ease up on the rant." He straightens. "A cop dies in an op that goes tits up. We don't all sit around stroking one another's arms, hand-wringing, drinking cups of tea."

"Prof Con say jump, we ask how high. That it? It's not only Trix, now. Right? We need to penetrate her support network."

"Don't obsess about the Professional Conduct boys or anything else. Okay?"

"Why don't I drop you off, pick you up later?"

He gives me his disappointed teacher face. "There's an expectation we'll both be there, with and for the top brass. Treat it as a door knock, unpleasant but compulsory. Besides, they'll want your view on progress."

"What progress? We've interviewed every jail mate Trix spoke to in the last eighteen months she was inside. Nothing. And nothing from social media, the fifty-grand reward, or from *Crimewatch*. Bad enough she got parole but skipping bail?"

"You'll grab a break. It'll come. Hold the faith, son."

"Short of searching more than ten thousand quake-damaged and abandoned homes all over Christchurch, it's hard to tell where any change in luck will come from."

We drive in silence until the next red light. Dowling leans forward and clutches his stomach. "Shit," he says.

"What the hell's wrong?" I ask. "That's not your diabetes. Is it?"

He shakes his head. "It'll pass."

"You need a doctor, mate."

"No. Had this before. I'll be okay."

"Okay? Bullshit. You're ill and you've been yellow round the gills for weeks. We need to go to an after-hours clinic."

"Too late, Solly."

"What do you mean too late?"

He sits up and takes a deep breath. "My health's fucked. Got the rust to go along with my diabetes. In the pancreas."

"Oh, Jesus." My thoughts flash to Mum—not cancer but slow suffocation by terminal emphysema, Eve nursing her, the gasping, the oxygen tank, the late-night panic calls, the undignified torture, the feeling of being useless, the end of hope.

He looks resigned, almost calm.

His daughter, Tracey, works on my team. The two of them went through a terrible time with Dowling's wife when she had brain cancer. He always limited information about why he was absent from the station, never wanting his family problems to become issues for his employer. I admire his self-reliance, his stoicism.

"It's passed," he says, and his shoulders relax. "Listen, I should've said, but this shit with Nick—well, there's never been a right time."

"Said what?"

"My last day is tomorrow, confidential to you, Tracey and Hockley."

His expression is one I know well—stern and doesn't invite debate. My tongue turns to old leather, like the strap Owen used to apply to my backside.

"I'm taking a less stressful job," he says, "a supervisory role in a security company. Desk jockey, managing staff rosters, those sorts of things."

"Treatment?"

His frown lines deepen. "I need to enjoy the few years I have left. Not sure about the chemo. Hit and miss success rate. Might go straight to palliative when I need it."

We arrive at the community hall car lot on the city's eastern boundary bordered by the Pacific Ocean. I park next to DCC Hockley's flashy white Nissan convertible. It must bother her to no end that since the February quake damage, the choice of venues is limited. She's forced to attend events in shit holes like this.

I say, "I'm comfortable taking you to the doctor, boss."

"I believe you. Always so earnest," he says, voice hoarse as if the words are near his last. "We've had some terrific times, though, eh? You and me."

"Well, a few more years is a bloody tough prognosis to take," I say. "Let's make sure we make the most of it. Right?"

I guess he'll hear my hollow rhetoric, but I can't help myself. In his silence, the waves roll in on the sand and the smell of the sea enters the dashboard air vents.

"What I'm trying to say, boss, is you leaving at this point won't help morale. Not after Nick."

He smooths down his thick hair and I imagine chemo washing it away.

"The ink's dry, Solly. I'm mentioning it because there may be talk of it inside."

I drop my chin and experience my guts in a clench. "Did Hockley make any attempt to change your mind?"

"Medical retirement, mate," he says at a volume suggesting I'm deaf.

"I don't want you going like this. Way too sudden. Not after all your service. What sort of a district crime commander have we got?"

"Some might say compassionate." He pulls an envelope and a plain-wrapped parcel from his suitcoat. "Got something for you. Switch on the interior light."

I frown at the distraction he's creating.

"All will be revealed. Parcel first."

I rip off the paper to see a chisel fixed to a polystyrene backing labeled with the name of the hardware store. Dowling grins.

"I don't get it."

"Card next."

In a plain white card, in Dowling's neat hand, "Caution. Use chisel to remove chips from shoulders and eat with humble pie."

"Hilarious."

"Heed the message, son."

"Well, here's something for you, as it happens." I withdraw the envelope addressed to DI Dowling.

He reads my resignation letter and then opens the car door with no reference to the content. "Borrow your lighter for a minute?"

"Thanks for trying to talk me out of it, boss."

He clicks his fingers, extends his palm, and gives me the disapproving eyes. I comply.

He activates my Bic and applies it to my resignation, letting the last of it go the instant before he burns himself.

"Seeing as you need cheering up, I do have other news. Someone else is in my life—at last."

"I can write another one after you abandon ship."

He pretends he hasn't heard me and says, "Can't say who. She doesn't want it out yet. Got a current partner to deal with. Sorry to be mysterious, but it's a bit complicated."

We exit the car. Across the roof, he says, "From now on, you'll be reporting to Mick Coman." He responds to my gaping mouth. "Yeah, he's old school, but he's not too bad."

"Well, my resignation is now all the more certain. How can you say not too bad when a couple of times a week you call him a lazy sonofabitch? Jesus Christ."

He places a hand over his heart. "The ultimate forgiver. Listen, you bailing along with me achieves nothing except a mess for others to clean up back at the shop."

"I'll work out my notice."

Martin Troup and Quentin Sinclair stand on the lower steps of the hall entrance. Troup is among the top brass, an assistant commissioner in crime prevention based at the national headquarters in Wellington, also known as Bullshit Castle. Two levels from the highest turret, he now towers over a diminutive Sinclair, chief executive of Earthquake Insure, our host.

Dowling gives me his crooked smile. "What notice is that?" He gives Troup a nod and thumbs up.

Troup calls out, "Catch you inside, Fergus."

We pass the men and I say, "I didn't know you and the AC knew each other."

"Friends for a long time."

"I don't recall you ever mentioning your friendship."

He glances back at Troup, an uneasy look. "Little secrets, we've all got 'em. Not so?"

I follow him to the hall. "Guess so."

"Know so. Our job is all about uncovering them. Can't do that by quitting."

FRIDAY, 27 JULY 2012
19.20 HOURS

After a flight of stairs, we enter the double doors of the function room, a space resembling a school assembly hall with an elevated stage situated at the far end, a podium, and a projection screen. In the lingering mustiness, I notice a faint incense smell. About sixty guests in suits and cocktail dresses gather in pairs and small groups. A few glance my way, furtive little checks, no one wanting eye contact. Troup is Dowling's only friend here and Dowling is mine. I stick a couple of fingers inside my collar, looking for breathing space between skin and cotton. For the first time, I notice Dowling and I have dressed in matching pinstriped suits, black leather shoes, and white shirts. His tie is navy, mine crimson. But for my olive complexion, we could be father and son.

Dowling sets a course for the bathroom and when I feel my temple pulse, I move to the edge of the room for a familiar perspective, comfortable even. From here, I have an outside-in view of the assembly.

Behind me, District Crime Commander Yvonne Hockley's loud voice jolts me away from the view. "Lovely vista, under the full moon."

"When your eyes penetrate the sea salt off the windows, boss."

I turn. In her white suit and shoes, she's a contrast to others in their charcoal gray, relieved only by small flourishes of color in shirts, ties, and scarves. An expensive-looking gold necklace settles above a discreet show of cleavage.

"Important people here tonight, Jonah." She nods to reinforce her condescending message, something she's famous for.

Dowling returns and nods at Hockley. "Boss."

Her frosty smile reappears, the same untrustworthy expression I learned to read in adults after Mum died and Owen went to jail. Visited by social workers, I lied and said I was seventeen and we were managing fine. I showed them the fridge and freezer, the pantry, offering the contents as proof. I got the smiles—smiles of deceit, smiles with words of comfort, of support. All the while, they were planning to take Eve from me and place her in foster care.

After I take a low-alcohol beer offered on a tray, a functionary escorts us to a small area in front of the stage with "Reserved" signs on the seats nearby. In seconds, the government's Minister of Police, Amy O'Brien, and Assistant Commissioner Troup approach us. O'Brien dyes her hair a chestnut color to match her horse-like face, both frozen with chemicals. People who know her say she's a quintessential politician who can confound human lie detection because only her jaw and dark pupils are capable of movement. Botox controls everything else. She whispers something to Troup, who gives a grimace crossed with a smile.

When they arrive, Hockley assumes control of introductions. Troup's hand is clammy. I share his problem, but it takes willpower to avoid a wipe of my own after the shake.

When Troup faces me, I notice one eye is significantly hooded. He says, "Incredibly sorry to learn about Nick Jarvis, Jonah. Terrible to think I was at a bloody fancy dress party when it happened." He shakes his head in apparent disbelief of the coincidence. "Fergus here says you spoke highly of him."

"Thank you, boss. I'm sure he would've achieved great things for the police service."

Troup inclines his head. "What about you, son? How's the counseling going?"

I'm tempted to mention my resignation, but that might underscore Assistant Commissioner Troup's view that I need counseling. His question makes me wonder why I'm really here. "No time, boss. A bit on."

Troup nods. "Well, see you do. Speaking of great cops, have we all got something in our glasses?" He waits. "Here's a toast to you, Fergus, one of our finest detectives. I well remember when you were a sergeant reporting to me in the Foxton country station. A terrific experience for any cop, working in a rural town. And at police training college, you had a real eye for talent—Jonah Solomon here, a case in point. You'll be sorely missed but I wish you all the best in retirement." He holds up his glass like an Olympic torch. "To Fergus Dowling."

As we all echo the toast, I confirm from others' facial expressions I'm the last to know about this news.

Dowling's eyes are down. "Thanks, boss. Any success you attribute to me is a credit to those who put up with my little ways." He puts a wiry hand on my shoulder. "You can't beat an effective police team. Best in the business, I reckon."

Troup faces Hockley. "A disappointment Trix is still on the

run, Yvonne. Must be time to wind back the homicide team. Eh?"

"I was thinking the same thing, sir. This time we know who the killer is."

This is typical of Hockley. The best way to look after her own interests is to agree with the boss.

The two top cops discuss the search and the size of the team on it. O'Brien joins in, expresses some surprise Trix would still be in the country.

"Who's leading the inquiry?" Troup asks.

"With Fergus's retirement, another inspector will assume command," Hockley replies, "but I expect the day-to-day management will fall to Detective Sergeant Solomon."

Troup squints at me. "Ex-cop. We all want her caught. But can I give you some advice, Jonah?" He nods to his left and we both move into clear space. He lowers his voice. "Don't muck about on this. Get it done or move on. The public expects us to pursue Trix to hell and back." He shakes his head. "Not happening."

"Not sure what you mean, boss."

"In confidence." He leans toward me. "There's a bit more to my suggestion about reducing resources."

"Resourcing the capture of a cop killer would be a top priority. Wouldn't it, boss?"

"I assume you know we've got someone undercover in EI?"

I don't know this but I should. Has Dowling, mind on his illness, forgotten to tell me? No one's told me anything about undercover cops in Earthquake Insure. I cover my surprise by nodding.

Troup says, "Mick Coman's given me the nod Jarvis was

about to be arrested." He takes on a sour expression. "Fraud. Always a rotten apple to be found. Quentin Sinclair and I have it sorted. They've got enough shit going on without us dragging them down by adding our own. Right?"

I stop myself from asking what kind of bullshit this is. Instead, I shake my head and look away, unable to find alternative words. Dowling's talking to Hockley, who glares at him like she's been accosted by a beggar.

Troup fills the silence. "Understand, no one's blaming you. Okay?" He looks toward Hockley who's with O'Brien.

I want to ask Troup for the evidence damning Jarvis. In this group, I'm the only one who can speak for the murdered young cop. I'm outnumbered and it finally dawns on me, this is the reason I'm here. I sip my drink, worried if I challenge him, it'll come out wrong. I manage to say, "Thank you, boss." I take another sip and add, "Got to admit, hard to learn that about Jarvis."

"I understand," he says. "But don't let it get in the way of finishing the job." His directive tone emphasizes his view. Jarvis was a resource who turned to the dark. Life goes on.

We rejoin the others. Troup says, "So. Where's your guitar, Jonah?"

"Sorry, boss?"

"You boys. You'll have us up all night. Won't you?"

I force a smile for the racist. Fergus turns away, pretending an interest elsewhere. We once discussed the happy-go-lucky-Māori stereotype, too common in these large, white-faced gatherings. The Māori boy will bring his guitar and a dozen beers. He'll get pissed, drive home, rape the missus and, with a bit of luck, turn up to work the next day without throwing a sickie. Eh, bro?

"I never learned to play, boss."

"Really? I thought…"

"We all did? No, boss. Most of us can only play two chords." I give one of Hockley's smiles.

Troup frowns, unsure how to respond, and turns to Hockley. "I'll be staying for a few more days before returning to HQ."

We all take finger food, but my chicken and mushroom pastry blisters the roof of my mouth. I sip cold beer and delay swallowing.

Troup touches my shoulder, taps the side of his nose. "Might see a bit more of you, Jonah, while I'm here," he says, chewing. "A team player and a good Māori cop. Valuable assets those. Trust you're not losing too much sleep about the Prof Con inquiry."

Hockley brushes at a nonexistent crumb.

"Can't discuss that, though. Can I?" he says and gives me a wink.

"The inquiry? No, boss. Appreciate that."

FRIDAY, 27 JULY 2012
20.03 HOURS

Doctor Gwen Sinclair, Earthquake Insure's communications manager, taps the mic. The effort proves ineffective. She waits, appearing determined not to repeat herself. Somebody behind me gives a sheepdog whistle, and it quietens the room. Gwen apologizes for interrupting, thanks her audience for coming, and introduces her CEO, making no mention of their personal relationship.

Dwarfed by his partner and most of the men in the room, Quentin Sinclair prances to the podium in shiny shoes. He wears a gaudy tie on a puffed chest, apparently unconcerned by the daily diet of negative publicity his outfit receives.

Behind him, the giant screen provides harrowing and unnecessary reminders of the quakes—battered and bleeding people running away from collapsing facades in the inner-city red zone.

Sinclair trots out statistics, replacing insensitive images with dry and impersonal data. He avoids referring to EI's tortuous and prolonged approach to quake victims' assessments and claims.

Hockley, next to me says, "Powerful speaker. Isn't he?"

I whisper back, "Well-practiced."

"Despite the magnitude of this disaster," Quentin Sinclair says, "we've completed forty percent of household damage assessments. Tonight, I'm announcing, in the short time since the disaster, we've doubled our staff and implemented robust procedures to expedite claims and prioritize the most vulnerable in our community—the elderly, the frail, and the disabled."

Loud applause.

"I only want to say two things tonight. The first is, despite what some parts of the media might say, we've dealt with people infiltrating our ranks whose integrity failed them, failed us, and failed our customers. I apologize for what people have put up with, but we've taken action."

I cross my legs, wondering how this guy sleeps at night, whether he's written this bullshit or paid someone to do it for him.

"On a more positive note," Sinclair continues, "I also want to thank Minister of Police Amy O'Brien for her leadership in enabling the police to partner with EI in preventing earthquake insurance fraud. It's one thing empowering those responsible. It's another thing ensuring it happens. In that light, we're all very grateful to our wonderful District Crime Commander, Yvonne Hockley, ably backed by Assistant Commissioner Martin Troup at Police National Headquarters."

I glance at Troup, wondering whether his wink was to assure me I'll come out of the inquiry okay or an attempt at manipulation. I'll ask Dowling. He'll know whether Troup's another wannabe politician in a police uniform or a genuine cop. And Dowling must know something about the source of intel on which Troup condemns Nick Jarvis.

"Martin's resourced local police to combat suspect claims,

helping us put tens of millions of dollars back into the community. I'm sure I speak for others when I say Martin Troup continues to prove himself an extraordinary leader in crime prevention. I'm sure we're all extremely grateful for his support."

Another long round of loud applause. The adoring audience in front of Quentin Sinclair reminds me of the North Korean leader's rent-a-crowd. Troup smiles at Gwen. She reciprocates, catches me looking at her, and quickly flicks her eyes back to her partner.

"Despite all the aftershocks," Sinclair says, "we now have crime prevention strategies in place to make this city a safer place for rebuilding. Ladies and gentlemen, please join me in toasting the New Zealand police."

The audience responds, little more than duty in the applause, and Troup touches Hockley's arm.

"Last, but by no means least, I want to acknowledge my partner, Gwendoline." The camera recording EI's leader in action now goes to her. On the big screen she's elegant in her fitting red dress and blonde bob cut. "I could not have achieved what I have without Gwen's support every step of the way."

Gwen puts her hand to her chest, appears to mouth a silent thank you.

When Quentin leaves the podium to the rock star applause of his sycophants, everyone stands. Troup gestures me closer. "What do you make of Quentin Sinclair, Jonah?"

Is this some sort of test? I sense Hockley's challenging stare and wonder why this senior cop wants my view about a man who's given him and our organization high praise. Hockley won't want me to mention the thousands of people under EI's duress, how they're using contract law as a weapon to target what they can get away with, not what's fair. Mentioning blameless people, overwhelmed, and driven to despair by the exercise of power against them. I imagine that message would be poorly received. Instead I say, "Clearly competent in giving speeches, boss. He's got a difficult job at a difficult time."

Troup smiles at Hockley but her attention is diverted to Sinclair moving downstairs.

I'm over sucking up and the corporate pantomime. I text my offsider. *Now*.

My mobile sounds. The rest of the conversation around me stops and my ears burn in response to disapproving stares. I answer, eyes down.

"Having fun?" Blain asks.

"What location?"

"That good, eh?"

Amusement in his voice.

"AOS on standby?" I ask.

"The only armed offender is you, peppering me with blanks."

"The intel solid?"

"Are we done?" he asks.

"On my way."

I face Hockley. "Boss, a woman fitting the description of Trix is on the move in North Canterbury. The Kaiapoi cop's in attendance." To Troup, I say, "There's only one in that station so I'm sorry, I need to leave."

He nods but says nothing.

If this was a real breakthrough, I would be miffed at the lack of excitement in either of them.

Troup frowns. "Sure you can't delegate this, Jonah? I'm keen to share my insights on how you might develop your career opportunities."

I catch myself about to rub behind the back of my neck and pull my hand down. "Love to benefit from your wisdom, boss, but we're understrength and the team knows I'm at this party. If I don't front, it might send the wrong message."

Troup gives me an appraising stare followed by a grin. "Lead by example. Can't fault you, son."

Hockley heads downstairs and Dowling wishes me luck. "I'll get a cab home," he says, "but I'll catch up with Marty first. My tenant's moving out of town and I want his advice about the property now it's red zoned."

"Ask him whether he's heard anything about Nick, any details I should know."

He gives a small shrug. "Don't obsess."

I can read nothing in his response.

"Sergeant," Troup calls. He moves a finger across closed lips. "Take care of morale. All the best, son."

Down a few carpeted stairs, I hear Hockley's agitated voice beneath me. I pause, still wondering about her admiration for Sinclair, what this might mean for the police relationship with EI. In a hushed tone, she says, "It's not like that, Quentin."

Sinclair says, "They're threatening our complete existence and I can't find anything on them. You must be able to help."

I take a next step and a board creaks under my weight. I continue and nod my good night. Outside, the moon is bright and the sky clear. More frost is on the way.

FRIDAY, 27 JULY 2012
21.35 HOURS

I ride the lift to the top floor of Griffin Pollard's club, mostly undamaged due to high compliance with 2010 building code changes. My pulse quickens with the rising floor numbers and I wipe my palms before the doors part. At the reception area, a man with a butler's air and rat-like wrinkle of his nose greets me, oozing suspicion. A Māori with an unbuttoned collar and crooked tie? I see his point. I sometimes believe I won't be visiting for much longer. He picks up a phone, pushes three keys, and within minutes, Griff is with me.

He thanks the man, who replies, "Very good, Your Honor."

I check he's closed the door behind him. "Tuxedo tonight. Special occasion, Your Honor?"

Griff hugs me. "Law Society dinner. Got back seconds ago. How was the Earthquake Insure gig?" I stand back and see evidence of spray on his cornsilk hair. His skin glows with face cream.

"Don't know what was worse." I tell him the headlines, beginning with Fergus's health and ending with me contriving to escape.

Griff's mouth gapes. "Oh my God."

"I knew it was a bullshit PR event, but I didn't expect the stuff about Nick."

He gives me a sympathetic smile. "I'll run us a bath. What say you pour the Bombay?"

I put crystal tumblers on the marble benchtop. He's rearranged the kitchen slightly. His Italian double espresso machine, with its copper dome and brass eagle, sits next to a posh commercial juicer, its tube full of oranges, a cannon ready to fire. Both appliances are flashy, and he insists they were gifts—not his choice—but from a grateful importing client when he practiced at the bar. "They do make beautiful coffee and juice," he once said, almost apologetically.

He stands at the bathroom door while the water thunders behind him. "Fergus knew about Nick. Yes?"

"I can't see how he couldn't. I mean, if Troup got it from Hockley, which would be the normal chain of command, one of the inspectors would've told her. You can't keep that stuff quiet."

"You'll rest easier when you talk to him about it."

I take the drinks to the bath and place the one with ice at Griff's end. I strip, feel the heat of the water on my feet and ankles, and gingerly lower myself, taking time to achieve full immersion. He likes the water hotter than I do. The deep, cream oval spa swallows us both. Three jet settings offer underwater streams to stimulate and relax according to whim. I'm doubtful whether nurturing is what I want now, but he's put a full stop on me sounding off about the hierarchy. He's right. I need to talk to Fergus.

After a few minutes of dimmed light and the low, soothing sound of jazz through Bose speakers, my inner gloom lifts.

Over the last seven months, these have been times when I haven't felt intellectually inferior to him, when not having the right kind of family didn't matter and when I thought my mum's instinct to bring us up in a Pakeha world was correct. She believed I could pursue my Māoritanga when the opportunity was right, but where I work, I see that time as elusive.

Griff's blue eyes narrow, not in concentration. It's his worried face.

"Forget it, Griff. We're not going to talk any more about any of tonight's shit, okay?"

We absorb the skin-wrinkling water in silence until he says, "You'd have been better off coming to the event with me tonight. With most people in attendance as couples, I missed you."

"Well, that would've raised eyebrows and prying questions. Not helpful to secrecy."

"I know you want to keep our relationship a secret."

"I believe we both do."

He gives a throat-clearing noise. "I agreed because it was what you needed, and I wanted to make it work."

Past tense. "I want us to work too."

He reaches forward to my left calf, the problem one before physio. He massages it, his thumbs roving over the muscle gently.

I put my head back, close my eyes.

"That's it, Solly. Relax."

After a few minutes, he works on the other calf. "Talk to me, Solly."

"What's to say? We're either in a relationship only we know about, or not. Straightforward. Isn't it?"

"Maybe, but not my ideal world," he says.

"In my ideal world," I reply, "I win the lotto."

"I'm not talking about big windfalls."

"I know about offenders' ideal worlds too, people like Trix," I say.

He stops massaging my legs and I open my eyes. "They want to do whatever they want and not be held accountable. I'm sure you like to deliver judgments and not be appealed to a higher court. We've all got ideal worlds, Griff. Few are relevant or practical."

"Appeals against my decisions are not as important as us being a normal couple, guys who can talk about what's going on in their personal lives as people do. That's my ideal world—us together, out with other couples, groups of people enjoying life, not closeted away."

"Not so easy for me, though. Is it? The system frowns on personal relationships between cops and judges."

"And you've had a life of being frowned on. Right?"

I note his empathetic tone. I see what he's doing. It's what we're taught when interviewing suspects—a prerequisite in making connections, building trust. The more we dislike a suspect, the more we work to sound empathetic. I dismiss the thought and say, "It never stops. Don't you hear the anti-gay conversations? I listen to long-serving detectives, their references to shirt-lifters and fudge packers, how other forces let them in, and how police standards plummeted." I rub the back of my neck. "You don't want me to be the subject of that. Do you?"

"C'mon, Solly. You always say that."

"I say it because it's true. But you want to pretend like it doesn't happen."

"I'm not pretending at all. I'm saying gay cops reflect the reality of the population they serve. Not those old dinosaurs." He sips his drink. "Are you saying you want us secret because you accept the bullshit, the need to conform to macho masculinity?"

"That's an old argument and I'm over it. People are either with you or against you. In my world, the number against far outnumbers the rest. No point in giving them more reasons to be against me and I'm not going to create enemies within the force when there are so many outside."

"I don't want to argue," he says, disappointment in his tone. "Your need for secrecy is now only important to me because it's important to you." He pauses. "But here we are, you early forties, me not far off fifty, both in professions dedicated to restoring some natural order in the world, professions predicated on some understanding of the truth. Doesn't it strike you as ironic?"

"So, you have a problem with secrecy. What about my privacy? Sacrificing that comes at a huge cost. I lose credibility. I'm in a minority now and I don't want to be further marginalized."

He wipes sweat from his forehead. "I have been unhappy for the last few months—slinking off to movies and shows we visit, sitting on my own with you somewhere nearby, thinking we should be together. To be honest, it feels like our relationship is living a lie by omission. It's hard when I love you. You get that. Right?"

I nod but hold my breath, my fist to my mouth. Nobody's said they loved me for twenty-four years.

"It feels to me," he continues, "like we're living some shame-based life bound up in you avoiding the rejection of others."

"I'm not ashamed of us, Griff." I shake my head. "I don't choose to be gay." I spread my hands. "How can I be ashamed? This isn't about us."

"What is it about?"

"Have I not made myself clear? I need to be so careful about who I can trust."

He gives me a pitying look. "Such a bleak view, even for a cop. How can you say you're not ashamed when neither of us can talk about what's going on in our lives with others, what's important to us as a couple?" His voice is up a notch.

I wave a dismissive hand. "What about the issue of professional distance?"

He shakes his head. "I'm sorry, but that's a deflection from the real issue and easily mitigated. I can recuse myself from any proceeding before the court involving you and your team. Likewise, if I was ever investigated by police, you would ensure you weren't involved. Let's not allow an imperfect system to mess with our good relationship."

He stares at me for a bit before saying, "Where do I fit in your life relative to Eve?"

"Eve knows I'm gay, if that's what you mean."

He turns away.

"Look, Griff, I'm sorry this isn't what you want to hear, but despite being together seven months, I'm not yet feeling the same way about us as you."

He covers his mouth with a hand.

After some silence he says, "Have you debriefed with the police psych?"

"Jesus Christ. I tell the truth about how I feel, and you hit me with that."

I push myself up on the sides of the bath. The water

rushes off me like a car wreck winched from a river. I step out, dripping on the mat. "I'll use the police media unit. Shall I? Detective sergeant out and proud with local judge. Would that kind of headline make you happier?"

"No, Solly." He shakes his head. "I'm thinking about the trauma of your work, not what you said about how you feel. I get how you feel."

I wrap myself in the super-soft white bath towel. "Maybe. But we've still got an issue. Haven't we?" I pick up my clothes and exit the bathroom door.

Behind me I hear, "Don't go, Solly. Not like this."

"I'm sorry, Griff. I'm not saying it'll never happen, but if we both can't be happy with what we've got, I don't think this can work. I don't need that pressure now."

SATURDAY, 28 JULY 2012
07.32 HOURS

I arrive at the office intending to ask Dowling about the intel on Nick and find him packing his personal items.

"Come on, boss," I say, "don't leave like this. At least defer till Monday and say the proper goodbyes."

He fixes his jaw like concrete. "It's best this way, Solly, with minimal people around, no awkward goodbyes."

As Fergus Dowling packs up his belongings, my throat narrows. He adds contents to three full boxes on his desk—a few folders, a framed photo of him and Tracey the day she graduated from police college, and a dozen books.

"Boss, you're exiling yourself from your police family, setting yourself up to reject future support, but you don't need this hard exterior cover. Even if you had a relationship of friction with Hockley, it's not like this team is going to get a better deal if you're out of the picture."

His jaw softens but not enough to speak. He's not going to budge.

"Fine. I get it. Need a hand packing?"

He doesn't look at me. "I'm sorry." He points to a sheet of

paper at the side of his desk. "About that."

An email from Hockley dated yesterday. "Please instruct DS Solomon, if Trix isn't found within twelve days from the date of this instruction, I want him and the rest of his team engaged in the search to be reassigned to other duties. As you can see, I've copied your colleague Inspector Coman, and he'll reassign the relevant staff."

"For Christ's sake." I toss the memo toward his desk and it floats to the floor. "Not even two more weeks."

He faces me and in a tired voice says, "Don't blame her. You heard Troup. She's only following his lead. You know we're stretched on all fronts. And you needn't ask. I tried to persuade her to give you more time."

"With Nick gone and you going, we're down here." I rub the back of my neck. "How's this going to help?"

"You have to pick yourself and the team up. The essence of leadership, right?" He gives me a palms-up gesture. "Hockley said we're the only two cops who believe Trix is still to be found. We're swimming against the tide, son."

"Has this deadline got something to do with Nick Jarvis's character?"

The lines in his forehead deepen. "What are you talking about?"

I tell him exactly what Troup said.

He exhales loud, drops his shoulders. "The first thing you need to understand is Marty Troup's rock solid on the job. I should know after all these years. He's not wearing a police braid as a politician-in-waiting."

"And?"

"Solly, Mick Coman and Marty were once good mates.

Like Marty and me are now." He sounds tired.

"Are you saying I can be their mate, a lowly DS and two brass?"

"No reason why not."

"Because according to Troup, Inspector Coman is behind the Jarvis story."

Dowling, eyes on the floor, shakes his head. "If Marty said that, it will be because Coman's giving him snippets of information, working overtime trying to repair his relationship with Marty."

"Why would he do that?"

"When he was a DS, Troup busted open a huge narcotics op. Took half a million worth of ice off the streets. Stupid Coman, same rank at the time, tried to take the credit. His second wife left him. I'm sure he wasn't thinking straight. Marty and Mick had the inevitable fallout, made the Hiroshima mushroom look like a little toadstool. It's mended now, and Mick sucks up to him because he needs a friend in the castle. Hockley hates him. Well, hate might be a bit strong, but he's embarrassed her on district crime stats. Several times."

"You never mentioned this before."

"You didn't think it strange Coman wasn't at EI's piss up? I'm only telling you now because you're going to be reporting to him. You're not resigning. You run away from your first major setback, you're not the bloke, much less the cop, I think you are."

"Politics and alliances. And the Jarvis story?"

Fergus scratches his head. "Did Marty tell you to keep it to yourself?"

"More or less. Said to take care of morale."

"He's done the same thing to me in the past. It's a clumsy attempt at appeasing you."

I give him a palms-up gesture. "Appeasement?" I remember Troup telling me no one was blaming me. "What makes him think I'm in need of his appeasement?"

He stares out the window before he answers. "Guilty." Back at me, he says, "I told him how Nick's murder impacts on you. He's inflated an error of judgment Nick made on a claim involving his mother's church. Nick submitted it without disclosing there'd been building repairs before the quake. The omission puts the value of the claim under scrutiny. Coman took a call from EI. And you know our risk management policy. Someone farts and the place prepares for chemical warfare."

"How is telling me one of my team is a fraudster supposed to appease me?"

"As I said, clumsy. He wasn't thinking about Nick or his reputation. This is also part of Marty's history. Like you, he lost a colleague in the field. An AOS op, two cops shot, one killed. The IPCA determined the dead cop screwed the shooter over a cannabis deal. His plan was to cap the dealer and defuse a shit bomb, but he came off second best. Marty knew none of that going into the op. But when it came out, it helped him sleep at night."

"Ugly."

"Got it in one. If you want to put your mind at rest, you need to talk to Coman about his history with Marty, but the source of your intel will be obvious. Up to you. I'm not asking you to protect my reputation given what's happened to Nick. So, when you talk to Coman, try and get on his good side, or your life will become a whole lot more miserable."

I nod. "Is this why you and the AC are close?"

"Spend enough time in this place, you make some friends. You gotta know who's in your camp and who's not. I doubt I'll see much of him when he goes back to the castle. So, what are you going to do?"

"I'll have to take my chances with Coman on the deadline. If we run out of time, I'll cross that bridge somehow."

He picks up a file. "Check this out. Will you? I haven't made much progress."

"Passport fraud? Should be Wellington or National Crimes. Why've you got it?"

"Favor to a mate, Head of Passports at Internal Affairs. The suspicion is the main activity for the inquiry is here in Christchurch."

I nod as I glance inside the file. "On your desk for four weeks?"

"Done nothing since Nick. Lacked the energy. Tracey might like it. She reckons she's good on research."

"Who am I reporting to on this? Coman?"

"He knows nothing about it, and I suggest you keep it that way. I'll tell Troup I passed it to you."

"Bit irregular. Isn't it?"

"Could have significant implications." He faces the rest of the packing he needs to finish, picks up a book, and holds it like a shield. "Crack it, who knows what might happen for you."

"Significant implications?" My voice is louder, and I look around to see if anyone heard. "You'd have investigated. Right?"

He gives me the familiar expression. The one that says, grow up, take the order, and see the opportunity.

"By the way," he says. "If you pull any more stunts to deceive

Troup and Hockley like you did at the party, you should let me know. Or, more to the point, Coman from now on."

My guts tumble. "What's happened?"

"Nothing serious. I followed up on what you told us about the Trix sighting. I rang the Kaiapoi cop and when he said he knew nothing about it, I apologized and said, I must've misheard the location. If Coman found out, he'd introduce your rectum to his blowtorch."

"Have I compromised you?"

He waves at the boxes. "Give me a hand with this lot to the car park."

In the lift and through the foyer, the silence between us is like a tombstone around my neck. We load the boxes into his Honda Acura. At the driver's door, he says, "You haven't compromised me, Solly." He stares at me, moisture in his eyes not there earlier.

I wait for more, but he offers his hand. I want to give him a bear hug, slap him on the back, and assure him of my support. But it's awkward. His eyes are on his shoes as we shake hands.

"What is it, boss?"

"These are due for a polish." Head up, he gives a false smile. "Could be said, not only the shoes. Eh, son?"

I can't speak, try to swallow spit that's absent.

Fergus gingerly eases himself into the car and lowers the window. "Take care, Solly. Not everyone comes at you from behind."

I sense a sudden increase in the air chill around me and step back. He raises his eyebrows and drives away from our workplace for the last time. I don't move until he disappears out of sight.

MONDAY, 30 JULY 2012
11.23 HOURS

Detective Lyall Blain drives us to the end of the Jarvis's tree-lined street and parks along the cracked and broken curb. We both hesitate to get out. Blain sighs as we watch an elderly woman in boots and dressing gown exit one of thousands of community porta-potties. This one is a fixture near the Jarvis's yard. The woman hobbles halfway down the street, toilet paper in hand, and enters her unrepaired home.

Blain says, "If you want to assess how well politicians understand the plight of Christchurch people, listen to their lectures about grand rebuild plans when people can't crap inside their own homes."

I say, "Eve and I are back to the luxury of an inside flushable toilet. Our neighbor, Ken, is on the local council. We got our pipes fixed when he did."

He shakes his head. "These weekly visits to Nick's mom keep getting harder."

"Look, we'll just tell her about the time limit to catch Trix and nudge her for anything she suspected was bothering Nick. Maybe she's far enough in her grief now we can gain a breakthrough."

The expression on Blain's long Scandinavian face suggests I don't deliver empathy. Maybe he's right, but I believe it's our job to help the dead speak about what happened to them. Dowling always says, "Don't visit the bereaved as funeral directors but as angels of revenge."

We step out of the car to a skin-penetrating southerly. It hustles an empty beer tin off a weed-strewn berm. It rests again under cover of the gutter. The red brick Jarvis home in Linwood resembles an over-sized dollhouse, something you find in a kid's storybook, although the picture is far from perfect. The front corner lists to the east and a log fire flue emerges through brown tiles, no longer in straight lines. The concrete foundations reveal jagged cracks and I see where Nick filled money-box slits between bricks and wooden windowsills. Skeletal standard roses appear cryogenically preserved in frost so thick that winter rain doesn't wash it away. A shovel buried in the cold hard dirt stands nearby.

Blain, tall and straight-backed, carries a framed print of Nick I organized in the last week. Keen to get to the door, he says, "Christ, it's cold."

I struggle to keep up with his long stride.

Alice Jarvis appears in a sliver of the open door, gray hair, puffy eyes. Her face hardens when she sees me. "I'm sorry if this sounds rude, Detective Sergeant, but unless you've come with positive news, I'd prefer it if you stayed away. It's too upsetting."

I take a step back. "Mrs. Jarvis, we're on your side."

She glances at Blain, then back at me. "Well, you're here now, but I'm sure you understand. We need action not sympathy." She points down the hallway. "C'mon, I don't want the house getting colder."

In a room off to the right, Nick's father sits in a wheelchair, wrapped in a woolen blanket in front of a two-barred heater. The TV is on with the sound muted. I slow, intending to say hello, but he's asleep. In the kitchen, the last of the funeral flowers from our previous visit are gone. Blain hands over the framed print of her son holding a beer as he grins at the lens.

"This is nice," Alice says, voice flat, tears emerging.

I reach for the nearby box of tissues. Alice ignores the offer, knuckles her eye sockets, and places the photo next to another of Nick on the table. She pulls her pink cardigan together. "Your *priority*," she says, emphasizing the word, "should be locking up the evil bitch who killed my boy."

"Mrs. Jarvis, our resources for finding Trix are to be cut back in a little over a week. My superiors think, despite our best endeavors, she's left the country."

She stares at me through uncomfortable seconds of silence. "Rachel Trix. The shit never sticks. Nick said she was proud of that. Did you know, detective?"

I glance at Blain. He gives a barely perceptible head shake. I can tell he's not going to join in this discussion.

Alice says, "She was a lot smarter criminal when she came out of prison than when she went in. Corrections has rehabilitation down to a fine art. How do a vehicle and its driver vanish, never to be seen again?"

"We swarmed over all possible escape routes within minutes. No doubt Trix has been helped by someone, in all likelihood, close to where she attacked."

She shakes her head. "How do the police lose at hide and seek? She should never have had a chance."

"Mrs. Jarvis, were you aware of anything bothering Nick in the leadup to Trix killing him."

"How does his state of mind help find her?"

I think about the answer, but she shakes her head. "You can go now." There's more sadness than anger in her voice.

I face Blain and nod my head to the front door.

We're on the porch, Alice behind us, when she says, "He didn't tell you. Did he?"

"Who didn't, Alice?" I ask.

"Nick. He broke it off with her."

I feel off-balance and steal a quick glance at Blain, more white visible in his eyes than normal. I stammer, "They were... in a...? When did it end?"

"You don't know?"

Blain spoke up. "He was a private person at work, Mrs. Jarvis."

"They split up about three months before she killed him," she says.

My heart knocks on my chest wall. "What happened?"

"It was so acrimonious. He found out she was seeing someone else. She accused him of spying on her, being secretive."

Dowling's comments about avenging angels flood back. I'm about to ask if Nick knew who else she was seeing when Alice steps back and closes the door on us.

In the car, I ask Blain, "Who else is keeping secrets that prevent me from doing my job?"

Deep lines appear on his forehead. "What do you mean, who else?"

"Nothing. Just an expression."

His mouth tightens before he speaks. "May I give some advice?"

"No."

He shakes his head, gives me his expression that I'm a lost cause. "We've been working together too long," he says. "One of us is in need of respite care."

I say, "If there'd been the animosity Alice said, the squad room would've been alight with the gossip about Nick and Trix."

"You think Alice's wrong?" Blain pulls away from the curb and indicates left. "Maybe Nick saved it all for his mum."

"Maybe the relationship stuff might explain why he was keen to be involved. But he was troubled. I put that down to the fact he missed checking the firearms box in the vehicle."

He says, "One thing we've learned—Nick Jarvis has been less than open."

I'm in two minds about whether to tell Blain about Troup's comments, how he attributed fraud allegations about Nick to Coman and how Dowling was dismissive about it. If I do, it will reinforce Blain's conclusion Nick was secretive.

I decide the timing isn't right and say, "Which raises an important question."

"Which is?"

"With Dowling gone, do I tell Coman?"

"How can you not?"

"Like any brass, Inspector Coman can help or hinder us. With our resources under threat and his eye on doing what he can to impress Hockley, I don't see him being in the helpful category. Which means I'm unsure of his judgment. If he doesn't have our backs, and everything Dowling says about him suggests he doesn't, there's a bloody good reason to keep this intel tight."

Blain frowns, says nothing.

MONDAY, 30 JULY 2012
12.35 HOURS

Despite being on the phone, Mick Coman calls me in. He's eating a salad, a dietary change he makes a month before his medical rolls around. His struggle with weight and the police physical exam is legendary throughout the station, perhaps beyond. I walk along the trail carved by the hulking man into the cheap public service carpet. It runs from inside his door to the right side of a desk, the width of a judge's bench in court.

He points at the raggedly upholstered chair, the varnish on the armrests embalmed with the sweat of nervous visitors. I want to know whether I can trust Coman, tell him stuff without adverse consequences to me or my work.

Coman continues his call, "Yes. No. Yes." The replies must be to several closed questions.

I conclude he's getting another Hockley pep talk before he says, "Listen to me. Right? You must finish the program. The whole point of it is to... Hello. Are you..." He slams the phone down and shakes his head.

"Problem, boss?"

"Bloody kids."

"Yours?"

"Only child." He gives the loose wrist gesture. "One of those. Know what I'm saying? Young, dumb, and full of cum, etcetera. I'm too old to cope with that caper."

I work on not showing my disgust at what he said by sitting upright and focusing on slow breathing.

He continues, "Blame myself. Had him too late, wife number two. She wanted kids."

I chew the inside of my left cheek.

"And a twenty-fuckin'-four-year-old baby as well," he says. "Like I need that now, with this." He points to his computer screen and shakes his head. "Fucking rosters, fucking software, fucking overtime. How's anyone supposed to get anything right using this?" He pushes the keyboard aside and reaches for a file. "Says here, you failed to complete the staff management course you attended." He lifts his chin, the coal-dark skin around his eyes like a bad make-up job. "That right?"

"It wasn't practical, boss. All theory."

"Got no ambition, then. A cruiser. Yes?"

"Not how I'd put it, no. Boss."

He frowns. "Okay, what?"

"My ambition is to lock up scum bags. I have no ambition to sleep through some kid's wet dreams of man management, sitting cheek to jowl next to blokes with bad breath and stinking feet."

"Yeah? Well, I liked the good old days when you could give a stone-throwing kid a kick up the ass and get a thank you card from the parents. But life's moved on."

"I don't think we should be navel-gazing about spreadsheets and coding systems and new-age ways to give people feedback."

A fleeting smile on Coman's face. "Agreed. Still, not flash walking out." He leans back and links hands behind his bull neck. "Walking out is your way, according to Professional Conduct."

I look away. "Those pricks interviewed me when I was tired, stressed, and grieving."

"You agreed to an interview. I'm told when they offered you a chance to do it later, you insisted on continuing. Then despite walking out on them, you show some pull."

I resume eye contact. "Pull, boss?"

"The political influence to attend the wank-fest at EI the other night. How did you manage that?"

"I was under orders, boss. To be frank, I preferred not to be there. Not my scene."

"Mine neither." He stares through a grimy window. Outside, gray clouds scuddle north. "I couldn't go. Bit of a blessing." He sits forward and the chair groans under his weight. After a rummage through piles of paper, he uncovers a sheet. "DCC Hockley wants this done." He hands me a typed list. "These are the names and contacts of people who've responded to the DCC's appearance on *Crimewatch* seeking information about Trix. She's not optimistic. Most of these sightings occurred well before Trix murdered Jarvis and none since. Follow them up, pronto."

"What you're saying is, the DCC's sniffed and declared them dead. Right?"

"I'm saying, after bailing from EI and failing to apprehend Trix, you need to rebuild bridges. You need to hunker down, be seen to conform, do what's expected, and keep your nose clean."

"Get better at police politics. Right, boss?" I snatch the piece of paper.

"Frame it any way you like, but it's usually what passes for normal around here. What's not normal is a failed pursuit and a dead cop."

"It wasn't a pursuit, boss. It was an interception."

"A major fuckup, son. That's what it was."

I try and give him my version of the story including our lack of manpower. He's more interested in scraping the detritus from under a fingernail before he replies, "Well, our superiors will consider your excuse in the fullness of time. No cars in the car lot sounds like running an op on out-of-date information. I expect you boys to have better attention to detail."

I stare back, hearing the term boys as a racial slur.

"Perhaps Dowling recommended your promotion to sergeant a bit too soon," he says. "Equal employment opportunities are all very well, but you need to be seen doing the right things. In view of unnecessary public scrutiny you subject us to, the Trix inquiry stays under my command, which means you do what you're told. Can you grasp that?"

His appraising gaze reminds me of my first school headmaster, a Pakeha who talked about equality of cultures but strapped us for using our own language.

"Meanwhile," Coman says, "you are to prioritize a visit to the shrink. Is that also clear?"

"You lost me at equal employment opportunities, boss. I interpreted you to mean my promotion was only because I'm Māori. And, given your neck is pink, I'm unsure whether your earlier reference to 'you boys' was actually about attention to detail."

He slams a desk door closed and glared at me. "Be careful, son. You're not speaking to some fuckhead crim, here. I'll be clearer. Based on recent performances, I can't see any sane person punting you up for a senior sergeant role. With me now?"

The blood in my own face and neck spikes. "With respect, boss, there's no link between the management course and what happened to Nick Jarvis."

"You think I'm the only one making the link? Jesus Christ. Wake up and smell the coffee, son. And not seeing the police doctor—trauma relief 101 for most people. Not you, right? You know best."

"I've put the murder of a police officer first."

He leans back and his chair protests again. Arms across his girth, he asks, "While I'm thinking man management, what's happening with the complaint against Blain?"

Thrown by his change of tack, I blink a couple of times. "In my view, there's an absence of detail to justify any finger-pointing except at EI. It appears to be one in their catalog of cock-ups."

"How so?"

"You remember former detective Kevin Yan, headhunted by EI?"

"I do. Based on his performance here, I need some convincing they found the best part of his body."

"Well, Yan and Blain seldom saw eye to eye on issues."

He sticks his jaw out, showing a little thatch of whiskers that survived this morning's machete. "Well, this needs to be on the record. So, if you whitewash this to keep Blain happy, make sure you're thorough. Okay? AC Troup recruited Yan before he did a runner to EI. So do it right. Keep it tight. No smudges in the ink. And don't muck about."

I'm at the door when I hear from behind, "And clean out

Dowling's office. Keep only the useful stuff. Don't get used to occupying the space."

On the street, wind cooling me down, I shelter the lighter's connection to the Camel and draw on the nicotine, filling my lungs with pleasure. My phone vibrates—a text from Griff. *Sorry about the other night. Are you okay?*

Is he sorry about asking if I've seen the shrink, or because I said I don't feel the same way about us as he does? If he hadn't pushed about us being out, would I have been so open? Maybe Griff, Coman, and Eve have a common view about me. They see me as a defective detective. Time to hunker down and be more selective about who I let in on what subjects.

Calmer by the end of the Camel, I walk back into the building as DCC Hockley heads toward me. She slows. "AC Troup asked me to pass on how much he enjoyed his chat with you. He said you looked a bit stressed and should take some time off. I could approve special paid leave."

It's an invitation to show weakness.

"I'm not likely to take that, boss."

"No?"

"I hear you put me against the clock."

"We've always got important choices to make. I'm accountable for the efficient use of resources. You heard the AC give me that reminder." She gives me the frosty smile. "I hope you make the right choices."

Back on our floor, I go to Dowling's daughter, Tracey, temporary cover for another detective on maternity leave. Since she's the boss's daughter, the top brass okayed her reporting to me. She sits with elbows on her desk, her head in her hands. I look around the squad room to see if anyone else notices.

"You okay, Trace?"

"Yes, boss. Going through the internal emails about the CCTV images, hoping someone will inspire us with new intel."

"I'm tiring of the dropped chins around here, including my own. Let's pull the team together at sixteen hundred hours."

MONDAY, 30 JULY 2012
14.45 HOURS

Blain joins me in the lift along with someone neither of us knows. We're silent until the unknown man exits two floors below.

"There was a time," Blain says, "when new people in this place used to be carted around and tortured with introduction after introduction. I miss that. We could now be sharing the lifts with all sorts of undesirables, a violation of our security. Like the Christchurch Cleaver. He was a police station cleaner."

I glance at him, unsure whether he's serious. "The Christchurch Carver was the character's nickname in a work of fiction—by Paul Cleave, if memory serves."

He sniffs. "Can't be too careful. I spend hours thinking about how fictional our world is."

"In your own bloody time, I hope. I could help fix your insecurity. After Coman's chat I may have just enough influence left to transfer you to Human Remains—officer in charge of inductions. Has a certain ring to it. Yes?"

"Sounds like you received Coman's testicular tuning call. His normal coaching MO, I'm told."

I tell Blain what Coman said about my choice of place for Trix's interception. He winces. "Coman thinks a visit to the shrink is a cure-all prescription," I say.

Outside the station I ask, "Have we got Tracey back in Trix's neighborhood?"

"We've done that."

"Yeah, but when we cross-referenced her neighbors and their addresses with airport departure cards, it explained why we hadn't been able to talk to some of them. It's worth another shot."

We head to Cashel Street's RE:Start Mall, shipping containers transformed into coffee bars, boutiques, and souvenir shops. Others, out toward Sumner are in place to stop falling hillsides from crushing motorists. But these are a huge step up from the widespread city trauma created seventeen months ago—something constructive out of the carnage of broken buildings and smashed bodies.

I set down the coffees as Blain says, "Don't sweat Coman's rant, mate. Normal transmission—a snowdrift in an already unclear picture."

I sip my coffee, feeling more assured he's right. For some reason, Blain's grip on politics is better than mine. "This beats the floor sweepings back at the factory."

The place is quiet—one white male, twenties, one older Māori female. They appear to have reached an uneasy place in their conversation. A smiling man in his sixties, freckled head and a comb-over uses his forefinger to swipe across his device screen. I think he looks familiar and ask Blain whether he recognizes the man.

He glances. "Should I?"

I say, "Feel like I should be able to place him."

"Witness, juror, burg victim, sacked court officer. Could be anyone. Occupational hazard thinking you know people you don't." He takes a sip. "What's this about me and a complaint?"

"Coman's on the case. EI says your claim was dodgy and their overpayment was caused by you putting in photos of a later model Audi than the one you owned."

Blain pulls his head back, gives me a disbelieving look. "This is bloody Kevin Yan covering up his fuckup—blaming me, the slimy prick."

"I know you wrote saying they overpaid you. Not much of a fraudster. Are you? There's not a bloke in the shop who EI hasn't shat on."

He folds his long arms. "Bloody Yan. That bloke couldn't detect a stiffy in a brothel. He was useless with us."

I give him a sympathetic smile. "I think Coman agrees. He said when the headhunters recruited him, he doubted they got the best part of his body. Still, some care is justified here."

He raises his eyebrows.

I clarify, "Troup recruited Yan."

He breaks eye contact. "I always wondered how the cheeky prick got into EI. Yan rang me. Did I say? The day after Nick died."

"No. You didn't say. What did he want?"

"Reckoned my letter didn't exist." He looks back at me. "I said to him, once a dumb fuck, always a dumb fuck. I don't think I helped my cause much."

"Penetrating analysis, on both counts."

"Where's this going, you reckon?"

"Coman wants me to formalize the investigation."

Anger flashes over his pale face.

I show him my palms. "It's Coman trying to stay clean with Hockley. She hates him."

"Yeah?"

"I heard he's embarrassed her by supplying incorrect performance stats, which she passed on to the castle."

Blain frowns, still looks uneasy.

I prod, "Something else I should know?"

"Listen, Solly, if I said it before now, you might've felt compromised in front of Prof Con."

I finish my coffee. "Not sure I'm going to like this. Mentioned what?"

"My statement to Prof Con." He pinches his left ear lobe. "I said I was present when Dowling briefed you in his office. I said you told him the interception of Trix was risky without a chopper."

I stiffen in my chair.

Blain says, "I added Dowling insisted there were enough resources."

"For Christ's sake, mate."

He nods.

"Why didn't you tell me earlier?" I ask.

"To avoid allegations that we conspired to blame the senior officer."

"Jesus, how do you think Ferg feels about this. He'll think I'm behind it."

"Solly, Fergus Dowling is toast. You need to be thinking about your career, mate. I'm trying to help minimize the damage to you and, judging by what Coman said, I did the right thing. The tapes show you didn't challenge the change in the plans. I helped them see why. You already had the debate and lost."

"I could still have challenged it in the moment. Mate, you put yourself at unnecessary risk."

He empties his cup. "Sticking together is always better. Right?"

He's done me a favor and expects one in return. I cover my feeling of being compromised. "Want another? On me. Enjoy while you can. It mightn't be long before we're both selling cars in Moorhouse Ave."

He shakes his head. "That was my third today."

Back on Cashel Street, I say, "We'll see the Yan thing off, mate. You still got our surveillance photos of him?"

He grins. "From the vault? I forgot we hadn't presented them."

"Well, a relief to us all when he resigned. Flick them to me. They might help in some way."

MONDAY, 30 JULY 2012
15.40 HOURS

Strolling over the Hereford Street bridge, Blain stares up toward our workplace, a famously ugly building resembling a car lot with an afterthought of windows. He asks, "Do you feel secure in there?"

"Define secure."

He maintains his gaze, doesn't respond.

I say, "If you can believe the top brass, we'll be outta there by the end of the year."

"Forked-tongued, they are. We're on the move, yet we're supposed to be safe. I reckon it rocks in a decent breeze."

"Those despair-gray concrete panels have defied what killed 185 people elsewhere."

Inside, I punch in Dowling's speed dial code, unsure what to say if he answers. Straight to voicemail. At my cluttered desk, I stare into his office, missing the old bugger. He'd gone to bat for me. As the most senior of our team, I could move in on a temporary basis, but it doesn't feel right.

I sift through case files mixed with admin files mixed with department propaganda known as circulars and instructions. Some I read. I view identikit builds of suspects in other cases, scene of crime materials, unread Police Association newsletters, and an impatient note from the court asking when I'm going to take away our exhibits from Trix's old fraud trial. They pointedly said the time for her appeal against conviction had long since passed. I review personnel files, think about people I might interview to replace Nick. My heart isn't in any of it. I need something on Trix, something concrete, something to boost our flagging morale.

At 1600 hours I'm at the whiteboard on the far side of the briefing room. "Let's get cracking."

Blain and Tracey join me. I don't see Detective Vincent around the squad. "Anyone know where Mr. Vincent is?" I ask.

Blain says, "Urgent personal business to attend to."

I stare at Blain until he slides a finger back and forth in a hole he makes with his other forefinger and thumb. "Didn't actually say, to be fair. But we know he likes to offer attractive crime victims comforting intercourse, not always in the verbal form."

"He better not be. Given we're down twenty-three days since Nick was killed, we need all hands and no shirkers. Also, the DCC's alarm clock is ticking. Ten days from today, if we haven't got her, we're on other duties." I turn to Tracey. "You get anything from the Fendalton addresses around Trix's last known residence?"

She flicks a strand of brown hair from her face.

"Might have a new angle," she says. "I met up with a woman coming out of Trix's house. She was locking the door after taking in junk from the mail box." She opens her notebook. "Name's Linda Nichol. She and Trix looked out for each other, neighborly stuff. She reckoned she hadn't seen Trix for more than a couple of months. She said, at first, living next to a cop gave her a feeling of security."

Blain said, "What?" He crosses his arms. "Trix hadn't been a cop for something like two years."

"Nichol said Trix not only claimed to be a cop but talked like one. She didn't know Trix did time in jail because she only moved to New Zealand in the last couple of years." Tracey inspects her notebook.

I say, "You said before, Nichol used the words, 'at first' living next to a cop helped her feel secure?"

"Yes, boss. Trix's behavior changed. She became paranoid, very suspicious, accused Nichol of coming over to her property without her knowing. And she'd go running late at night, complaining she couldn't sleep."

Blain raises his fair eyebrows and I suspect he thinks what I'm thinking. The paranoia and hyperactivity suggested she was back on the meth. "Anything else?"

She says, "Nichol also said a man used to visit Trix a bit, stayed the odd night. Described him as short and bald, a Danny DeVito with a little beard." She mimes a goatee shape. "He drove one of those sporty types of car."

"Helpful," Blain says. "Narrows it to about fifty thousand men with small man syndrome. Where's this Nichol woman been and why have we only found her now?"

"She's returned from a short holiday to Queensland. Used to live there. And that reminds me of something she said when I first talked to her. Trix told her she had a holiday coming up and would have to choose between using her New Zealand passport or her British passport for when she went overseas."

"Legit passports?" I ask.

"I accessed all the background on Trix, boss. There's nothing in her or her family's history to entitle her to a British passport."

"On his way out," I say, "DI Dowling gave me an inquiry file, possible passport fraud. Can you pick that up and see what else you can get from Nichol on Danny DeVito?"

"No problem." She extracts a photo from a folder, puts it on the whiteboard. "Some positive leads apart from Nichol," she says. "This is an enlarged but grainy image of Trix facing a service station security camera out into the forecourt. The facial isn't great, jail's aged her a bit. The height's right and the cheese-cutter cap is what she used to wear off duty.

Blain says, "I wish, just once, we could have crystal clear footage like the lucky bastards in the movies."

Tracey says, "To be honest, I was surprised we got anything useful with the old tech they were using. Until now, we've had Trix and an unidentified male Māori, no shot of the Chev or the two of them leaving." She posts a police mugshot of a thickset man offering an intimidating stare into the camera lens. "Recall, we got this CCTV footage the day before the EI function, boss. You'll see from the timing on the photos, Trix and the guy in this photo met about thirty minutes before she came charging down car yard alley. You asked me to run this pic through our facial recognition software but the quality's not up to it. Working on internal email tips about who it might be, I've identified him as thirty-nine-year-old Walter Te Pou Edgar."

Blain says, "Rap sheet?"

"Multiple counts of fraud. One demanding with menace, as a debt collector for Earthquake Insure. Baseball bat his preferred tool of trade."

"Why don't the pricks just cancel the insurance contracts?"

"They do. But they figure they're entitled to collect unpaid back premiums. After speculating who helped Trix elude us, I trawled records to find if Nick was threatened by any of his offenders, the crims who did time. Edgar has jail time and wrist slaps all the way back to the youth court."

I ask, "What else do we know about this guy?"

She flicks a page in her notebook. "On the day he was jailed, media described security dragging him off to the cells kicking and screaming. He said he'd break every bone in Nick's body before he put him out of his misery."

Blain says, "Old habits die hard."

I ask, "Nick was arresting officer on the menacing charges?"

"Correct, boss. Since his release, the same day as Trix was released, Edgar's been clean, working for Comfort Cabs."

Blain says, "Doesn't make him clean. He could've escaped further detection."

I say, "Trace, no phone records for Trix but have we got them for this guy?"

"Only identified him this morning, boss. No known phone number. Like Trix, he's probably using a burner."

At the whiteboard, I draw four circles and inside them, write the names of Edgar, Trix, Nichol, and EI. "At the moment, only fraud connects Trix and Edgar, possibly an intent to commit violence. I put EI up here because, at their function, CEO Sinclair said they've had people who lacked integrity infiltrating them. He didn't actually admit to fraud inside his house, but no one's in any doubt that's what he means. Nichol may be unconnected except for being Trix's neighbor. I don't doubt there'll be more names, more connections. It's important to establish whether Trix and Edgar left the service station together. Let's get him in here ASAP. We have analysts checking CCTV for license plates and owners and cross referencing those names to registered mobile phones in the area at that time. The goal is to find numbers known to us from previous intel that might give us connections through records to either Edgar or Trix. We might get lucky.

"Tracey, another long shot, but check the Corrections property records and see if Edgar and Trix turned in mobiles when they were locked up. A surrendered smart phone and a nosy Corrections officer might be the combination we need to turn up new phone numbers."

Tracey says, "Have we had any responses to our media coverage?"

"Yes. DCC Hockley's got some calls she needs following up on." I decide not to say she thinks they're dead. "Tracey, can you work with Detective Vincent on those when he decides to show up?"

"Sure, boss."

I ask, "Have we gone another round of her picture in all social media?"

Blain says, "From day one, continuously."

Tracey says, "Those threats to Nick. I wonder if we should broaden our inquiry."

"In what way?" I ask.

"Well, we sort of knew Nick as a workmate but maybe there was stuff we didn't know, stuff that might help us find Trix? Apart from the funeral, I met his mother once, more than a year ago. What say I make a reconnection?"

Blain stares at me.

I tell her what Nick's mum said. She widens her eyes and moves her head back.

"I take it from your reaction, this comes as a surprise to you, as it does to Detective Blain and me."

She says, "Wow, he kept that quiet."

I'm uneasy about telling either of them what Troup or Dowling said. It might make them more vigilant and productive, or it could send them down an emotional rabbit hole like it did to me. I decide against it.

Back at my desk there's a message left. *Alice Jarvis. Call her back.*

When she answers she says, "Before you arrived this morning, EI gave us a low-ball settlement offer. A hundred grand less than what it will cost to fix the place. I'm afraid you copped my anger."

"I'm sorry to hear that. There are far too many cases of this. Aren't there?"

"Might be nothing, but can you meet me at the Avonhead Cemetery tomorrow morning at ten thirty?"

This isn't where Nick was buried. I check, "Avonhead?"

"Yes, the plot reserved for earthquake victims."

TUESDAY, 31 JULY 2012
10.32 HOURS

At the cemetery gates, my mobile vibrates. Twice. *Can we talk soon? G x*. The second text is Tracey: *Have Edgar. Vol i/v booked for 14.30. Under obs in case he runs*. I don't answer either of them.

Alice is enveloped in a navy-blue winter coat, buttoned from the neck to her knees with a pink scarf around her head. Blain and I shake her gloved hand. Despite the conditions, her greeting is warmer than yesterday.

"I visit the fourth Tuesday of every month, rain or shine," she says with a wan smile. "Seems like yesterday my sister Peggy sent me a text that terrible Tuesday afternoon: *Trapped but okay. Love you x*."

I saw many of these poignant text messages between families and victims trapped in fallen buildings in the first hours after the disaster. While batteries had juice, they continued throughout the major after-shocks into the small hours of the following morning.

The three of us walk past the concrete pillars of the cemetery gates, an easterly breeze pushing at our backs. Blain and

I dwarf her. I imagine it as a pitiful sight—a small woman, a guard on each side of her in case she collapses, braving the winter chill down the asphalt road to the cold graves ahead. Her sister's remains are in a plot reserved for many of the quake victims.

Blain and I stand back a respectful distance from her quiet communion in front of Peggy's plaque. After a while, Alice's lips move, perhaps in a quiet prayer. It takes several minutes, and it crosses my mind she's underscoring the extra grief I've wrought upon her.

When she rejoins us, she says, "I suppose when there are so many dead from a single event, it's not easy to have a grave as nice as Nick's. Is it?"

I shake my head.

We walk toward the huge gum trees dividing the perimeter of the park from the cemetery. Alice asks to do a lap of the park. It will cost us time that we need to prepare for Edgar's interview.

Halfway down the northern pathway, she says, "You knew I chaired the vestry at The Word of Life Church, the one that caught fire?"

I say, "Nick mentioned it, yes."

"He was enthusiastic about me retaining an interest after I retired from teaching. Bless him. He ended up helping me with the church's accounts, the insurance claim. And he helped with our house too. That lowball offer, I mentioned. I suspect EI came up with that when they figured out Nick was no longer around to help us."

We walk a few more paces and I glance at my watch.

Alice says, "I don't want to talk about that awful woman

who killed my son. But there was someone else, a woman. Christine. I thought that if Nick hadn't told you about Trix, you might not know about Christine."

"Christine? A girlfriend?" I ask.

"I used to think so," she says. "He visited her often, perhaps once a week, at Earthquake Insure. I'm not positive about how often. I remember one time he was leaving to see her outside of work. I was about to serve dinner. I asked why he didn't call her by phone, make it easier on himself. He smiled at me. Records, he said. I didn't understand and let it go. But he said they often talked about his job," she says.

"He loved his work," Blain replies with a nod and a smile. "There was never a day when the job's challenges didn't enthuse him."

She shakes her head. "I think there might've been one or two. Anyway, I got curious about Christine and rang the receptionist at EI asking for her. I was told two Christines worked there. Christine Inkman and another whose name I forget. I knew it was the Inkman woman because Nick referred to her as his CI. I thought it was a term of endearment."

I know what CI means and, from the concern on his face, so does Blain.

What we don't know is why Nick Jarvis was running a confidential informant.

Alice nods. "I hope this isn't wasting your time, Jonah, but Nick seemed to be concerned about her, often looked preoccupied in the days leading up to… you know."

I ask, "Can you tell me more about Christine and Nick's concerns about her?"

"Not a lot because you never knew with Nick. His affair

with Trix was over before I heard anything about it. I'm not sure why, but I now think with Christine, it might've been more police business than personal."

Blain's expression suggests he is as ignorant of this intel as I am.

Our pace is funereal, and I glance at my watch again. "What did this woman do at Earthquake Insure?"

"I never found out."

Alice spends the last few minutes talking about loss, grief, and the counseling she's having. We say goodbye and walk back to the car. I ask, "So, what the hell was Jarvis up to running a confidential informant?"

"You didn't think you should push her for more?"

"I think we got all there was to tell. Is it only an oversight he didn't tell us?"

He says, "I hope so."

"What if he got too close to something?" I ask. "Better check her out. Will you? Christine Inkman."

"Probably in the typing pool."

"I thought I was the dinosaur here. No one has those anymore."

A silent moment between us. "You have a theory?" I ask. "About the intel Nick might've been gathering?"

"Thing is, everyone knows theft has been occurring over there. Maybe it's more systemic than we think."

"Organized, you reckon. Widespread insurance fraud?"

Blain runs a finger down his cheek. "But why keep his inquiry a secret? He wasn't the most experienced cop in the shop, but he wasn't dumb enough to run an informant without telling anyone else."

We step inside the car. "I want to tell you something that stays between us."

He gives me a questioning look. "Of course."

"At the EI party, Troup confided Jarvis was suspected of earthquake fraud."

He points to himself. "Fuck, who isn't? Another of Yan's vengeance games?"

"Not this time. I got the sense Troup meant more. A lot more. Why else would it reach the AC?"

"What's Dowling say about it?"

"Dismissed it. Reckoned Troup was trying to make me feel like I didn't get a good man killed."

I tell Blain the story Dowling told me of Troup's similar experience. He remembers the drug case and the cop getting killed. He says, "You think with what Alice says, there might be more to it than what Dowling knows?"

"I'm thinking whoever Nick called his CI might be an accomplice to a crime. That might explain his secretive behavior. Those informants are tricky if there are issues of immunity."

Blain says, "You made no mention of this at the team briefing."

"Observational power. Ever think about being a detective?"

"The question is, don't you think that information might be important to the rest of the team?"

"Don't you think there's enough against me without dropping shit on my own people?"

He frowns. "So, what now?"

"I don't like where it's heading—secret relationship, rumors of a false claim, now a secret informant. Let's hope we get somewhere with Wally Edgar."

TUESDAY, 31 JULY 2012
14.34 HOURS

"So, how's the fishing going, Wally?" Blain asks.

In the stale air of a bland interview room, Walter Edgar leans back, shoves meaty hands in the well-worn pockets of his jeans. His greasy hair is overdue a shampoo and his pear-shaped body spills over both sides of the plastic chair.

We're recording the interview but as Edgar isn't yet a suspect, we haven't read him his rights.

He says, "Don't tell me I'm in here 'cos I caught a few more cod than I shoulda."

His eyes droop, no sign of nervousness.

Blain says, "Trying to break the ice, Wally."

He sniffs through his broad nose. "Get to what's under it. I'll manage."

"We want to talk to you about your driving business," Blain says.

Edgar smiles. "Not for sale. I'll tell you when it's comin' on the market, eh."

"We were wondering," Blain says, "how you managed to pick up those jobs with your history?"

Edgar faces me, forced humor gone. "You the token brown boy? They wheel you in to stop the white pigs from fitting up the likes of us?"

I say, "You're here at our request. But if you don't cooperate, we're prepared to arrest you and read you your rights. Your talk of filing charges against you on false evidence only makes us curious why an unplanned winter fishing trip is a sudden priority."

He leans back again. "I'm a cab driver, but I'm not dumb. I get how you pricks work."

Blain gives an expansive gesture. "You want to cut to the chase, Wally?"

"Sure."

He pushes our clipped mugshot of Trix at the gas station across the table, withholding pictures of Edgar and Trix together. "Ever met this woman before?"

"You guys need better photographers. How's anyone s'posed to know who this is?"

"Don't fuck with us, Wally," Blain says.

"I seen her. So what?"

"When did you last see her?"

He grins. "On the telly."

I intervene. "Has she ever been in a vehicle with you?"

Edgar glances at the photos. "Coulda been, once or twice, eh. In the cab."

"When did you have her in your cab—the last time?" I ask.

"C'mon, mate. How can I remember?"

In my silence, Edgar examines the ceiling, no doubt musing the fly shit up there.

"Six or seven weeks ago," he says. "Maybe." He casts his eyes down. "At least, yeah."

Blain leans forward. "Pick her up from home?"

He smirks. "Give 'em rides, mate. Don't write their fuckin' life stories."

Blain points to the picture in front of Edgar. "What was your connection to Rachel Trix beyond giving her cab rides?"

He sniffs. "Said I'd seen her. Didn't say I was connected."

Blain turns up the pic of Edgar with Trix. "You were both paroled on the same day. How did you arrange to meet at this service station?"

"She called me."

"How?"

A small shrug. "Mobile—how else?"

No one speaks for long seconds. Edgar's admission Trix called him after he threatened Nick's life and met her at a service station minutes before she killed Nick is a crucial admission. I'm wondering whether Edgar's status as a witness is changing to a suspect. He is close to being cautioned he's not obliged to say anymore. I still don't know whether he was in the car with her or whether he may've helped her escape. He's clenching his fists when he says, "She rang for rides. Not a biggie if cab drivers take exclusives."

I need Edgar's phone number to get to Trix's number. I rip a blank sheet from my notebook and hand it to Edgar with a pen.

"Write down your name, address, and mobile number please, Mr. Edgar."

Edgar sounds surprised. "You got it all. Why?"

"If we find documents relevant to our inquiry, we may need a sample of your handwriting. Voluntary, of course, but your refusal will be noted. We can speed this up and get you out of here."

He complies, and I call his number. His phone vibrates in his jeans hip pocket.

I nod at Blain.

He asks, "So how often did you see her after your release?"

"Dunno. Mighta been one time. No reason to remember her, eh."

I say, "Since she ran down and killed one of my team and attempted to kill me, Trix has vanished."

Edgar shrugs. "Sorry for your loss." Hands behind his head, he exposes dark underarm sweat patches on his red shirt. "Got nothin' to do with me."

Blain places his palms on the table. "On the day Trix slammed into young Nick Jarvis, you didn't meet to talk about little tax-free cash jobs. Did you?" With the tone of a patient parent, he continues, "She asked to see you that night. Didn't she?"

The only sound in the room is the hum of fluoro lights.

I speak again. "Mr. Edgar, let me share some information with you."

He swivels to me. "Fire away."

"When you came to our attention, some members of our squad expressed surprise about what you did for a living, given your colorful history."

"So what?"

"So, we assume conversations between you and your current employer excluded your secure kitchen and laundry work for the government on the western outskirts of the city. Are we accurate?"

Edgar lowers his arms. "You bastards. I'm getting my shit back together and you..."

I hold up my hand. "We've said nothing. Yet. Our first step is to offer you the chance to show your community spirit. No threats from us, Wally. We don't need to threaten you. You're a witness whose cooperation is important to us. All we need to do is find out where Trix is and who's been hiding her."

TUESDAY, 31 JULY 2012
15.15 HOURS

Blain turns over all the stills from the CCTV that show him and Trix at the gas station and talks Edgar through the timing of the pics. Edgar stares at them but gives nothing away.

Blain folds his arms. "Your explanation of why you met Trix about thirty minutes before she killed Detective Jarvis is important to us both, Wally. I'm assuming you'd rather be a witness than a suspect."

More silence.

Blain's eyes invite me to speak. "Thing is, Wally, your profile screams suspicion more than innocence. We have a theory about why you'd meet Trix."

"You pricks've always got theories. Provin' 'em's somethin' else, eh?"

"Well now," Blain says with confidence. "We know you used to kneecap slow payers for Earthquake Insure. You did six months for that. And it's more than an unproven theory you planned some unique medical treatments for Jarvis. You were as loud as a cannon with your threats when you were sent away."

"Heat of the moment. You think I wanted to swap my bedsit in Barbadoes Street for a jail cell? Didn't mean any of it."

Blain says, "Nick arrested you and you claimed you were framed. You still believe that. Don't you?"

"Doesn't matter anymore. Someone else got him for that. Karma's a bitch eh, mate?"

I say, "Trix and Jarvis had a bitter breakup. She knew what you thought of him. Some people might think the two of you met so you could join her on her murderous trip and help ensure her safe escape. Maybe there was an offer of money for your help. Why you'd help her isn't so important. A man of your intelligence knows helping her murder Jarvis means you may as well have done it yourself. Right?"

Edgar grimaces. "What?" He shakes his head. "No fuckin' way, mate."

Blain asks, "So why did you arrange to meet Trix that night?"

His eyes go down and to his left, a sure sign a porky's on the way. "I asked her if she could get me a couple of tires. I didn't have the readies. These driving jobs don't pay well. I reached out for some help."

"Come on, Wally," Blain says, disbelief in his tone. "Why would she have access to tires?"

"I'm not sayin'."

"Let's say that's true," Blain says. "A need for tires didn't require a meeting in the early hours of the morning with someone you say is a near stranger."

He waits for a response but only gets a cold stare in return. Blain continues, "So, when you agreed to meet, it was to help her, rather than the other way around."

For the first time, Edgar stares at the Black Diamond video-audio recording system.

I say, "If you need to tell us things in confidence, Wally, we can help you. But your information must hold up. It must be truthful."

He rubs a cheek and says, "Put the tape back. Scrub what you said, and say we're stopping for refreshments or whatever crap you usually say."

Blain's lips are tight, his "I don't know about this" worried look. He'll recognize I'm creating the opportunity for another challenge to our interview process. The videotape counter will show a break in the continuity of the time record. He rewinds the tape until we hear him say, "...rather than the other way around." Blain pushes stop, looks to me for a signal and pushes record.

I say, "Mr. Edgar needs a break. Interview suspended for ten minutes." I record the time shown on the tape and Blain pushes stop.

Edgar takes a deep breath, exhales slowly. "She pulled up, outa sight of the cameras. She came over, asked me to walk back to the car, talk to some bloke. I wouldn't have said more than three words to her."

Blain asked, "This bloke was in the car?"

Edgar nods. "Driver's seat."

Blain, "What did he want?"

Edgar, "He was wearing a mask. He told me people called him the Putis."

Blain, "Tell us about the mask."

Edgar, "Rubber I reckon, gray face, pink teeth, mouth red to look bloody. It had holes in it for the bloke to see through."

Blain, "You notice his eye color?"

Edgar shakes his head. "The light was shit. I was starin' at the vampire teeth. Fuckin' creepy."

Blain continues, "What about his hair? Color, length."

Edgar, "Hair coulda been part of the mask. Mighta been glued on. Stringy lookin', down to the shoulders. Black, I think."

Blain shows photos of Edgar's associates, but he's confident it wasn't the voice of anyone he knew.

I ask, "So what did the Putis want with you, Wally?"

He points at the photo of Duffy Quip, one of Edgar's associates, a man who died of an overdose not long after he was released. "To contact Duff to do a job."

"What kind of a job?"

Edgar says, "Duff had connections with someone at EI and the Putis wanted this person to help him get a piece of the action, something to do with dud claims, some fraud to cash in. The Putis offered me twenty big ones if Duff could come up with some insider. Someone who knew somethin'. I says to him, how did he know there was someone else in this game if he didn't know the name. All he said was someone knew about untraceable payments. He wanted in."

Blain, "Why go through you?"

"Dunno and don't care. Duff never found the person. I asked around. No one knows anythin'."

"We can get all your bank records, transactions, everything," Blain says.

He shrugs, appears genuinely untroubled.

I ask, "Had you heard of the Putis before the night of your meeting?"

"Not much. No rumors, nothin'. He strokes the underside of his chin with his thumb. "Been to the earthquake office, though."

"Earthquake Insure?" Blain asks.

"Took some suit there who reckoned he knew the Putis. The guy pretended to be some corporate bigshot. Don't ask me the name of the company. Meant nothin' to me."

I ask, "When was this?"

"Can't be sure." He points to the pictures Blain showed him earlier. "Long time ago before this."

I lean forward, "Is it possible the Putis and the suit you gave a ride were the same bloke?"

He scratches his cheek. "Not if the suit said he knew the Putis."

"If the suit knew who you were, he could've been checking you out—looking to recruit you for work."

"Maybe. But I didn't think that, eh. I'd already got the ass from EI by that time."

I ask, "Would you recognize the voice if you heard it?"

"Maybe."

"Wait here a minute."

Blain frowns as I leave the room. I bring back my laptop and pull up a radio recording of Quentin Sinclair. I select an audio clip that doesn't identify him. "Listen to this, Wally."

I play the recording. "Recognize the voice?" I ask.

"Could be him. The Putis. Yeah. I can't say I'm sure."

"This suit you once took to EI. What's his address?"

"A sidewalk pickup." He sounds frustrated and shrugs. "Wouldn't have a clue, mate."

"Okay. Enough for now, Wally," I say. "We'll turn the tape back on and you'll demand to see a lawyer, refusing to say any more. Okay with you?"

"That's it?" he asks, disbelieving.

"For now. We'll check out your story. If it holds up, we may need you to identify the mask."

The one-eyed squint returns. "You know who the Putis is. Right?"

"We'll see you out. Appreciate your cooperation."

In the corridor, Blain says, "We better hope we won't need Edgar's statement as evidence against himself. Who was the voice?"

"Quentin Sinclair."

He tilts his head. "And you went for him because?"

"I could say inspired guess, but at the EI function, I overheard Hockley and Sinclair talking about some threat to EI. As to the name Putis, I'll get Tracey to do some research. But is it a coincidence, concerns about fraud at EI, and the Putis, now appear on our radar together?"

"You ever asked a question you didn't know the answer to?"

"We ever had a conversation not peppered with your insubordination?"

He grins.

"I'll download the data off Edgar's phone, get Trix's number. Bit of luck, might take us to other numbers."

"Good."

"Comfort Cabs," he says. "We give them the prick's full CV. You reckon?"

His question takes me back to when I was eight years old, hanging out with two Pakeha schoolmates who set fire to our school in Port Banks. They told the cops about my father's petrol can, about how I'd used it to make my headmaster pay for trouble he caused me. Kids understood old-world prejudice. The grilling I got lasted hours, and the attending social worker said nothing. I suspected she was a plainclothes cop. My father couldn't be found, and my mother wouldn't come because she'd lose her job if she left the sewing factory. I was about to be charged in kids' court before one boy's conscience got the better of him.

"Since he's been out," I say, "Wally Edgar's resisted temptation. Do what you think's right."

Blain looks pensive, turns and departs as Coman approaches. "How did it go?" he asks.

I wonder if he's here to give me more of Hockley's dead leads and time wasters. He should have our backs, but he's more interested in trying to get into Hockley's good books than help me. I need to keep him at arm's length until I can trust him to do the right thing but give him something without getting orders to do unhelpful stuff.

I tell Coman what Edgar said about the Putis. With our no surprises and risk management rules, Coman needs to authorize an interview of Sinclair, and he'll know Hockley will never approve of him doing so. I decide to keep the lead to the team until I figure out how to reach Sinclair without being blocked.

"Internal fraud at EI? I'm not going to the DCC without hard evidence on that. On another front, what's happening with Trix's neighbor. Nichol, isn't it?"

His question tells me he's using job sheets to check on what I'm doing. "Gone to ground," I say. "We're still looking."

"It's fucking action I want, son. Not chasing your tail. Get back into the black. With me?"

"Yes, boss."

"Edgar's interview transcript. I want it."

TUESDAY, 31 JULY 2012
18.01 HOURS

When Coman leaves, I go to the whiteboard and my diagram of circles. I draw a spider web of lines with Nick's name centered, adding circles for Duffy Quip (deceased), and replacing EI with Sinclair's name and a question mark. The movements, background, and associates of Nichol the neighbor, Jarvis, Trix, and Edgar provide six focal points for the inquiry. My hunch is Nichol's identification of the DeVito character who visited Trix is important. What about all the praise Sinclair gave Troup and Hockley for their help rooting out corruption? Could that be a diversion—a pretense at being helped by them while Sinclair's trying to muscle in on organized crime? Could Trix, rather than Hockley, be his real asset? In which case, why ask Edgar to uncover intel for him? My head starts to hurt.

Linda Nichol also bolsters the theory Trix was back on the meth—her paranoid behavior, a normal circadian rhythm upset by the mind-altering substance. If so, she would, in her disorder, think herself invincible. The sight of Jarvis under bright car-yard lights, her seething resentment about his suspicions of her, meth in her system... These might've been the lethal combination producing an intent to kill.

We acted too late pulling her out of undercover. The hierarchy believed she was functional and didn't notice drugs changed her thinking.

Starting to feel overheated, I stride away from the whiteboard and pull a Camel from the packet so I can light it the second I exit the building. In the early evening dark, I walk against the Cambridge Terrace traffic coming my way, thinking about Griff. *Let's not allow an imperfect system to mess with our good relationship.* Does a good relationship allow for resentment? The answer eludes me. Despite the bullshit served up to him and his parole board colleagues, I still resent his decision to parole Trix. Unfair? Maybe, but I believe, in the same circumstances, with someone else like Trix, he would make the same decision.

I pause at the courthouse side of the Armagh Street bridge with an uneasy feeling of being watched. I check for who's around but discover I'm on my own. This place could be named Justice Bridge with courthouses to the north and south. Before the damaged inner city was cordoned off from all but the army and us, hundreds of people—judges, lawyers, witnesses, jurors—would pass this point every day.

I light another Camel and draw the nicotine's rawness to the pleasure center of my brain. A solitary duck rides on the dark current beneath me while a frigid easterly rips the smoke from my lips to deny me a more lasting moment of peace.

I punch in the quick call number for Dowling. Nothing. Last night, Blain said Dowling might be leaving space for a new relationship with Coman. To hell with that. I need to know he's okay.

I burn through the Camel and stare at the town hall. From this distance, it doesn't appear to be the write-off claimed by engineers. For a while, the quakes that broke the city repaired community spirit. Everyone's earthquake stories infiltrated the briefing room, the talk at coffee and meal breaks with no escape possible. In some ways, sharing common experiences brought workmates closer. Some were lucky—only minor or cosmetic damage to their homes—and you saw their guilt, a sort of survivor syndrome. Being part of a wounded army served to remind us all about the scale of the problem. Earthquakes and their aftermath mirrored our work—no end to it.

I draw the last of the smoke, grind the end into the concrete, and begin the walk back to the station. Something flicks into my peripheral vision near the shrubbery outside the abandoned cafe on the Port Hills side of the bridge. I'm being watched. Despite the weak riverside light, I see enough evidence that Detective Vincent needs to improve his technique. I cup my hands to amplify the call. "Vincent!"

No response. Gone. Or will be by the time I reach where he stood. This will keep until tomorrow. Someone else to distrust.

WEDNESDAY, 1 AUGUST 2012
09.07 HOURS

When I enter the squad room, Tracey, Blain, and Vincent are together. Other detectives are busy on phones, talking in pairs, or riding keyboards. Before I greet anyone, the floor jolts us, and the building sways. Here we go again.

Blain yells, "Three point seven, I reckon."

Tracey counters, "No. A four."

No one makes a move for safety under a desk.

"What's your score, boss?" Tracey asks.

Her question pulls me from wondering whether Vincent is on some folly of his own or someone else's. Perhaps some-one on the other side of the law. I didn't want to think about that.

"Three point nine. I reckon Blain's buying the coffees."

Tracey approaches me and lowers her voice. "Contact from Fergus last night, boss. A text. He's in Sydney. Asked me to tell you."

At last. I thank her. "Need a quick chat with Vincent. Catch up after. Okay?"

I lock eyes with Vincent, blond hair, pin-striped suit, pink shirt. Dowling recruited him from the fraud squad. I jerk my head in the direction of Dowling's old office. I wonder what Dowling would say about Vincent's performance last night.

I close the blinds and door before leaning against a filing cabinet. Vincent's hands tremble and his eyes dart between mine and over my right shoulder. "Two things," I say. "Detective Blain tells me you made an arrest on the insurance scam case. Well done. Dodgy earthquake claims, eh?"

"Cheers, boss. Variety of false claims but always involved vehicles. The offenders timed their work to coincide with the quakes."

His voice is squeakier than normal. He knows what's coming.

He adds, "With the current pressure on the insurance companies, they hoped their claims would attract less attention."

I decide to prolong his discomfort a little.

"How did you make the breakthrough?"

He strokes the top of his left hand, something he does when he thinks he's been clever. "Found an informant. After the principal offender took about seventy thousand from several victims, he decided to scale up and recruited others. Worked well for a while until one of them asked for a bigger cut. Principal turned him down." Vincent grins, not an eye-crinkling show of humor but more forced. He says, "After some heat, his lawyer came to us asking for immunity. Inspector Coman signed it off going to the crown solicitor."

"And what about you, Ian. How are you doing?"

His smile fades. "You inquiring about my health or..."

"Your future. A subject of some importance to you, I imagine." I share one of the thousands of con artists' plastic smiles received over decades of policing. "Not only dependent on arrest numbers. Right?"

He touches a cheek. "Is this about me not being here for the briefing yesterday?"

I fold my arms and offer a silence designed to solicit unguarded statements. Blain once asked me if I practiced in the mirror.

Vincent studies his shoes.

I say, "You might think you can rely on DI Coman to protect you. But when a shit-sensing blowtorch comes near his ass, he'll put distance between you and his big frame quicker than you could imagine. Me? I'm disinclined to that form of management. I like to think I'm in a bloke's corner when the time comes. That I have a bloke's back, Detective. Grasp what I'm saying?"

"Think so, yeah. Boss."

"So, engaging in some spook shit for him is unbecoming."

Vincent restores eye contact, blinks, and blinks again. He can't sustain it.

"You're not going to tell me you don't know what I'm talking about. Are you?"

"No, boss."

"Your technique's piss-weak, son. The whole idea of a bloody covert op is you're not seen. Right?" I pause. "What's your situation with Mr. Coman? You squared your cover being blown with him?"

"I told the boss when you left here, you went to the Armagh Street bridge, you met no one, called no one. I said it appeared like you wanted some time out."

"Have you disclosed you were busted?"

"No, boss."

"Right. How long am I to be surveilled?"

"No timeline, boss. I don't know what evidence I'm supposed to obtain."

This is Coman's MO with sergeants he hasn't brought through the ranks. He likes to maintain a personal vault of intel, unveiled, and later extracted to be used to his advantage. I stare at Vincent until his discomfort is strong enough.

"I'm not happy about this, boss."

"He's testing you. This is as much about you as it is about me. You're his spook because you're heading back to single life. Got the spare time."

His eyes narrow. "Jesus, I haven't told anyone."

I give him a small head shake. "No need to, Ian. Your fashionable clothes don't hide the drooping shoulders and the sullen face. You mope around here like a dog whose master kicked him up the ass for licking his own balls. Alternate that with leering at every bit of skirt walking through this cesspit. You think we miss what's going on? And you boast about your betting and eating out. We're detectives. Remember?"

I wait through a long pause. "Payback, boss."

"You're paying for what?"

"The same night Nick was killed I was out on a date. She drove through a red light. About two a.m., no one around except for the patrol car she T-boned. I got out and argued with the uniform, behaved like a dick. It got to the boss. Me watching you is off the back of that. Plus, I'm paying for the panel beating."

"You didn't think to tell me? No surprises. Remember?"

"I did, until I received the punishment. Telling you after was kinda too late. Know what I mean, boss?"

"When shit goes down, I'm first cab. Not the last. When

I'm first, I can help mitigate, help you avoid stuff you're rubbish at. Like spook duties."

"And I end up on a charge."

"If everyone got charged with being a dick, son, the squad room would empty. Sort your shit out. Please. For all our sakes. Don't ever leave me guessing where you are, or when you're on your next mission. If I arrange your transfer out of here, you'll be recycled somewhere with a warning sign on your forehead. With me?"

"Understood, boss."

I remove the voice recorder from the pocket of my blue checked shirt and push the stop button.

"Oh, shit," he says, and the hangdog expression of defeat reappears.

"I need loyalty from my team members, Detective. I'm protecting my interests until then."

He looks down.

I ask, "So, why are you absenting yourself from team briefings?"

"Personal business yesterday, otherwise crime prevention work at EI."

"What crime prevention?"

His expression suggests I'm giving him a new test. "Anti-fraud, boss. DCC Hockley says orders from the top."

"AC Troup?"

"I understand so."

"Who's suggested you don't tell me what you're doing?"

"No one, boss. I assumed your bosses would keep you informed. No reason to keep it a secret."

Blain knocks, pauses, and enters. "Got a result on the Trix tip-off to Dowling, narrowed it to a few public call boxes in

Hornby. We're canvassing, but so far no one remembers seeing anyone going into the five phone boxes within the four-mile radius we gave to uniforms."

"Any CCTV around those call boxes?" I ask.

"No. Only the one catching Edgar at the service station. Nothing else. No one's identified any suspicious behavior after midnight. Unlikely to change, but that might just be me."

"I'm in need of uplifting news. Have any of that for me?" I ask.

"Mixed news would be more accurate. The techs exhibited the audiotape tip-off, but no one here can ID the voice.

"Ian, you understand surveillance. Make sure you give the help needed. Trawl through phone surveillance tapes in the last six months. Listen for a caller ID we can match to the tip-off."

"Boss."

To Blain, I ask, "Any activity on Trix's bank cards?"

"Nah. The cash from her Bank Secure job could be keeping her going."

As I pass Tracey's desk, she fishes out her mobile and shows me the text: *In Sydney, on way to Mexico. Some med help there. I'm okay. Will text again soon. Tell Solly.*

I return her phone. "Too bloody independent for his own good. Still. Relief to hear he's okay."

WEDNESDAY, 1 AUGUST 2012
11.57 HOURS

While Vincent's off the floor, I saunter over to Blain's desk near the squad doorway. He removes his headphones.

"Eagles or Air Supply?" I ask.

He gives me his contemptuous face. "I do possess others."

I point to the *Woman's Weekly* on his desk.

He says, "Trace's, I think."

"Likely story. I did one of their quizzes once. Got the top score for road rage."

He grins, "That could be discoverable information."

I check no one is nearby and then fill him in on Vincent. "Take a sniff will you. Find out what you can about the woman and the vehicles involved."

"Can I ask if this is a priority? Head down, bum up here."

I pick up the magazine. Underneath it, a couple of glossy real estate brochures. I know these are his.

My phone beeps with an incoming text from Coman. *If you're not more proactive, I'll require hourly updates. WTF's happening?*

I show it to Blain and draw an eye roll. "Christ, we're one

and a half men down. Hockley must be riding him again." He mimes being whipped. "My sources in HR tell me she's been taking their advice on a performance improvement plan for him."

"Well improvement's unlikely. Isn't it?"

Coman appears and asks, "What improvement is unlikely?"

Blain and I speak together. He says, "Insurance problems." I say, "Staffing."

His eyes move from me to Blain and back to me. He frowns. "You blokes are doom and gloom."

"I got your text, boss. Getting an update from Blain now."

"Forget that for the moment. Both of you move yourselves to Windsor. Reports of a body found. Might be suspicious." He hands me a note.

I say, "This is DI Dowling's old address."

WEDNESDAY, 1 AUGUST 2012
12.56 HOURS

Blain and I crumple steak pie wrappings and jam them into the vehicle's takeaway coffee holders. Ahead of us, crime scene tape flutters across the street end of the driveway on the property Dowling once lived in and now rents out. I send him a text as we arrive. *Body found at your Windsor house. Investigating. Hope 2 talk soon.* That will get his attention.

Beyond the tape, a tidy garden reveals trimmed lawns and edges and a hose connected to a faucet at the side of the house. All the windows are intact, a stark contrast to other houses around it. As in the Jarvis neighborhood, porta-potties dot most blocks, though fewer are here since the departure of many residents. Angry clouds hover, threatening to make forensics difficult if we're not quick enough to beat the rain and protect the scene. The darkening sky helps intensify a front porch light. It's an unusual time for it to be on.

I pull the edges of my suit coat together. In the front yard of the house, a uniformed cop talks to a man wearing sunnies. Tats cover the man's forearms, and he holds a lead to a dog wearing a studded collar around its thick neck, stalactite slobber hanging from its jowls.

The cop's face is like a fourteen-year-old's without the pimples. He's logging movements to and from the scene. I point to the clouds. "We got cover for the scene?"

"Tent's on its way, sir, but the body's undercover."

"How is that possible?"

"The deceased male is in a utility shed around the back, boss."

Blain and I walk down the driveway along the north side of the house. A wooden picket gate separates the drive from the back section. With the shed in view, my guts instantly recoil from an internal boot. I'm back to being fifteen years old and in full-time work to help with Mum's medical costs. Instead of going to uni, I'm helping Owen keep the house going. A utility shed forms part of the slaughterhouse where Owen and I work, the place where smoko breaks are taken. As the last stragglers return to their workstations with knives and saws, I get a message to go to the shed and help clean up after smoko.

The foreman waits for me. I don't like him. He winds Owen up, plays favorites, and allows mates to take cuts of meat home without paying. We could do with those favors, enjoy the longer lunch breaks, start a little later, and finish a little earlier. When I reach the shed, chairs are positioned around a table and against walls, a green-topped pool table in the far corner. But the foreman's the only one there. He holds up a boning knife. "Got a tip-off. Found this in your backpack. Attempted theft, son, fireable offense. What's your old man going to say? How are those medical bills going to be paid now, boy?"

My eyes well with frustration and anger at the bullshit. He says, "Don't worry, boy. We can put it behind us." He gives me a false smile, shows me his smoke-stained teeth. He limps to the door and slides a bolt not there the day before. Color in his cheeks and a sheen on his forehead, he takes his bloodied apron off and unzips his fly, withdrawing his half-erect penis. "I know you want this. Spotted you a mile off."

"Hey! Do you wanna talk to me or what?"

The man with the dog raises his voice and jolts me back to the present.

I turn and say, "Sorry. You shouldn't be here, but I do need a word with you. Please go back to the front yard."

He shrugs. "Already been in the fuckin' shed, mate. Seen the body. Called you lot."

"I understand," I say, "but you can't be here now. Okay?"

He jangles the dog's leash and the minifridge on short legs gives him an admiring gaze. "Bin Laden here found the bloke."

I nod, offer a smile and point to where he needs to go. "I'll be with you in a moment."

To Blain, I say, "Might be an idea to run the protective sheet from the shed door to the back door, or spread it as far as it will go."

"You think I need to be told that?"

"No. I think you might be oversensitive at times. My confidence in you to run the ops with the techies is high." I pause. "Redeemed myself?"

He frowns.

"I'll check out the front yard," I say. "Try and get a read on the bloke with the dog, whether his involvement here is beyond an innocent reporter."

Blain looks at the retreating man and dog. "Good luck with that. The dog might be more knowledgeable."

The techies arrive while I'm back with the dog man. The image of my father's foreman exposing himself reoccurs. My pulse is trying to escape from behind my temple but I will myself to stay focused.

To the dog man I ask, "Do you know the deceased?"

"Nah, sorry, mate."

My mouth is out of spit. "You walk Bin Laden around here often?" I sound like I'm slurring my words.

He stretches, exposing the armpit of a bush shirt long deprived of laundry service.

"Every day, sometimes twice. Depends on how frisky she is."

"Most of the neighborhood is redded around here. You see anyone else on your travels?"

"Nah, mate." He coughs a small bark. "Why she's off the lead."

The Techies step into their forensic suits. Blain has donned his from the car in which we arrived. They all apply masks over noses and mouths and Blain slowly escorts them down the driveway. While preserving evidence is critical, there's never a rush to reach a covered body.

My guts give me grief, rumbling like an old washing machine on the spin-dry cycle. "Appreciate your help," I say. "I'll take your name and contact details and you can finish your walk."

He leaves and after I suit up, I move to the front door. Locked. On the porch I think about what's happening inside the shed, hoping I'm not missed. Is the porch light a sign someone searched for something in the dark, something that might offer a clue about who was here with the deceased?

On my haunches, peering at the ground, I realize I need the porta-potty outside the next-door property.

When I return, the medical examiner arrives and Blain appears like the parent of a small child, a runaway from the safe grip of the hand that now consults his head for relief. When he spots me, he engages that long stride of his.

He says," I ah..." He clears his throat. "I didn't..." His Adam's apple bobs.

"What is it, mate?"

"I didn't know where you were," distress in his tone.

I point to the porta-potty.

His eyes dart everywhere. "It's Fergus, Solly."

I smile. "Relax. I told you this is his place."

"No, no. The body. It's Fergus Dowling."

"Dowling?" I step back. "Some mistake, here." I shake my head. "This is his property, yes. But he's on his way to Mexico. I texted him when I arrived here."

Blain's face lengthens. "I'm sorry, mate."

"I was with him Saturday morning."

Blain nods toward the shed. "I'll finish off in there."

In time, two morgue men wheel the body from the shed. Blain follows, carrying evidence bags. I raise a hand for them to stop, unzip the bag and jerk my head away from the sight of Fergus Dowling's deformed face behind the torn plastic. His eyes and some of his bottom lip are missing.

One of the men says, "Pull the zip down a bit."

He wants me to see a wound. I hold my breath, ease the zip down. Fergus Dowling has an electric blanket wrapped around him.

I face the man. "Switched on, before you put him on the trolley?"

"It was," he says, as if this was an everyday occurrence.

The men rezip the bag and wheel him away.

Blain puts a hand on my shoulder, his face grim. He holds up one bag and says, "Empty whiskey bottle, ditto sleeping pills."

I can't speak.

He shakes his head. "I don't know what to say. He was more than a boss to you."

I shuffle back from him. "Not right. Makes no sense. Just not right." I turn away from Blain's gaze.

"We'll figure it out, Solly," he says.

The lump in my throat makes it hard to swallow. In my mind, I see the text Tracey showed me and replay our last conversation—Dowling stowing stuff in boxes, the apology for the time-frame Hockley imposed, his unsuccessful claim for more time. The talk about Troup and Coman.

"Why did he talk about that shit?"

"Sorry, mate. Fergus Dowling?"

"He talked about work. Why didn't he tell me—about this, how he felt? How did I miss this?" I sound like I've gone from baritone to soprano. "I need to find Trace. I have to be the one."

"Solly, you don't look too flash. I don't think you should drive. Your hands are trembling."

"A smoke. I need a smoke. You deal with the formalities here. Yes? You know what to do."

"I prefer it if..."

"Not a request. And make sure no one here releases any identifying info about DI Dowling. Nothing at all until I talk to Trace."

"Of course, boss."

WEDNESDAY, 1 AUGUST 2012
15.15 HOURS

On autopilot, I think about how I can support Tracey. At a red light in Hornby, I'm in a trance, close to the Hornby gas station where Trix and Edgar were caught on camera. But I don't know why I'm in this part of town or even remember how I've driven here. I'm jolted to start driving by loud honking from behind. My stomach settles but pain in my right shoulder tears at me, almost preventing me from smoking.

The text, the Mexico treatment. Did he change his mind? *I'm not sure about the chemo. Hit and miss success rate.*

I'd believed he'd give it a go. I call Tracey.

"Yes, boss." Same efficient tone.

"Trace, you in or out of the station?"

"Out, boss. Going back to reinterview Trix's neighbor. The six-pack mugshots. Remember?"

"Sorry. Been a busy morning. Need to meet you before you do that."

"You okay, boss? Don't sound too flash."

"I'm fine. Can we meet at the Coffee Co-op on Lincoln in, say, fifteen?"

I take a couple of turns to head back to the city and think about what I left unsaid to Dowling. Thanks for his support, encouragement, and guidance, basically everything he did for me. He, more than anyone, cajoled me into taking my sergeant's exam. I recall his comment about his shoes needing a polish, his false smile. *Could be said, not only the shoes. Eh, son?*

Now, I need to find a way to tell Tracey her father hasn't been overseas getting treatment but rotting in the shed of the home where she grew up.

Suicide? Grounds for it, yes. But not Fergus Dowling. What did he mean by, *Take care, Solly. Not everyone comes at you from behind.* How did I fail to ask him about that and his comment to me about not only his shoes that needed a polish? I let my own upset about his sudden departure override doing my job.

Apart from hospital staff, only Troup, Hockley, Tracey, and I knew of his ill health. I drive through a red light, avoiding a smash on my side by inches. The female driver's face shows more shock than anger. I'm doing fifty in a thirty-mile zone. I ease off the gas and think about the night Dowling said he was retiring. Was there more to Troup's speech than something smelling of haste and duty?

Out of the car and approaching the cafe, I'm surprised to sense my jaw quivering. As the cold gnaws at my bones, I attempt to speed up on the short walk from the car to the barn-like building, but my legs possess a mind of their own. At the Co-op, the warmth inside is a relief but I keep my overcoat buttoned.

Tracey arrives, a red scarf around her neck, her face pinched around the eyes, and her shoulders slumped. I order a double shot Americano for me and lemon and ginger tea for her.

Her eyes narrow. "You sure you're okay, boss?"

We find a seat and sit opposite each other. Noise and chatter reverberate around us.

I say, "Your concern for me makes this meeting more difficult."

She bites her top lip. "If I have done something wrong, you can spit it out."

I shake my head. "No easy way to say it, Trace. Your father didn't go to Mexico for treatments. He didn't go anywhere."

She stares through me and I wait for her to make the connection.

I blurt it out. "He was there, Trace. In the backyard, the old shed on the property you once lived in. We found your dad's body there."

She nods. "Why didn't he tell me he came back? Was he doing a property inspection there? I, I don't understand."

I let her replay my words. In seconds, she says, "Found his body? That can't be right." She says it like she's disturbed by a suspect's badly told porky.

"Been there a few days, Trace." I tell her about the bag over his head, the whiskey, the pill bottles found at the scene and the electric blanket.

"But... the text... just..." Her ashen face stares back at me. "And who takes an electric blanket into a shed and kills themselves?"

"A bit early to draw firm conclusions. We need a thorough account of the scene and the results of the autopsy. He told me he had a few years."

"His typical bullshit approach to life." She shakes her head. "Twelve months at the outside."

I reach over and grab a leather-gloved hand. I say, no great conviction in my words, "When Coman finds out who's responsible for Fergus's death, we'll all find out why."

Tracey snatches her hand away. "Coman? Oh, boss. No. They hated each other. You can't let Coman deal with this. Please."

She won't be the only one expecting me to manage the investigation.

"Trace, I'm not saying Coman will deal with it. Fergus advised me to work with him, but so far, I'm in the shit. Coman's watching everything I do. I'm saying he will need to decide what gets investigated and who will do it. But if I push the line Fergus was murdered when it appears he took his own life—that won't help me or you. I'm certain of that. We need a bit more than a text message before presenting a theory of homicide." I hope my argument sounds reasonable.

Her eyes drop. "This is… such a shock. Who found him?"

I tell her about the dog, the dog's owner alerting police, and how Coman directed Blain and me to the scene. I leave out the details of not going in the shed and how her father's eyes and part of his lip were missing from his face.

She squints at me. "When did dead men start sending texts, boss? Some new technology I missed there?"

"Suspicious, yes, but not conclusive. For whatever reason, people don't receive texts at all, or they turn up at times that make no sense. I agree the blanket is bizarre when he could've stayed warm in the house, but Trace, you know how it is. We need a steer from pathology, Cadaverman to come to the barrier, rule out suicide."

"I guess it's not easy to jump in and do what's right when the brass is watching you. Right? That's what you said. Wasn't it, boss?"

WEDNESDAY, 1 AUGUST 2012
16.55 HOURS

I'm about to go home, tell Eve the terrible news, and take Pugwash for a bonus walk when Coman calls. In a softer tone, he says, "Join us for a memorial drink."

In the background, I recognize Troup talking to someone. My scalp prickles at the surprise invitation and I suspect Troup has asked Coman to invite me. Perhaps there's another agenda in play.

Hockley is talking to Troup when I arrive. The Chivas Regal is uncapped on the front of Coman's desk—a tidy workspace, a state unseen in a while. The whole office smells clean with remnants of vinegar and other foods gone. I equate the sudden change to Troup's presence, which is not a common occurrence. The three brass all hold crystal tumblers containing the brown peaty liquid.

"Jonah," Coman bellows, like the greeting of a long-lost friend in a public bar. Hockley's eyes lock on the bottom of her glass.

Coman drops his voice. "Come in and join us. You and Ferg were close."

Troup offers his hand. "So sorry to be with you in

these circumstances. I share your loss." He whispers, "We were good mates." In his normal voice, he says, "But you know. Yes?"

"Thanks, boss. It's a big loss, not only for me."

"Quite," he says. "How's his daughter?"

My mobile vibrates with a text from Griff. *Heard news at court. So sorry about FD. Pls call. Need to know U R ok.*

"She's in shock, boss. Excuse me while I answer her text."

OK thnx. With brass, talk soon.

I look up from my phone. Coman lifts a glossy crime prevention poster off his desk and shows Troup. "Terrific. Aren't they? Just the ticket to motivate the squads." His eyes flick between Hockley and Troup. "Might add a wee jump in our next staff engagement numbers, I suspect."

He's as convincing as a novice perjurer. After Hockley's false smile, he puts the poster down and straightens it out like a proud parent. Three failed marriages and a division of his capital by half each time make this job more important to him than many his age. Not that Hockley would care. She'll peg him for 4E or 4J, our escort or court security duties.

When Coman sees me finish the text, he loses the happy face and pours whiskey into a tumbler. "Get this into you."

The peat fume could rip the tired paint from Coman's walls. "Cheers, boss."

I tolerate whiskey, just, but the energy to refuse or the will to cope with being judged ritually noncompliant is absent. The liquid turns the inside of my mouth to a kiln and my tongue to old clay. Troup and Hockley appraise me like invigilators in front of a class full of students, no doubt looking for signs I'm losing it.

"There'll be guilt involved," Hockley says, nonchalant in her judgment of me.

I wonder why they're still staring at me. "I don't think anyone saw this coming," I say, hearing my defensive tone.

They look at each other. Hockley says, "I'm talking about the bereaved daughter, guilt for the family, Jonah."

The second time she's called me by my first name.

Coman sounds unsurprised. "Terminal cancer. Not long to go from all accounts."

Troup says, "Don't be too judgmental, Mick. Jonah's right. I don't think any of us at the EI function believed Fergus was a danger to himself. Know what I'm saying?" His tone suggests he needs an affirmative answer.

Coman bows his head. "Of course, boss."

Troup gestures for me to sit in front of Coman's desk.

Coman says, "Not wanting to trivialize this sad day, but Fergus wouldn't be the first cop. Won't be the last. Understandable in his situation." He sits on the corner of his desk, belly swallowing his trouser belt. To Hockley, he says, "I'm sure many cops would consider it in similar circumstances."

Hockley gives Coman a sage nod and turns a hard budgie eye on me.

Coman reaches for his glasses. "This bit here," he says, pointing a finger to a sheet of foolscap inside a clear envelope. He reads: "'Jenny wasted away. It was awful. I'm not putting anyone through that.' And, of course, where does he do it?" Coman asks. "In the house where Jenny died. He went back. Didn't he? Some spiritual closure."

"May I see, boss?"

Coman hands it to me with a court prosecutor's flourish, a mix of triumph and condemnation.

Some form of percussion invades my ears and pounds away while my body temperature spikes. I want blood—their blood. It's difficult to concentrate. "How did you come to receive this, boss?"

Hockley answers. "As soon as we heard it was Fergus, and suicide, I wanted hard evidence there was no foul play. I directed the officer in charge of exhibits to bring me any available physical evidence."

"I was the officer in charge of the scene, boss." My voice is back to a soprano.

She frowns. "You know what I mean, Jonah. Besides, I understood you were not at the scene when this was discovered."

Blood courses through my cheeks. Finding it hard to concentrate, I force myself to focus on the unsigned, typed note, trying to gauge whether it could've been three to four days in a shed before being placed in the plastic envelope. It appears fresh, unexposed to cold winter nights. "Can you tell me whether this was handed to you in this envelope or in some other way?"

Troup says, "Good question. Ever the inquisitive detective, eh, Jonah. Fingerprints. DNA."

It strikes me this convivial meeting isn't about remembering Dowling. I'm here because I attended the scene and will talk with the pathologist. They want to manipulate me to suggest suicide in advance of an autopsy. With one cop's unsolved murder, they don't want another. They want a full stop on the dying Dowling's death, ASAP. The case Dowling took his own life is arguable. I could tell them about the text, but none of them have earned enough trust for me to share contrary evidence. Troup is a racist who thinks I'm in need of appeasement. Coman was an adversary of Dowling's, and Hockley will do whatever she can to keep in Troup's good books.

I could appear to buy their theory and appease them. I

would attract less scrutiny from Coman and gain more freedom to do my job the way I want to do it. Going along with them might bring me in from the cold, even like me a bit.

I face Coman and ask, "Are we still at the point where we're considering all options, boss?"

Coman looks to his senior officers. In their silence, he says. "Well, not an accident."

Hockley shakes her head. Troup covers his mouth with a hand, a picture of inscrutability. To me, Coman says, "Not with a plastic bag over his head. Maybe assisted suicide," he adds. "Can't rule out a helping hand."

Dowling's long-term mates are Catholics. Usurping God's right to choose the timing of the death call is a sentence to eternal damnation. He had help, but not of the type Coman's suggesting.

WEDNESDAY, 1 AUGUST 2012
17.25 HOURS

Hockley puts a hand to her chest. "I must say, early in the day, before he joined you in your attempted capture of Trix, Nick Jarvis came to me. We conversed for a long time. Well, truer to say, he had a long chat *to* me. He expressed concerns about Fergus, things he said he couldn't tell you."

The heat in my face flashes again and I bite on the inside of my top lip before answering. "Concerns about his peaceful retirement, whether he could balance out playing golf and catching trout. Those concerns, boss?"

She regards me like I'm an errant pupil, and I feel small in the silence she leaves.

His tone sympathetic, Troup says, "You're hurting, Jonah. Natural for you to reject this notion." He glares at Hockley.

"I am hurting, boss, but not so much that I don't wonder why Nick was so concerned. It suggests he was less self-interested than I've been led to believe."

"What do you mean?" Hockley asks.

She may not be aware of her boss's comments to me about Nick's criminal behavior, or his zip-lip signal to me to keep quiet. But I don't believe that would involve keeping Hockley and Coman out of the loop. I address Troup. "Apparent evidence Jarvis was involved with quake fraud, his imminent arrest. It strikes me he might've been too busy to think about the mental state of his superiors. I don't mean anything by it. I'm a little surprised."

Troup says nothing.

"Things said in confidence," Hockley says, "but I'll say this. He sought Fergus's advice about asking you to swap assignments. He didn't want to piss you off if he asked to drop the red zone Bank Secure robbery and join the interception. I advised him to stay on the robbery as that inquiry could lead to Trix and her associates." She swipes a lock of hair away from her eye. "My point is, when he met with Fergus, he observed him to be depressed to a breaking point. Jarvis told me he was worried about him." When she finishes talking, her neck colors to the pink of dawn.

"News to me, boss." I want to add she hadn't taken Jarvis seriously enough to go see the man herself or tell someone else.

"To be frank, it was news to me as well," Hockley says, "but the relationship and communication between Detective Inspector Dowling and me was not as good as it should have been when he retired. Not all his fault, to be fair. I accepted there might've been things about him I didn't know. As I said earlier, there are matters I can't speak about, but I advised Jarvis, given your relationship with DI Dowling, he should talk to you."

"I can say he didn't. I can also say Inspector Dowling talked about his significant travel plans at the EI function. He showed no sign of any distress whatsoever. In fact, he was in terrific humor. Told me he met someone new who might be special in his life."

Troup says, "No doubt all true, son. To your point about

Jarvis's concerns about Dowling, you make a good point. There may not have been too much in it."

Troup's authoritative manner is the tectonic force in the room. He continues, "We don't know who said what, or the extent people were depressed or otherwise because the two men involved are no longer with us."

Coman says, "This isn't your fault, Jonah. No one's blaming you for not seeing Dowling was suicidal."

Troup says, "To be honest, while I don't doubt Fergus committed suicide, I'm not sure I agree with my colleagues it was all down to depression. Despite his note, there's insufficient reliable evidence to conclude why he did it. More likely to be a combination of things. I don't subscribe to the view that you must be mentally unwell to take your life. Some do it to take an easy way out of facing their problems."

Hockley says, "Fair point, boss. I don't want to speak ill of the dead, but Fergus tended to do what he wanted—most of the time. He was quick to distance himself from problems of his own making and pass them to others to resolve. It gives me no pleasure to say this, but he wasn't a team man. Truly."

"Selfish, boss?" I ask. "Is that what you're saying?"

Coman spoke. "He isolated himself to the point of having no friends."

Troup was a friend. I wonder why he doesn't challenge Coman on his statement. Is Troup now embarrassed by his friendship with Dowling? Or does he want to keep Coman as an internal informant and enjoy the big man sucking up to him. Troup gives no clue when he checks his watch.

Coman continues, "I'm sure, after Jenny died, her death, his retirement and his lack of friends proved to be a fatal combination."

I could stay on to tease out more of their lies, gain more insight into why Troup felt I needed his appeasement about Jarvis. Something other than brass exists between these three, but I can't grasp it. I'm not staying to be part of this disgraceful besmirching of a loyal and dedicated cop. Troup is the least of three evils. Although he implied Ferg may've taken an easy way out, he seems more open-minded than the other two.

I will myself to show no emotion. "I understand. I need to leave, I'm afraid. Check on *Fergus's daughter*," I say, emphasizing the last two words, "before she goes on bereavement leave. Will you excuse me?"

Hockley says, "Of course. I need to leave too—call booked with the commissioner. Nice when the country's top cop takes an interest in how we're doing at a difficult time. Please tell Tracey she can talk to me any time. Stress no appointment is necessary. I'll support her in any way I can." She stands. "That said, I don't want you to waste precious time and resources resisting the obvious, Jonah. I heard your reference to being open-minded. But you're one and a half staff down, and now, an additional person going on bereavement. You understand what I'm saying?"

"Yes, boss."

She excuses herself and leaves. Troup extends his hand again. "All the best, Jonah." He follows Hockley out.

When Hockley and Troup retreat, Coman, sheen on his forehead, says, "The Commissioner's executive team has approved the coming year's development projects. When time's up on Trix, you'll be seconded to coordinate all twelve districts' feedback on our performance appraisal system."

I jerk my head back. "Excuse me?"

Coman repeats, "The performance appraisal system."

"A bloody admin role—at a time like this?"

"A prominent role for you there. Career enhancing."

My ears start ringing, a reminder of the first time I fired a weapon and forgot to wear ear plugs. "What? Is this ongoing punishment for perceived wrong-doing?"

He repeats the encouragement, as though parroting someone's lines. Hockley's, no doubt. It gives me a second to think. I tell him the names of a couple of sergeants likely to be more willing and interested in the project.

With a tone implying I'm stupid to resist, he says, "Listen. This isn't my idea. Okay? It's the boss's idea." His forced smile resembles an ugly grimace.

I see Hockley's strategy—jam me up with work. I need to buy time. "Bit awkward, boss. Tracey on bereavement, Vincent on crime prevention with Earthquake Insure, these are significant setbacks for us in case work."

"You need to play your part for our district. I've mentioned the importance of being seen doing the right things. How many fuckin' times must I repeat what everyone else understands? Besides, we can't let those HR people run amok with our appraisal system. Can we?"

"Okay, boss. Tell her how much I appreciate the offer. I'll be only too happy to consider it."

Coman glares at me. "I'll do that, Detective Sergeant. But you listen up for a second." He holds up a sun-spotted hand, index finger extended close enough to make me go cross-eyed. "You're not self-employed in this shop. You can't afford any more turds in your shitty CV. With me? You're fast running out of options with your benefactor gone. And by the way, with Dowling's death, I cut you slack on Yan's complaint against Blain. That doesn't last forever. Nothing does."

WEDNESDAY, 1 AUGUST 2012
17.57 HOURS

Back in the briefing room, I'm desperate for something to wash away the dead rat forced down my throat. Ten detectives are in the room. I call out, "Anyone got any news to give me, some light, some joy in a world getting darker every day? Don't we deserve that, people?"

One of the squad detectives calls out, "Technically, boss, the days are getting lighter now."

I shout back, "I want enlightenment, Detective. I'll trade sunlight for insight any day."

I get a text from Blain as I sit: *Vinny/me poring over audio tapes and DCC's list.*

Tracey appears with no visible sign she's heard about her father. "Boss, we've talked to a security guard in the Windsor red zone. He's given us a new video of our missing Chev taken two days before Nick was murdered." Tracey sounds excited. 'It might be a link between Nick and my father.'

A couple of seconds pass before I can ask, "Tracey, what are you doing here at work?"

"You can't make me stay away, boss. I looked into it."

I wince. "Sorry. Make you?"

"The light's not great in the video, boss, but the driver is bald with a goatee."

"Okay." I force a smile. "Trace, sit here at my desk while I have a quick word with Blain. Can I get you some tea or something?"

"I'm fine, boss."

I find Blain and ask Vincent to excuse us. I lower my voice. "What the hell's going on with Tracey. Why did you let her back in?"

"Let her in? What choice did I have? Do you not think she needs our support?"

"Of course she bloody does, but not here while we're trying to solve murders, one of which may be her father's, for Christ's sake."

"Take it easy, boss. She's in shock and she's safe here. Yes?"

"But she wants to work. On some bloody video in the red zone."

"Humor Tracey for a bit. Yes? People handle grief in different ways. Not so long ago, you demonstrated your own case for not being here."

"I'm fine. I have to be. Someone's got to run this bloody asylum."

Back with Tracey, I say, "Okay. Let's take a look at this video of yours at my desk."

We play the mpg file, its date and time showing the recording was made two days before Nick was killed. The entire clip is less than one minute long.

At its end, she says, "The guard was surprised. The middle of those red zones, like this one, is deathly quiet. So, he listened for any vehicles. When he heard them, he videoed any movement to help keep himself awake." She grins. "Kinda wanted people to show up. Make his day."

"Has he confirmed the accuracy of the date and time recording?"

"Yes, boss."

Although the footage is shot after dusk, the Chev's lights are on and we make out the *T* and *S* on the plate but not the first few letters. I'm betting it's the same make and model of the vehicle we're trying to find.

She says, "Now we know this vehicle pulled into the drive right next door to where I lived with my parents. You can understand why I wanted you to see this. The guy on the tape might be familiar with the layout of my father's old place, at least the section."

"Let's rerun it," I say.

She rewinds and plays, and I get her to pause at the silhouette of a short man exiting the vehicle and appearing to check no one else is around. He then disappears out of shot.

"What's happened here?" I ask.

Tracey says, "Mike, he's the guard who shot the footage, he filmed this guy until the lens was obstructed by a window frame. When he called this in, he was asked to get the plate number. But the short guy came right back out."

"Is that a firearm of some kind coming from the end of his right arm?" I ask.

Tracey says, "Could be a long-barreled pistol, perhaps.

Fifty-two seconds elapse between the Chev stopping in the driveway next door to Dowling's old place and reversing away in a hurry.

"How did you get this video, Trace?"

"A while ago, I had a fling with Mike. I called time a few months back, but he rang me. I think he hoped we might get back together. This is our Danny DeVito. Don't you think?"

"Could well be."

My mobile vibrates an incoming call. I check and recognize it's the head of admin. In no mood for more admin challenges or needless distractions, I kill the intrusion. Coman's proving more than enough to deal with.

"I'm going to brief Inspector Coman with a view to getting armed backup for searches in this area. It could even be the place from which they monitored your old family home."

"Why?"

"To see if it was vacant twenty-four-seven. I suspect Fergus was moved there close to the time you received that text. But a movement like that would be risky. Monitoring the place beforehand gives the mover some valuable knowledge of any other comings and goings in this red zone. They don't want to be seen moving him. Or it could be Trix or an accomplice has been living there. Who knows what we could find, which is why we need to upgrade this op to armed support."

Tracey says, "If this DeVito guy saw Mike trying to film him, he could've told Trix to get out. That's assuming she's been there."

I say, "Whether she's there or not, we'll get a forensic team to investigate, find something useful."

I issue an instruction for the techs to prioritize whatever enhancements of the video are possible and to call Linda Nichol in for a view.

"Trace, I gotta admit I'm not comfortable with you not being on bereavement leave."

"I know. And I get it, boss. But we're understaffed, and the way I see it, not likely to get replacements any time soon. I believe it's better for my mental health if I'm helping. If I get in the way, you'll kick my ass. Right?" She gives a wan smile.

"I'll have to. Let's all assemble at 1830 hours. Pizza is on me."

WEDNESDAY, 1 AUGUST 2012
18.34 HOURS

Corners of the briefing room are forested with boxes of files—some open, some closed, some on the floor by workstations, like sandbags to repel a never-ending tide. I bite my top lip. A clump of papers is spread by one of the whiteboards. This is how shit gets lost and we lose time trying to find things. Tracey is on the tidiness roster this week, so I quell the urge to complain.

Vincent places four large pizzas and a dozen low-alcohol lagers I ordered on tables in the center of the room. The fragrance is of yeast, cheese, herbs, and heated cardboard. The four of us—Blain, Vincent, Tracey, and me—take pizza and beer and move to sit at desks closest to the whiteboard. I say, "Don't leave trace evidence of what we're doing at your colleague's desk. I don't want accusations tomorrow I'm excluding people from squad parties."

This is our first gathering as a team since we found Dowling and I decide, given Tracey is still at work, to acknowledge the terrible event. "Before we get to discuss Putis progress, I want to say something else first. Trace and I discussed whether she should be here. I respect her choice, as I must." I look at her.

"We're here to support you in the way you need, not what I think's right. So please don't be backward in coming forward when it comes to asking for any personal help. Okay? We're all here for you."

"Thanks, boss." Her eyes well up. "Everyone's been terrific in letting me carry on. I appreciate it heaps."

"I need to tell everyone the collective brass view is that Fergus took his own life. To be fair, aspects of the scene pointed to suicide." I go through what I know about the scene. "Hockley instructed I'm not to put resources into what is a known cause of death when the team is under-resourced."

Tracey shakes her head and the others' faces are solemn.

"We need a definitive position on this. I don't like asking, but we need to do so off the grid, in our own time. Understood?"

Collective heads nod.

"So, no overtime, notebooks only, no job sheets until we've got clear suspects lined up."

Blain frowns. Perhaps he thinks this level of caution is paranoia.

"The other thing I want to talk about is the time proximity between the deaths of our two colleagues. I don't know whether this is a coincidence or a pointer to something more sinister. Given how Nick was killed and how Fergus was found, it appears unlikely their deaths are linked in any way other than time. But let's make no assumptions, take no shortcuts. We owe those guys our best detective work."

Tracey asks, "Don't we receive out-of-town assistance for an inquiry of this type, boss?"

"If we're struggling to identify an offender, yes. An independent review of the inquiry files would be warranted, but the hierarchy here won't support that. As for the Jarvis inquiry, we know the offender is Rachael Trix. We need to determine who helped her and who continues to do so. That inquiry's about finishing a job with clear parameters."

I face the board and write, "Sinclair—the Putis or access to the Putis?"

"This unidentified person has been in our National Intel for some time. We know Trix killed Jarvis and tried to kill me. The question is why she was using a vehicle with the PUTIS plate and whether she is connected to a person known as the Putis. What assistance did this person provide before, during, or after the murder? So far, our understanding of the Putis is this." I write on the board: businessman, head org crime, stand-over e.g., kneecapping. I face the team. "After talking to Walter Edgar, we might be getting closer to answering that question." I chug down some beer. "Let's be clear. No bigger opportunity exists for white-collar crime at present than earthquake claims. Quentin Sinclair, Earthquake Insure's CEO, admits this."

Vincent shuffles his feet. "Remind me who the PUTIS plate is registered to."

Tracey says, "John Jones, 2000 East Colombo Street, an address that doesn't exist."

Blain says, "It could be argued, Sinclair's been creating a smokescreen. His limited admissions are an opportunity to talk up EI and the tightening of its procedures. But in doing so, he could be deflecting suspicion away from himself and encouraging the public to believe he's an honest broker doing his best in difficult times."

I say, "Segues well. Play the tape."

Edgar's interview tape played, I tell the team about the

off-tape discussion and Edgar's voice ID of Sinclair. I spin the whiteboard around to show my previous diagram of names in circles and show the new lines I drew to make them into a web.

Tracey says, "I'm doubtful, boss. Based on Edgar's record, he's not the most reliable of witnesses. Also, he may have a lingering grudge with EI. They hung him out to dry when he was charged."

"Reasonable conclusions," I say. "As you saw, Edgar was moderately confident he was listening to the right voice. I was counting on it. Now I'm not." I play the security guard tape.

At its end, Vincent asks, "Didn't the guy Edgar describe have black hair? Sinclair's got black hair. Dyed, I reckon."

I say, "He also said it was possibly part of the mask. Here's how I see it. I was a bit trigger happy feeding him the Sinclair audio, a lesson for us all. I thought Sinclair might've been trying to learn how widespread the scam talk was and prep for more ass-covering. But why would he need someone like Trix, and how would the two of them be connected? He wouldn't, and we have no evidence they are connected. Edgar only ever saw the guy in the mask sitting in the car. You heard him say he was freaked out. He noted nothing else about the man's description, including his build.

"The guy in the red zone video, the guy in the mask, and the guy Nichol described as Trix's regular visitor could be our Danny DeVito. It makes more sense for this guy to be the Putis, not Quentin Sinclair."

Vincent says, "So, Sinclair's out of the picture?"

"I agree with Blain. Sinclair's covering up or deflecting attention. And I don't trust his buddying up with our shiny brass when his company is in the shit. Smells off to me. But our first priority remains finding Trix and her vehicle. If we identify the Putis, we get the person who helped her to escape, maybe more. Vinny, access to the staff list at EI. Can you get it?"

"It keeps changing from week to week, boss. They make Grand Central look like a remote country station. I guess I could get last week's version."

Blain asks, "Could Trix have come out of hiding to kill DI Dowling?"

I say, "We need to be open to that possibility. Anything more from those neighbors, Trace?"

She holds up a hand and chews to finish before she speaks. "I didn't go back after I heard about Fergus. I intended to go out with different mugshots."

"No problem, carry on. I'll take the passport inquiry back."

Blain says grinning, "Are you suggesting we keep running out with mugshots until we identify Danny boy?" He grins. "Why don't we show Sinclair's picture to Linda Nichol?"

Everyone laughs, including me. "Wouldn't I love to do that with the smug prick?"

Tracey asks, "How's it going with checking Nick's background?"

Blain gives me his might-as-well-tell-them expression. I recap for Vincent the intel about Nick's relationship with Trix. "His mother also informs us Nick used a confidential informant at EI. I found out that this informant is not registered with our human source management unit nor is our covert source supervisor aware."

Vincent says, "Well perhaps it was a one-off or intel situation?"

I shake my head. "Those are also supposed to be registered

with HSMU. Hasn't happened. So, while it now appears Nick was connected to a CI, we don't know whether this person was connected to Trix or knew what she was up to."

Tracey says, "Shouldn't we be rattling cages over at EI? Bring Sinclair in for questioning?"

I say, "I had inquiries made about vehicles registered to him and his wife. Nothing relevant there. I don't think we've got enough to question him about. Not yet."

I look at Blain, hoping he's prepared to add something to the Sinclair question. He avoids my eye and reaches for a piece of Hawaiian.

She asks, "Are you concerned about his relationship with the DCC, boss?"

I catch Blain grinning. "With Sinclair owning high-ranking allies, I don't want him circling the wagons to shut us out. More, rather than less, caution is appropriate."

She nods but gives me her face of doubt.

"You think I'm missing something?" I ask.

"No, boss."

"Right, enough for today. Detective Blain, can you give me five more minutes?"

He checks at his watch. "I'll ask my wife to lower the oven temperature."

WEDNESDAY, 1 AUGUST 2012
19.50 HOURS

Blain and I head for the police canteen. He says, "You're more comfortable now?"

"With what?"

"Tracey staying at work."

"I accept we might be all she has."

Another DS walks out of the canteen as we approach. We exchange eyebrow greetings. "Coming in from the cold," he says, grinning. "Everyone spends time in the fridge. Don't let the bastards grind you down, Solly."

This tells me two things, neither of which are surprising. My failure to find and arrest Trix is being talked about outside my team, and I'm offside with the brass. I raise a closed fist in response.

Blain finds a quiet leaner, away from the jukebox and where the light is low. He's picked a spot away from the two other groups of cops, which in my experience, only draws attention to us. I'm surprised, given the hour, more people are not in here. I figure the storm's not far away. I buy two beers and set them down on little cardboard mats. "Not quite the

Chivas Regal that Troup, Hockley, and Coman opened up this afternoon."

He smirks. "Generous."

I tell him about the shit they dumped on Dowling's memory. "Made my skin crawl. They wanted to sell me their theory that Ferg topped himself."

"Jesus, mate. That would've tested you. I looked for you when I got back from the scene. Thought you might need to… you know, talk."

"Appreciate your concern. I went from telling Trace straight into drinking with the brass." I take a drink. "I looked for you at the meeting back there."

He frowns and appears puzzled.

"Tracey. Pushing on Sinclair. I thought you might take the lead with her."

"Not an expectation you shared."

"I thought we were aligned. You didn't look comfortable."

He frowns. "Well, Edgar did ID his voice."

"Half-assed appeasement."

He sips his beer. "You ruling out suicide—is that for Trace's sake?"

"I knew Dowling a long time. Suicide's not his way. And bloody Coman revealed his true feelings. He was almost joyful about the unsigned suicide note. I assume you found it in the house, passed it to uniforms?"

He gives a quizzical look. "No mate."

"Who did?"

"No idea."

"Sure?"

"Course I'm bloody sure. Who got it to Coman?"

"Hockley. She said the OC exhibits gave it to her. I told her I was in charge." I take a swig of my beer.

"For the short time you were there."

The censure in his tone bites. "Couldn't be helped. Hockley was well-informed about it."

Blain drinks. "Don't look at me." He belches.

I say, "Can you imagine Ferg leaving an unsigned note about his intentions anywhere?"

"No. Although if he was suicidal..."

"Did Nick ever say he was worried about asking me to give up the Bank Secure robbery and work on finding Trix?"

Blain frowns, shaking his head. "Wouldn't be any point. Would there?"

"One hundred percent. Hockley reckons she and Jarvis had a heart-to-heart before Dowling died. According to her, Nick held serious concerns about Ferg's mental state."

"She elaborate?"

"Depression. And now Coman's pissed at my suggestion it might be premature to conclude suicide."

Blain gives me his sympathy face. "Bark at you, did he?"

"Lectured me on the pitfalls of shirking contributions to police administration."

"Can I speak in my usual unguarded way?"

"Do I risk that again?"

His eyes assess me across the top of the glass. "You overthink things and get distracted. No one knows when you're going to attack the brass or appease them. And your attitude to Coman—sure, he's not half the cop Fergus Dowling was. We all realize he's just seeing out his time."

"So, what would you do?" I return his look.

"Me? Try and stay on his good side," Blain says.

"Dowling's advice."

Blain caresses his cheek. "Coman's a slack-ass, but he's not stupid when it comes to reading people. He knows your history with Dowling, and he'll guess how you're feeling about reporting to him."

"Not guessing anymore."

"My point entirely. Try and lighten up with him. Find something to confide, work at getting closer, relationship management, that sort of shit."

"The bit of the management course I missed."

"I can promise you one thing," Blain says, shaking his head. "He's not going to change. If you want anything different from him, you'll need to initiate." He sips again.

"Be his only friend?"

"If need be. Think of it as something for us, the whole team."

"You mean you?"

He draws his head back. "What?"

Seconds of silence pass between us before I add, "Sweeten him up a bit, the Yan inquiry goes better."

He bangs his glass on the leaner. "Fuck this." He moves to leave.

I grab his sleeve. "Don't."

He wrenches his arm free. "I thought you knew me."

"I'm sorry, mate. Uncalled for. You make sense. I'm... I'm feeling under the hammer here. Sorry. I'm sorry, mate."

He stares at me. "Verbal fart. You know you don't get many of those. Right?"

I nod in relief. "Understood. Fair enough. Look, I'll think

more on the Coman issue. But Dowling—did it look like suicide to you?"

"Let me put it this way. If you told Coman it was premature to conclude suicide, how is it okay to be definite it isn't suicide?"

"I take your point. I just have a..."

"Gut instinct?"

I nod. "Who commits suicide in the middle of bloody winter by going outside and wrapping themselves in a bloody electric blanket?"

"Let's say you're right," he says. "Do you have any conviction these killings are linked? I mean, not only in the timing. Or that Trix might be involved in both?" He sounds disbelieving.

"If Dowling was murdered, it's possible the killer didn't realize Dowling was dying. At the EI function, Ferg told me that only Hockley, me and Trace knew. That's all."

He shakes his head. "Doesn't make a link. Apart from timing," he says, "anything at all?"

"What if this depression bullshit is to avoid a link being made? He was the one keen for the EI function, not me. He found some new woman and was as upbeat as ever. Why would DCC Hockley come out with that crap when there was nothing to point to it when he was alive? This is like the bloody Bain case—only it's not the defense attacking the character of the deceased, but our own people."

"Perhaps Hockley believes it to be true. Your point about the blanket could equate to a disordered mind. It's a piece of evidence that cuts two ways on the suicide question."

"Nah. I could tell she was embarrassed to tell the tale.

As Troup said, both men are dead—impossible to prove or disprove."

Blain says, "Tracey doesn't believe he killed himself. She mentioned a text she got from him."

I nod. "Identify the author and we've either got the killer... or someone connected. I reckon the killer used the blanket to speed up body rot."

Blain says, "Fire risk. Might burn the note."

"Fair point—if there was a note."

He says, "I don't get why a killer would make it look like a suicide and then send a stupid text pretending Dowling's still alive. What's that about?"

"A defense lawyer's question. The killer or killers have realized they've overlooked something, seen my missed calls on Dowling's phone, Trace's too. Perhaps they were buying time to limit forensics."

"Risky way to do it. I still don't see your link between Dowling and Jarvis."

"My point is, if Dowling's death is investigated, we may be able to establish a link."

"The text could put Trace in danger. And what about you?"

"No stranger to someone wanting to kill me. So long as doubt hovers over how Dowling died, the killer's identity remains unknown. You hold tight. Don't you? Any action's risky. I tell Coman that..." I shake my head. "I'm up against it there."

"Anything I can do?"

"You went above and beyond with Prof Con. I can't ask any more of you."

"Look, I'm over your brain fart. Ask what?"

"Vincent. He was Dowling's man but..."

"I haven't done the little inquiry. You want me to give it priority?"

"Not a priority." I look away.

"What?"

"Vincent's girlfriend or whatever he calls her. When she took out our rear support vehicle, it ended up weakening our position. Trix could've done a U-turn and scarpered. If I replaced it, she could see a hole in the block."

"You're thinking no accident?"

"Paranoia, you reckon?"

"Huge implications."

THURSDAY, 2 AUGUST 2012
16.25 HOURS

Coman's taken a sick day. It's respite from hounding texts or emails, an extension of the dream where I don't work weekends, take long walks around our broken streets, and lie on the couch watching rugby and meaningless TV.

In the late afternoon, at the last trees before the prison entrance, my throat is tight on the swallow. Countless times, I take this trip without these physical discomforts. Through the gates, past the warning sign to visitors, I steer my old Lexus around the winding drive between pines and eucalypts. Under a dishwater sky, I splay my elbows across the car roof and stare at the admin office a short walk away. Sweaty palms to the easterly wind, I stretch and roll my neck. I sense people looking at me. Some will know who I am.

The hard, cynical side of me says my father, Owen Webb, did the world a public service when he killed the man who raped me. I should be proud of him. But being a cop with a father as a killer doesn't make for easy family relationships.

Book signed, I'm escorted from the security arch to a private visiting room by a warden, an expression of annoyance carved into his face. We don't speak. I wait several minutes before he returns with my father in an orange jumpsuit tied at the back. He wears slip-ons. With an abrupt flick of the wrist, Owen's directed to sit in a plastic prison chair on gray linoleum. The warden says, "I know who you are, but if you want privacy, Webb'll be strip-searched when you're done. If I stay, he won't."

Owen gives me a shrug. "I had a dose of the shits this morning." He tilts his head to the warden. "I don't mind if he wants to experience the leftovers."

The warden stands, leaves without another word.

I can't remember shaking my father's hand the last time I was here. I wipe palms on my thighs while my shoulder and neck ache. Owen's gray hair, combed back, is wispy but clean. His sharp blue eyes are now set further back in a pale, well-lined face. The tussock hairs emerging from his ears need a trim.

"Happy birthday, for yesterday," I say. He's now sixty-nine.

He nods, as perfunctory as my greeting, his jaw set tight. "How's Eve?" he asks.

"Same. How are you?"

"Same."

"Owen, if you're the same, we wouldn't have a letter about your health and compassionate parole."

"I don't want any fuss."

"Would you like to come and stay with us?"

He squints at me. "What did I say? Only two seconds ago."

His incarceration hasn't wiped belittlement from his questions. "It wouldn't be a fuss."

"It would be to me. Why don't you tell me the truth about what you're here for?"

The physical distance across the Formica table is

measurable in inches, but as he sits there with folded arms and stone face, he's never been more unreachable. "We want you to stay with us, while you… you know, get something sorted."

"From here to death row. That it? C'mon, Jonah, end the bullshit. You want to discharge a duty to a dying father. You always wanted to do the right thing for you. This isn't about me."

I grind my teeth before I reply. "Who raised me with a sense of duty?"

"So, you're here to talk about your mother? Helpful."

"Can we start again?"

He leans back and folds his arms. "How many people at your station know you've taken your mother's name, know about my parole?"

My body temp spikes, and I let out a long breath. "I admit it. As a cop, I'm ashamed you're in here. And I plead guilty to avoiding you. Can't remember when I last came or shook your hand."

"For the record, seven hundred and thirty-three days ago."

I say, "And I realize, at forty-two, commanding men and women in life-or-death situations, I should be above this."

Surrender complete, Owen sags in his seat, chin on his chest. When he looks up, he says, "Old FD. Heard about him falling off his perch. A few boys enjoyed their dinner that night."

I ask, "How old was he when he arrested you?"

He shrugs. "He thought if I said what happened to you, it gave me extenuating circumstances. But I knew it also gave the cunning shit motive to use against me."

"I blame myself for telling you what that prick in the slaughterhouse did to me. I can never come here without thinking I should never have said anything."

Head down, he looks up at me under thatched eyebrows. "And if you hadn't told me, you'd have been his bitch again and again."

"You never said that before."

He shrugs. "Not many opp…" He stops.

I say, "You make it sound like you knifed him to prevent him doing it again."

"The fuckin' cop in you." He shakes his head, disappointment in it. "Dowling thought the same. But I knifed him to save myself. If I wanted to stop him ever doing it again, I would've sliced his dick off." He stops to give me a searching look. "The way I saw it, no good could come from saying what the bastard did to you. You don't need to beat yourself up about telling me. Right?"

I sense a turning point. "I can't imagine how I would've coped with all of it coming out in court."

"You were the Māori boy who got nailed by dumb and dumber. Never understood why you joined them."

"I didn't know it back then, but I had to become part of the system if I wanted to change it. Dowling was a huge help to me, gave me the chance I needed. Have I mentioned how long it took to get promoted?"

He gives me a pitying look. "More than once."

"And why?"

"More than once."

"My current boss made it clear I'm a beneficiary of so-called equal employment opportunities, the need for the force to have…"

"I know what fuckin' EEO is. They're full of it in here. Your problem is you don't quite fit."

"The point I'm making."

"No, Jonah. Being part Māori's one thing. Being able to talk like an intelligent Pakeha is something that doesn't make sense to cops. They don't get what they're dealing with. Can't handle it. Can't put you in the right box. That's your *real* problem. You can say stuff like, becoming part of a system if you want to change it. You don't think about it. Māori don't talk like that. They either settle for the system that rolls over them or they rebel and end up in here." He leans back with a little lopsided smile. "I blame your mother, all those fuckin' books."

"And where does that leave me?"

"A light bulb moment at three in the morning. Let's get back to what you want?"

I'm unsure what to say. I blurt out, "It'd be helpful if you could take Pugwash for a few daytime walks, and Eve's got nursing skills when you require them. I don't want you going to emergency housing or some doss house when you can stay with us."

"All about what you *don't* want. They call that loss aversion in here." He gives a sardonic grin and shakes his head. "Let me tell you what I think you want. You want me to absolve you from your sins—to be rid of the shame and guilt you finally fessed up to."

I swallow but can't find my voice.

"Am I wrong?"

I force a throat clearance. "Right now, I want nothing more than to find Rachel Trix and lock her up. The longer, the better."

He offers a sad smile. "Suit yourself." He looks around the room with a pained expression. "Now Dowling's dead, you might have a chance. You can benefit from favors I...," He grimaces and brings his right hand to his chest. "Maybe I can hel... Je... sus."

"Owen, you need a doctor."

I leap up.

"Leave it," he whispers, hunched. "Indigestion. Had it before."

He closes his eyes, and his face contorts. When he attempts to stand, he collapses back into the chair, still clutching his chest. I run past him and bang on the door. "Help. We need medics. C'mon. *Help!*"

When I hear no sound of a key turning, I bang again. The door opens and the warden strolls in, holding an electronic card.

"Get help now. He's having a heart attack."

He gapes at my father, who's slumped to the cold floor.

"Now!"

The warden jerks his head back, his open-eyed, deep sleep, disturbed. He leaves in what passes for a hurry.

Is this angina or a genuine myocardial infarction? Will chest compression help or harm? I roll him on his back and thump my fist into his heart once before starting compressions. I pull at his jaw to open his mouth and cup mine to his. After blowing air, I try three more sets of chest compressions.

I can't find a pulse, but I don't trust my finger is over his carotid. I repeat the process until two guards arrive with a defibrillator.

THURSDAY, 2 AUGUST 2012
17.45 HOURS

They said he was dead before he hit the floor. After the medics left for the morgue, I drove home, past Denton Oval, where I had my first game of rugby after moving south with Mum and Eve. We moved to leave Owen behind. I was a nine-year-old beanpole who locked the scrum, standing on my toes to catch line-out throws when other boys needed to jump. Mum took me to rugby games in her Morris Minor when I whined that if I biked, it would take too much energy from my game.

When Owen discovered we moved to Christchurch, he came after us and pleaded with Mum to let us all live together again. But he didn't come to my rugby games. Saturday mornings were always hangover recovery time and remained so.

I drive to my local supermarket intending to get Pugwash a treat. I focus on other shoppers as though they're offenders, noticing their physical details, their demeanors. This is nothing more than a distraction from an unpalatable fact that twice in a month, I failed to save two men who died in front of me.

The normal grocery shop is delivered Saturday mornings so if I'm at work, they leave them in a cool disused coal box on the property. It makes me pissed that Eve won't bring them inside, even after the delivery person has left the property.

People dress down to come here. One woman in her forties wears soft cloth pajamas with a red teddy bear motif. A male, late teens, Māori, displays half underwear, half trousers. He proves gravity still reigns in the absence of contrary effort. Another woman, riven skin, and a peculiar substance in her hair, snap freezes her at sixty. I struggle to date the creeping loss of community pride and sense this is worse than it was before the quakes.

I load eggs, butter, bottled water, Pugwash's favorite dog biscuits, and a treat for him, a piece of rump steak on the black belt.

I navigate holes in the tree-lined road leading to my broken street, peering through a windscreen smudged by demolition dust. A ginger cat, ribcage in view, lies lifeless on an overgrown berm. The number of broken windows increases every day.

Rodents scurry along the banks, burrows, and drains of the Avon River looking for cast-offs from the lost and angry who squat, piss, shit, vomit in, and spray-paint houses no longer under the scrutiny of neighborhood watch groups. The despairing malaise of vandalism keeping us, and security guard companies, in work.

I stop short of the dodgy garage door that won't close, leaving several inches of space between it and the sunken concrete floor, also alleged by the geniuses at EI to be buggered through wear and tear. Inside the house, I glance at the hall ceiling. The plasterer was supposed to come last week, but there's no change. I failed to argue, to push our case, to cajole others to do the right thing by us. And Eve won't call because making the necessary appointment means opening the door to a tradesman.

I swig from the water bottle and the sight of flaking paint and cracked kitchen ceiling summons the red mist. I almost puncture the bottle with my grip. I drop the supermarket purchases, launch the water bottle, and yell, "You miserable assholes." It hits the target, rebounds to the kitchen sink, and destroys two glasses.

Pugwash barks from somewhere inside the house.

"Solly!" Eve comes running out with an anxious face. "What's wrong? What's happened? Are you okay?"

"It's Owen."

The room is quiet. I don't know what to say next.

"Please don't stare at me." She reaches out and touches my arm. "What's happened?"

On the sideboard, the bill holder is no longer empty. "I went to the prison. He dropped dead in front of me."

She jerks a hand to her mouth.

"I tried to save him."

She gasps. "Oh, my God. How awful."

I ball my fists. "I was there with some asshole warden who couldn't win a race with a lamppost."

Eve shakes her head in apparent disbelief.

"It's true," I say, my voice starting to crack. "You should've been there with me. I was on my own. *Again.*"

She splays a hand across her chest and steps back. "What could I have done?"

"I couldn't find his pulse."

She looks down. "I'm so sorry."

"You're always so sorry."

"What can I do?" She turns on the tears.

"Stop making your problem my problem. That'd be a

spectacular start. I have enough of my own, a deep serving dish full of them."

She turns, reaches to the sideboard, rips tissues from a box, dabs her eyes, and blows her nose. "What the hell am I supposed to do—in my condition?"

"Time you took some more responsibility for improving your condition."

"By doing what?"

"Stop firing people I bring here to help you. Or better still, organize your own counselor."

"I didn't fire anyone."

"You refused to talk to her, Eve. You may as well have said, 'Piss off and stop wasting your time.'"

She continues to sob, but it fails to impact me. I say, "There could come a time when you'll be forced to leave the house."

"In a pine box. I won't be worried."

"Given a fire, would you burn to death?"

"Might be better than putting up with your bullying. This isn't about me. This is about you and being unable to live with what happened." She dabs her eyes again. "You should get the counseling."

"What the hell are you talking about?"

"Your constant lies to yourself. That you were responsible for Owen killing someone. And you put your guilt on others." She points at herself. "Easy for you. Isn't it? Right or wrong, guilty or innocent, healthy or sick. Do you feel lucky being able to get through life with such simple judgments of others?"

"Not a lot of luck in this house. Time it was on the market."

I stride to the TV where a reporter promises to bring us

more heart-breaking insurance stories. From behind me I hear, "We both own the house now."

I switch the TV off. "True. I can choose where I live, though. Can't I? Unless you buy me out, I'll put a tenant in here to look after my half of the asset. And best of luck getting them to change their life to make yours functional."

I walk past her to my bedroom. She's in a trance, staring at the black screen.

In the hall, Pugwash stares at me. His eyes, little wet marbles, ask if everyone's okay. I bend and ruffle his head. "Good boy." I force a smile but he's too smart for that. "Come on, Pug."

He follows me to my bedroom door and stops at an invisible wall before him. After years of training, he can read the sign—"no dogs allowed." I'm a dumb ass for doing this, but I slap my thigh in encouragement, and he trots in. I lay out a towel on my bed and lift him. "Don't get used to this I say," with all the conviction of a defense lawyer pleading his client is now sober. He farts in gratitude.

Three pillows behind my sore head, I watch a Clint Eastwood rerun, stroking the silky fur on Pugwash's brown and gray head. Fiction, yes, but how I wish I had the man's balls: his self-assuredness, his ability to be who he is regardless of circumstances, regardless of opinion, regardless of consequences.

Twenty minutes later, a gentle knock at the door diverts my attention. I mute the volume. "Yes."

Eve enters and Pugwash turns, a preemptive and silent plea that says, "It's okay. I was invited." When he realizes he's safe, he turns his focus back to me and I reassure him with further strokes.

"What's happened to Owen?" she asks, softer tone.

"Hospital morgue. I might be able to swing it, so they can bring him here."

Her vigorous head shake leaves no room for misinterpretation. "I couldn't cope, Solly."

"Okay, can you do something for me? Can you arrange the cremation? Ring the outfit at Harewood. We don't need a funeral director or a so-called celebrant."

"A sudden death. Won't there be an autopsy?"

"Pretty unlikely given he was up for compassionate release parole. I'm sure the prison doc will sign off the death cert."

She gives the ceiling a wistful look. "I guess we're orphans now."

"We're a bit old for waif and stray status, eh."

She asks, "Lasagna for dinner? Only needs reheating. Will you eat some with me?"

After I agree and return to the living room, she fixes dinner and I read the paper, taking nothing in. Food in front of us, we toast Owen with a, "Rest in peace" and sip Merlot. Neither of us shed a tear, though I was close when I threw that water bottle.

Eve says in a soft voice, "Since Nick Jarvis, I worry about you. It keeps me awake. You're close to a boiling point. You should talk to someone."

"I will if you will."

She frowns and shakes her head.

I say, "I'm required to talk to the resident shrink. Made an appointment to stop the brass harping on."

"Well, don't do it for this Coman guy. Do it for you, Solly. The counselor might be able to help."

After washing up, I remember Owen's meager possessions in an old sports bag on the back seat of the car. On the cleared kitchen table, I place an old and battered three-head shaver with one of the heads missing, a charger, an Old Spice stick deodorant, a faded green toothbrush, bristles almost flattened, some clean underwear, and two shirts: one brown polo, the other with a blue check and a whisker-frayed collar. At the end of my rummage, I find an unopened packet of Rothmans, and plastic Bic lighter, a Mars bar, a half-completed book of cryptic crosswords, a pocket notebook, and a couple of Bryce Courtenay paperbacks—a lonely man's life.

I take a pill to help me sleep.

FRIDAY, 3 AUGUST 2012
07.45 HOURS

I'm entitled to bereavement leave but I don't want the questions. I realize not taking it also makes it harder to pressure Tracey. Driving early to beat the traffic, my chest and head coordinate a complaint about last night's sleeping pill. It didn't do the job. I woke every couple of hours. I spent some of the time awake thinking about better ways to challenge Eve to be more proactive. Using Owen's death wasn't great—my own fault for enabling her dysfunction for so long.

Trotting Pugwash around the block for twenty minutes before getting in the car hasn't helped. I swear he reads my mind. Normally, the pooch likes being off the lead and wanders away from me but not this morning. He stuck by me and kept glancing up.

Toward work, I pass the shiny, undamaged office of Earthquake Insure. Protesters are assembling outside for their daily vigil. Signs of "Earthquake Inept," "Earthquake Insult," "Earthquake Inane," are on display again as they have been for many weeks.

At the station, Coman joins me at a urinal. "You're in early, boss."

"Prep time before the DCC. She wants to put my balls in a vise at 1100 hours."

Blain's advice plays in my head. "Anything I can help with?"

He glances at me, a look reeking of suspicion. "She needs reassurance you're not spending resources on an inquiry ahead of Dowling's autopsy."

"No, boss. How's it going with the roster spreadsheets?"

"You trying to be funny?"

I finish and wash. "No, boss. I could lend you some of Vincent's time. With his fraud experience, he's a bit of a whiz on spreadsheets."

His head's down with no flow. "Prostate. Fucking doctor's visit coming up. Just what I need. You can spare him?"

"He's fast. Leaves me for dead."

"Well, I won't say no. The boss loves those pictures. What do they call them?"

"Charts."

"Charts. Charts and so-called formulas. Give me a break."

"I'll send him up at ten o'clock. That suit?"

He finishes. "It would."

"On the Dowling file, okay with you if I obtain evidence supporting he typed the note?"

He walks to the basin, looking uneasy. "I emailed you last night. We've confirmed Dowling's fingerprints and DNA on it."

"With respect, boss, those findings indicate nothing about when the evidence was left on the note."

"How do you think you'll get this confirmation?"

"Visit his West Melton house. Given no suspicious circumstances, I thought Tracey should have moral support when she visits."

"The two of you will go to his house?"

"We'll suit up, just in case. She believes his PC will be there. Our techs tell me there's no sign of anything on his work laptop."

He nods but looks disbelieving. "Jesus, imagining a man typing a suicide note on his work computer. How bad is that?"

I nod.

"Don't waste too much time on it," he says. "For all we know, he could've typed the note anywhere."

As I return to the squad room, the building rumbles its usual complaint about an aftershock. Instability passes through the floor and into my feet.

Within a minute, someone yells, "GEO NET says 3.6."

It's like a game of fastest finger after a quake.

FRIDAY, 3 AUGUST 2012
08.05 HOURS

Tracey in forensic coveralls is at the wheel of her car. I say, "I'm not sure this is the best idea for you, Trace."

"Don't worry. I'll take my bereavement leave, boss. I'm here because I need moral support." She turns and winks, both of us knowing they were my words.

At this hour of the morning, most people head east, which makes for light traffic out to West Melton, through the city's less damaged suburbs. Blain had lamented not having the capital to purchase commercial buildings in this part of the city. He foresaw a financial boon for those landlords, and he was right. Reliable and profitable rents, but also the power to lock businesses into longer-term leases.

"Would've been sweet," he said, last year, "having snake-lipped lawyers pay me rent while they give us grief in court trying to defend scumbags."

Owen's last words are in my head. "Now Dowling's dead... Maybe I can hel..."

Help. It was the only word he could've been trying to say. And the wary look beforehand, instinctive, like he was checking for eavesdroppers. Why did he think I had a better chance of getting Trix now that Ferg was dead? The thought makes me go cold.

Tracey takes her red Mondeo off SH1, down a side road as long and straight as an airport runway. Now in a semi-rural location, the pale light of another winter day creeps over frosted paddocks. On my side of the car, a few yards beyond the seal, a ditch runs parallel to the country road, knee-deep with stiff grass either side. It's a natural place to hide a body.

In time, we come to a turn-off and see the gables and long-run iron of Dowling's empty farmhouse.

"I never understood why Ferg came out here, Trace. So much work to do."

"I think he saw that as a positive. He was always going to shift out here for more peace and privacy at some stage. No putting his feet up and watching soaps all day. Not his thing. In a way, he kept a promise to Mum. They talked about it. Also, he couldn't stay where he was in town. Not after she died."

Her lip trembles.

"You sure you're up for this? We can do it another time."

"Sooner the better I reckon. But thanks, boss."

Through a copse, unwelcoming in their cold stillness, we come to a pebble apron offering parking in front of double Rimu doors. As we slow, the light gravel crunches under the tires, and we stop in the same position where I last saw Dowling's blue Honda. Uniforms discovered it locked in the garage of his former house. Another unlikely action preceding suicide. Too tidy.

The rural frost pinches exposed skin and arrests warm breath. I slip on black leather gloves.

My phone vibrates, reminding me to send Griff another text.

"I need a smoke, Trace. You okay to open up?"

"Sure, boss."

She puts booties on and moves to the house, key in hand.

The text is from Griff. *So sorry about the other night. Apprec txts but can we f 2 f soon?*

I'm unsure, given our polarized views, what the benefits of face-to-face chats will be. I respond, *Agree. But flat out. After shift, eat and sleep.*

I don't wonder for long how he'll react. He comes straight back with, *Hope work not all-consuming.*

Of course, it's bloody all-consuming. But I reply, *Promise to be in touch when I can.*

He'll recognize the blow-off, but I can't handle him trying to manage my time.

I blow smoke rings into the still and frigid air and watch the perimeter of the house, looking for signs of forced entry. Perhaps Dowling welcomed his killer or killers inside before he was driven away? Or did they try the door, push it open with a tentative press? With no fear of being discovered, they must've concluded Dowling's tenant at the city house was away. Perhaps they knew a lot about a man who kept his life to himself. Which, in turn, suggests Dowling knew them and may've been satisfied to let them in.

Rural people seldom lock up—one reason why we make them targets for crime prevention strategies. But I don't buy it for Fergus. Despite working in a police station, and in a force with minimal corruption, the man locked his office, filing cabinets, and desk drawers every day. If I didn't know him so well, it would be suspicious.

I suit up, extinguish my cigarette on a tree trunk, and drop the butt into a plastic envelope. I grab a police camera from the back seat and check the date and time functions are on.

Inside the house, cracks run through the lemon-colored walls and white ceiling in the kitchen.

Tracey sits at a wooden table, hands either side of a coffee mug with the stenciled words, "Worlds Greatest Dad," no apostrophe. An item from a two-dollar shop. As I walk closer, she lifts her head and offers a wan smile.

The grandfather clock calls me to the adjacent living room. It takes me back to a time when we talked about secrets, how uncovering them often led to solving crime. I was mesmerized by this clock and affected by wine, and at the time, I believed Fergus knew my own secret. Part of me wanted to tell him and I came close to it. Somehow, I pulled back from the brink.

Back in the kitchen, I say, "Don't take this the wrong way, Trace, but this place is tidy. Almost too tidy. And the cleaning smell. Was that normal for him?"

"From the carpet, I think. He wasn't big on regular house cleaning. Used to save the work for when hours of labor were involved and get someone in when he couldn't tolerate it anymore."

"When were you last here?" I ask.

She touches her chin. "Not sure. I'm embarrassed. I should be able to say. Shouldn't I? But I agree with you. The place feels like a commercial cleaner's been through."

"I'm hoping you'll detect anything odd, or out of place."

"Understood."

"Let's have a decent sniff." The expression was Fergus Dowling's.

FRIDAY, 3 AUGUST 2012
08.54 HOURS

A comfortable gray leather sofa faces a gas fire at the north wall of the house. I sense an eerie chill in the poorly lit room. To the left is a wall-mounted plasma TV screen. Below it, a sound system. To the right are ugly fake logs in a gas fireplace, an antique wooden desk, and a leather, high-backed ergonomic chair, an incongruous mix of old and new.

On the desk, a silver-framed photo of Tracey holding her daughter Rebecca's hand aged about five. She's in an oversized school uniform, wearing her mother's helmet. It covers her eyes and the top half of her freckled nose. I hold it up. "First day at school?"

Tracey takes a deep breath and exhales slowly. "Mum used to take photos of me, first day at school every year. By high school, I was sick of it. Fergus shot that. Becky wasn't going to cooperate unless I let her wear my lid."

She always refers to Fergus by name rather than Dad but refers to Jenny as Mum. No point asking about it now. "We haven't seen her for a while," I say. "You used to bring her in all the time."

"Oh, God. You know what it's like. School stuff, childcare, after-school activities. All go and Nigel's no help."

One night, Tracey ended a shift earlier than expected and caught Nigel in their bed with his secretary. She gathered up his clothes, toiletries, and other items in black rubbish bags and heaved them onto the front lawn, telling him he was lucky she didn't have sharp scissors. Some of the team thought she was referring to castration.

"Can't be easy being a solo parent—like your dad was after your mum died. He did a terrific job as a husband and father. Right?"

She gives me a look of incomprehension. "All due respect, boss, but you don't know the half of it. You are much more like a father than he ever was."

"C'mon, Trace. That's not very fair. With all he did for Jenny?"

"We both nursed her, yes. He helped when he could. You want to know why?"

The twist in her face and her cold eyes tell me there's something I mightn't want to know. "I'm sorry. I'm presuming too much."

She steps toward me. "Projecting, boss. Not presuming. You're projecting the decent, loyal man you are on my father. Like you, he was tough, determined, and successful. But he was never faithful to Mum."

I cringe. "Other women?"

She raises her eyebrows.

"I thought the scuttlebutt was police politics, the usual undermining of brass."

"You only ever saw the good in him. Didn't you? It used

to piss me off you didn't understand what he was like, beyond what he wanted to show."

"I'm sorry."

"I'm sorry, too, for bursting the bubble." She throws her arms around me and I hold her, feeling awkward, trying to make sure she senses my support.

"You still want to be here?"

She pulls back and nods, her eyes full of tears.

"Take your time, Trace. I'm going to look at his desk."

"Thanks, boss. For… you know."

"Appreciate you being straight with me."

I tell myself to block this information out and stay focused—Dowling's frequent request. I pick up a referral letter from Dowling's doctor to an oncologist. Reading it feels like an intrusion.

From behind me, Tracey says, "What about your own parents, boss? Are they still around?"

"Dad was a Vietnam vet, never recovered. He's no longer with us. But Mum could sew anything and that kept us afloat. When Mum wasn't working as a seamstress, she smoked. Eve nursed Mum through emphysema until it killed her."

She says, "Tough, real tough."

So many half-truths in so few words. I hate misleading her, but not trusting people with the truth is ingrained, a safety net, and besides, she doesn't need any more burden today.

"We coped," I said. "Did all right in the end."

I pick up an unconnected computer cable, still plugged into the wall below. I photograph it. "Ideas?"

She says, "I'm assuming you would've told me if you found his computer back at the old place."

"Correct. Nor in his car. Did he say anything about taking it to a repair shop?"

"Let someone tinker with his computer? He said, ages ago, he had something important to finish. I got the impression it was fixing up the house. For me, I guess. But perhaps he was writing."

We move through the living room. I take a picture of a small video camera on a tripod standing between two floor-to-ceiling bookshelves at ninety degrees to each other. I say, "Fergus never talked about videoing anything. Did he have this interest for long?"

Tracey shrugs. "News to me, too."

New, dust-free, it's connected to power. "Check for a memory card in it."

As she looks, I say, "Knowing your dad's sense of humor, he might've recorded some memoirs or riding instructions for the rest of us. Still plugged in, so my guess is he used it within the last few days."

This, it occurs to me, would've made an ideal suicide note. Put the matter beyond doubt.

"Nothing here," she says.

The rest of the room is as I remember it: a library with shelving on every available wall space; biographies, military and naval history, books on finance, property development, and leadership. His lightest material would be classified as literary fiction. I pull out the autobiography of the police chief in the Moors Murders case and hold it up to Trace.

She says, "Fergus expected more on the man's life in the police but it's all about the old case. He said, when he was reading it, he'd do a better job of his own autobiography. He laughed about rattling some skeletons. At the time, I thought it was the wine talking. He never said any more about writing a book."

Through Fergus's bedroom window, the day's new light enters and reacquaints itself with the hall. The brown and beige top hat and cane wallpaper with black musical notes and clefs are out of place. I shake my head but say nothing about how dated it is.

Tracey, beside me, says, "You're thinking, if it was me, changing this décor would've been the first change. But no. He had his heart set on a new roof and those new doors at the front. The most expensive jobs first." She frowns. "You reckon I should cancel the new kitchen and bathroom installations?"

"Well, not to put it indelicately, but you inherit his estate. You don't have to do anything. Sell up if you want to."

At one end of the hall, a heavy brown door leads to a veranda.

"Did he like morning coffee out there?"

The embarrassed look returns. "I don't know, boss."

At the eastern end of the veranda, potted plants and rustic wine barrels contain skeletal rhododendrons, bent and beaten down by the cold. Beyond the tubs, a round iron table and two chairs, the white paint starting to fade. On my haunches, I peer at the veranda surface, looking for marks. Nothing. The back of one of the chair legs is scratched, metal on metal by the look of it. I take a photo. The damage is new, no grime in or around it, and nothing nearby to have caused it.

Near one of the table legs, I find a tiny orange plastic cone, no more than fractions of an inch in length. I photograph that as well. "Fergus was diabetic. Wasn't he?"

"Type one," she says.

"Insulin dependent?"

"Yes, but don't ask me how much or how often."

"Know what this is?" I ask, pointing to the cone.

"A needle cap, to stop you pricking yourself."

"You check out the cabinet in the bathroom," I say. "I'll do his bedroom. We're looking for needles, syringes, and insulin. Check the trash but be careful. Call out if you want anything photographed."

In half an hour, we find one unopened bottle of insulin in the bathroom cabinet with a syringe set. There'd been nothing medical on Fergus's body, where we found him, or in his car.

I try to picture him traveling back to the Windsor property and conclude an unlikelihood of him intending to drive without life-saving insulin. The suicide proponents would say he was past caring, but I don't believe he would risk hurting others.

Much more likely his killer came through the house or through the lattice gate between the garage and the corner of his house. Except for the chair, no signs of a struggle are evident, but any effective cleanup would overcome a fight without blood.

He was killed out here, no doubt. The killer or killers took the computer and any backup system on the premises and wiped the place from ceiling to floor. They got him to Windsor in his own car, parked it out of sight and then placed his body in the shed, adding the elasticized bag to show he wanted reinforcement to end his life. I make a note to check possible CCTV for his car between when he left work for the final time and when the car went back to Windsor.

The fact his cell phone is still missing tends to confirm it's still in the killer's possession. Forensics on the Honda could be useful, but after Hockley's instruction not to waste resources,

I can't justify requesting them yet. When we're standing back in the Broadway hall, I say, "Let's conduct a proper search back in the house for the computer. If he was writing a memoir, he may have hidden it."

"Also, memory sticks," she says. "I once saw those sticking out of his laptop. But something else is missing, something he never went without."

"Yes?"

She's unsure before clicking her fingers. "Barley sugars—he always had a supply."

"He was diabetic, though."

"Yes, but you need sweets to bring your blood sugar up if it drops too far. Insulin's here, but no barley sugars."

"Did your dad ever ferry anyone around in his car?"

"Not that I'm aware of."

I think about telling her what Dowling told me; a new woman in his life. Given how Tracey feels about him, I'm in two minds. I say, "Trace, I don't know if there's anything in this, but your dad told me he'd met someone else. I got the impression it was recent. Did he tell you?"

"I guess I can't be surprised. But no. As far as I know, when he bought the car after Mum died, he was the only person ever to be in it."

"Any thoughts about who the woman could be?"

She shakes her head. "Based on what I know about his infidelity, someone younger, possibly a lot younger, would be my guess."

I say, "It appears he had no money problems with what he spent and planned to spend on this place."

"Correct. He'd invested, seed funding I think they call it. Those books in there, some of them are about venture capital lending. He told me he got into it after the GFC, when everything was cheap as."

"He never mentioned it. These ventures he invested in. You know any of the people involved?"

She shakes her head. "Are you thinking fraud, that he was onto fraudsters who killed him and removed all his records?"

"I'm thinking we're unable to find a single clue he typed a suicide note and all means of doing so have vanished along with his mobile. I'm thinking that's circumstantial evidence beyond the text, suggesting a person or persons were involved in his death and, for whatever reason, have attempted to show Fergus killed himself. Could that be fraud, jealousy, revenge? I can't rule anything out."

"Now we can go to Hockley, do this right, and get an investigation team assembled," she says, enthusiasm in her voice.

I look out to where the sun begins to melt the frost. "If this was someone other than Fergus, I'd agree. Blain and I want to find who wrote the fake note and how it got to Hockley. I'm sure Fergus knew his killer." I face Tracey. "So, until I can trust her or Coman to do the right thing, we'll remain covert."

What I'm not saying is that Tracey's new information about her father's character and his financial circumstances gives me pause. Serious pause.

FRIDAY, 3 AUGUST 2012
13.00 HOURS

The courier bag addressed to me is from Latham and Co., one of several law firms forced by the destructive quake to relocate to the suburbs. I knew the name. Barry Latham represented Rachel Trix in her fraud trial.

> *Dear Mr. Solomon,*
>
> *We represent retired Detective Inspector Fergus Dowling in matters pertaining to his property and estate. We hold instructions from Mr. Dowling, that upon three consecutive days passing without our firm being in personal contact with him, we are to provide you with the enclosed digital file. Those days have passed, and we have not heard from our client. Please note Mr. Dowling instructs us that for reasons which will become obvious to you, there is no copy of the file enclosed.*

I wait until quiet descends in the squad room before moving into Fergus's old office. With the number of lawyers in this city, I wonder about the coincidence Latham acts for Rachel Trix and the senior cop who authorized her arrest.

On screen, Fergus looks like a stern judge about to impose a severe sentence on a cringing prisoner—a familiar expression to me sitting on the other side of the inspector's desk.

"Solly, you have this recording because I'm dead before my time. More about that in a minute," he says, his voice sounding like the first words after a night of debauchery. He breaks judicial inscrutability and gives the familiar wry grin, where half his mouth turns down a little. "Sorry about the mysterious parcel from the lawyer. Given I made no copy, it was the safest course I could think of." He reaches to his right and takes a sip from a tumbler. It's his never-ending supply of Glenfiddich, as certain as the identity of the man staring into the camera.

"The guts is, I'm overdue for some home truths and I figure you deserve them."

My shoulders tense up. He's so still, I think the video has malfunctioned. As I peer at the millisecond timer, he says, "I know, Solly. Have known for a long time."

I grab the mouse and click pause. Feeling uneasy, I move to a window, open it, and light up. I draw on the nicotine to bolster me for what's to come. I do this twice, then extinguish the barely smoked Camel.

Little secrets, we've all got 'em. Haven't we?

I lock the door, check the screen isn't visible to others, and put on headphones.

"Bit of a shock. Isn't it? I was always curious why you never said. I used to think you trusted me. Well, you did, but only to a point. In the end, I never said anything. Your business, not mine or anyone else's. You didn't tell me everything about you and I didn't tell you everything about me." He takes a swig of his drink and holds the glass up like he's making a toast. "Hence this video.

"I told you Marty Troup was rock solid on the job. It was a half-truth. His operational decisions in crime prevention are second to none. But he hasn't been without a streak of the devious either. The stuff about Jarvis was bullshit, and it surprised me. I covered for him and I'm going to tell you why. But you'll have to hang on. I need to pee." He stands, an unsteady movement and shuffles out of vision.

I hear his shortness of breath before I see him reappear. A simple bodily function tests his respiratory system in a way I haven't seen. When he returns, he uses the arms of his desk chair to lower himself and reaches for the whiskey.

"Let me start at what I believe is the beginning. It'd been hush-hush," he says. "Unbelievable the media didn't get tipped off. Marty was a superintendent at the time, same rank as Hockley now. He was only weeks away from being appointed assistant commissioner. The others were three-legged horses in Marty's race. All he needed to do was to keep his nose clean."

Dowling pauses and his eyes shift away. For a second, I think someone else is in the room. "One day, close to three years ago now, we were at a national police conference. Marty copped a bollocking from the minister—budget overspends, traffic ticket targets, that sort of crap. On the final day, when he believed his race was over, a bunch of us went for drinks and dinner. A lot of drinks. I couldn't stay with him like I often did—he had some family in his spare room—so I stayed in a motel nearby. Meant we both had a car. He followed me into my lot space and smashed his vehicle into the back of mine, pissed as a fart. I was close to the limit, but he was in a shocking state.

"His car was drivable, but the front fender was demolished. I reversed it out, drove him home, then taxied back to the motel. We knew he'd have to account for the smash. When he sobered up the next morning, stupid prick filed a hit and run. Said he dropped me off at my motel, went on to his place, but a guest staying overnight had blocked him getting up the drive, so he parked on the street."

Dowling runs a forefinger in the crevice of his chin, a tell sign for him. "I knew investigators would want to talk to me. As you know, we investigate our own with more rigor than we apply to crims. I got hold of the CCTV tape. It showed the crash and Marty staggering around in the parking area like he went too many rounds with Tyson. I stripped the content, told the motel manager I must've given him the wrong date, that there was nothing useful on the tape. As you can imagine, Marty was more than grateful.

"About that time, Jenny was diagnosed. We needed cash to get to the States. Best cancer hospitals in the world but a trip like that costs a fortune. With two months off, I worked it so we did a cruise on the *QE II*. Wouldn't have been possible without Marty's help. He was a bit coy at first, claimed there might be issues with the leave."

Fergus holds up his glass, stares into the amber liquid. "Let's say I provided him with some clarity of thought—a witness who saw him crash into a car in a motel parking lot."

Dowling smiles, the crafty grin I know well. "Unfortunate, but I reassured him I could fix it. When he was in the clear, Jenny received a sizeable dividend check from some outfit called Putis Insurance. Putis bought and sold shares on our behalf. I had nothing to do with the transactions, never heard of Putis. Marty told me he formed a trusted relationship with a guy who was an informant for him. Putis was the informant's company and between them, they cooked up an idea for covertly winning all EI business through internal espionage. Clever Marty helped to embed this informant in EI, got Quentin Sinclair to hire him."

The stern expression returns. "Years ago, I'm going back to when Marty was your rank in Wellington, I believe this informant got him out of tight spots—helped plant evidence against suspects to secure convictions, find witnesses to fill gaps in case evidence, that sort of thing. It all helped Marty climb the greasy pole. He was getting rich but also getting lazy. Any problem, his new mate would fix it. I tried to find out who it was, but the bloke's identity was well-sealed."

Fergus takes a slug of Glenfiddich. "Coming to the present day, this bloke told Marty he believed the best form of insurance for Putis, and its continued success, was to have police inside EI working with him. I think the guy headed up the claims department and handled all the payments. Marty never said what he did, but the guy was in deep and had Sinclair's ear with access to all sorts of records. I imagined he was undercutting their premiums, telling all the Putis clients, and Marty was clipping the ticket.

"Late one afternoon, I got a call from a woman calling herself Harriet, an EI employee. She claimed to have discovered examples of fraudulent payments. One of these frauds involved payment for earthquake damage to your rugby club. There was no way I was going to tell you. Right? I wasn't going to compromise you based on her say-so.

"You said your club's claim for damage was declined. So, I thought she'd gotten the facts wrong. I assumed your club made another claim and provided EI the data it needed to justify a payment.

"Then she called again, told me about Alice Jarvis's church and its claim. She implied the scams were to benefit families of police officers. It started to reek of a lot more than commercial espionage. Sounded to me like someone was taking information from declined claims and turning them into approved claims, with the money going to this Putis outfit. I didn't know enough to tell you anything, so I said nothing. Until now. I mean, I had no idea how they could do that. Still don't.

"I went to Yvonne with my concerns. At the time, she was Marty's local police relationship manager with EI. She was also next in line for AC, so she took care to follow Troup's direction and make sure EI got the police cooperation they needed. Marty's mate, now deep in EI, stayed out of the limelight and no one, apart from me, realized Marty and his mate were connected with EI and Putis.

"The ministers of police and earthquake recovery were aware and happy with our contribution to crime prevention. So, it was obvious my concerns were as effective as a quiet fart in a wind tunnel. I decided to cash in. Fuck 'em. Take what I could for my silence. I mentioned to Marty I knew what was going on and keenly anticipated a top-up in the old Putis shares."

I feel breathless, heavy in the stomach, and push myself back from the screen.

"I got a third lot of shares, but the climate cooled soon after. Who knows what'll happen? Sinclair's just a puppet in charge of minimizing the government's financial exposure so they're not kicking him out for poor performance. Hockley's got her eye on the totem pole, so she's trying to help Sinclair stay out of the PR shit heap EI keeps building."

He reaches for his tumbler. "I'm heading away to a warmer climate for a couple of weeks. I did have a cancer scare but I'm clear. Haven't told Tracey. You probably guessed we don't have the best of relationships. I used the oncologist's letter about potential treatment to engineer my departure, so needed to keep the truth hidden. Hockley and I are like cat and dog. But apart from diabetes, I'm fit—need to be, with the woman I told you about. Met her when I was doing the prison inquiry interviews. Modern girl, unlike me, understands all about IT. She's involved with Marty." He does the curled finger quote gesture with the word involved. "Twenty years younger than me, both of us. She might have Daddy syndrome, but I don't care—take what you can at my age. Good to get one over Marty. I know you'll be happy for me."

His face takes on an expression of regret. "You asked me today if you'd compromised me. Well, this is how compromise works. I suspect if you find a way to use this tape, it won't be the conventional way." He repeats the toast gesture. "Cheers, mate."

He stands awkwardly and his trembling hand comes at the camera. The screen goes black. I lean over the rubbish tin, prepared to retch.

Safe from embarrassing myself, I take some deep breaths and exit the building. I don't believe for a minute Putis has anything to do with corporate espionage or that Dowling believed it.

My hands tremble. I light up and take the deepest draw I can. If Tracey burst a bubble, what the hell is this?

I can justifiably destroy the tape. I can't see how I can use it. As evidence implicating Troup, its value is questionable given the statement is from a self-confessed criminal who can't be cross-examined. And he knew if I attempted to use it, I expose myself to all the inevitable questions about my life, my secrets. My privacy would be in tatters. It doesn't matter Dowling never used the word gay. The intrusion would be relentless. I'd need to make stuff up to silence the questions.

FRIDAY, 3 AUGUST 2012
17.00 HOURS

I search the register of companies for Putis. Nothing comes up, which tells me the entity must be something other than a limited liability company. It could be an unregistered trust and therefore have no tax number. Apart from trying to track down Putis and locking the video file in the trunk of my car, I remember nothing of the first few hours after watching Dowling's confession except walking to the botanical gardens and a loose sense of people who came and went from my office. I must've appeared normal. I don't recall anyone saying or doing anything different.

At home, the unmistakable fragrance of roast lamb, rosemary, and garlic hangs like a fragrant curtain inside the back door. Potatoes and carrots are ready for the oven, long beans in a pot of water. Eve loves the dish, also a favorite for me, but I want little food and less discussion. I don't know what I need. Sympathy? No. That's weak. Besides, I don't deserve it from Eve.

Pugwash jumps down from his low-seated chair, my purchase from a local kindergarten rummage sale. I covered it with a sheepskin. He trots over to say hello.

I give him his usual head ruffle. "Good boy. How are you, mate?" I straighten. "Smells delicious," I say with a false heart. "What's the occas..." I drop my head. "Your fortieth. I'm supposed to cook on your birthday."

She puts a hand on each hip, "Well, you forgot. Didn't you? With Owen's death yesterday and you heading to Dowling's place today, I'm not surprised."

"I'm sorry, Eve. Forty, eh. Bit of a milestone. Can I do dessert?"

"Also, under control," she says, smiling. "I opened one of your better pinots. Call it my birthday pressie."

"I'm getting off lightly."

She points a directive finger at me. "But Pugwash gets the shank bone."

Over dinner, she talks about two of her old nursing mates, their visit with coffees and iced cupcakes in frilly paper, but I struggle to take in the details. "How did they enter the house?" I ask.

"Who?"

"Your friends with the little cakes."

"Monica's got a key. Remember, we agreed someone other than you needed one if you couldn't get here quickly."

"Doesn't Ken next door have a key?"

"He does, Solly. But I'm not going to phone up Ken to let Monica in. Know what I'm saying?"

I know exactly but refrain from arguing she wouldn't need to if only she opened a door. A small task to make life easier for her, both of us.

I say, "Pleased you enjoyed celebratory company." Dowling's image comes to mind, the whiskey tumbler thrust toward the camera. *Cheers.*

"Monica and Ken. No one else, right?"

"You shouldn't worry about me handing my security to all and sundry, Solly." She giggles.

I smile at the speed with which the wine works on her. "Does Monica still write mysteries?" I ask.

Eve rolls her eyes. "Her editor sent back her latest manuscript. Says things like, 'reduce this to one sentence. I don't buy this. You need a bigger secret,' and so on."

Just be aware that everyone's got secrets.

"I thought more about Owen today," she says, moving off her writing friend. "I once asked Mum how they met. She said he came out of Vietnam with hepatitis, bad enough to be hospitalized. After his discharge, he went into a private boarding hostel."

"I didn't know. I thought it was the hospital where she first saw him?"

"No. Soon after. He got better and joined a horse-riding group. They galloped along New Brighton Beach. She said he later told her he was unofficially paired up with the sister of a war vet he served with, but she was ill on the day." Her voice rides up. "Owen on a horse. Can you imagine?"

I smile at her animation but I'm not taking much in.

Got secrets.

"His horse was at the rear of the group. Mum started after the others and caught up quickly. Guess what she said?"

I shake my head.

She mimes two hands on a steering wheel. "'This isn't a Sunday drive, Grandad,' and she sprinted past him to the front of the field. He couldn't cajole his horse to pick up the pace and later told her he tried to copy how it was done in Western movies."

You've got this recording because I'm dead before my time.

"Anyway, she eased back until she was level with him again and she said, 'I can give you lessons on how to ride, mister. Would you like that?' Her cheek won him over."

I know I'm not taking in what she says. I pretend to smile.

Eve moves to the stove and turns on the heat under the beans. "Do you remember the day Mum rounded us up to come to Christchurch?" she asks. "Solly. You okay?

"Sorry, nice story."

"It was like packing our bags for a new world. Don't you think there was something dreamy in all that?"

I force myself to concentrate. "Not so much dreamy, more like an adventure."

"Like living in the movies," she says, eyes wide. "Something you treasure but for the seriousness. And the ferry over Cook Strait? We knew nothing about sea sickness. I guess we were lucky we didn't suffer, but I was so frightened to see her retching. It was awful. Then there was Mum finding out Owen had followed us to Christchurch. She looked like she turned into a Pakeha, she was so white. I didn't mind when he came after us."

Take what you can at my age. I know you'll be happy for me.

"Me neither. I thought he wanted to be with us all. Back in those days, kids lived with both parents. I already hated being called a half-caste kid in redneck Port Banks, so having no dad in the house made things worse."

Eve appears pensive. "Mum never said, but I think he sort of proved to her he loved us all. For a few years, I remember us as the happiest ever as a family until Mum got sick and you started work at the god-awful slaughterhouse."

Tears well and I let them roll down my cheeks. Eve reaches across the table for my hand.

My voice cracks. "I'm sorry."

"No, no. Don't be sorry," Eve says, concern in her eyes. "Tears are a positive thing for you."

I withdraw my hand, grab tissues from the sideboard, wipe my eyes, and take the box back to the table. Pugwash, sensing a change in the room, comes to me. I stroke his head.

"You're right about my guilt over Owen."

She waits for me to say more but I avert my eyes.

"You got to an understanding, though. Didn't you?" she asks. "Made a connection?"

"Of sorts. He called me on it, drew me back to being a boy again. More or less said I was too smart for my own good, why I hadn't been promoted. He kept asking me what I wanted, and I tried to change the subject."

She nods. After a few seconds, she says, "I'll put the apple crumble in the oven, and you can tell me what else is bothering you."

"Only work stuff."

"Here's the deal, Solly," she says, sitting again. "You forgot my fortieth, so in return, you spill the beans. Okay?"

"I thought you already helped yourself to a birthday present."

She lifts her eyebrows.

"It's not only Owen," I say. "Fergus Dowling. The man I thought was like a real father. He looked out for me," I say, looking up through fresh tears. "All those years I wanted to be sergeant. I got to where I thought it wasn't going to happen. There was always someone who had some policing experience I didn't have, something perceived to be important. Ferg persisted, got it over the line for me."

I dry my eyes with the heel of my hand. Her neutral expression is effortful, another tell. "Something you want to say?" I ask, keen to focus on her thoughts more than my own.

"I thought… Okay, I'll say it. When Dowling came to the house last year, I thought he was a bit of a sleaze. I never said anything because I knew how you felt about him."

"Sleaze? An interesting description based on a one-off meeting."

She studies her hands. "He didn't make any advances if that's what you're thinking. He did ask if I had a younger sister. It was disturbing."

"Turns out, you're not far off the mark," I say, moving to the kitchen sink. I run the hot water.

"What are you doing?" she asks. "We still need to eat."

I point to a few things on the bench, the pot in which she's parboiled the spuds before roasting. "Thought I might get these out of the way."

Eve picks up a tea towel and joins me.

"No, you go and put your feet up," I say. "I'll sort these. Go and preserve some of those valuable looks you think you still possess as a forty-year-old and after this, I'll carve the meat."

She flicks me with the tea towel, and I tell her what Tracey said.

"There's more, though. Isn't there? Something else," she says. "You may as well tell me. Is it something about how you found him?"

I half-smile at her imagination. A couple of years ago I told her about a deceased male, a case of autoerotic asphyxia.

"No. Me being bloody stupid, facing a day of reckoning about my judgment."

She waits me out.

I tell her about the video. "He arranged it so only I would see it. And if I show it to others, it means I'll breach my privacy."

She frowns. "Nasty. Is this something you must deal with?" she asks, drying the pot. "If you ask me, I think you have enough on your plate without a dead man's past."

I nod, more acknowledgment than agreement.

"It isn't only what he said. Is it? You look wounded, betrayed."

"Sleaze isn't a crime. Being bent is the crime. That's the betrayal. Taking from the most vulnerable citizens in this city, when he gets daily reminders from his own team affected by quake insurance problems. That he could be so much like Trix, so selfish... is... is shocking."

"Didn't you say it was to help Jenny fund specialist treatment?"

"Can I rely on it being true? I think he wanted to spend it on some gold digger twenty years his junior. I need to find out more."

"Why? He's dead." She holds a pot lid to her chest, like a shield. "You can't go after Troup or other senior cops, Solly. What if you're wrong. What if this, this confession, is a... I don't know, some sort of windup? You always said he loved his practical jokes."

"I wish. He wouldn't joke about this. He's pissed Troup off big time, putting his hand out again. No. Corruption fits with so much money being paid out as proceeds of crime, but so many claims still outstanding."

"Well, why you, Solly? You work so hard for recognition. I don't want you to put it all at risk."

"Because he confessed to me. No one else can take this up."

SATURDAY, 4 AUGUST 2012
10.00 HOURS

With eight of our twelve days gone, the team is at work today. I'm wondering if Blain's got anything useful from Edgar's SIM card when Vincent approaches with the satisfied face Pugwash once had when he brought a dead rat to our door.

"Detective. You appear pleased with yourself."

"About to see if the DCC will take my call. I uncovered what I think's a huge lead on Trix. A sensitive matter—involves EI, boss."

"Do you not recall our discussion about me being first cab?"

He offers a tight-mouthed grin.

"Well?"

"I'm in a tight spot, boss," he says. "I don't much like having things over me. Can't imagine anyone who does."

With Dowling's revelations, Vincent's my only chance for understanding more about what's going on at EI. "You want an exchange. Yes? Recording for information?"

"I wouldn't think that too unfair, boss."

"I might have a copy. Thought about that?"

"In your situation, that's a probability. But you say you're a boss who backs his staff, so if I give you something of value, I'm picking you might return the favor—do the right thing." He appears confident in his unblinking attempt to read my reaction.

"Perhaps we could complete this negotiation over coffee."

At RE:Start, I buy Vincent's quad shot half-decaf latte and an Americano for myself. The faces of four other customers suggest they are engaging in life-changing conversation. Vincent glances at them looking like he wants to make a run for the door. I wait him out. His first sip of latte leaves him with a cream fault line above his top lip. I run a finger under my nose. He gets the message.

"I prefer not to move from being under one shit heap to another, boss."

"Not a dumb preference."

"DCC Hockley's made it clear I'm not to discuss what's been happening there."

"I recall you said something different. Something about not being a secret what you were doing at EI. Standard CP, yes?"

"It is, boss. From what I can understand, the DCC's received a lot of praise, but now the media know we're helping EI, some of their shit's landing on her. Unlikely to help her in any race for AC." He pauses, peers over my shoulder. "Sinclair." He grabs a menu from a bronze holder and pulls it in front of his face.

I half turn. Sinclair walks in with his partner, Gwen. Both of them look like they've had a brisk walk around Hagley Park. They smile at me and I wave back.

From behind the menu card, Vincent says, "You said coming here meant some privacy."

"He's not your boss, Ian. The longer you try to cover your face, the more ridiculous you appear."

He peeks over the menu. "He's got his back to me."

"Okay, you need an out? I'm doing your performance appraisal. I like to run those things informally. More pleasant surroundings to help with difficult conversations."

Vincent lowers the card. "Cool."

"Anyone asks, you can say I rated you as meets expectations."

"Generous, boss."

"Given your failed spook duties, I agree. Let's start with what made you smile before."

He glances over my shoulder again. "I gave the latest staff list to Blain as requested. Nothing of interest." He lowers his voice. "But when I went to HR, I overheard some talk about a guy called Oliver, who's close to Sinclair. He's not on staff, no file on him. People say he's an external consultant. A business process engineer, whatever the hell that means. They pay him a lot."

"Something to be excited about?"

"Well, he's got something to do with the payments processes and he's brought someone in who's on staff, name of Harriet Volp. One of the payment team leaders but she's been full of excuses for avoiding an interview with me. Last-minute canceled appointments, been sick, that sort of crap. Makes me a bit suspicious. I mean, I know we can cause anxiety in some people who've done nothing wrong, but I had a sense..."

"You sure of the name, Harriet Volp?"

He nods. "Sinclair hired her."

"He involved himself?"

"Correct. With a bunch of managers under him, he personally hires this one person. That's why HR staff talked. They got their noses outta joint. After Nick Jarvis was killed, no one saw her again. Hasn't been seen since." He pulls a folded sheet from his jacket. "Passport and photo," he says, checking no one's watching before he hands the document to me. "Copied from her staff file."

"Jesus Christ." I lower my voice, but my pulse knocks loud in my temple. Rachel Trix is now Harriet Volp. Longer hair, over-sized glasses. "When did you discover this?"

"Last night. Not interviewing her nagged at me, made me suspicious. I wondered if she was a phantom employee, someone on the payroll who doesn't exist. So, I pulled her file from HR."

"What claims work was she doing before she stopped turning up at EI?"

"Her file says residential. Apparently, she led one of four teams, managed five staff. They make sure the…"

Dowling's statement comes to mind and I interrupt. "This Oliver bloke who introduced her to EI, did he ever appear to be connected to any senior ranking cop?"

"Don't know. I haven't seen him either. This is only off the back of me hearing whispers. Right? You got a name for this cop?"

"Fergus Dowling believed someone close to Sinclair was also close to a senior cop. Unlikely he was talking about you."

"Well, if we're talking brass, the DCC visits Sinclair. Quite a lot. I guess, she's a possibility."

I ask, "Could there be anyone else?"

His doubtful face. "I wasn't in a position to monitor who was talking to who and how much. Not without drawing attention to myself." He nods toward Gwen. "As chief spokesperson for EI, she must know what's going on. Is this important?"

I make a mental note to dig around, see what I can find out about this woman. "Not sure. You said the claims officers make sure about something."

"Yeah. The assessments are signed off and validated with correct claimant addresses, identification of bank accounts, all the expected stuff. My job is to check claimants against our intel, make sure their identity can be double-checked so we identify known offenders or find fake claimants with dodgy bank accounts. EI are diligent with payment signatories. I added a step to ensure independent identity checks. Not popular and it meant I slowed things down a bit. So, is there payment fraud? I can't see where or how. We need an informant to open a door."

"How long had Trix worked there as Volp?"

"Three months on permanent staff. Before that, she was casual, a few days here and there. I didn't find out she became permanent until after she went missing. I'm not in there every day so I didn't think much about not seeing her around."

"Before she went missing, did you tell anyone you thought she was dodging you?"

"I emailed Sinclair. He said he talked to her, and I didn't need to be concerned. He also said because she was a team leader, she was there for people management skills more than technical or system knowledge. I could make her a lower priority."

I raise my eyebrows. "Anything else?"

His shoulders drop. "No, boss."

Does he want me to do cartwheels? "Appreciate you came to me. Well done."

Vincent's intel is the extra requirement to justify interviewing Sinclair. I need his answers about how their external consultant could introduce a staff member to him with a false identity. Was he duped, or was he in on something Vincent had not yet detected?

I say, "I mentioned at the team meeting about Jarvis having an unregistered confidential informant at EI." I stare at him looking for a reaction.

"It was news to me." He looks pensive.

"What?"

"Well, might be nothing, but a day or two before he was killed, he was hanging outside the EI building when I returned from lunch. He looked at me. I waved at him, but he ignored me. I think he still held a bit of animosity after his girlfriend and I got together."

"Long time ago. Police College, wasn't it?"

"He never let it go."

"Ian, what if he turned his back on you for a different reason?"

He shakes his head, unsure of where I'm going.

I'm not entirely sure myself. I say, "We know you never worked with Volp. No grudges between you. We also know you went into EI without my knowledge. We don't know why."

He folds his arms. "Previous fraud squad experience."

"Perhaps. Also, common knowledge you scramble from one payday to the next, courtesy of investing in horseracing, your personal life being in turmoil."

His empty cup becomes a source of silent fascination.

"Who does the finger get pointed at when EI goes tits up, son?" I pause, silently counting to five. "You need to be careful. Sinclair's relationship with the DCC is close. When the excrement hits the aircon, you'll be Hockley's cover, the one who forward rolls off the high ledge. You will be positioned as the key holder to dirty corporate secrets, experience in fraud. They might say with your life in disarray, gambling issues, you became corrupted, gave advice on systems to help you steal, switch sides."

"Me? No way, boss." He sounds horrified.

"Think about it, Ian. She put you in there. You said yourself, she's ambitious. That much is common knowledge. She'll need something when their demise is shown as systemic fraud."

His mouth turns south. "I can't find any systemic fraud."

"Not found any yet. Doesn't mean it's not happening."

"You think it is, boss?"

"I'm thinking there was a different reason why Nick was avoiding you. He didn't want to be seen with his CI."

"Volp, you reckon?"

"It worries me no one knew about their relationship or their breakup. But if it was Volp, we're all in serious shit. It would mean the whole story about an acrimonious breakup with her is rubbish and they ripped off EI as a team."

Wide-eyed. "Holy crap. Then she's betrayed him?"

"Open mind on the possibility. A plausible explanation for now, but what we know increases the importance of uncovering who else she was involved with. This Oliver guy—I reckon no coincidence he's introduced her, the reason I asked whether you saw another cop with Sinclair."

He nods, but I suspect from his vacant expression he's struggling to take in the gravity of the situation.

I say, "I think Hockley might be in the dark, but she hasn't become a DCC because she's stupid. You're still potentially in the cross hairs. I'm guessing she's destabilizing our relationship. Am I right?"

He nods. "It wasn't DI Coman who instructed me to spy on you. It was the DCC. She said if it unraveled, she would blame Coman because he owns that MO."

"You get an offer of promotion?"

He nods.

"What's her beef with me?"

He pulls an ear lobe. "Not my place to ask, boss. She made some comment you were a disciple of DI Dowling, now in a team of one. It was in my interest, as well as hers, if I held something on you. Sorry, boss."

His expression of relief is akin to an offender after confessing.

"Would've appreciated knowing this a bit earlier, Ian."

"What would you do in my situation, boss?"

I give his question some thought. "Can't change what's happened. From here, make reassuring noises, say how much tighter things are over there. Say nothing about Trix. I'll work out a way forward without compromising you."

"And the tape, boss?"

"It's safe for now."

SATURDAY, 4 AUGUST 2012
12.30 HOURS

I find Blain in the canteen having lunch—homemade ham sandwiches with white bread.

"Not a vegetable in sight," I say.

"Rabbit food in a sandwich?" He gives me his contemptuous face. "Not my thing."

"I need you to do something for me."

He strokes the back of his neck. "I hear you took Vincent out for coffee."

"I take you out for coffee."

He sounds miffed. "You normally keep us informed, that's all."

"Someone else monitoring my movements now? Finish your sandwich. We need to take a walk, take advantage of what passes for sun in this climate."

He gives a sardonic smile. "Ride the camel would be a more truthful account."

Blain's expression is a reminder he doesn't like the smell of my Camel brand. The weather's brighter but the southerly is still cruel to exposed skin. We walk in the direction of the city's museum.

"When Trace and I went to Dowling's West Melton place, a video camera and tripod were set to go. Made sense for a farewell message. But we found nothing in the house to assist typing a suicide note."

Blain raises his eyebrows, not a reaction of surprise.

"Yesterday, I received a recording, held by his lawyers."

"Intentions about his will?"

I tell him the content, except the bit about Dowling knowing my secret.

"Hang on. You're saying Fergus Dowling was involved in this Putis scam?"

"That's what he says. He played the informed spectator to what Troup and his mate did and became a beneficiary in the process."

"Paid for silence?"

I nod. "Can you discreetly find out how much money is in his estate?"

"Of course. Now we have a motive for murder, yes? Every day Fergus was alive was a drain on the cash flow." He gives me an appraising look. "You seem somewhat at ease about this."

"Only because I'm twenty-four hours processing time ahead of you, including time to observe some interesting complications."

"I'm guessing the coffee meeting with Vinny is one of those?"

We pass the museum, the wind now at our backs. Two buses pull in and offload tourists outside the Gothic-style building. It's come through the quakes well, unlike much of the Arts Centre opposite.

I say, "A complication as big, possibly bigger than what

Dowling said. According to Vincent, the Harriet woman is Harriet Volp, hired personally by Sinclair, a woman whose true identity is Rachel Trix."

"No fucking way. Oh, fuck. How much better does this get? What about Yan? He allegedly works there. He must have known."

"I checked. Big place. He had no contact with her and the name Volp on the staff phone list wouldn't ring any bells for him." I hand Blain the copy of the passport.

He says, "I said Sinclair was in on something big. Didn't I?"

"You didn't have evidence. With all the minions over at EI, I don't know why Sinclair interviewed Volp/Trix, but she was introduced to him by a business consultant named Oliver. We need a way around Hockley to interview Sinclair."

"Vincent's found nothing. Right?"

"Nothing he's seen as dodgy."

"Who else knows about this?"

"Closely held secret, I reckon." I cross two fingers. "With Hockley and Sinclair like this, we need to know whether she's ignorant or turning a blind eye about Trix and her fake identity. She's not going to tell us, which brings me to what I want you to do."

"Not sure I like the sound of this."

I stare ahead. "Given the Hockley/Sinclair relationship, we will be blocked if we try and interview Sinclair or his partner, even if we say our only interest is to learn who their consultant is. I suspect if we mention this guy's name, a huge red flag will run up the pole for them. So, we need a surprise, our only viable way forward."

"What's my part in this magic trick? Get my head sawed off, do I?"

"Such little faith. All I need you to do is to call Sinclair's secretary and make an appointment."

He frowns. "Oooh, I feel so exclusive. Why do you need my secretarial skills, which, by the way, are nonexistent?"

"Mine are worse. I already tried, which is why I know I blew it. I think she'll recognize my voice. You can be a newbie to her."

"Why would a lowly senior detective be more successful?"

I fold my arms and grin in silence.

"Jesus, you want me to pose as Troup. Don't you?"

"Close. As his liaison officer, from an unlisted number. Frankly, I'm out of options."

He frowns, which creates a vertical ravine between his eyes. "Makes it okay. Does it? I mean, you're asking me to impersonate a police officer."

"No, you *are* a police officer."

He shakes his head. "Yes, but someone in Troup's office? Put aside, for the moment, my obvious reluctance." He juts his chin to emphasize his point. "I don't see how the benefit outweighs the risk."

Blain lying to the Prof Con artists on my behalf was undoubtedly worse, but I decide not to bring it up.

"I'm not guaranteeing it will. But a full identification of Oliver at this point is also critical. Given the daily shit flung at Sinclair, we can expect the CEO's list of approved callers to be extremely short. A few pollies, Hockley and senior residents of Bullshit Castle."

"I suspect you have enough from Dowling without this charade?"

"No. Only the stuff about Harriet's calls. Given his admissions of his own criminal dishonesty, we need to corroborate what he says. So, storming over to EI demanding info to nail Oliver-the-bloody-consultant's identity isn't going to cut it. Hockley would blow a fuse. It would confirm for her Dowling was a mental case."

Blain bites his bottom lip. "Am I the only one who thinks this is hare-brained?"

I stare back, hoping he'll be persuaded.

He shakes his head. "The only reason I'm considering this is because your idea these murders are linked might be right." He peers at me. "What I don't understand is why Dowling's confessed to anything. He was never under suspicion."

"Agreed. He's either relieving what little spark of conscience still lived in him, or he wants me to take on the challenge of removing tarnished brass to benefit my career."

"Or kill it, mate. Ignore him and we're no closer to ending this. Act on it, you set off the biggest shit bomb to ever hit the service. Neither choice is tasty."

I point to my neck. "I'm up to here with placating and doing what others think is right. But I still need your help."

He nods. "Dowling's revelations mean we need to dig deeper. I'll call EI."

I slap his arm. "You up for a beer after work? I'll fill you in on everything else we failed to find at Ferg's place."

His mouth turns down. "Nah. The wife's dragging me to the theater. Won't get a decent meal. All fancy hors d'oeuvres and bloody chardonnay."

"Bit of culture. Admirable character building for you, mate. By the way, I appreciate the vault contents on Yan. I think I can do something for you in return."

"Better coming from you than me," he says, smiling.

SATURDAY, 4 AUGUST 2012
15.55 HOURS

Two stragglers from a previous funeral service head for cars next to mine. After handshakes they both depart, leaving my vehicle the sole occupant of the parking lot. The hospital van left without me noticing. The box of beers I brought for the guys delivering Owen's body will wait.

I walk into the chapel of the Harewood Crematorium with five minutes to go. The place is quiet, almost ominously so. Only Owen in a cardboard coffin in front of 150 empty blue seats. A young man, business-like in his dark suit and stride, enters and taps the microphone. "Are you the Mr. Solomon who indicated he would be the sole attendee?"

I want this over. "I am."

"Would you like to say a few words, sir?"

Words. Words about our relationship, my inability to face our history square on, to rise above what should have made us closer. I steel my mind not to think about lost opportunities with my father, but the thought is like an insomnia-driven music track the mind can't dump. Was it too much to hope Owen and I reached some understanding about our emotional distance?

"All been said, I think."

My thoughts go to the tiny bit of newsprint in my pocket, the announcement of Owen's death to anyone reading the newspaper. Eve cut it out and put it on the kitchen table. Owen's name, place, date and time of cremation, a reference to his service number in Nam. No reference to surviving family. I placed this ad in case an old ex-con was tempted to drift out of their bed-sit, doss house, or shelter. I'm now thinking, if anyone shows up, they might regret the effort. None of the ubiquitous pastries, sweet slices, and egg sandwiches. A long shot, but if someone comes, it might be a chance to discover what Owen knew about Dowling.

"Short and sweet, that's what we like," the suit says.

The funeral functionary says the words of the committal and, with a flourishing finger, pushes a button and the final form of my father disappears behind a velvet curtain and will be ashes within hours.

I turn to leave and see Mick Coman exit the chapel. Does he not want to be seen? He turns when I catch up and call out.

He's in a white shirt and dark suit. "I saw the little death notice and thought, with your sister's condition, you might be here on your own. I'm sorry for intruding."

"No, not at all, boss. Appreciate the gesture."

His hands are mobile, finally settling in front of his groin. "Service was short."

"Not a service, more an acknowledgment, eh. You knew he was my father."

"Your business who you tell," he says, face serious. "I was around at the time you moved to Christchurch for the job. As far as I know, only Dowling and Hockley knew."

"The prison term?"

He shrugs. "Yeah. My father died after a long period of silence between us. We're all different, but when he died, I couldn't stop thinking about all the years lost, years never recovered."

"I suspect yours didn't go to jail?"

"Well," he says, drawing out the word, "different kind of jail. Bit of a rat bag. Missed the conventional slamming of steel bars by a nose hair. Sort of bloke, if he had an asshole transplant, the asshole would've rejected him."

I chuckle, which makes Coman smile, releasing a little warmth. I can't remember seeing him like this. Ever. It occurs to me Blain might've been right. Offering Vincent's help was a good thing. "Meant to ask, boss. Was Vincent any use to you with the spreadsheet issues?"

"He was," he says. "The DCC was happy."

"Excellent," I say, wondering if and hoping Coman was seeing me in a different light.

He offers his hand. We shake and he says, "Given current circumstances, I don't want to talk about work here. Take the time you need, Jonah. You may not've been close to Owen, but these things impact in unexpected ways."

"Thanks, boss."

In the car, my phone vibrates. "Yes, Tracey."

"Been talking to a farmer who says he rang us a few weeks ago, boss. Reported a burned-out car at a riverbed on his farm up in Oxford. Claimed a woman picked up a guy and drove away from the fire."

"Not Crimewatch material, I'm afraid."

"No. Except, the farmer said he gave Comms the license plate and they said the owner would be asked to remove it as it wasn't a police job. But here's the thing. The plate was PUTIS, boss."

I curse.

"Another thing, boss. Bit awkward."

"Speak freely."

"I asked about the delay on this info being passed on when it was relevant to our inquiry."

"With what result?"

"The head of admin, boss. He said he called you, followed up by email three days ago, after the farmer rang back, but he received no response."

"Jesus Christ." I hit the delete button believing it was another complaint about me.

It's not always about you, son.

"Sorry, boss."

"Appreciate the heads up. Locate the farmer who called it in. Try and obtain more description on the couple who left the fire scene."

SATURDAY, 4 AUGUST 2012
16.50 HOURS

Forced laughter pushes its way through the glass in Dowling's former office. Coman sits, feet on the desk, with Vincent and Tracey in front of him, an attentive audience.

Coman calls out, "Ah, our sergeant returns." He swings his legs down.

"Comfortable there, boss? Are you going to add DI Dowling's workload to your own? Save a bit of the police budget?"

The long jowls of grumpiness return. "My office."

On the way, he says, "Did I not say take some time?"

"I appreciate the offer, boss. No one can say I'm stricken with grief, and to be honest, I have pressing things here I need to discuss regarding Dowling."

Side by side in the corridor, he says, "I'm reliably informed you chatted with Alice Jarvis?"

"She likes to tell me stuff, how disappointed she is in me, and so on."

"She could help me do your appraisal. Boss would give me marks for initiative." He glances at me. "Make sure Victim Support's in the picture."

"She's connected, boss. Also, I want to say thanks for being at the crematorium this afternoon."

"Doubled the turnout. I don't often achieve that."

"The living, yes."

He gives the hint of a smile.

His desk is back to its normal state, a position between disorder and chaos. He points to the seat opposite before fishing around in piles of paper and folders. He finally extracts a sheet from the mess with Hockley's writing visible.

He says, "So you want to talk to me about your visit to Dowling's place."

I try but fail to read Hockley's notes. I can't do that and keep eye contact with Coman.

"Yes. It was unsuccessful. We found nothing to corroborate he wrote the note. No computer, no disks or memory sticks, nothing from which an unsigned note was composed."

"Shit." He folds the page to make it invisible to me, stares out the window, and frowns.

I sense he's aware of something I'm not. "Not in his car," I add, "or anywhere at the property where he was found."

"He could've done it anywhere. I said that. Didn't I?"

"Yes, boss. You did. Right to ask, though. Isn't it?"

He resumes eye contact. "Ask what."

"Well, Tracey says he used a laptop, he wanted to finish some written work, a memoir or something. She remembers memory sticks plugged into a laptop. The question is, how come none of these things are to be found?"

Coman blinks, looks uncomfortable, and shifts his sizeable frame in the chair.

"You're not suggesting, are you, boss, that Dowling

borrowed someone's computer to write a suicide note, only to hide the fact he wrote it? I mean, what would be the point?"

He runs a finger along the lines in his forehead. "Point taken. But he still topped himself. You can understand why?"

"What I can't understand, is why put his fingerprints on the note but dispose of the evidence to prove he created it. We can't find his mobile phone either. And what of the man himself?"

Coman's forehead lines deepen, subjected to their own quake. "What?"

I think about how he and Dowling were not close. His issue is a lack of motivation, an eye on the sunset, driving him to avoid conflict. His appeasement of Hockley is the politics of survival, not corruption. Can I risk more discomfort for him?

"Dowling knew, like the rest of us, not every suicide leaves a note. You leave a note, you want people to believe your intention. You don't print it without signing it, as well as hide or destroy every piece of evidence corroborating your intent. That gives it no more authenticity than finding it on a computer screen. I'm thinking if he didn't craft it, who did? If someone covered up a homicide, they might produce a note as a panic measure. Maybe figure they could use the circumstances of illness, his wife's death, the method of his own death, to suggest suicide. A note? Last piece of the puzzle, isn't it? Not to cops like us, not to anyone in their right mind, right? The note in these circumstances, with this man, it doesn't fit."

He leans back and folds his arms. "Why would anyone kill him when he was dying?"

"A defense lawyer's question, boss, and it assumes the killer knew. And if they did know, there might've been some risk associated with a lingering death. Boss, if I obtained evidence, circumstantial or otherwise, would you review your position about further inquiries?"

He unwinds a paper clip, starts cleaning his fingernails, and glances at the folded foolscap sheet. "I need something meaningful for the boss, though."

I ask, "How many people knew about Fergus's illness?"

Eyes still on his nails, he says, "I guess when you're taking an early retirement, it's no secret."

"Did you know?"

He shakes his head. "Not about his cancer."

"Until the EI function, I didn't know. I understand he hid his illness from everyone except those who needed to approve his early retirement."

He discards the warped paper clip and leans forward. "What are you saying? Someone in here killed him? Jesus Christ."

"What I'm saying is, circumstances suggest a suicide conclusion is too soon."

The windows have his attention again. "Fuck. I was going along with the DCC's conclusion. The note was brought to her and she brought it to me. She said so."

"She did, boss. She did. Do you mind if I attend the autopsy?"

The color of his face and neck rise. "Go for your life."

I head for the door. He calls out, "Your father. Did I suggest some bereavement leave? I think I did."

"You did, boss. Thank you."

"We can leave family bereavement off the record. Call it special leave. Between us."

SUNDAY, 5 AUGUST 2012
10.30 HOURS

Driving east toward Griff, I'm counting the number of days since I walked out of his bathroom. The fourteen level Radio Network House disappears from my vision; there one moment, gone in three. I forgot sixty kilos of explosives inside it would be detonated today. Onlookers stand behind a cordoned area. The event was streamed live into homes in case people hadn't witnessed enough destruction in the city.

Near Griff's apartment, a man, early sixties, jeans, and green bush shirt kicks over orange road cones. A group of five youths stand around him, some egging him on, others taking pics. He's going to be a star on social media any second now. I check for cuffs and pepper spray—you never know.

The man tosses a couple of cones into the middle of the street, incoherent in rage. Others laugh and jeer, call him a retard and fuckwit. He drops to his knees and sobs.

I pull my ID and hold it up to the small audience and shout, "Police. Move on, please. You're not helping."

Some redhaired-runt, no more than fourteen, says, "Fuck all other entertainment, around here."

"I won't ask again."

They shuffle off, shoulders slumped.

I approach the man, call to him, ask his name, and tell him mine. The sting in him evaporates and snot arrives to accompany tears, running from nose to chin.

Evan wipes his face on his sleeve and tells me his elderly mother suffers quake-related, post-traumatic stress disorder. Many elderly, with no time to gather up treasured possessions, were transported out of the city due to damage to their residences. They went to places and people they didn't know.

"Taken to strange places, concentration camps, some of them said. She doesn't know if or when her handful of friends will return," Evan says. "She got through the quakes okay. Those bastards at Earthquake Insure continue to inflict secondary trauma."

He tells the story of the multiple visits by assessors, engineers, and others now all inured to the stress they create due to their own housing issues and workload stress. Evan says, "I helped mother battle missing assessment reports and pathetic inaccuracies in reports. They couldn't even get the number of bedrooms or water cylinders correct. I mean, how hard is that? And now, finally, a lowball offer, well under EI's own assessment of the cost to repair damage. I was forced to use the Official Information Act to claw every scrap of information from them."

I say, "You're one of thousands, mate. They don't know what to do with us all."

"She lives in the Flockton Basin," he says. "The quakes changed the whole floodplain. Two winters now with water lapping at her front door." He pulls a newspaper cutting from his shirt pocket. It's a cartoon, in this case with cutting accuracy. In front of broken buildings, overfed rats scurry around baring sharp teeth and dagger-like claws. The cartoonist's label across the vermin—"Insurance Companies" and in an anonymous speech bubble to the side of the picture, "Show 'em half a crack, and they'll find a way through."

Evan shakes his head, "Says it all. Doesn't it?"

I nod. "Not easy seeing this shit happen to your mum, though."

His jaw quivers and his eyes fill again. He's unable to answer.

I think of his cone-throwing performance on Facebook, perhaps with me looking on, a bored bystander. Some people will expect me to charge him with disorderly behavior, a legitimate but heavy-handed response.

Calm restored, he says, "Are you going to arrest me?"

"No, mate. Now you're rid of some pent-up adrenaline, why don't I help you put the cones back in place?"

By the time we're done, broken pavements re-shielded from the unwary, he's told me about his nightmares and flashbacks—seeing the feet of dead under the Cashel mall rubble, a young woman reporter in tears, comforting an injured woman, severe injuries, the cameraman she's with, unwilling or unable to continue taking photos.

At his apartment building, Griff responds to my text and meets me in the unstaffed reception.

Our hug and kiss are not lingering, more like a couple who've endured a relationship for years, an unbroken habit, not dysfunctional. He tells me nine days have passed and he's missed me.

In the first months, despite our busy jobs, we would see

each other no less than every second day. It became twice a week including time somewhere on the weekend.

In the elevator I say, "I don't know where the time's gone." It sounds lame, and when I said it, I realize it implies I haven't missed him.

We don't speak again before we reach his dining table. He picks up a tiny piece of paper from the glass top and shows it to me. It's Owen's funeral notice. He releases it from his thumb and forefinger and lets it float back to the table. His silence sings my indictment. He breaks it by switching on the coffee machine. Over the motor, he says, with exaggerated volume, "Will you watch a *60 Minutes* doco with me? It features one of my judicial brethren's family being interviewed."

I suspect not talking about my silence over Owen is a new tactic in the debate about my personal communication, or lack of it. I say, "I don't know why I didn't tell you, Griff."

"His son says he discovered a thing called a 'Fair Insurance Code.' It requires insurers to settle claims quickly and fairly but, as we know, insurance contracts are filled with arcane and abstract concepts, which give the companies significant discretion. Until a court case."

Persevering, I say, "I think I wanted to get through the funeral on my own. He was a virtual stranger. I made that clear."

"These battles are unequal," he says, matter of fact. "His son pulled no punches. He invited *60 Minutes* to get someone undercover in EI. Said, they'd soon uncover a strategy where every dollar the insurer avoids paying is another dollar on the profit line. It can soon become their default policy. Perhaps we should buy shares."

I rub my forehead.

He says, "Can you see why these battles are a mismatch."

"I think so."

"Communication, isn't it? The will to do it and the skill to be effective."

Here we go.

He adds, "You are not short in the skill component. No one can deny it." He pauses to let me think about the will part of the equation. "I'm assuming," he says, "you know when he died?"

"Late on the afternoon of the second of August."

"Three days ago. And I texted you two days ago. Right?"

"Honestly, Griff. I'm sorry. I can see by not telling, I hurt you, but truly, this isn't about you, or us. I was already dealing with Fergus's death. His autopsy's tomorrow and I think you know I once believed he was more of a father to me than Owen."

"How much have we talked about Dowling's death and its impact on you?"

A rhetorical question. "You're excellent at being open, talking things through. I'm hopeless at that. Work, fine. Personal? A dead loss."

He has a faraway look. "You said you once believed Dowling was more of a father to you than Owen. What did you mean?"

I nod to the coffee machine. "Am I still welcome?"

While he pours, I see I'm in another dilemma. To share Dowling's video or not. It would be a positive gesture around sharing, but if he knew Dowling knew about me, he would renew his efforts to persuade me to come out.

"Over here," he says directing me to the comfy chairs, the manner of a judge inviting counsel to sit in his chambers.

I decide if Dowling knew about me for a long time, he

must've kept it to himself. I tell Griff about Dowling's relationship with Troup and the payoffs he received.

He opens his mouth, more width than is necessary for words.

"Yes, disgraceful. Isn't it?"

"Awful for you," he says with a sad expression.

I say, "Buried in the enormous pile of shit I'm dealing with, I need to prove two cops were murdered to cover up organized insurance fraud."

MONDAY, 6 AUGUST 2012
14.00 HOURS

I head toward the hospital morgue, past the city's shit-brown river, hoping for causal evidence of Dowling's death the brass can't ignore.

This is my ninth visit to the body store, and it's thirty-nine degrees chiller. From prime minister to pauper, the standards for autopsy health and safety are universal, almost comforting in their impersonal coldness. After I don the lightweight layer of protection over my dark suit, a technician leads me through the changing area and into an area of stainless-steel slabs and gravity drain systems. Low-pressure water runs continually over the shiny, nonporous surfaces.

The pathologist is Professor Pat Cadveron, known to the force as Cadaverman. After greeting and pleasantries with him and his assistant, Cadveron says, "Middle of winter, no maggots to hose off." He gives his cheery smile. "Your average female lays her eggs in the eyes first before rigor sets in."

"You used that line on me before, Cadaverman. You said, the way the eggs decorated the tear ducts, they looked like finely grated Parmesan."

"An excellent pupil." His mask hides the familiar and

inevitable dark grin. Cadveron goes to the slab. I point to Dowling's missing eyes and chewed lips. "I'm hoping what happened there was post-mortem."

"Without doubt. Earthquakes have more to answer for than meets the eye if you'll pardon the pun. Your average moggie," Cadveron says, "is pretty determined when hungry. Your faithful dog will sit by your side for days, starving. Not your cat. Eat you right away without qualm. Mr. Dowling is a classic presentation."

The torn plastic covering Dowling's head indicates where the claws penetrated before feline feeding. He says, "Decomp is a little more advanced than one might expect for the three days between when you saw him and when his body was discovered. Bloating around the abdomen. That's where the electric blanket appeared to be doing its work in countering the cold evening temperatures. We will step well back after incision to avoid the full toxic gas balloon. After death, bacteria go on a more voracious feeding spree than any predators. They feast on the body's proteins comprising our cellular structures."

"In your debt, professor. You never disappoint on the education front. And the frequency of your reminders means I must be slow-witted to forget."

Cats feeding on Dowling is unsurprising. Frightened by persistent quakes, lost to owners, and unable to find new feeders, some will still be scrounging to survive.

Cadveron applies light and magnification to inspect all surfaces of Dowling's body. He pauses at the right wrist. "Some lateral ante-mortem bruising here. Not wire, no pattern indicating rope either."

I peer at the bruising, remember the metal-on-metal scratches on the veranda chair. "Handcuffs?" I ask.

He nods. "Consistent with handcuffs." He examines the left wrist. "No similar bruising here, though."

His assistant moves in to take close-ups.

"In theory," I say, "if he played a sex game, would this bruising be consistent?"

"Are you suggesting I possess expertise in that domain?"

"I'll take your answer as don't know."

The men turn the body.

Cadveron says, "Post-mortem lividity confined to the lower limbs but absent on the buttocks. Consistent with how he was found in a sitting position."

I ask, "Why no lividity in the buttocks?"

"They take the pressure of sitting on a hard surface. Blood doesn't flow to and settle in that part of the body."

"Isn't it the same if he's lying down?"

"Lying down would result in greater discoloration in the parts of his body not in contact with the ground. Little evidence of it in this case."

"What if he died somewhere different than where he was found?"

"Not as certain, but he may well have been sitting up when he died. Timing is important in such a case because the time when blood will no longer settle and produce evidence of discoloration is limited. It can take up to six hours post-mortem for some change of lividity with a change in body position. After that, not much. Do you want to test a theory?"

"Only what was in my question. I'm concerned his death might've been made to look like suicide."

"Well, best we get on with it." Cadveron makes the first scalpel incision from the edge of each collarbone to the breastbone, pushing through the skin and muscle of Fergus's chest and from there all the way down to the bone at the front of the pelvis. He steps back, and I follow his lead.

In time, Cadveron removes and weighs the individual organs. In another setting, he could be showing the care of an obstetrician in a difficult birth. "Lungs discolored, a long-term smoker but still functional," he says.

With all major cavities open, and clear of fluids, the pathologist takes tissue samples and places them into a formaldehyde solution for later examination. In the stomach, he finds undigested whiskey and what he suspects are undigested sleeping pills, more than twenty of them.

I ask, "Would these have any impact on his death?"

"I don't know yet," he says, impatience in his tone.

"If pills were forced into him there'd be bruising inside the mouth," I say, "perhaps chipped teeth."

"I would expect bruising on the lips, but because there is not much of that flesh present, difficult to say. The teeth are a little loose, attributable possibly to gum shrinkage. I think what I have here is interesting."

From a stainless-steel bowl he takes something in tweezers and holds it up. "My guess is testing will show this small oval-shaped pill is for sleeping. Same as those in his stomach," he says. "This one lodged in his throat. The whiskey hasn't sluiced it all the way down."

"But wouldn't he cough it into the bag over his head?"

"If he was conscious. It would not be possible for him, anyone for that matter, to tolerate this in their throat and not attempt to clear it. Being suicidal makes no difference. Reflexes take over. In my view, he ingested the pills and alcohol when he was either unconscious or deceased."

"Surely an attempt to make his death appear like suicide when it wasn't. Leads you to conclude a suspicious death. Yes?"

"There is no blunt force trauma or wound penetration on his body. The real question is not what happened after he died but what caused his death. I'll need all the biochemical analyses."

I mention Fergus's diabetes. "Given no evidence of trauma, is it possible he was deliberately deprived of what he needed to balance his blood sugar ratio, forcing him into a diabetic coma?"

"Of course, although quite difficult to prove as a cause of death. I expect I'll find some indicators of hypoglycemia or hyperglycemia if that was the case, but it might depend on how soon he went into a coma. There could be any number of conditions influencing the onset of a coma."

"Which is which?"

"Hyper is too much sugar. Hypo is too little."

"There was insulin in his house but no sweets."

"The problem here is blood glucose values continue to fall after death. A normal or raised glucose concentration would exclude hypoglycemia as a cause of death but low concentrations wouldn't be helpful in determining the opposite cause."

"What happens to someone in this situation?"

"Fatal cardiac dysrhythmia, if caused by hypoglycemia, tends to leave no histopathological clues."

"English, please, professor."

Cadveron rolls his eyes. "When I open his heart for further study, it's almost impossible to identify issues solely attributable to a hypoglycemic attack."

"So, no forensic clues?"

"Limited. The brain often undergoes significant stress. I

might find damage to the cortex and regions within the hippocampus. Quite a brutal way to die. If aware of your diabetes implications, you wouldn't choose it as a form of suicide."

I leave, optimistic the autopsy proves suspicious death rather than suicide but unsure whether the quantity of evidence is enough to show murder. The pills washed into his stomach with whiskey wouldn't have been helpful evidence of homicide. If anything, they point to suicide. But a pill lodged in his throat is a game changer. That was bad luck for his assailant. But on what Cadveron said, I can't prove intent to kill unless the assailant already knew Dowling was unconscious, and the pills were to finish him off while he was in that state.

On the way back to work, I call EI.

Kevin Yan says, "What do you want, Solly?"

"I'm investigating your allegations of a fraudulent claim by Lyall Blain."

"Not by me. By EI."

"A fine, but fair point."

"You have a conflict of interest, yeah?"

"Not according to my superiors."

"How's Coman doing?"

"I'll pass on your best regards. Can we meet?"

"I can do after work. Pomeroy's Brewery. It's on my way home."

"Admirable choice. Owned by a former cop."

MONDAY, 6 AUGUST 2012
17.55 HOURS

I'm across the road from the pub. Under a dark sky, I take a few seconds to identify Yan at the entrance. He wears a beanie and he's lost his thick-framed glasses. His slate overcoat and royal blue Cashmere scarf suggest he dresses differently at EI, paid more than when he worked for us. He still walks like a tall man in low tunnels. He checks his watch and buries his hands in deep pockets. He fidgets, makes multiple checks of anyone in the vicinity.

I walk through the gloom, slowly making myself more visible. It feels a bit le Carré.

"Kev," I say smiling. "How are you?"

"What do you want, Solly?"

"I want to ask you about Blain's claim."

He makes a little head movement, impatience evident. "No, no. I know you. You want something."

"I want everyone to be reasonable, help you see that casting a shadow on Blain's integrity might give you the satisfaction of revenge but nothing else."

"Not revenge, Solly. A false claim."

"I also want you to see revenge would require you to lie, to expose yourself to the risk of jail for committing perjury. But the fundamental reason is why. Why go through this?"

He exhales in frustration. "For the last time, what do you really want, Solly? Fuckin' cold out here."

"You wearing a wire, Kevin?"

He points to his coat. "Under this? You joking, man?"

"Let's go inside. Comforting glass of Bin 389 if I remember."

"You're paying."

After the quakes, Pomeroy's was reconstructed in the style of a traditional English pub. Yan says, "The owner lost sixteen thousand dollars stolen from here, stolen when everyone ran for safety."

"No shortage of quake predators around, Kev. Just need to point the finger at the right people. Hot fries to go with the red?" These are his weakness. He lived on them when he was with us.

He hesitates. "Sounds good."

I place the order. This is not a place that offers Bin 389. An alternative red in hand, we head to a table by the internal brick wall separating the dining and drinking areas. It's noisy, not with music but voices.

"How did Blain come into your crosshairs?"

He shrugs. "Nothing particular. The claim didn't look right."

"Come on, Kevin," I say with some disbelief. "Who's pushing you down this track?"

His eyes dart. "It's my job. I don't need to be told what to do. I'm trusted over there." He says the last words with a teenage tone of resentment.

A beanpole of a man nearby guffaws while his mate necks a generous quantity of beer.

"Were you pointed in his direction, Kev?"

"No."

Too quick.

His response deserves my iron face and laser stare, but Yan's discomfort with prolonged eye contact is still with him. I avert my gaze again.

A waitress brings a low-waged smile and dumps the fries at our table.

When she leaves, I say, "My rugby club made a quake claim. You know about that?"

"No."

Again, too quick. Didn't ask which club. He picks up a couple of fries and munches.

"The claim was declined," I say.

He finishes chewing, takes longer than necessary. "Satisfying fries."

I eat a couple, too salty. I wait.

"What do you want me to say?" Yan asks. "Claims are declined. Plenty of unhappy customers at EI. So what?"

"Dowling said, after it was declined, a payment was made on the claim, but not to the club's bank account."

He takes a handful of fries and says, "Perhaps he made a mistake." He bites fries in half and mumbles. "A checking process is thorough, but it doesn't stop typos in a bank account number. But we're here to discuss Blain's claim. Yes?"

I take a punt. "Instead of the club's account, the payment was sent to the account of another insurance company."

"Your club is with Putis Insurance. Not a problem."

"So, you do know about it."

He gives me the eyes of an animal about to become roadkill. "The payment to Putis, probably just a timing issue. No big deal, Solly. I can find out more if you want." He gulps the wine like he's about to leave.

"Putis Insurance. What exactly is this?"

"Private Company, some sort of consortium. I don't know, none of my business. EI is their admin agent."

"Kevin, mate, you're working to someone's agenda and it suits you because you can take a shot at Blain for being an asshole all those years."

He shakes his head vigorously. "You're wrong, Solly."

"Let's talk about Rachel Trix."

He grins, showing Cabernet-stained teeth. "Who could forget?" He makes a fist, pulls up his forearm."

"Kev, you didn't!"

He nods furiously. "She was a bit pissed, also coke." He loses the smile. "Consensual, though."

"She was tidy, yeah?"

"Not much in the tit department, but deluxe elsewhere. Friendly pussy. Know what I'm saying, Solly?" He laughs.

I think about the likelihood of him not seeing her, despite the disguise. Perhaps she saw him first, his name on a staff list. "Back in the day," I say, "before EI stole you from us, do you remember us investigating Trix's scam on the elderly?"

He looks wary. "What about it?"

"You resigned during that inquiry."

"As you say, I got a better job. So what?"

"You see Trix at EI?"

"No." His eyes move everywhere until he fixates on the entrance. I'm now certain he's seen someone who worries him.

"What about Harriet Volp? Ever meet, see or work with her at EI?"

"What's this got to do with Blain's claim?"

I withdraw an envelope from inside my coat and lay out pictures for him from our vault—private collections of documents held by detectives never destined to be produced in evidence but stored for a rainy day to induce cooperation from the unwilling. Yan's rainy day has arrived. One picture shows him with his arm around a naked woman, about eighteen, in his lap. Another with the same girl, snorting coke we believed he supplied. Another of Kevin, when he wore the black-rimmed goggles, snorting coke. "You left your résumé behind, mate."

His color resembles the inside of the chips. "I'm in the vault? Blackmailing me?"

"Do I need to blackmail you? I understood you knew about these, which is why you resigned. Not the case?"

"What do you want? Money?"

I put a hand over my heart. "Kev. I'm insulted, mate. I don't want your bloody money. I'm not blackmailing you. I'm giving you back your privacy rights."

He brings his thin eyebrows together.

I say, "You think I want a high price for these? I don't. What I want is for you and your conspiracy theorists to pick another target. Give up the idea your old place of work is a target for revenge."

His eyes roam again as he tries to appear relaxed.

"You can keep those," I say.

"So what? You'll have copies."

I stand. "I need a piss, mate. I'll leave you with those, give you some time to think about doing me a favor in return. Or you can give them to your mate Oliver. Seek his guidance. Is he watching us?"

A vein in his pale neck pulsates.

"I don't want you to stuff up your new career, Kev. When

I come back from emptying my bladder, we'll talk about how you can crawl out of your self-dug shit-hole."

Near the bathroom, a short man in a puffer and hoodie scuttles toward the exit. I think I glimpsed him earlier, changing direction to enter the pub about the same time we did.

I return to the table, chips and wine left unfinished. No Kevin Yan.

Frustrated, I pay the account and walk back to the pub's parking lot. The cold drizzle arrives. It was never Yan's style to seek advice. If someone else is behind the fraudulent claim allegation, he's in a bit of a bind. It won't be easy to quietly withdraw it. At our end, it doesn't matter much what he says—some mix-up of photographs, perhaps reconsidering Detective Blain's account convinces EI of his honesty. He could admit to zealotry, too distrusting due to all the media shit they copped. We'll accept an apology for wasting our time, no matter how stiff-jawed it is.

In the shadows, I spot something not there earlier, a dark bundle of clothing. As I get closer, the glint from a metal object reflects the lights from Fitzgerald Ave. A shiny belt buckle. I recognize the overcoat. I remove the photos from inside Yan's coat and keep firm pressure on his bleeding chest while I call an ambulance. Despite a short distance to the hospital, I think he will die before the medics arrive. I feel selfish thinking that because I will be a witness, it will be a homicide investigation passed to someone else.

TUESDAY, 7 AUGUST 2012
08.45 HOURS

In Dowling's old office, I sit with Blain. He asks, "Is he still alive?"

"Unconscious, on life support. Rod Black will probably be OC."

He rubs a spot between his lower lip and chin. "Will you tell him why you were seeing Yan?"

"Of course."

"Jesus, I could be a suspect. I have a motive."

"And two police alibis last night, Vincent and Tracey."

He sits back, appears to take comfort from this.

I ask, "You stayed away from him. Right?"

"Of course. Nothing since I wound him up on the phone. I guess he might have that on tape. Why do you ask?"

"Forensics. We don't want the complication of having something from you on him."

"Can't happen. Not unless someone's trying to fit me up. What happens to his complaint?"

"It becomes part of the evidence gathered in the inquiry, but background, I reckon. The worst thing we could do would be to try and cover up his allegation. But we can deal with it on its merits. As far as our response to EI is concerned, our experts say their provisional view is your Audi photo appears not to be an original."

"Doctored?"

"They're not going that far yet. But EI also needs to confirm no one mixed up photos with other inquiries. When I mentioned conspiracy theorists, Yan looked shaken."

"Do you reckon Coman'll go with this—EI's internal cockup?"

"He's coming round to my way of thinking, gave me the okay to go to Dowling's autopsy. As for Kevin Yan, I think we should be more concerned about why someone's tried to kill him. I'm sure he was under observation at the pub where we met. He claimed he knew nothing, yet he was shitting himself." I tell Blain about the man I saw.

"What did he look like?"

"Couldn't see much—seemed to be bald, had the height of the bloke in the security guard's red zone video. My presence may have been injurious to Yan's health."

"Something was," Blain says. "I don't believe in coincidences."

"Have you made any progress with Edgar's call logs?" What Vincent said about Trix working at EI makes the logs more important.

"Bit of a setback there, I'm afraid."

I cross my arms. "What bloody setback?"

Blain's eyes go to his toes. "Got the telco to give us what they had on Edgar's number, other numbers in and out. I passed the material to the analysts. Heard nothing by the end of Friday and paid them a visit. Turns out, they misplaced them."

"Misplaced what?"

Blain grimaces. "All the call numbers to and from Edgar's phone."

As I shoot to my feet, my chair crashes into the filing cabinet behind me. "Misplaced? You gotta be kidding."

Blain turns, checks if anyone else heard me. He holds his hands up. "Not me. Only the messenger, mate."

I shake my head as I open the call log on my phone. "We can start again. Edgar's number is still logged. What the hell happened?"

"They say they don't know. Significant ass covering, I'd say. I instructed them to open every paper file on every desk and if that didn't work, in every fucking drawer."

After Blain leaves, soreness in my neck and shoulder strikes. I open an email from Coman, following up on why my appointment with the shrink is so long in coming. It reeks of Hockley's voice. He finishes it with, "Re. Trix and her possible support. You could maybe consider checking out who posted bail for her on those fraud charges a couple of years back?"

The letter from the court about Trix's trial exhibits catches my eye. I decide to call them when Tracey phones. "On my way back in, boss."

"You have an update?"

She gives a little cough. "Mixed news, boss."

"After last night," I say, "I have a strong preference for beginning the day well."

"Well, Nichol was unable to ID anyone from the mugshots. But this time she referred to him as Cole. Nothing on our intel about any Cole."

"What about the other neighbors? You tried the mugshots on them?"

"No luck there either, boss."

I rub the back of my neck, hesitant about giving her more jobs to do. "A couple of jobs I need to do at the court. You free to help with one of them?"

"Only five minutes away, boss."

"Might be a bit of a punt, Trace, but can you uncover who posted bail for Trix when we pulled her in on the frauds."

"Sure, boss. Shouldn't take long."

I spend the rest of the morning learning about Yan's health and being interviewed by a colleague about meeting Yan. My colleague wants my perspective of Blain's claim, the alibis, Blain's general attitude toward Yan, any tendencies toward hot-headedness. At lunchtime, Tracey calls. "The guy who posted bail was one Oliver Collinge, boss."

What did Vincent say when he went to HR at Earthquake Insure? *I overheard some talk about a guy called Oliver, who's close to Sinclair. He's not on staff, no file on him. People say he's an external consultant.*

I key the name into the desktop software and ask, "We got an address?"

"Have now, boss."

"Got any form?"

"No convictions. Nat intel says investigated for arson over his boat. He insured it heavily six months before it was destroyed in an explosion, believed to be caused by transporting LPG tanks to a holiday house. A couple of witnesses went AWOL on us. We couldn't pursue the charges."

"Superior work, Trace. Call you back in a second."

I try another couple of searches including pics but find zero internet footprint for Oliver Collinge.

I weigh up the grounds for moving on Collinge with a search warrant. With an established past link to Trix after her fraud arrest, his introduction of her to EI with a false ID, and his own prior arrest, there's enough. If he's the Putis, and I move now, I increase the risk of him making his broader crime network untouchable. I call Inland Revenue and explain I'm looking to identify whether one Oliver Collinge is a taxpayer. I give them the address and explain it's all the information I have. They confirm no one of that name or anyone at the address is a taxpayer.

I call Tracey back. "When you're back, grab some uniforms for a search. Blain will apply for warrants on Collinge's place, his vehicle and whatever else you can find he might own. The warrant will say he's suspected of aiding and abetting a fugitive for whom there is a warrant for arrest for murder. But we're looking for passports with Trix's picture, any documentation to help produce false passports or anything pointing to Collinge having another identity. Grab all phones, despite expected denials of ownership."

"Got it, boss."

I stand, observe Blain at his desk, and motion him into Dowling's office.

"Meant to ask before. Got our appointment with Sinclair yet?"

"A message on my mobile, just now. Tomorrow, 0900 hours."

"Well done."

He grins. "You bring me in here to check on my secretarial skills?"

I tell him about the lead on Oliver Collinge and get him to draft the application for the warrant. He holds up both thumbs.

Tracey's news spurs me to the passport inquiry file. I call

the Department of Internal Affairs in Wellington, but when they understand my inquiry, they refer me to the Home Office in the UK. After establishing my credentials, I explain the purpose of my inquiry and ask about the e-Passport chip.

A woman says, "The chip in an e-passport can be read at a short distance without its owner's knowledge. But it isn't a question of whether the entire passport can be forged, but whether the identity can be stolen and aligned with a different digital photograph."

I say, "Stolen with electronic readers?"

"Well, yes, but these are not readily available," she says, tone defensive.

"But they can be bought on the internet. Right?"

"Maybe, but someone would need the software know-how."

"To download data from a reader onto a chip?"

"Yes."

I thank her for the call and withhold my conclusion—that such know-how could easily be bought for the right price.

TUESDAY, 7 AUGUST 2012
13.02 HOURS

After uncovering Oliver Collinge, I'm researching public information about Gwen Sinclair at EI. After Vincent's comment about Gwen being chief spokesperson, a person who must know what's going on, I think she might be more influential than previously thought. But after twenty minutes, I'm left with a puzzle. A search return on Gwen's name returns a piece on the local victim support service. I scour the article, but the only name mentioned is the local VS manager's and her report of a new patron for the agency. As I give up, Tracey appears at my workstation.

"Boss, got an appointment at 1400 hours with a contact at *The Press*. She's the business editor, access to a confidential source who might add something about Putis. You interested in coming?"

On our way out, I tell Blain, "Check with our Victim Support people. My hunch is they may've helped or been associated with Gwen Sinclair in the past." I explain how the search link on her name and the VS service seem to have been associated at one time.

After the February 2011 quake, *The Press* moved from

its wrecked Gothic building in Cathedral Square, a building demolished soon after. Staff now herd into temporary accommodation near the airport, reminiscent of huts inside prisoner of war camps. Tracey introduces me to Ursula Ryder, stocky woman, sporting a black eye and a dyed bob infused with the orange streaks of a hot day's sunset.

I say, "I'm led to believe you've been making inquiries about the Putis company and you're willing to talk to me about this."

"I'm hoping we can collaborate," she says speaking at a volume that leads me to think she's partially deaf.

"The police and media have a reasonable relationship. There is cooperation between us, certainly."

She says, "We've found Putis is a privately owned entity, an insurance consortium that funds individuals with dividends from profits. But we've found no records of the registered directors or company annual returns."

"That's not news to us," I say. "I'm not trying to be rude, but I heard you may have an informant who could take us beyond the simple fact Putis exists.

"You know the war stories out there about increasingly unaffordable premiums," Ryder says. "And the hot topic about what to do with the uninsured?"

I want to say police don't live under a rock, but I cut her some slack. "We know."

"Well, a lot of people talk to us in ways they might not talk to you."

I want her to speed up and glance at my watch. "Sure."

"It might be a coincidence, but when we did our obit on Nick Jarvis, we were contacted by a source who said a woman by the name of Harriet Volp was involved with Putis."

My eyebrows are up before I realize.

She says, "I can tell this name is familiar to you. You remember the prison corruption inquiry led by DI Dowling?"

"Of course. I recall he used an informant by the name of Harriet." Ryder couldn't know I was stretching the truth.

She smiles. "Our source isn't called Harriet."

Now Dowling's dead, you might have a chance. You can benefit from favors I've...

Recalling my father's reference to Dowling, I take a punt. "Was the late Owen Webb one of your sources?"

"Owen's dead?"

"He is. Very recently. Anything we discuss must be confidential if we're to help one another. No mention to anyone, including other cops."

"Of course."

I say, "We believe Volp was a false name used by Rachel Trix."

She blinks several times, perhaps giving herself time to digest this. "That is indeed news to me."

"Trix and Jarvis were a couple at one time. Webb didn't tell you that?"

"No. Can I ask how you knew?"

"We discovered the fact through the course of the investigation but I'm not able to disclose how."

Ryder says, "Owen also indicated documentation about Putis is not sent electronically anywhere, which suggests those involved are concerned about interceptions. Whoever Volp was communicating with about potential crimes was contacted through dead drops. There's also this possible link to another company." She extracts a file from a desk drawer. "Myles Holdings Limited. A single registered director, Edward James

Myles, registered office is the premises of lawyers, Latham & Co."

This Myles name is familiar, and I ask Tracey to check criminal histories. I face Ryder. "So, what's the link with Putis?"

"With Owen dead, I don't know. He gave us the name to check out. I was wondering if this was a possible person of interest to you. Strictest confidence of course."

"I think the expression is can't confirm or deny. Not at this time."

Ryder leans back in her chair. It gives a small squeak. She grins. "In other words, you have someone or something but don't want to tell me."

"I can say we have a different name but I'm unable to say it. Not yet."

Ryder tilts her head. "You guys have one of your team over at EI. Is that correct?" she asks. "Crime prevention strategy or some such?"

"We have a detective working there helping EI with anti-fraud practices."

"Owen told us there might be some heavy hitters behind insurance scams, but with so little to go on, we have no confirmation."

"Any names to interest us?"

Ryder grins. "What do I say here? Can't confirm or deny?"

"Perhaps a senior cop?" I ask.

"Someone said to be involved with Rachel Trix. Hence my interest in your person of interest. Can you tell me anything at all?"

There is a plea in Ryder's eyes. It won't hurt to keep her

investigation going. If I can't make an arrest, it would be useful to have criminality in a media exposé.

"Still confidential between us. Right?"

"Of course."

"We're interested in a person who appears to be close to Sinclair. I can't yet say who, what or why, but I'm happy to tell you if, and when, we make an arrest."

"A tip-off. We like those. Not often we get them." Ryder gives a half-smile. "At least it suggests holding my focus is worthwhile. Do you think this person uses an alias?"

"It's possible we could be talking about the same person."

Back in the car, Tracey in the driver's seat says, "I didn't think you wanted stuff about Trix out there."

"I'm creating a possible ally. Ryder and I might have the public interest in common."

She looks pensive. "I think we can rule out Trix killing Nick as some form of revenge, boss."

"Never rule anything out too soon."

She glances at me. "How did you know her informant was dead?"

"It would be more useful if he was still alive. I went to see him on an unrelated matter. How did you say you were connected to Ryder?"

"I didn't."

We're close to the station when a man, mid-twenties, black leather jacket, faded jeans, staggers toward us. He almost falls over as he steps off the footpath. With one hand, he steadies himself on the roof of a Corolla, fishes around in his pockets. "Call for assistance," I tell Tracey, "a van, washable floors."

The driver's door is half-open when I yell, "*Hey!*"

He ignores me and pulls the door fully open. I quicken my pace and arrive as he attempts to shut it.

He says, "Fuck off."

"Or you'll do what?"

His head lolls.

"Driver's license," I say, producing my ID.

He gives a stupid grin. "Yep."

"Show me. Now."

He tries to withdraw the wallet from his pocket but can't manage it. I help him. James Alexander Coman, born 7 August 1987. "Happy birthday, James. Your celebrations are over."

The plate check shows the Corolla doesn't belong to him, but he can't tell us anything useful about why he's attempting to drive it. He struggles to focus when the uniformed cop and I pull him to his feet and guide him to the van. "Farver," he mumbles. Talk ta my farver."

"Would your father be Inspector Mick Coman?" I ask.

His head lolls again and he appears to have lost the ability to speak.

In the process of falling into the van, a small white plastic package exits his right trouser leg. Unseen by the constable, I retrieve it and slip it into my pocket.

TUESDAY, 7 AUGUST 2012
15.30 HOURS

James Coman is on his way to detox by the time Tracey approaches with a phone to her ear. She mouths the name of a detective recently recruited as a temp while she listens, a picture of focused intent. She asks, "Did he say if he could identify either of them?"

A pause.

"Cheers."

She gives a long sigh. "Our visit to the Oxford farmer—you remember—the one reporting the abandoned..."

"Paid to remember, Trace."

"Well, he says he was a fair distance away, on a quad bike. By the time he got closer, he saw a man getting into a car with a woman driver. He said he wasn't great on cars, but he was certain it was a two-door convertible. White Nissan he reckons. Not enough plate numbers to help us unfortunately."

"There could be a few dozen of that type and color of Nissan in the city. DCC Hockley has one. What did he say about personal descriptions?"

"Not a happening thing. Reckons the bloke was short to

average height. He thought he might've been wearing a mask but wasn't sure."

"And the woman."

She gives a look of frustration. "Not much there either. She never got out of the car. Blonde, shoulder-length hair, nothing else."

Back on our floor, I sense we could be closing in on the Putis. I anticipate Linda Nichol picking him out in an identity parade after Collinge denies his association with Trix. Despite the hour, I decide I'll take an actual lunch break. I text Coman requesting time to update him and get a reply he's visiting his doctor. Vincent tells me Blain's taken the search warrant paperwork to the court for signing but he's drawn a blank with Victim Support. He gives me a concerned look.

"Dead ends," I say. "Comes with..."

"Dead people," he says.

It was a Dowling expression. Too many dead ends, and a homicide quickly shapes up as unsolved. He said it often and it's true.

On my way out of the squad room, a men's health magazine catches my eye in Vincent's in-tray. A headline, "Gay Cop Tells All." I point to the mag. "You still believe in the muscle supplements?"

"In moderation, boss."

"This mag a good read?

"Help yourself. There's usually a couple of interesting articles. Bloody thing's full of advertising, same every month. I was about to bin it."

I pick it up. "Out for half an hour or so. Contactable on my mobile."

Back at my car, I check the envelope containing Dowling's video recording is still safe in the trunk. In the driver's seat, I open the magazine and read the article interviewing a police inspector.

Interviewer: *Did you ever think coming out was risky?*
Inspector: *Of course. I mean, I'm about forty years old. I've known I was gay since age ten or eleven. But I finally decided I'd had enough with the secrecy and shame.*
Interviewer: *Is there an anti-gay culture in the police?*
Inspector: *There are probably still small pockets of it. Social change attitudes are not lightning events. We're all a bit better educated about harassment and procedures for managing anti-harassment.*
Interviewer: *So, what's your take on why people stay in the closet?*
Inspector: *For me, I knew I was gay about the time sex between NZ men became decriminalized. It has taken until now, in 2012, to have draft legislation widening the definition of marriage beyond a heterosexual couple. That was significant for me, but many young men have been out for a much longer time.*
Interviewer: *What about gay men your age or older—are you saying that's not the case?*
Inspector: *I think I'm saying some older guys believe they benefit by adopting and maintaining a kind of double life. Especially Pakeha guys who have always had the comforts, dare I say it, from a society where a white heterosexual man always held privileged positions,*

often with power and control over others. The thought of giving up those privileges so you can be out—well, could be unappealing to some.

Interviewer: *But discrimination on the grounds of sexual orientation has been illegal for nearly twenty years.*

Inspector: (chuckles) *Sorry, I'm laughing anyone would think because a law was passed, it would change society's behavior.*

Interviewer: *Isn't it much simpler? Some guys are conservative in what they reveal to others. Or they might be wary of how information about them could be misused. A trust or privacy issue?*

Inspector: *It runs with the society point I'm making, not counter to it. Damage occurs when people keep secrets. For me, it's just easier to be out.*

I put the magazine down wondering how the article will be received in the hierarchy. They'll say all the right things, have our police diversity liaison officers engage in loud cheering.

I try Griff's number. He answers on the third ring. "I'm worried I pushed you further away on Saturday. Can you imagine how hard it's been not to keep texting, not to call?"

"Well, I don't... I'm not being pushed away and I'm calling now. Right? How are you—apart from being stressed about not hearing from me?"

"I'm congenial. All the better for hearing your voice. But are *we* okay?"

"I think so. Just don't go taking time off someone's jail sentence because we're okay."

He chuckles. "I'll try and remain judicially temperate."

"That's what worries me."

After a pause, he says, "I'm away for a few days at a judicial conference. Can we..."

"Make an appointment?"

"Get together when I'm back Friday night. I'll cook for us."

No suggestion of a public restaurant. He's heard me. "That would be great."

TUESDAY, 7 AUGUST 2012
16.40 HOURS

I sit opposite Coman who's perched on a bar stool in an almost empty canteen. His sausage-like fingers envelop a coffee cup from a vending machine. In front of him, a white plate holding a couple of ham sandwiches. He's eating a party-pie. Taking coffee with me, I sit opposite.

"Not eating?" he asks with greasy lips.

"Not hungry."

"Since when did that matter?" He takes a savage bite of a sandwich and mumbles. "The investigation into our process the night Nick was killed. Heard chatter in the castle about progress. Guts is, no causal link between you overseeing the pursuit op and Nick Jarvis getting killed. Wrong place, wrong time. Jesus, the poor prick could've taken the final curtain at Lyttelton if you let it go that far."

I let his use of "pursuit" pass. "Hope your intel turns out to be true. Thanks for telling me, boss. Grateful for all news. And I have some for you."

He takes another bite and mumbles, "Have you, now?"

"The tip you emailed me about Trix? Paid off. Search warrants will be executed on one Oliver Collinge."

"Form?"

"Suspected arson but Vincent tells me this guy could've gotten Trix into EI."

"As what, an employee?"

"Yes."

He shakes his head, but his look is one of disgust.

I touch my cheek. "Some other news, boss. Concerns one James Alexander Coman, aged twenty-five."

He swallows the rest of his party-pie then wipes his mouth with the back of his hand.

"What's he done now?"

"Gone a little far with birthday celebrations."

He closes his eyes, the prolonged action of a tired man suddenly put to sleep. He looks at his watch and sighs. "That's why he's not answering my dinner invitation. Where is he?"

"The drunk tank. About to drive someone's car before I stopped him. You won't extract any sense from him now." I glance around, check no one's looking our way. "When we helped him into the van, this appeared to fall from his trousers." I put the packet on the table.

Coman is flushed. "Dopey bastard. I demanded he stay in the program. Booze and crack. Have you charged him? Enough there for a charge of dealing. Jesus Christ. No prior convictions, but ... he's fucked now."

The inspector's right. Too much here for a first offender diversion—a slap on the wrist and community service before the charge is finally withdrawn. I wonder about the lad's upbringing, possible similarities to my own—an absent father, this one working to climb to the rank of inspector. Was he a boy who needed support but got it too late to make a difference? Heard only his father's demands, never quite good enough.

"Not your fault, son," he says. "You do what you need to do. Yes?"

I look away. "I prevented him from driving. No charge there, boss." I nod at the package, choose a tone of uncertainty. "I could be mistaken. The uniform didn't notice it. Was it impossible it was already on the bitumen, dropped by someone else and he scuffed it, drawing it to my attention? Who can say? And with natural uncertainty about what it is, we still need to get it tested by ESR."

He looks around. "Getting busy in here. Let's retire to a more private setting."

He gathers up the sandwiches, wraps them in white paper napkins and, in a movement smooth as fine olive oil, inserts the food parcel into the side pocket of his suit coat. I don't want to think about what might've gathered in those seams over the years.

In his office, he says, "I'll get him straight if it's the last fuckin' thing I do. But politically speaking, might be best to inform the boss about Jack being in the tank. Avoid any suggestion I have a conflict of interest."

"Sure, boss."

"But listen up. As much as I'm grateful you want to give him a break, and it embarrasses the shit out of me, it doesn't help him. He's gotta take a fall, the only fuckin' way he's going to learn. But more important than that. Never do anything to compromise you as a cop. Now, that's me giving you a break. With me?"

I feel the rising heat in my skin. "I hear you, boss. Understood."

"By the way," he says, "the grapevine tells me the DCC might not be around much longer. A more senior role in HQ.

Not sure whether we'll get a resumption of normal transmission or something worse."

"You in line to replace her, boss?"

"Too old school. The castle doesn't want superannuated pricks like me who wear department store shirts and never touch hair gel. I give the odd kick up the ass every now and again but also enjoy taking the boys to the canteen for a few beers. The powers say my class of man management sailed off with Noah. A lot of fun's gone from the job."

I smile. "Every chance we could get another DCC like the current one, I guess."

"Or worse."

"What will you do?"

He plays with the turkey skin under his chin. "Take some retirement package if I can head off HR. They can't afford to make people like me redundant and they can't make us retire." He gives a weak smile. "Know what they call these HR wankers?"

"Well here, human remains. Isn't it?"

"Not talking about here, son. Up in Bullshit Castle—HQ." He points a fat finger toward the ceiling. "Up there, they call them the modern Hitler Youth. Navy shirts in Pierre Cardin suits and hair standing on end like they received thirty thousand volts before the photo shoot. That's if they can find an actual bloke to do the job. They're getting their picture in the Commissioner's bloody newsletter. Seen that?"

"No, boss. To be honest I can't tell you when I last read one of those from cover to cover."

He nods sagely. "Sensible man."

I thank him again for the news about the inquiry and stroll to his door. I'm sure his eyes are boring into my back as I head for the door. He says, "Oliver Collinge, eh?"

I turn.

He adds, "Given Sinclair's hired Trix, you're not going to make any friends over there."

"I don't make them anywhere in this job."

He gives me an inquisitive look.

"It's making the right calls in the right moment. Isn't it, boss? Something you often remind me of."

He nods slowly, perhaps assessing my authenticity. "Of course."

"Sinclair's not my only focus," I say. "We need to go wherever the evidence takes us."

"Police rule number one," he says.

"A question, boss. The EI function you couldn't go to."

"What about it?"

I pause. "To be honest, I'm a bit nervous about provoking something resulting in a shit shower for me."

He gives me his expression of silent appraisal. For some reason, I cope with it now. He says, "We don't think that's likely. Do we?"

I say, "The AC pulled me aside at the function, just the two of us. He said you received credible information Nick Jarvis committed earthquake claims fraud."

"What?" He looks incredulous.

"Fergus Dowling backed him up. The AC also said you had someone working undercover at EI. I believed he was simply mistaken, that being based in Wellington, he wasn't across all the fine details."

"Vincent's on crime prevention," Coman snaps, "not fucking undercover." He squints at me. "Why have you waited so long to tell me this? What else don't I know?"

I walk back to his desk. "I'm still unhappy about some

matters concerning Fergus Dowling's death." I tell him about the text from Dowling's phone, the pill lodged in his throat and its significance.

He leans back, strokes his chin, and folds his arms.

I say, "I told Tracey texts can be delayed, hang in the ether, silent and invisible. Arrive at awkward times. Dowling could still've sent it. Dowling also told me he met a younger woman, said it was all a bit mysterious."

"And I assume you still haven't found his phone or evidence of him typing that note?"

"No, boss."

After a long pause, he says, "Okay. There's something I need to tell you. The DCC was tipped off about Dowling's suicide note."

I frown. "Sorry, boss. Not with you."

"She said a bloke claiming to be an old drinking buddy of Dowling's was concerned about his welfare. Apparently, he told her Dowling was distressed and suggested she check him out at home. The note was found in his West Melton property not in that fucking shed."

"She went there?"

"More likely had someone go for her."

"Did you know this when I said we found no evidence of his ability to write a note?"

He gives a small cough as his ears redden. "Guilty, Your Honor."

"Jesus Christ, boss. We're two peas in a pod."

"Keep going on the Dowling inquiry. But between us, okay?"

WEDNESDAY, 8 AUGUST 2012
08.58 HOURS

Blain overhears Tracey tell me Edward Myles has no criminal history and asks, "Who's he?"

I tell him about our visit to *The Press*. "They had an informant who thought Myles had a holding company, an outfit with possible connections to Putis."

"Does that put us any further ahead on the Putis front?"

I shake my head.

Blain and I leave the station to attend EI at the appointed time, only to learn Quentin Sinclair left in a hurry. We ask to make an urgent appointment and get a stony tone, "I'm not authorized to do that," the young woman says.

"You're his PA. Aren't you?" I ask, layering on the incredulity.

"When it suits him." She yawns.

I suspect Sinclair is hiding inside, seeking guidance from Hockley on how to deal with impertinent impostors.

Back at the office, the radio informs listeners the minister of police is to visit the city today, escorted by New Zealand's top cop, the police commissioner. It's a bullshit PR exercise about the proposed justice and emergency services precinct, how cops and judges will all work together in the same place, a happy family bound by the pursuit of justice. I can imagine the judicial reaction to the bureaucrat's plans. The visit provides another chance for Hockley to ingratiate herself with the top cop. I can almost smell the shoe polish and carpet cleaner in preparation for the royal tour around our damaged station.

At 1030 hours, Coman calls my desk phone. "Can you be at the courthouse in ten minutes?"

"What part?"

"Durham Street, foyer. Immediately before you go through security."

"What for?"

"Morning tea with the minister."

"Is she not coming here?"

"The minister doesn't share her schedule with me. That much I can tell you."

Despite admitting withholding information, Coman still sounds pissed with me. It's made me less sure of who to trust, who not to, and whether to tell him about Vincent, who at Hockley's instigation, attempted to poison my view of him.

"Boss, on the subject of being more open, I should say Blain and I went to EI at 0900."

"What for?" His voice is full of concern.

"Given Vincent is helping EI, and Yan worked there, I thought we could help on the Yan case by chatting to Quentin Sinclair. It's already a warm relationship. Isn't it? Nurturing important relationships was something I remember from the management course. Plus, we can check on Vincent's work, see if Sinclair's still happy."

"DCC Hockley know?"

"That's why I'm mentioning it. I couldn't get hold of the DCC, so I'm telling you in case we've set off any alarm bells. But it came to nothing. Sinclair did a runner, but if anyone asks you about it, you'll be able to head off any possible grumbling."

"Forewarned. Appreciate it."

Walking to the courthouse, dark clouds hang low. I realize our visitors are breaking the normal protocol of meeting in Hockley's office. The uneasy prickling scalp returns.

At the appointed time a cream limo pulls up to the main courthouse entrance. First out is O'Brien's personal assistant followed by O'Brien and Assistant Commissioner Troup. They wear dark suits, funeral faces, and tight jaws. No sign of the police commissioner.

The PA's tone is formal. "Lead the way please, Detective Sergeant."

We place cell phones, keys, and wallets in a tray, walk through the security arch, and retrieve our items. No one says anything in the elevator. We move into an empty court waiting room and the PA acts as sentry outside the door. I flick the light switch and the single tube blinks. It shoots tiny light bursts into a dim room with little natural light and continues to blink. Troup arranges the chairs in a triangle around a small shin-high table piled with worn magazines. I'm at the sharpest point, facing a sliver of window to the outside world. O'Brien thanks me for coming—like I had a choice. "Understand," she says, "this meeting is not taking place. Yes?"

"Plausible deniability, I think it's called, Minister."

"Strictest confidence is required."

"Applicable to the territory I work in, Minister."

She looks at Troup, who shifts in his chair, refusing to meet my eye.

"Right," O'Brien says with authority. "We're here to promote the new justice precinct but I understand you have concerns about Quentin Sinclair, some criminal investigation. Is that correct?"

I get a fluttering feeling in my guts. How the hell does O'Brien know this? Has news of our attempt to make an appointment already gone to the top of the organization? My suspicion about Sinclair contacting Hockley seems on the mark but what does she know. Is Vincent still in double agent mode? Is a reluctant Blain, the man more in tune with office politics than me, hedging his bets on my future?

"We have a range of ongoing criminal investigations, Minister." I tell her what I told Coman, trying to make my tone sound casual. "I'm also investigating whether there's any connection between the disappearance of Trix after killing detective Jarvis and Earthquake Insure."

Troup shifts in his chair.

"How could there be?" she says, surprise in her voice.

I say, "We know Mr. Sinclair interviewed and hired Rachel Trix before she killed Detective Jarvis. He did not use one of his many managers to do so. Trix was supplied with another identity. These events occurred before Mr. Sinclair publicly spoke about suspicions of fraud at EI. I would be negligent, Minister, if I failed to make some inquiries about that and his knowledge of her true identity."

O'Brien is still and her Botox blocks any facial reaction. I glance at Troup to gauge his reaction. He maintains a close watch on his footwear.

I add, "I'm also concerned to learn Sinclair engaged a consultant, a person of interest to us for a long time and believed to be involved in organized crime. Until now he's only been known as the Putis, but we believe the person can now be identified as Oliver Collinge."

Troup's chin is now up, eyes bulging. "You're not suggesting evidence of Sinclair's criminality in any of that. Are you?"

O'Brien faces Troup and gives him the smallest of headshakes. To me, she says, "Ordinarily, Jonah, I wouldn't be taking interest in any case."

"I understand the government's desire to be independent from police investigations, Minister."

"Of course, you do." She attempts to exercise the smile muscles around her mouth, but it becomes a grimace. "But in this case, there are significant competing interests about which we must all be cognizant. Yes?"

"Yes, Minister."

"To be frank, Earthquake Insure is nothing short of a public relations disaster, Jonah. It's the only reason we went to their function the other night—an attempt to boost the flagging morale of EI's troops. Quentin Sinclair is guilty of presiding over a poorly run organization, unable to pull itself out of a crisis of its own making. Poor leadership, poor recruitment, complete disorder to name but a few problems, piled on top of the country's worst natural disaster. But let's be clear. Shall we?"

She checks with Troup, who makes a noise in his throat, like the growl Pugwash would give in response to my command to be quiet.

"I have Sinclair's word, his guarantee," O'Brien says, "he's not involved in any criminal activity, any fraud. That's rock solid. He's shocked to learn you wanted to speak to him."

Troup says, "Given your concerns and our public profile

with EI, I find it extraordinary you didn't seek to discuss this with either your inspector or the district crime commander."

"Can I ask you a question, sir?"

He gives a look more from one eye than his full face.

"Have you ever met Oliver Collinge?"

"Never heard of him, much less met him. What are you…"

"The real point, Jonah," O'Brien says, cutting in, "is if citizens understood Earthquake Insure's CEO was under investigation for any criminal offense, after what he said at the function, I shudder to think about the political consequences for my government. I'm sure you haven't forgotten his praise of Martin, here, or DCC Hockley."

"I understand your point, Minister."

"Their PR campaign is no longer effective. People have switched off listening to data about the size and scale of disaster, etcetera, etcetera. Our polling suggests as political stewards of the recovery, we could be heading for trouble. Hence our move to put out the rebuild blueprint, balance up the doom and gloom, offer some positive news in a community drowning in sadness. You can see that. Can't you?"

"I see some utility in the strategy, Minister."

Troup, assuming his boss's calmer approach, says, "Let Vincent continue to do his work for Quentin in a low-key and supportive way. We'll continue to build cases of fraud perpetrated against EI. Superb results there so far, Jonah, so pat yourself on the back." He waves a dismissive backhand in the air. "Some misunderstanding about hiring Trix. Either that or Jarvis left a shit bomb behind him. Rotten apple. Good riddance."

I feel my blood pressure rising and want to ask him if the

career pathway to Assistant Commissioner is based on condemnation without evidence. I chew my bottom lip.

The minister says, "What the AC said about Vincent's work, it all helps to build confidence, not only in the anti-fraud measures in place but our reputation in crime prevention. The optics are good for my government," She looks at Troup.

He says, "No ripe fruit to be picked by going after Sinclair. Okay?" He doesn't wait for my answer. "And think about your career, too. That's important. Isn't it?"

"Sorry, boss?"

"Not talking out of school here, but it's no secret Mick Coman is close to retirement. I see you in his role in six months."

I tense, and the old shoulder pain returns. "Isn't there an appointments process?" I ask. "Others must be in the running, I'm sure."

"We'll put you in an acting role to ensure you get any possible leg up needed. From there it's easy unless you commit an unpardonable sin. I'm confident you'll keep your nose clean. Neither complicated nor difficult for a successful cop like you. A man with leadership skills too, I recall."

The Minister attempts another smile. "I can't imagine you're the sort of man who needs to be on some form of probationary period. Quick learner, I heard."

"He is, indeed, Minister."

My mobile vibrates in my pocket.

"What do you think, Jonah?" asks Troup with a plastic smile. "I'll tell Yvonne to make you a senior sergeant. Promotion of a team player well earned. Yes? Makes the transition to inspector easier. What do you say?

"There are benefits to be had, boss." I give them a tight smile and they both force a laugh in palpable relief.

A momentary pause before Troup says, "I understand you live with your sister, Jonah."

I feel my pulse elevate and crack my knuckles at him.

"Don't be concerned. I'm simply wondering how she's getting on with her condition."

"Not easy for her," I say. "For either of us."

"And Judge Pollard? How's he doing?"

I slip my hands under my thighs. I've run out of saliva and can't speak. The best I can do is give him a head shake. He stares at me, no doubt enjoying the moment.

"Anyway," Troup says, "Quentin's incompetence is something we need to keep between us. Yes? Keeping confidences is the sign of a good cop on an upward trajectory. Breaking them," he points his left thumb at the ground, "usually comes with unpalatable consequences, often with unintended fallout."

He gives a wolf smile and hands me his card. "Happy to take your call, son. Any time."

I leave feeling like Little Red Riding Hood.

WEDNESDAY, 8 AUGUST 2012
11.15 HOURS

Back in the station's lobby, I check for messages and see one from Eve.

"Solly, Ken, next door. He's been burgled." Her voice is shaky at a higher pitch. "He told me through our bathroom window. He said nothing taken."

I shake my head in disbelief at his decision to tell someone incapable of letting him in the house, much less offering tea and comfort.

"He's tried to calm me, I know, but police officers are in the street. Can you come home?"

I light up and as the nicotine does its work, I wonder why Ken, with a spare key, simply didn't come into the house. I let the question drift into the cool breeze.

I can't shake O'Brien and Troup from my mind. The fact there were no explicit threats somehow makes it worse.

They want a grateful foot soldier, someone who'll stay in line and accept his mentor was stressed and depressed, realize Dowling was suicidal.

And Nick Jarvis? A man with a secret life. In a relationship with a bent cop, perhaps benefiting from her frauds before a crisis of conscience. Had he blackmailed her for a share of her takings from EI, thus creating a motive for his murder? What about his secret informant, off the books, unsafe and against procedure? Could've been part of a double cross. Could've been anything. It all pointed to a pattern of a man living a dangerous life, a man who made himself vulnerable to rough justice. Some might call it poetic justice. He reaped what he sowed. *Rotten apple. Good riddance.*

Eve's right. It's possible to let it all go. Justice is such an ephemeral thing when you think about it. You win cases and you lose cases. You can pour thousands of person hours into an inquiry and get no result. What do I have? An identification of Collinge as the Putis, passport offenses. Big deal. We've got little to go on to pursue Sinclair for being party to frauds we can't find, much less prove, with only a dodgy voice ID from a convicted criminal.

On the other hand, Senior Sergeant Solomon has a nice ring. But for how long? Why wouldn't I meet an unfortunate accident as part of a later cleanup? If Dowling and Nick were both crooked, justice still demands accountability, the truth. There've always been dodgy cops, self-entitled over one thing and another. But crime on this scale: greedy predators feeding off a catastrophe, causing more misery to innocents. I can't turn away from this kind of corruption.

My mobile vibrates again.

"Yes, Eve."

"I'm worried, Solly. Ken's back home, the locksmith is changing his locks. Will you be home soon?"

"Unlikely. I've still got a day's work ahead of me. Are all the doors locked?"

"Course they're locked. What do you think I am? An idiot?"

"Okay, okay. Wedge one of the dining chairs under the handle of the back door."

"What about the front?" Eve asks.

"Shift the dowel rod lying in the well where the door slides open. Bring it forward so the door won't slide back. And turn the stereo on."

"I think you should come home, Solly."

I rub my forehead. "I'm about to go into an important meeting with Blain about a development in Nick Jarvis's case. I need to do this face-to-face, reduce the risk of eavesdroppers. But look, no need for alarm, Eve. If Ken's been burgled, the guys who did it won't be hanging around to burgle us. Okay? Any half-brained thief won't want police dogs on him."

"Please, Solly." She sounds terrified.

I take a deep breath. "Okay, I'll be there as soon as I can."

I call Blain and tell him about Eve.

"You want us to get some uniforms over there?"

"The neighbor's called them. I'm on my way to see if I can calm her down. Listen, I've come from a meeting with O'Brien and Troup."

"Tea and cupcakes?"

"Carrot and stick, more like it. The Minister's presence is disconcerting. We can take nothing at face value."

"The plan from here?"

"A gamble."

He gives a throat clearing sound. "Don't like the sound of that."

"The good news is the ice wall between Coman and me is melting. We've had a little talk."

"That sounds g… Hang on, boss. Tracey's got something urgent."

"Boss?"

"Yes, Trace."

"A body in Wainoni about to be concreted over." She provides the address. "See you there."

WEDNESDAY, 8 AUGUST 2012
12.05 HOURS

I expect to see Eve racked with anxiety but she's calm, drinking tea, and reading today's newspaper. I balance my resentment at the time-wasting trip with comfort at feeding Pugwash. Given where I'm heading next, who knows how long it will be before I'm back? I tell her I must leave straight away, and she says she'll cook something I can reheat.

At the Wainoni property, two blocks back from the river, a green tarp provides cover for a broken chimney on an old two-story house. Shrouded in a forensic suit, I duck under police tape and stride down a broken concrete driveway bordered by a brown paling fence, twisted and buckled, on my right. The section is subdivided. I pass the old house and come to the back half, all shingle and concrete boxing, ready for a new townhouse.

In the corner of the back section, one of our protective tents is up with two builders' vans and a small tip truck close by. In the gloom, I count twenty people, including media, most on mobile phones. The cops are well outnumbered and forensically, this is bad form. A red mist forms behind my eyes as I charge ahead.

Vincent, his back to the growing chaos, writes in his notebook. With him, a man in green overalls leans on a grubby earth compactor. Walking toward him, I yell, "Why hasn't this scene been cleared?"

Vincent points behind me. "A work site, boss. Everyone, media excepted, is legitimately here."

"Get a perimeter tape up. All persons not investigating, outside. Damn it. That's Police 101. Isn't it? Or am I crazy?" I point to the man beside him. "Who's this?"

"Noel Franklin, boss. He found the body."

Franklin is tall, muscular, a block head making his protective earmuffs look like a kid's toy.

I point at the tent. "Been in yet, Detective?"

"No, boss. Sergeant Blain directed a priority on witnesses while they were still here."

I turn to Franklin. "Appreciate you waiting for a bit longer."

Franklin scowls, shakes his head in silent protest.

Inside the tent, Blain is upwind of a putrid body. I walk around the grave to join him, peering into the hole, jerking back at the head-turning stench. This isn't the four-to-six-foot deep grave of a cemetery, but it's a lot deeper than the shallow grave typical of many homicides. This took time to prepare. Most of the lower body is cleared of stones, crushed brick, and sand.

Blain, hand over his mouth, says, "Identifiable, but dead for a while, I reckon. The winter earth has probably preserved her."

"How soon did the tent go up after Franklin's call?"

"I can check with uniforms, but Franklin said he kept people away until we got here."

"Some sense."

Blain points at the body. "Are you thinking what I'm thinking?"

"If you're pondering our inability to find her, then yes."

"A lot of unproductive man hours until now, I reckon."

"Okay," I say, "I'll admit it. I was wrong."

"I'll get Vincent in to witness that admission."

"Don't bother. Vincent's a bigger idiot than me."

Blain tilts his head as though he wants more from me.

The techie's portable lighting and gentle excavation help us see Rachel Trix's sunken chest, her blue shirt heavy with blood around the neck and down the front. A large hole in the front of her face takes the place of her right eye.

"Sight for sore eye, you reckon?" says Blain. "Decent exit."

I look at him as he stares into the grave, unsure whether to comment on his black humor or not. "I'd say a forty-five, point-blank range. Also blows this inquiry wide open."

Blain's phone buzzes. He coughs behind me. "Cadaverman will be here in two minutes."

We move outside the tent. Vincent has cleared the scene of people and a skinny man in a navy suit talks to Franklin, both now behind a taped boundary.

"I don't imagine this is a rebuild site," I say to Blain. "Not in this part of town."

"Not like you to lack imagination. According to the guys on the site, the owner must have some pull or know the builders. People this side of town would be lucky to get an outside shit-house built for them."

Blain owns and lets a two-bedroom somewhere in this suburb. He's not averse to having tenants on government benefits, and families are even better. He cops good-humored ribbing about living off beneficiaries but his heart's in the right place.

"Where's your rental from here?"

He points north. "Two blocks up there."

"Your wife still pushing you for doing it up?"

"I said the dough would be better spent on a trip to Bali," he says. "We won't recover the capital spend on such dodgy land and you'd be lucky to find affordable insurance. The talk is, people will take cash settlements and sell livable houses—as is, where is."

I nod and decide to refocus. "What's the timing here?"

"According to Franklin, the concrete was supposed to go down the day after this shingle and boxing settled in. Meant to be six weeks ago but higher priorities for repairs at other properties ruled."

"So, we can date her burial at a minimum of six weeks. Probably longer."

"If the project had gone according to plan, we might still be looking for her. Now we can tell Alice her son's killer won't be doing time on the taxpayer."

I frown.

"What?"

"Something doesn't make sense."

Blain gives a wry smile. "Replaced one unsolved with another."

"Yeah, but there's..." I shake my head at something inaccessible in my mind. I rub my temple and it comes. I ask, "Could the date and time stamp on the gas station CCTV be dodgy?"

"Don't go there," he says, frowning. "Jesus, I hope not. Although, those sorts of errors would be consistent with the rest of their recording system. Why are you asking about that now?"

"Think about the timing. When Nick was killed and how long she's been dead."

Cadaverman and an assistant arrive, along with a forensic scientist from ESR. Cadveron says, "I hope you don't think you have me on some personal retainer, Detective?"

"My generosity stops short of helping you with your performance targets, Professor."

The forensic scientist says, "I've shot you a note about finding traces of foam rubber on DI Dowling's clothing."

"Whereabouts?"

He points at his arm. "Left sleeve of his jersey," he says. "Nothing on the right, though. Mean anything to you?"

I turn to Cadveron. "Wasn't there bruising on Fergus's right wrist?"

"There was."

"One wrist possibly handcuffed, the other one protected. What the hell does this mean?" I ask.

Cadveron checks at his watch. "I'm only the butcher. You're the cop. I'll crack on if you don't mind."

"Thank you, gentlemen." I turn to Blain. "There's a few people I wouldn't mind slicing up, and they don't have to be dead."

A worried-looking uniform cop approaches. "Sir, Franklin and the suit with him want to know how much longer they have to freeze their balls off. The suit reckons we don't understand time's money."

"Sorry," Blain says, "have we been focusing on the wrong thing?"

The cop doesn't answer.

I walk to the tape and face Franklin. "I'm told you saw the depression in the ground, and you started digging?"

"Yep. Sometimes we have to excavate and repack to make the ground level again."

"What was the first thing you saw?"

"Looked like the soles of two running shoes, toes up. Weird, eh. It was only a bucket and a half deep."

"What depth from the surface are we talking about?

"About a couple of feet, maybe a little more."

"What did you do next?"

He looks at the shrouded site. "I got out, had a squiz, then scraped away dirt, stones, and shit from the shoes—enough to see feet in them. Fuckin' freaked me out."

"But inside the tent," I say pointing, "more uncovered than the feet, right? The body's clear from the knees down to the ankles. You do that?"

"I thought, feet in shoes, it was one of those mannequin things, ya know? I dug a bit more out. I didn't think it was a fuckin' corpse, mate. Why would I think that?"

"Okay. Where's your car?"

Franklin points.

"Warm up over there. I'll have someone take your formal statement. They'll tell you what we need from you to account for your presence at the scene before our team arrived."

He and his companion head to the car, hunched like two headless zombies.

"Get any grief from the suit?" Blain asks.

"Might have if I asked your questions. Let's try you on answers." I nod in the direction of the smoking, coffee-drinking media. "I'm sure the vultures await you, eager for your pearls of wisdom, appreciative of a newbie's unguarded offerings."

He nods with enthusiasm.

"Except, you'll have bugger all to say. Not releasing the identity until next of kin, that sort of thing. Nothing about the gunshot wound. Any questions on cause of death, tell them we're asking for an urgent autopsy."

"I'm not hearing a lot of opportunities for initiative here, boss. Or is that just me?"

"Perceptive. The making of a competent detective. When you're done in two minutes, I'll have a more interesting job."

Blain claps his gloved hands twice. "Eternal gratitude, that's me."

A uniformed officer approaches with an evidence bag. "Told to show you this, boss, before it goes off to the ESR for analysis."

One clear plastic bag contains shell cases. In another, a handwritten note—Trix's writing, if my memory's any good. It makes fetching her fraud trial exhibits for a comparison a high priority. The note contains names and amounts.

Silvertops RC: $137,685

The Word of Life Church: $234,113

Butterworth Cars Ltd: $321,765

Kirby Kitchens: $296,657

Dessler Ltd: $316,528

De Vries Business Supplies: $129,694

"Shells and list in the pit?" I ask.

"Yes, the shells, sir. This note was partly visible on the underside of the deceased's bra. Protected, not much blood on it."

I photographed it on my phone. "We need a rush on the science."

"ESR allocates priorities between rush jobs," he says. "Would you like to know the criteria, boss?"

"Do I look like I want to know?"

"No, boss."

Blain returns. "So, what's the next exciting adventure?"

I show him the picture. "Silvertops RC is my rugby club."

"Insurance payments?"

"Some of them dodgy."

"The others, fictitious companies?" he asks.

"Not the church."

He scratches his head. "Records'll be somewhere?"

"I know one thing," I say, "the days of running this covertly are over."

He says, "Which corrupt cop do we trust—the living or the dead?"

"He's not going to like it, but it's gotta be Coman." I tell Blain I finally told Coman about Troup's intel on Jarvis and his disappointment at not knowing sooner."

His expression suggests I've no reason to be surprised by the big man's reaction. "What's our strategy for Troup?" he asks.

"I'm going to call him, tell him about today's treasure hunt. You head back to the station. Troup denies he's ever met Collinge. I want you to help me flush him out, photograph them holding hands, kissing." Blain grins. I add, "When I've called him, he's not going to want to use the phone, any phone. Call me on my personal mobile."

"When?"

"When he's moving." I think about Vincent's attempt at spying on me. "Only, don't be seen. Right?"

WEDNESDAY, 8 AUGUST 2012
16.45 HOURS

Extra lights erected to combat the creeping darkness also help us keep to the protective ground covers and preserve what little evidence remains uncontaminated. Vincent shivers despite gloves and a greatcoat over his suit.

"Eaten today, Detective? Helps keep the bleak from your bones."

He doesn't look at me. "Sandwich and a pie at thirteen hundred, boss."

"Detective, every time I talk to you, you examine your Italian leather shoes, looking distraught about the permanence of dog shit."

"I thought I might've had the tape by now, boss."

"I'll give you the tape, son. Dead bodies are the priority now. You can grasp that. Yes?"

"Boss."

Over Vincent's shoulder, I see Tracey escort an elderly Māori woman entombed in a long coat to the perimeter of the scene. I remind Vincent I have his back and he loses the aura of a dead man walking.

Tracey says, "Spoken to the head of the local Neighborhood

Watch, boss." She points to the two-story place next door. "She lives there on her own. Says this house owner's Victoria Milburn. Lived here many years. This is a recent subdivision, why the roller and concrete mixer are here. I have a spare key. Mira," she says, nodding in the woman's direction, "collects Victoria's mail and helps keep the appearance of the place being lived in. This development's in the hands of a construction company, has been for the last eight weeks."

"I was thinking," I say, "this property's been an easy option to access with no fencing or gate from the street."

She says, "Under surveillance by a property management outfit while Victoria's been away on holiday. Front garden and security checks."

I point at Mira's house on the boundary. "An open window up there, the frosted glass suggests a bathroom. See if anyone's stayed with her and if they heard anything unusual going on down here in the last couple of months. Also, ask around the neighborhood for strange night-time noises, digging and the like. No fences, the burial would've happened at night, difficult to keep quiet. Somebody other than Mira might've noticed something, had their citizen spirit aroused."

"Sure, boss."

Vincent returns from the driveway to say he's due at EI the day after tomorrow.

"I want to talk to the property owner and the outfit managing this section for the owner. Can you make it happen?

"Yes, boss."

"And see me before you resume duties at EI."

"Yes, boss."

Rubber gloves on, I enter the kitchen door at the back of the house and detect the same sickly cleaning odor as at

Dowling's place in West Melton. Could his killer have been in this old villa? It's the type of house, if you lost your yale key to unlock the place, you could pick the simple little lock, or if you knew the code number on the key, buy a duplicate. Could the killer know about this property because they once lived here? Maybe kept a key?

At the sideboard, I rifle through retail advertising and fliers. A utilities invoice confirms Victoria Milburn owns the property at this address.

Blain calls my personal mobile. "I'm in our car lot," he says. "Floodlights are on, so I'll keep my head down."

"Roger. Stand by."

I withdraw Troup's card, turn on the speaker function and punch the numbers into my work mobile, keeping the line to Blain open so he will hear the call.

Troup answers on the third ring. "Jonah, terrific to hear from you. Give me a sec while I leave this meeting." A short pause. "What can I do for you, son?"

"Wanted you to be first cab, boss. We found Trix."

"Where?"

"In a stony grave on a building site."

A longer pause.

"Are you still there, sir?"

"Sorry, yes. Someone trying to get my attention. Superb work, DS Solomon. You cracked it. I always thought you would. I should call you senior sergeant, now. Eh?"

Knowing Blain is listening, I wince. "Thanks, boss. Much appreciated."

Another pause.

"Recent burial, is it?" He makes his question sound casual, but I know he wants my view on how long she's been dead.

"Difficult to say, boss. Autopsy will confirm."

"Excellent. Your discovery, that is. What will you do now, apart from celebrate?"

"I'll inform the DCC. She'll be pleased too. As for Trix's killer, like you said, boss. Rotten apples. My recommendation is someone else should head the inquiry. I need a holiday. Been a while since the last time, boss. I'm buggered."

"Couldn't agree more. Take as long as you want. I'll fix it with Yvonne. Well done, Jonah."

"Thanks, boss."

He disconnects the call.

"Get it all, detective?" I ask.

"Yes, thank you, *Senior*. You're buggered? What about the rest of us?"

"Camera locked and loaded for brothel light settings?"

"Affirmative."

An ambulance siren penetrates the quiet. "Anything new on Yan's health?" I ask.

"His parents are on their way from China. Word is they might be asked to pull the plug. How long do you reckon before I see any action here?"

"Enough time for one of your master house inspections."

"Seconds?"

"I'd say."

Outside, the scene is occupied by a few police and scientists. The media have gone. Tracey's taking Noel Franklin's statement.

In minutes, Blain calls, "Here he comes. He's almost running."

"Don't lose him."

"Roger. Standby."

I wander outside, have a conversation with Tracey about bereavement leave. She promises me she will when we've made an arrest. "No problem after that, boss. We got some interesting stuff from the search of Collinge's place."

In twenty minutes, Blain's call interrupts. Before answering, I tell Tracey, "First thing tomorrow for Collinge?"

She gives me a thumbs up.

When I answer Blain's call, he says, "Blenheim Road, warehouse. Will email you photos."

THURSDAY, 9 AUGUST 2012
08.02 HOURS

Pictures of Troup and Collinge on my phone, the likeness of Danny DeVito to Collinge is justified. Blain catches them both with the grim expression of mourners departing a funeral wake where there'd been no beer or food. After Troup's denial of knowing Collinge, these pictures are exactly what I want. The concern on their faces is a bonus.

In the squad room, Tracey approaches with her own photographs and a broad smile. Got a minute, boss?"

She points toward the fishbowl office with a latex gloved hand. Inside, she lays out photos of a walled property resembling a gated community. They reveal security cameras on high fencing, a Porsche and its interior, one of the shelves inside a wardrobe, and one of what appears to be a workbench in a garage with various articles and pieces of equipment. Another photo reveals a dark plastic container the size and shape of a water bottle on a shelf underneath the bench. Tracey hands me a pair of rubber gloves.

She shows me a passport stained from the residue of the fingerprinting process, the original of the copy Vincent took from Earthquake Insure's HR department. The biographical details of Harriet Volp sit next to Rachel Trix's picture.

"Found here," she says, and points to a photo of the black Porsche Cayenne Turbo. "Parked outside Collinge's garage, but you can't see it from the street. His mansion is surrounded by this eight-foot-high fence. She moves her finger. The Volp/ Trix passport was in the wheel well of the trunk inside that plastic bag."

"How did you access it?"

"Collinge unlocked and opened the trunk at my direction. Looking into the trunk, I saw finger smudges near the wheel well, so I directed him to remove the spare. We videoed him complying. There was a bag and I asked him what was inside. I mean, hard to tell from this picture, but looking in, at the time, it was obvious they were passports. He said he never laid eyes on the bag before."

"A most unfortunate moment for him. Had time to check them out?"

"Nine digitally chipped, all with details of the holder's identities and photographs. Put the names through our system—all clean skins, of course."

"After his denial, I took the bag out. I didn't want him complaining if we found his prints on them it was because I made him touch the passports."

"Good work."

"He wasn't happy. He said Harriet Volp sold him the car and he could show us the bank transfer as proof."

"I expect he could. Same account he set up in her name using her flash new passport as an identity. The one from which she withdrew her EI wages."

Tracey chuckles. "He said after he took ownership of the Porsche he never went to the wheel well."

"Of course. Another Trix victim. Very sad. You running prints on the other passports?"

"On everything, boss."

"What does the passport office say about how identity was proved before its issue?"

"Online applications. The applicant for the passport has to get other passport holders to verify their identity. Some of those other passport holder names are on this list." She hands me her phone. "I didn't print this off for reasons that will be obvious."

The screen photo is a register of names, addresses, contact numbers and emails, family members and financial loan payments going back to the beginning of 2010. She says, "Collinge told me the Underwood group manage his debtors. The manager periodically updates him with repayments and new loans."

I say, "I'm not sure what I'm looking for, Trace."

"They're alphabetical." She uses her finger to advance the screen and points to a name. Ian Terrence Vincent.

I shake my head. "So, dealing with loan sharks. Wonderful. Isn't it?"

Vincent's reassurance the punt no longer grips him sounds hollow.

"On a related matter, boss, Detective Blain's asked me to serve a summons on the woman Vincent was with the night Nick was killed in relation to careless driving."

"Yes."

"She's part of the Underwood family. A few months back, I charged the mother with abduction and assault with intent to injure. Sorry to be the one with this news, boss."

"No issues. Well done, Trace. I'll have a little chat with Mr. Vincent. Talk me through the rest of these photos."

She shows me a pic of the inside of the Blenheim Road warehouse and a forty-four-gallon drum. "I expect forensics will tell us the contents of the drum are burned clothing," she says. "But we found this bronzed shape of NZP, letters joined up. Wasn't this Trix's bespoke buckle?"

"It was. The question is why was Collinge in possession of it. Anything else of interest?"

She flicks to a photo of books inside a wardrobe.

"I can't quite make out the whole titles. I assume you brought back the originals."

"I did. The one on the left is Lyman's 49th edition of *Reloading Handbook* and next to it, *The Cast Bullet Handbook*. And the little container there," she says pointing at her screen, "I believe is a bottle of gunpowder. Now being tested." She smiles. "He's worried about something. He called when you were off the floor."

THURSDAY, 9 AUGUST 2012
09.45 HOURS

At Oliver Collinge's request, Tracey and I enter a cafe in Madras Street. Inside the cafe's swing door, we're greeted by the comforting fragrance of roasted beans. Sacks of them are piled up against the back wall. The cafe is noisy with machinery, cutlery, crockery, and chatter accompanied by the odd shriek of laughter.

I'm focusing on how to out-maneuver Collinge—help him tell lots of porkies. I flinch at an electric shock to my chest before realizing my phone is vibrating in the shirt pocket. Coman's text says, *Trix found means I don't have to reassign you or your team. Well done.*

The tone of his text is a first, at least for him. It tempts me to ask for forensics for both Dowling's properties and now, the Blenheim Road warehouse. I decide to defer the request until after we've interviewed Collinge.

Tracey points him out. He wears an orange shirt and black pants, possibly the same clothing in Blain's pics.

At a leaner, coffee in front of him, Collinge wipes the lenses of his black-framed glasses and says, "The organ grinder I want, not the fuckin' monkey. Otherwise, I'm outta here."

Tracey's with me as a witness to our chat, but I must accede. Because he's not in cuffs yet, he controls who he talks to.

"Give us a minute, Trace." I hand her a ten-dollar note. "My shout. Mine's an Americano. I'll tell you if Mr. Collinge says anything useful." My mouth is suddenly dry, and the radio's volume bothers me. I search for a staffer to assist but no one's in sight. My left shoulder pain is back, an omen we're off to a terrible start.

Tracey's tight lips and pinched expression suggest something malodorous is under her nose. Without moving his hand from the table, Collinge shows her his middle finger. When she leaves, he strokes his goatee and says, "Thought I mighta received the courtesy of an invitation to chat, rather than your little Rotty being set on me."

"This is a courtesy. We're here at your request. It suits us while we run the prints on what we've seized from your car and premises. But I'm curious why you want to talk."

He lifts his chin, revealing a thin scar at the top of his neck.

"For a start, your key witness is missing, presumed dead. Despite what I understand is a determined effort on your part to find her. On its own, reason enough, yes?"

"What key witness is presumed dead?"

He raises a thumb. "You're not catching me out. Wall-to-wall media, this case. I said nothing the whole city doesn't know."

"We've never said who it was," I say with a smirk.

"You're not the only one with reliable sources. Point is, I'm a businessman who's reasonable. I'm good at what I do. You can't be successful in life without being reasonable." He gives a lopsided grin. "Can you?"

I say nothing.

"If you must," he adds, "you can rap me on some old traffic fines your little friend dredged up. Won't amount to much. But I'm suggesting no other charges of the kind mentioned in your trumped up warrant some pissed court official signed. Only a suggestion, but I hope I'm speaking plainly enough?"

I lean forward, detect cologne on his skin. I'm sure it's the same as Griff's but on Collinge it smells cheap. "The passport offenses are only the beginning." I sit more upright. "My detective is helping me place you in the vehicle that ran down one of my team, reversed over him and back again to make sure he would die. Now, is that plain enough, businessman Collinge?"

I pause for a denial.

Nothing.

"So, if you think for one second this all ends with you fixing up a few unpaid traffic fines, you're deluded."

Tracey returns with my coffee and takes hers to a table. She opens the newspaper. Turning away from her, Collinge says, "We know one another. Don't we?"

I maintain an unblinking stare. "I don't recall arresting you before."

He gives a loud belly laugh. "Let's be thoughtful for a minute. Yes? As a successful businessman, a lot of people depend on me. You understand I work for Earthquake Insure. I'm trying to help them fix all their systems and security problems."

"By managing the Underwoods and their system of knee capping slow premium payers. Also a crime. Known as demanding with menace."

He exhales loudly. "So, part of my job over there is to review their business processes, including integrity tests. I expect Vincent would've mentioned my new, 'prove your identity policy.' Familiar with it? That's the reason I borrow other people's passports—perfectly legitimate."

My turn to laugh. "The passports you told us you've never seen before? Of course, makes perfect sense to me and, I predict, a smart jury."

Collinge gives me his best sneer. "I'm not surprised you find it funny. Happens with the simple-minded people who become cops because they can't get into university." The grin reappears.

"All sorts of people with false identities, Mr. Collinge. Got a couple yourself. Have you? Thing is, I never met anyone who needed one for an honest purpose."

"You're not listening, Solomon." Anger replaces the fake humor. "I can't afford to waste time defending myself on dodgy charges. I need your help to shift the misunderstanding."

"You want us to turn a blind eye to all the forgeries some weak bastard at the passport office supplied you."

"All I know is, if those passports are not Harriet's, someone's planted them. What's the court gonna think about you appearing on my doorstep lookin' for dodgy passports? Give me a break." He removes his glasses, huffs and wipes his lenses, his squinting face vulnerable without them. "Fuckin' impossible to remove some smudges," he says. "Same in life, eh?" He replaces them on a nose listing to the right, poor surgery after a bad accident or alteration. "Your old man, a case in point. Miss him, do ya? Your old man?"

My skin tingles as sweat starts to bead on my forehead.

Collinge points to himself. "Believe me, no one sorrier about his untimely death. Thing is, me knowin' Owen doesn't help *you*. Comprende?" He pauses again.

"Yes. Eddie Myles, reinvented as Oliver Collinge. The pimply little kid in the courtroom public gallery, sitting at the opposite end of a row of seats while my father sat in the dock."

His sneer reappears.

"Foreman at the slaughterhouse," I say, the recall setting off the drain cycle of an old washing machine in my guts.

"Murdered by your old man," he says, his voice louder. "Is that when you got the green light to start fucking your sister?"

Tracey glances across.

I clench my fists under the leaner, and my heart thuds inside my chest. I'm torn between wanting to reset his nose and hiding in some dark corner cubby hole. "Do you believe I give a shit what you think about me through your seriously warped filters. You think being friends with cops gives you leverage to come asking for favors?"

"Don't know what you're talking about. Why would I meet you without knowing your full pedigree? If you're not worrying about what I know, how come you're sweating? Not hot in here."

I *am* sweating, but only because the restraint against violence requires huge effort. I suspect he wants me to succumb. I stand, take a pace toward the door, make eye contact with Tracey. She closes her newspaper. But if I walk out now, Collinge will take a victory. He's presenting me with a lose-lose choice. I resume my seat, feign a smile, and decide to persevere with the strategy of encouraging lies I can later use against him.

"Let's be clear," I say. "You want me to forget about the results of our little treasure hunt, including the blank passports in the trunk of your car. Sorry, not in the trunk, where everything might've fallen out of a bag. But all under the spare wheel. The normal place an honest bloke like you would store the necessary tools of your job."

I push a copy of the false passport his way, face down. He turns it over, studies it, pushes it back. The grin disappears. "Solomon," he says, "when I bought that car off Rachel, I didn't know about any falsie under the spare. How could I?"

"It was Harriet before. Excellent. Nothing to worry about. There'll be none of your prints on anything in the wheel well. Won't be long before we can confirm your innocence for you. And your wardrobe books—enjoy those, did you?"

Collinge finishes his coffee and bangs the cup into the saucer. "Made a few fireworks in my time, bit of a hobby. So fuckin' what? Let me leave you with a little friendly advice. Don't underestimate me."

"Please, enlighten me."

"I'm aware of your pep talks in certain quarters."

I show the photo of him and Troup together. "These quarters?"

Collinge rolls his right shoulder. "Here we are, two blokes having a coffee, one asking the other to consider being a bit less heavy-handed, to pull his overzealous team member into line, given the lack of witnesses. Nothing more, mate." He leans back.

"Excellent. We understand each other." And Troup will know what I know before the hour is out. "Got an alibi for 7 July?" I ask.

"As it happens, I have. But I'm not dragging her into this."

On his way out, he clips Tracey with his hip. "Sorry, we all need to be more careful of those around us. Eh?" His face is full of pure menace ensuring his last words are not lost on me.

THURSDAY, 9 AUGUST 2012
11.55 HOURS

Blain approaches my workstation, frowning and tugging at the cuffs of his shirt. "Yan's still on the critical list. His parents have arrived."

"I can only imagine what that's like," I say. "Regarding Trix, any ballistics results?"

"On the positive side, a second slug in Trix. The other, forty-five caliber, in her heart, or what passed for a heart."

"Well, a fraudster and robber. At least not a cop murderer."

He says, "Still a disgrace to the force."

"What about prints on the shells recovered in her grave?"

"None. Homemade. A gun like that, my guess is a gang weapon, unregistered of course."

"Forget gangs. It's the same homemade firearm pointed at me, the one we seized on her arrest for fraud, the one ruled out in the Selgin case."

"A huge disappointment, that case."

"The offender was more disappointed. The techies found shoddy work. It repeatedly misfired when the safety was released. That was the only thing that saved me."

He thumbs his ear. "You sound sure."

I hand him the shitty note from the court telling me I'm overdue to pick up the Trix fraud trial exhibits. "They included the forty-five involved in Trix's case."

"So?"

"So, finding Trix and the search warrant harvest spurred me into phoning the High Court. The clerk who sent me this note is now holidaying somewhere in Europe. But her colleague told me the gun was uplifted by police. They emailed this to me seconds ago."

Blain scans it on my phone. "Coman. Why would he uplift your old trial exhibits?"

"Not all my old trial exhibits. Just those we produced at Trix's fraud trial."

I show him the card Dowling gave me about eating humble pie and removing chips from my shoulders.

He grins. "Some might think he knew you well. What's this got to do with the case?"

"Take a close look at the word, 'Caution.'"

He does.

"And?"

"Now compare it with Coman's signature on this." I hand him an internal memo.

His eyes move between the card and memo and back. "Not much different. Not a bad job."

The gun's been picked up without me knowing, but not by Coman. Whether Dowling did or handed it to the killer, we don't know. But the court receipt shows they returned the gun thirty-two days before Nick was killed.

He gives a migraine grimace. "Gets better and better. Doesn't it?"

"We need grooves and lands from the slug we've recovered

to test them against the forty-five—when we find the bloody thing. The firing pin impression on the spent shells will also be handy."

"So, given the misfiring gun pointed at you is the same gun that killed Trix, the killer knew the gun was in court custody?"

"I'm sure of it. In theory, court staff could've contacted Nick, as he was OC exhibits. But I'm thinking when they saw me as tardy, or uncooperative in uplifting it, they went over my head and that signature is Dowling's forgery. Someone needed an untraceable weapon and used knowledge of the court exhibits procedure. Had to be Dowling. Or Vincent, at Dowling's direction."

"Vincent?" Blain pulls his head back. "He wasn't with us when Trix worked here. Plus, he's helped you ID Collinge and Volp."

"Not sure they're relevant factors given he was hand-picked by Dowling for our team. Remember? Trace printed this for me after the Collinge search. Spot the debtor names."

He drags a sun-spotted hand over his face. "The Underwoods and Vinny. Gambling debts?"

"He and I need a serious talk." I walk to the window. Outside, the lunch crowd scurries for cover from an unexpected cold shower.

Blain says, "If Dowling supported Troup and, indirectly, Collinge, what's the motive for killing him? Or Jarvis?"

Hearing his skepticism, I swallow hard. "Questions about motives are less important."

"C'mon, boss. We've only got circumstantial evidence of connections. Nothing puts either Troup or Collinge in the fucking Chevrolet. The passport charges stick if we show

Collinge's prints on them. But false passports are chicken shit, well short of murdering cops." He shakes his head. "Plus, we never proved Collinge was Trix's partner in the original fraud on those old folks, and we didn't prove he supplied the firearm to her. We've also got contradictory evidence—Wally Edgar. Remember? What he said about Sinclair is helpful to Collinge, not us. As for Vincent, so what? He went to Collinge's loan sharks, but the ledger shows he drip-fed it back. Are you suggesting Collinge incentivized him? Debt write-offs for favors? No evidence I can see."

"I need some help, mate, not a bloody defense lawyer."

He gives me his nasal exhale of contempt.

I say, "Coman says Troup's story about Nick is complete bullshit."

"Or a misunderstanding, based on some mistaken facts about who does what at EI. What else?"

"What the hell's up with you? You came in here looking like you had a gerbil up your ass."

He clasps his hands and taps upright thumbs. "I'm unclear. Unclear why my team leader refuses to share important evidence with me, unclear about what issues he no longer trusts me with and why."

"Mate, come on. You know better than to think I don't trust you."

He glares at me. "No. I don't. Dowling's tape—who have you trusted with that?" He points at himself. "Not me."

"Listen, Dowling said some things on the tape directed to me. Discreet and personal things. Things he called secrets. Right?"

"So?"

"So, do I not have the right to privacy over my personal life?"

Color in his cheeks. "What? Your privacy ahead of solving homicides?"

We glare at each other until he breaks the silence. "Do I think you're entitled to privacy? In a word, no." He spreads his arms, looking ready for take-off. "There you go. If we can't be open doing our job, I reckon we've got a problem. It makes us vulnerable. You think you're the only one who cares what people think of you?" He gazes into the squad room and I know more is coming. Back at me he says, "How about this? We start by getting really honest. I'll even go first. Once, I met an escort in one of my vacant rentals. I couldn't get it up, so we had pizza and beer, filled the evening with fucking talk. And you, mate, are the only person I've ever told. Now your turn."

"I wish I had the balls to be so open."

"I'm not going to broadcast it. Listen," he says, with gravitas, "unless you committed offenses on the job with Dowling..."

"No, no, nothing like that. I... I blurred professional boundaries."

He stares at me.

I add, "With a judge."

Blain gives a half-smile, underneath it, some grudging admiration. In a softer voice he says, "And Dowling refers to this on the tape?"

"Not exactly."

"Well, what are you worried about? Is she on the criminal court bench, a family court judge, what?"

"No." A flush emerges from my shirt collar and I clear my throat. "And it's a bit tenuous. Look, I just don't want the inevitable questions. It's not only privacy for me. There may be repercussions for others, and I don't want to be, or the judge for that matter, the talk of the station. Know what I'm saying?"

He nods.

"But I take your point. And now I need a bloody smoke."

THURSDAY, 9 AUGUST 2012
12.30 HOURS

On the Armagh Street bridge, I bring Blain up to date with the search warrant harvest and the discovery of gunpowder in the bottle in Collinge's garage.

He says, "You don't think he was into fireworks?"

"Lyman's 49th edition of *Reloading Handbook* and *The Cast Bullet Handbook* in his bedroom wardrobe don't suggest fireworks to me. Stuff about grain measurement by volume, risk of primer catching fire, or popping in your face, the importance of sticking to the published data on primer quantity and not touching it."

"Touching?"

"Finger sweat causes bullets to misfire. His claim about making fireworks is bullshit."

He tilts his head. "You were going to tell me about your little tête-à-tête with O'Brien and Troup."

I light up a Camel and tell him the details.

He says, "I take it our discussion means your invitation to be their team player is rejected."

"And as a consequence," I say, "the probable deferral of your promotion to my job."

He pokes his bottom lip out. "I was counting on that. Still, I carry hope, a great deal of hope." He cracks a smile. "Someone wants you dead."

I blow smoke. "Heartening support. At last."

"Where does the DCC fit in all this?" he asks.

I remind him about her Nissan vehicle. "Same type of vehicle seen by the farmer in Oxford when he went to investigate the Chev on fire. Then there's the bullshit she fed me about Nick's concern for Dowling's mental health. Now Coman tells me she responded to an anonymous call from one of Dowling's mates, someone who said he was worried about him. She responds by sending someone to visit and the person comes back with a suicide note."

Blain frowns. "Coman told you this?"

"He did, under the pressure of being unable to explain why a cop would type a suicide note, not sign it and remove all possible evidence he wrote it."

"So, she's in the mix—Hockley."

"Guilty of telling porkies but I'm struggling to see her as a Section 66 conspirator."

"Then why the lies?"

"Self-interest. Protecting important people, those who'll help push her to the upper levels of the castle."

He pinches the tip of his nose. "The Underwood mob could be the cleanup party, find the note, dispose of the computer?"

"Too risky. Debt collecting with violence is their pinnacle. I can't see Troup or Dowling trusting them simply because Collinge uses them. Risky to do so."

"Something else doesn't make sense," he says, concerned.

"What?"

"I'm not trying to be obstructive here, but it makes no

sense to delay taking Nick out if the reason they did so was his relationship with Trix. If anything's too risky, it's having Nick still breathing."

I massage my forehead. "Opportunity? Maybe a need to discover if anyone noticed her missing amid all the chaos. Remember, this operation's been run so we'd believe Trix was alive after skipping bail."

"No one at EI missed her?" He sounds incredulous.

"With Collinge in there, Sinclair, any number of stories or reasons would've accounted for her absence."

He saws his chin with a long finger.

"View it this way," I say. "If I tell you Nick's on leave for a month for family or personal reasons, you don't conclude I killed him. Do you?"

"Take your point about them wanting us to think it was Trix. The woman wearing Trix's cap was a nice job when we were predisposed to think it was her, right down to the choice of gas station and dodgy camera lenses. Now I'm wondering if it was even a woman who tried..."

"Hold that thought. On that night Dowling said he got an anonymous tip Trix was on the run, he said, 'You and Jarvis with uniform support.' Now we know Trix wasn't in the vehicle, what if the call was only to get Nick and me to the scene?"

"A setup to kill you both," he says. "Well planned but not the sign of risk takers, though. Is it?"

"What do you mean?" I ask.

"Collinge and Troup are not your average white-collar, bathroom coke snorters. Their biggest risk was someone finding out how they were making these frauds work. Their next biggest risk was a blabber."

"But they wouldn't know about the first without the second. What's your point, mate?"

He says, "The little list in Trix's bra when she died. It makes it clear she found out about frauds. But delaying the hit on Nick is like waiting for a shit bomb to go off. Why would they wait all the weeks Trix was dead before killing Nick if their relationship imperiled the fraud scheme?"

"They'd have to know what we'd found out from Alice Jarvis. Let's say it took them some time to figure out her connection with Nick. When Collinge attempted to induce Edgar to cough up some intel, he was trying to find out if Trix had blabbed to anyone else. Fraud's their primary interest. Right? Not murdering cops. I don't think the delay between the murders was intended."

"Really?" he says, disbelieving. "Nick coulda told me or anyone."

"Agreed. But they can't murder the whole force. Besides, their security was in us chasing our tails and getting nowhere on Trix."

Blain says, "If it's not Trix and it's not Hockley, who the fuck pointed that gun at you?"

I gaze out the window and mention Troup's admiring glances at Gwen Sinclair and hers at him, how she looked away when I saw them make a connection. "*The Press* had a cameraman at the EI function. Grab me the video. Will you? And the call into comms with the tip-off to Dowling. I need to listen to the voice again."

He says, "Will do." The he pauses before he adds, "We're closing in. Aren't we?"

I nod. "But it's just us until I get Coman over the line.

Okay? So, from here, only fluff on the job sheets. I can't be sure whether we've found all the malignancy here."

"Of course."

"And Victoria Milburn. We'll talk to her. Who knew she was away and the layout of her place? I don't believe with all the vacant land in the broken city, the choice of her place as a burial site was random."

THURSDAY, 9 AUGUST 2012
14.00 HOURS

Blain and I sit in the harshly lit office of Latham and Co., Barristers and Solicitors, waiting to interview Gwen Sinclair. We've been told this location with its smell of fresh paint is the only place she'll talk to us.

A tall brunette escorts us to Brian Latham, who's in blue shirtsleeves and ruby red braces. Gwen sits next to him sporting an expensive-looking haircut and wearing a tailored black jacket over a white shirt. She sits motionless, like a lawyer waiting for a trial to start. Latham stands and I introduce Blain. He closes a briefcase lid; we shake hands, and he motions to two chairs in front of his desk. "Please, make yourselves comfortable. As you know this is my client, Dr. Gwendoline Sinclair."

To me, Latham says, "We've met. Yes?"

"Your client, Rachel Trix."

"Indeed." He runs thumbs down his braces. "Now, before you question my client about the affairs of Earthquake Insure, you must understand she is, without mincing words, in danger."

I glance at her. Her face is unreadable with no hint of worry or concern.

I ask, "How so?"

"Let's say, for the moment, Gwen's aware of possible frauds carried out at EI." He gives the fingered speech marks when he says, "aware."

Blain scribbles in his notebook.

"We can pursue witness protection status," I say, "if you can demonstrate necessity." I glance at Gwen, impassive back straight in her chair.

Latham pauses while his assistant delivers a tray of glasses and a carafe of water. Interruption over, he says, "Protection isn't the only important factor at play. We're also looking for immunity from prosecution."

"Prosecution immunity from what?" I ask.

Latham glances at Gwen and back at me. "What everyone believes is happening."

"What does everyone believe is happening? I mean, you indicated a desire not to mince words, so maybe we can cut to..."

Gwen interrupts, "How about the killers of Nick Jarvis and Rachel Trix?"

Blain's jaw is slack. I try to pick whether this is the undisguised voice of the recorded tip-off.

Gwen says, "Compelling enough for you, Sergeant Solomon? But if I identify the killers, my life's at risk. You understand. Don't you? I'll need a new identity."

"Slow down, please. Are you involved in the murders, Gwen?"

"Of course not."

"You were the anonymous tipster, though. Right?"

"Tipster. What are you talking about?"

I stare at her and she doesn't blink. "The woman who

phoned in the night Detective Jarvis was murdered and said Trix was about to leave the country."

"Not me. I don't know anything about it."

"You realize we can obtain voice analysis?"

"Go for your life."

I explain the rules of Solicitor-General immunity. Latham is unimpressed. He wants a guarantee. I say, "Until I know more, I can't ask the crown prosecutor to pursue this with the SG. We need clarity that without the evidence given under immunity, a prosecution is unlikely to succeed. We're nowhere close to meeting that standard."

Latham shifts in his seat and frowns. "You don't need to tell me the law."

"Well, I'm sorry, but the ball's in your court."

Latham turns to Gwen. "Start with meeting Quentin before moving to the frauds."

Gwen tells us that after the September 2010 quake, she targeted Quentin Sinclair on nzdating.co.nz for a relationship. She said she did so, encouraged by her long-term boyfriend, Martin Troup.

I ask, "How did you meet the Assistant Commissioner?"

"The old-fashioned way. A mutual acquaintance."

She explains she and Troup intended she would seduce Sinclair into an intimate relationship. Once in EI, she put her doctorate in software engineering to use.

"To what purpose?" I ask.

She looks to Latham for approval to continue. He nods and she says, "I always knew I'd get revenge for what Fire and General did to me."

"Did what to you?"

"Marty gave me financial help when a house I owned was

destroyed by fire and the insurance company refused to pay a penny. That's what they're like. All of them, parasites. After we pay policy premiums, all we receive is their delay and deny strategy, and if that doesn't frighten you off, they 'lawyer up' on false pretenses. So in EI, I used my privileged position to do what millions of people would, if they could."

"Why EI?"

"Fire & General is EI's re-insurer in the UK, where the delay, deny, and defend policies come from. That was good enough for me. The UK had control of EI, but my focus was to make Quentin appear to everyone else as though he was in control. I told Quentin I could program code to speed up the assessments and payment process without compromising security. I explained it was bespoke, difficult to write, and extremely difficult to pull apart. Compared to my work, NT 5 with forty million lines of code is child's play."

"NT?"

"New Technology. A Windows family of operating systems. What EI thinks they're using." She grins. "They were, until I got hold of it. Let's say, if you can write something down for others to follow, it's no longer expert knowledge. Not everybody can be an expert—knowledgeable yes, but not an expert. Am I making sense?"

"Go on," I say. "Tell me how this coding works—simplify the expertise. Isn't that a sign of an expert too?"

She lifts her eyebrows and tells us the instant a search of payment records happens on EI systems, the search activates a code to alter the retention date of customer records and bring the scheduled destruction date forward to the date and time of search. "The internal records destruction log is also shredded," she says, "completing the steps to cover our tracks."

I say, "But when you delete any file, the data is almost never destroyed."

"Of course. Your forensic people rely on that. The operating system removes its memory of the file but keeps the data. The system gives itself permission to override the physical disk space occupied by the data before you hit the delete button. But that only makes the deleted data fuzzy, and not obliterated. Sensitive pieces of data, like bank accounts, can be reconstructed using software or advanced forensic data recovery techniques."

I ask, "So how did you prevent forensic recovery?"

"Overwriting or shredding the file requires my encrypted software to replace the original file. I crafted code, randomly generating noise in the right fields as well as instruction to delete all metadata, including those little thumbnail caches the forensic nerds sometimes find. The final step is to replicate and apply the delete code commands in the backup system, an automated step. To say Marty was thrilled with this process would be an understatement."

"To be clear," I say, "You're stating Assistant Commissioner Martin Troup conspired with you to commit fraud against Earthquake Insure."

Latham answers for her. "Yes. So, you understand why my client wants immunity from prosecution. But all this is relevant to the killers of Rachel Trix and Nick Jarvis."

I encourage her to continue.

Gwen confirms the details given by Vincent and Dowling. She discovered Trix obtained Vincent's password to obtain notes of claims from EI's master record. These, she says, revealed all claims and their stage in the payments process but not the bank account details. That data was only accessible if someone opened the claimant's individual approval file, but if staff did so without Gwen's encryption code, the records would self-destruct. She says, "Vincent did it once." She giggles. "Poor boy was mortified."

"Did staff try and retrieve backup files?"

She flaps a dismissive hand. "Of course, but as I said, I dealt to that issue in the setup. The simple answer is, I wrote code that performed an operation so when the operation was carried out, the code ate data and itself for dessert. It's devastating, not least because no one has done it before, not to my knowledge."

I nod. "Go on, please."

She says, "Our policy of firing people who destroyed records proved an effective cover because we could blame staff problems for delays in processing claims for payment. At first, I destroyed too many records, setting up a PR disaster."

I ask, "Are you saying you pulled back?"

"I decided to limit the destruction of claimant records to cases where we siphoned off payments over $100k."

"Why?"

"Because anything lower than one hundred would've resulted in more staff queries and the high staff turnover would've increased the risk of the government firing Quentin."

Blain asks, "When did you set this coding system up?"

"Following the September 2010 quake. But the scale of February's disaster required some refinements."

"I'm assuming," I say, "the accounts receiving the fraudulent payments were Putis accounts?"

"A whole lot more complicated, but essentially, yes."

"Complicated how?"

Gwen explains how she generated pseudonymous and

random accounts where one account would split off into a hundred account number options. "It's computationally explosive."

My brain is overloading and I focus on her enthusiasm for her cleverness. The more I ask, the more she sparkles in the telling.

I ask how they managed internal alarm bells and political concerns.

She gives a smug smile. "Think about it. If staff discovered they were unable to trace payments, they would be suspicious. Better they thought, like the public, that we had an intermittent problem causing system instability. Most intelligent people understand those kinds of problems are the hardest to solve. One moment, you have a problem and then you don't. Then the problem reappears. I convinced Quentin to assure the government that we would implement a new payment system, but it would take time. All of which diverted attention from the frauds. Meantime, he instructed staff to be super careful to avoid destroying the records, so our internal culture of fear of doing that helped in the coverup. Staff didn't want to be sacked with no reference and no chance of coming back."

"Where did Trix come in on all this?" I ask. "What happened?"

"She used Vincent's research, some spot checks he planned to do. She got greedy and blabbed. Before we canned the payments on decline method, she made notes of claims approved in the system and of course, she tried to track where they went. She found the church to which Nick Jarvis's mother belonged. We believe, to settle an old score, she taunted Nick there was a scam going on, involving his mother's church. She gave him enough detail to be credible."

"When did you discover this?"

She shakes her head. "So much was going on. I can't remember. I think, probably about the time when Detective Jarvis was killed. I only heard about that from the radio."

"And Martin Troup. What did he gain?"

"I can't tell you an exact amount. Millions, not thousands."

"Oliver Collinge. Tell us about his involvement?"

Her head recoils. "Nothing to tell. He has no idea about any frauds. Why would you think he did?"

I pause, waiting for more, but she shakes her head.

"And Putis Consortium," I said. "What's the link there?"

"Putis kept two-thirds of the net sweep after costs and paid me the remainder. Marty said to keep the Putis operation going, he spent significant costs."

I recall Dowling's tired face into the camera lens. He would've been one of those significant costs.

Blain asks, "What sort of amounts are we talking here, for you, Gwen?"

Her eyes meet Latham's, and he nods. "It was automated. My estimate is an average of a couple of million per month, over the last year. February 2011 was brilliant, way beyond our expectations, anybody's expectations."

Blain asks, "Brilliant?"

She nods. "The severity of the quake and the subsequent damage meant an untold number of claims, which in turn, meant huge takings for me and Marty."

Latham says, "My client is able to make significant reparations, which I submit can be taken into account with an immunity decision."

"I need to confer with my colleague in private," I say.

"Of course. My partner's office next door is available and unlocked." He nods in the direction.

We walk into the vacant office. For a second, we stare at each other.

Blain, in his quiet voice, says, "This is a shit bomb like no other we've ever seen."

"Agreed. But I'm torn here. I want them all in the dock, but we won't nail Troup without her."

Blain nods. "She seemed a bit too confident our voice analysts wouldn't have any joy."

"She could've had help, and no shortage of funds to pay for it. To find the evidence without her, we're going to need some superb coding and tracking experts. And if we do, we also need to track those changes to her because we won't be able to use her statement if we don't give her immunity. I can't recall anything like this being discovered in New Zealand before."

Blain says, "That morning Nick was killed, and they tried to kill you. You still can't identify her at the other end of the forty-five?"

"No. And we've got no evidence putting her in the vehicle and little chance of finding trace evidence of her at the burial site. I suspect she was too smart to go there."

We sit for seconds of contemplation before Blain breaks the silence. "You're thinking of supporting immunity for the person who attempted to murder you? Jesus Christ, Solly, a huge call."

"Never mind me. Justice for Nick. And if we drag Troup and Collinge into court, I'll need to discover why she's protecting Collinge. I reckon we restrict her immunity to fraud—find what she's got on Troup. She gets no immunity on conspiring to murder or attempted murder. According to her, she doesn't need it."

He shakes his head.

"What?"

"Everything turns on her reliability. And we'll need to make first base with Coman on any immunity. Or higher."

"If I had the authority, I'd do it. But now I can show Dowling forged his signature, I think Coman will support us."

We return to Latham and Gwen and I explain what we need, including significant and credible evidence implicating Troup.

She says, "What if I give you what you want but you don't give me my immunity?"

Latham answers. "No immunity, your statement's out. They can't use it against you in any fraud prosecution you might face. Given what you said about how you committed the frauds, prosecuting you without your statement will be difficult in the extreme."

I lean forward and say, "Now's the time to identify who was in the Chevrolet."

She shifts in her chair. "Well, I can identify Marty, and I believe I know who the other person was, but I have no proof. And for what it's worth, I have an alibi."

I jerk my head back, "Let's talk about alibis in a minute. "Are you saying, Assistant Commissioner Martin Troup killed Nick Jarvis?"

She looks surprised. "Of course. Who else?"

"I'm sorry," I say. "But asking who else suggests you might be speculating."

"I'm not speculating. For the record, Martin Troup killed Nick Jarvis and I'll tell you why."

THURSDAY, 9 AUGUST 2012
15.33 HOURS

I ask, "Who or what is your alibi?"

"The night Marty killed your detective," she says, "Oliver Collinge and I slept together. Well, in a manner of speaking. Not a lot of sleep was involved."

I catch Blain's raised eyebrow at me.

"To be clear," I say, "you're telling us you and Troup, in an intimate relationship for ten years, targeted Quentin Sinclair. You seduced him *and* you slept with Oliver Collinge. Is that correct?"

She laughs. "I tell you I helped commit millions of dollars of fraud, yet you seem to be worried about my virtue, Detective Sergeant."

I give her one of Hockley's frosty smiles. "It's not your *virtue* I'm worried about."

She rolls her eyes.

I say, "How did you make the two-timing work?"

"With a bit of imagination. I lived with Quentin in his apartment in Peterborough Street. Marty owns a place round the corner in Park Terrace. Not a difficult assignment."

"Tell me how frauds against Earthquake Insure turned into murder."

Gwen explains, at first, the insurance chaos was an excellent distraction for Quentin Sinclair. He always focused on assessment and payment data and how to recycle excuses about the unprecedented severity of the disaster. She says, "I'd estimate two-thirds of the claim payments to date are legitimate."

Blain, head down, mutters, "Generous of you." No one speaks until he says, "Sorry. I'm struggling to get my head around the enormity of this."

Gwen gives a plastic smile. "Well, that's unsurprising, detective. Rachel Trix didn't only taunt Nick Jarvis with what she knew. We believe she told one of Marty's ex-cop friends that EI made payments to nonexistent companies, other stuff too. Marty was furious. Our little operation..."

"I'm sorry to interrupt. How did you know the person was an ex-cop?"

"Marty said. You're going to ask me his name, but I can't remember if he told me, not with everything else going on."

"Please continue."

"Well, the operation went from enormously successful to enormously threatened. This mate of his talked of specific claims. One from a rugby club EI turned down but later paid to Putis. As soon as Marty heard that, we knew we were in trouble."

I ask, "Who else knew about these frauds?"

"As far as we knew, only Marty and me. Until Trix started snooping and, we believe, talking to Nick Jarvis."

I say, "Oliver Collinge tells me he's in charge of system security at EI. How could he not know about the fraud?"

She shrugs. "He didn't know. It was just Marty and me

until Trix let the results of her spying out of the bag. With expenses, Collinge made a million a year from EI and billed other clients as well. His overcharging six days a week when he worked four or five days wasn't criminal behavior. You could argue moral fraud."

I say, "You confirmed earlier Collinge introduced Trix to Sinclair as Harriet Volp. He placed a fox inside the hen house."

"But he didn't know. Did he? I mean, Marty helped Trix establish the false identity of Harriet Volp with a verifiable employment background of a woman who once worked with Bank Secure."

"Why? I mean this fraud gig was designed to be you and Troup. Right?"

"He admired her fraud knowledge and ability, thought she would be an early warning system for us, a kind of canary in the coal mine."

"And you don't think this compromised Collinge's ability to manage EI's security processes."

"No. Marty convinced him Trix had reformed, but she'd never get the job with her old identity. Having her inside EI meant she'd be valuable as an informer and early alert to security breaches. Marty persuaded Oliver to head hunt her in the name of Harriet Volp and he gave Oliver her new passport for the staff file. At least that's what he told me. It must've worked because Quentin told me Volp came with Marty's intel and recommendation." She shrugs and pulls a face of bad luck. "With so many staff coming and going, EI was like an airport. If Volp's true identity as Trix was ever discovered it would be dismissed as one of many recruitment mistakes at a time of huge recruitment pressure."

Blain says, "Tell us how Kevin Yan fits into your operation."

She strokes an eyebrow. "We got Yan to make a complaint against you to divert attention away from us and to reinforce Vincent was helping us with good antifraud work. Marty knew Yan worked for the police before he came to us, so he saw Yan as a credible complainant."

Blain says, "And when you were done with Yan, you attempted to kill him?"

"Not me. No one here wanted him dead. Whatever happened to him was nothing to do with us."

I say, "Let's get back to why Troup killed Jarvis."

Gwen tells us Troup knew Jarvis was on the team to apprehend Trix. She says, "I didn't know how or when he knew, but I assume Marty had inside information."

"Who drove the car at Nick?" I ask.

She defers to Latham. He asks me if I want to hear hearsay testimony.

I say, "Your client indicates Troup and another person were in the car. I'm asking for details about a co-offender that might show Gwen's credibility."

Latham nods at her.

She says, "Until yesterday when you found Trix, I assumed it was her."

Blain asks, "Why?"

She frowns. "Because you people had been all over the media telling us you were looking for her and why. At the same time, I knew how angry Marty was about her snooping into Vincent's records, winding up her ex, telling Marty's mate about what we were doing. He felt betrayed by her. So, when I confronted him, after hearing news she'd been found dead, he said he took her out weeks ago. He used another woman to help you believe it was Trix, but Marty drove the car."

"And you think you know who this woman is but can't prove it?"

"Linda somebody. I was in shock he admitted killing Trix and Jarvis. I don't remember much more except Linda and Trix were neighbors. Marty said Linda was in a relationship with Nick until he had sex with Trix. Of course, Marty paid Linda for her help."

I glance toward Blain. He says, "If Marty wanted to kill Trix because she turned her knowledge of the frauds against him and blabbed to Jarvis, why delay killing Jarvis?"

"I don't know if there was any delay. But when I asked Marty how he kept the forensic trail away from himself he said he organized getting the right firearm, one that couldn't be traced to him. Perhaps that was delayed. I couldn't say."

I wait for Blain to record her answer. I ask, "So, you say Troup goes on a murderous ride with a woman called Linda. Yet he's a high-ranking cop, a public figure with a national responsibility for crime prevention and he makes no effort to hide his identity?"

She leans back and shakes her head. "I didn't say that. I believe he wore a disguise."

"Why do you believe that?"

"He had a fancy-dress party to attend. I heard him ask Oliver for costume ideas. Oliver said he could help with a mask if he needed. Marty borrowed it and gave it back to him after the murders."

Blain massages the skin under his chin. It's his tell sign for trying to decide if someone's feeding him bullshit or not.

"It will help your chances of immunity if you can give details about how Marty planned and carried out Trix's murder."

"He told me he shot her twice. I don't know where or when

he killed her." She glances at Latham and lowers her voice. "But I know where Marty got the gun to do the job."

Latham leans forward. "We need assurances about immunity before you acquire this evidence, but my client can say more about the weapon."

He pauses and I hold my palms up.

He says, "We hold digital evidence of Assistant Commissioner Troup receiving the weapon used to kill Trix. And that file is secure."

Latham faces Gwen. "I know you're concerned about revealing this, but the photo is the credible evidence to back your request for immunity and it supports your account."

She nods but says nothing.

Latham lifts the lid on his briefcase and hands me a photograph. It shows Dowling handing Troup a firearm, halfway up the barrel, handle toward Troup. The background shows a room with a table and chairs behind the two men and a print on the wall, a scenic view. No one else appears in the picture, taken side on to the men.

I face Gwen. "I gather, from your lawyer's comment, you took this?"

Latham nods at Gwen and she confirms.

"Who's the other man with Marty?" I ask.

"He didn't say. Marty's secrecy was symptomatic of the one problem between us. He told me what he wanted me to know. As a cop, I assume you know what I'm saying."

"Tell us how you happened to be in a position to take this photo because I have a problem with that. On your own statement, you took it before you knew what happened to Trix. It suggests you knew a crime involving a weapon was being planned. What do you say about that?"

Again, deference to Latham and again, he nods.

"Marty used a burner to text his mate about the handover of the gun. Except, he texted me instead."

"An accident?" I ask.

"Oh, yes. I deleted it because I didn't recognize the number it came from and the message didn't mean anything to me. All it said was, *Good to go re transfer. Peterbo St 1615 tomorrow, after YH meeting.* That night, I caught him looking at my phone. I confronted him and he got all flustered in a way I hadn't seen before."

I glance at Blain and wonder if he believes Gwen's story. I'm thinking, why, if she didn't know it was from Troup, and if it didn't mean anything to her, did she remember the details?

I put the second of these questions to her.

"Because of his behavior, getting flustered when caught with my phone. I then realized he was scheming something behind my back, possibly a transfer of secret funds."

I'm not convinced but say, "Go on."

She pauses. "Well, the rest of this story doesn't reflect me in a positive light."

She takes a deep breath. "He didn't know, but I copied a key for his place early on. I'm not the one to crash and burn in the EI operation, at least not on my own, so I kept tabs on his movements. On the day I took this photo, sometime in early June, I got him to take me to the doctor for my smear at three o'clock. I knew he was going back to the police station to meet Hockley. As soon as he drove away, I took a taxi to his apartment and waited for him to arrive."

"And you now say you're in danger because he knows you got a text intended for his mate."

"Exactly."

"By my calculation, from the date of the photo to now is over two months. If you're so concerned about your safety, why wait this long?"

"I guess it's not just the photo. Because the operation's over, I'm no use to him and I'm at risk because of what I know. I wouldn't be talking to you otherwise. It's everyone for themselves now. Isn't it? I might be a fraudster, but I draw the line at murder. Murder wasn't in my game plan."

"We know the man who handed Troup the weapon was a police officer, and we know where he got the gun from."

I look at Latham. "It would've been two years ago wouldn't it—Trix's fraud trial?"

"In the ballpark. Where's this going, Detective?"

"There was huge publicity about Nick's murder and our hunt for Trix."

She says, "I'm aware."

"And you still say you didn't know she'd been murdered. That's what you're saying. Right?"

"Correct."

"What did EI do about Trix failing to turn up for work, presumably from 4 June, when you took that photo of Marty receiving the gun?"

"I don't know. She didn't report to me. She wasn't my problem or concern. My focus was on stealing money."

Latham leans back and smiles.

"My point is, Gwen, you know Trix went AWOL almost immediately after you witnessed Marty receiving the gun that killed her."

Latham says, "You can't prove either of those assertions."

Gwen says nothing but just stares at me. I sense the temperature in the room has changed.

I ask, "When you took this photo, where were you?"

"Hiding in his kitchen/dining room, expecting to see a secret handover of money."

I nod. "This Linda somebody. What did Marty do about her?"

"While you were looking for Trix, he put her on the first plane out to Brisbane the following morning. I understand she may've returned, so perhaps I'm not the only one in danger."

I turn to Blain. "We can do something about Gwen's security. Can't we?"

He answers affirmatively and with confidence, but he'll be wondering what the hell I'm doing.

To Latham, I say, "I need to see the original digital file of this picture."

Latham arranges for the camera memory card to be brought in.

While we wait, I face Gwen and say, "Troup was an old friend of the late Detective Inspector Fergus Dowling. Did you ever meet him?"

"No."

A quick answer, too quick. She says, "Is this man helpful to you in some way?"

"Troup didn't mention him?"

She shakes her head.

"Dowling and Troup were both at the EI function the night Quentin made his rousing speech. Dowling had terminal cancer and, in the end, took his own life." It's now easy to repeat this lie. I hand her the picture. "Are you sure the friend of Marty's you've referred to isn't the other man in this picture?"

She stares at the picture, draws breath, and tilts her head. She looks uneasy, perhaps sensing that I notice her discomfort.

She says, "I don't want to put you wrong. I didn't see or meet him at the EI function. Perhaps this is the ex-cop he was getting information from?"

Latham's PA knocks and then enters with a clear plastic envelope, a small blue memory card inside it. Latham opens his bottom drawer and withdraws a camera. "Battery's charged," he says.

I ask Blain to look while I maintain a focus on Gwen. I give her a little smile. "This reminds me," I say. "Dowling made a video, a sort of memoir about old times. Before he died." I smile at Latham. "Thanks for sending it through. My DCC holds it now. She's going to play it at his funeral."

Latham puts his hands in his pockets. "Fascinating."

Blain pulls up the picture on the camera's screen and shows it to me.

I thank Latham and face Gwen. "We'll be in touch soon, Gwen. I appreciate your cooperation."

***

Back in the car I call Tracey. "Have Linda Nichol on standby to ID Collinge as the visitor in her neighborhood."

"Will do, boss."

Blain asks, "You don't believe it was Nichol on the other end of the gun that night?"

I smile. "Do you?"

THURSDAY, 9 AUGUST 2012
16.35 HOURS

Vincent's face of relief is that of a man receiving parole before his due date. We are in the canteen for what he thinks is a convivial chat and a handover of his recorded confession about spook duties. We sit twenty yards away from three uniformed cops at a round table.

In a soft voice, I say, "When we had coffee at RE:Start, you told me you were done with the gambling. Now I learn you're indebted to the Underwoods, one of whom took out our rear support the night Nick was killed."

I show him the extract of the Underwood debtor register, his name highlighted. I hold up the tape, reminding him of his lies claiming Coman was responsible for the surveillance order. "And this tape you want reveals nothing about your date being part of the Underwood family." I lean forward. "Scumbags stand over merchants and knee cappers for Oliver Collinge."

Vincent rears back and puts his hands up. "I knew nothing about that, boss. I swear."

I check if his protest attracts attention. It hasn't. I stare at Vincent for long seconds, and he shakes his head.

"So, it's a coincidence. Is it? Using loan sharks, you happen to be dating one of them. And you want me to believe you're not paying off your loan by providing inside knowledge? Can you grasp how this *looks?*"

Deep lines in his forehead."The Underwoods killed Nick?"

"No, Sherlock. Oliver Collinge owns the Underwoods."

He turns his head.

"Played, were you?" I ask.

"Honestly, boss. I've never given out anything to anyone about any operation or inquiry. Never!"

"Well, the problem with being in debt and preoccupied with where your next root is coming from is you're not first choice as Detective Reliable."

He slumps and reddens around the eyes. "The job's important to me, boss."

I study the canteen blackboard with the chalked numbers for raffle results. "I don't know why, but I'm giving you a final chance, subject to you getting back into credit. Right?"

"Yes, boss." He grimaces. "Where do you want me to start?"

"With full information about EI. No pussyfooting around with half a bloody story."

In half an hour he outlines the specifics of his role. He includes how he overheard staff discussing a strategy for challenging claims based on pre-existing damage, and describes a picture of chaos, staff overwhelmed with workloads, and the firing of workmates. He steers me through different fraud opportunities he analyzed.

"Simple verses complex pieces of work. Take the auto-repair business. They charge you for a full tune-up, but they only change the air filter. It's a scam that can work at EI. They can list stuff on the scope of repairs after a customer signs off, amounts to the same thing. You end up with the right amount paid in the system, but some of the money goes into the fraudster's account. But remember, I examine fraudulent claims by customers."

He explains the fraud opportunity with discounts, where EI unbundles a scope of repairs after a discount is applied at a defined cost point. "The invoice code used is for the discounted job. But in the payment process, the discount code is changed for itemized codes, each with their undiscounted cost. The building company still gets paid what it invoices for. No complaint from them. But when you unbundle all the items, they can be coded and individually paid to another account."

I can't see this type of fraud running to millions, but I ask for an example.

"Let's say a firm replaces double-glazed windows," he says. "They agree, with labor and materials, twenty jobs might be two hundred thousand dollars but it's at a bulk-funded discounted rate. In this job, it's not only the glass. There're frames and sashes, seals, plus all the factory work going into assembly as well. Right? So EI bulk pays the two hundred thousand to the contractor. No complaint. But in the payments system, the fraudster catalogs all the individual items and labor. Let's say this calculation comes to two hundred and thirty grand."

"And the extra thirty goes to another bank account."

"Correct, boss."

"Do they ever analyze and compare job costs verses contracted costs?"

"Part of Collinge's workflow checks."

I decide to test Gwen's statement. "With customer payments, did you ever do a search on payments made—authenticate approved payments went to the correct bank?"

"I did and somehow crashed the system. Don't know

why. Because I'm a cop, I was safe. But others were sacked. Disastrous for customers because if they become shitty, they go to the bottom of the list."

I receive a text from Blain. *Need 2 c u urgent!*

I tell him where we are. He arrives with the grin of a naughty boy. "Hockley's home's been burgled."

"Really?" I say, trying to sound surprised.

"Happened when she and Troup lunched together."

"Take the gloss off a delicious meal, I imagine."

"Leave a sour taste," he says, grinning.

I face Vincent. "You're supposed to be in with Hockley. Can you shed any light?"

Blain, hand over mouth, suppresses laughter.

"Me, boss?" Vincent says.

"Yes, son. You got an alibi?"

The question tips Blain into hysteria.

FRIDAY, 10 AUGUST 2012
09.30 HOURS

Victoria Milburn, slim and tall, wears a white shirt under a gray woolen suit. She strides with purpose into the living room, her lilac beaded necklace bouncing on her chest.

"My team met your neighbor, Mira," I say, breaking the ice. "She was good enough to let my colleague and me into your house."

"She was so helpful to me when Ivan died. I wanted her to come on the trip, but she convinced me she wouldn't be able to manage the travel." Victoria gives a sad smile. "Do you mind if I smoke, Detectives? We'll go to the back door."

We leave our cream sofas and follow her down a hallway lined with gilt-framed paintings. The ceiling's recessed and dimmed lighting gives the feeling of a museum display.

After we've both had our first drag, I say, "I'll come to the point if I may, Mrs. Milburn."

She blows smoke beyond the porch where we're standing. "I think we can drop the formality, Detective. It's not every day someone returns from a trip to something like this. To be frank, I expected the concrete would've been poured. I'm not sure whether to complain or not."

"How long were you away?"

"I went to visit my sister in Australia in the beginning of June."

"Based on the condition of the body we found buried on your property, it's likely the burial happened soon after you left for your holiday. Who knew you were away?"

"Let me think." She draws on her cigarette. "Mira and Mrs. Mott, my neighbor on this side." She points. "Also, the property management people who liaised with the building people. I have a card somewhere so I can give you their details. My cleaner has a key. I asked her to come in while I was away."

Blain takes her details and the additional names of the golf and Probus friends Victoria gives us. "I think that's about ten."

I say, "I'm told you live here on your own. Is that right?"

"Yes, since Ivan died, ten years ago. This place is a bit big for me now, which is why the section subdivision happened. When my new apartment is ready, I'll move in and sell this house." She takes another drag and blows the smoke up. "I only hope having a body buried on the property won't interfere with that."

"I hope not, Victoria. How long have you lived here?"

"We moved in the year after the stock market crash, in the spring, I think."

Blain says, "That would be 1988, so twenty-three years."

"I'm sure you are correct."

I say, "The woman buried here, her name was Rachel Trix. Did you know her?"

"Never heard of her, much less knew her. Of all the abandoned places in this city, how on earth did that poor woman end up here?"

"We suspect knowing you were away was the first thing," I

say. "And it's likely the person or persons responsible also knew concreting was imminent."

"That sounds dreadful. So, perhaps some good has come from the delay."

I say, "Mira informed one of my team a Mrs. Mott mowed lawns late at night. Does that make any sense to you?"

Victoria laughs. "No. It would be years since the old dear mowed her lawns. She uses the same gardener as me. In fact, once he's done mine, he does hers. I don't know what Mira would be… wait a minute." She brings a hand to her chest. "No, it couldn't be…"

"Tell us," Blain says, keen.

Victoria returns to the kitchen and rummages in drawers under the sideboard. Holding a key, eyes gleaming, she says, "Follow me."

We walk along a gravel path to a woodshed at the side of the house. The lock fitting for the little building is undisturbed. Blain follows her in, and I stand at the door, pretending to finish my Camel. A few garden tools sit clipped to walls in designated places. In one corner sits a small piece of machinery, shrouded by a green tarp. She lifts the cover and reveals a yellow digger, incapable of any significant excavation and in pristine condition.

"Your late husband's?" Blain says.

She nods and asks, "Could the noise Mira heard have been made by this?"

"Quite possibly. Has the digger ever been used on this property?"

"No. Never."

I say, "We'll need the digger examined."

She winces a little and looks unsure.

I say, "I promise we'll take good care of it. I want to know if someone's started it recently and match any materials with the shingle and dirt outside. If I understand you correctly, your fingerprints should be the only ones on the digger. Yes?"

"Well, you'll know better than me whether Ivan's might be present after ten years."

"How long has the digger been on the property, Victoria?"

"It was a retirement present for Ivan. Let me think." She pauses. "Yes, 1992 when he retired. He removed some old tree stumps next to Mrs. Mott's woodshed. More sentimental value than anything else and I haven't been able to part with it."

"Apart from the two of you, who else might know about the digger?"

She moves a hand over her heart. "Ivan, so overcome by the gift from his former work, seldom mentioned it. I'll make us some tea."

Back in the sunless sitting room with a wall heater on, steam from the poured tea wafts into the cool air.

Victoria tells us about her unwell sister in Australia. "Our other sister died several years ago, and I always regretted not spending more time with her."

Blain says, "Understandable."

I take a sip of the tea. "You said before you made the tea, Ivan seldom spoke about the digger. Did anyone apart from the two of you see it?"

"Only my nephew and niece. I can't think of anyone else. They lived with us for a while, after my sister died. A terrible time. In hindsight, I think I was so grief-stricken I wasn't a competent mother. I couldn't have been." She bites her bottom lip and looks away.

Blain says, "I had a younger sister die. Leukemia. Quite a long time ago now, but you're never the same after. I wasn't."

I can't recall seeing this softer, empathetic side in Blain. Not to this extent. But I have a dilemma now. The cop in me wants to explore whether the kids lived in Christchurch and may've been on our radar. On the other hand, that might take Victoria back to something painful and have no benefit for her.

I take a punt. "I think it's quite normal for kids to go off the rails Victoria, especially after a parent dies."

"Oh yes, and both their parents died within a year. My sister was depressed and hanged herself. The children's father was stabbed and killed. Ivan and I took on emotionally damaged teenage orphans at a time when I wasn't only in grief, I was riddled with guilt, missing the signs of my sister's decline, and not helping the kids out more."

I lean forward, my hands in my lap, and nod.

Victoria's chin quivers and she pulls at her collar. "I should've done more," she says. "Took some counseling at least. Might've stopped my nephew going off the rails." She looks away again.

Blain frowns at me.

I say, "Well perhaps you can take some comfort from the fact he didn't end up with a police record."

"I can't. He probably should have. He ran some scheme at the university. A lot of people lost a lot of money. An awful situation. He fell out with Ivan over it and he hasn't been near or communicated with me in years. He didn't come to Ivan's funeral."

I say, "I'm sorry to hear that."

"Over time, I've accepted if my sister was right about him

being abused by his father, that was more significant than my failings as a mother."

Blain said, "Your sister told you your bother-in-law abused his son?"

"Abused them both. My sister suspected her husband, Eddie, was a pedophile. I can't remember all the details. I suppose I've blocked them out. She was worried for the children. I remember she convinced herself his own children were safe, but in the end, toeing the line must've become too hard for her."

"What about your niece?" I ask. "What became of her?"

Victoria wipes away tears. "A bright wee thing, from the moment she could talk. I let her go on a school trip with a friend. The friend's mother took them to the North Island. I never saw her again."

I say, "That's terrible. I hope the police were helpful."

"Oh yes. They and the Social Welfare Department were very kind. Couldn't have done more. Wendy, my niece, phoned me. Quite unexpectedly. I was having dinner and she said, "I'm fine, Aunty Vic. I'm going to uni next year. She wanted to know if I heard from my nephew, Ollie. They lost touch with one another. I don't suppose this is any help to you. Is it? You've been kind and patient letting me prattle on."

"Ollie, being short for Oliver?"

"Yes. Wendy and Oliver Myles-Milburn. They took our name when they lived with us."

"Victoria, how long is it since you've seen Ollie?"

"I should think twenty years."

I pull my phone out of my jacket. "I'm going to show you a picture of two men. They are not alike to look at, but I'm wondering if you might recognize one of them." I scroll to Blain's email, open the pic, and hand her my phone.

Not an immediate answer but she says, her soft voice, "They don't look happy. Do they? But I think I recognize the look. It is twenty years, after all, and children change more than adults. Don't they?"

I say, "I agree."

"Ollie is standing next to the tall man. He was short and stocky back then. I think that's him. Why do you have his picture?"

I stand, and Blain follows my lead. "We think he may be involved in the insurance industry and, I'm sorry to say, not all his work may be legal."

"Well. I'm not surprised to hear you say that. The university scheme I mentioned. I don't recall all the details, but I remember Ivan said it was fraudulent. Will you keep me informed?"

I say, "You've been very helpful. I'm sure we can do that."

I look at Blain. He nods.

We're at the front door, when I say, "Your late brother-in-law. Eddie, I think you said. What was his full name?"

"Myles. Edward Myles."

FRIDAY, 10 AUGUST 2012
11.46 HOURS

I call Griff at his judicial conference in Queenstown. I detect a lilt of joy in his description of the beauty of the mountain range and lake. "But I'm missing you," he says.

"I need a holiday, and having one with you in Queenstown sounds lovely. Sold. At my end, some promising news. We're inching toward an arrest for Nick."

We end a ten-minute call with no deeper discussion. I think we're both pleased to talk without conflict.

I'm loading a few supplementary groceries into the car when Blain calls. "Two developments. I talked to Linda Nichol."

"And?"

"She's been to Brisbane, but Tracey told us that. Never heard of Martin Troup before she saw him on the TV after Nick was killed. I had no sense she fed me a fine line in bull-shit. None at all."

"Anything else of interest?"

"Yeah, the night Nick copped it, Linda visited her mother—in care. The old lady mis-behaved and they called Linda in to help them settle her down. Something about not having the right people on the night roster that night. She left her mother's care home after 23.30 hours."

"Meaning no alibi for Nick."

"Correct, but an interesting little side note. The old lady settled down, and when Linda left, she noticed a dark-colored Chev parked on the other side of the road. At the time, her ex owned a Chev and stalked her. She relaxed after she saw a blonde woman in the vehicle so was unconcerned about taking a plate number. Admitted some paranoia."

"Jesus Christ. How the hell did that come up in your conversation?"

"Did the usual ask. Anything else, no matter how trivial etcetera."

"What are the odds this was another Chev and not the one that plowed into Nick?"

"You're more of a gambler than I am. You tell me."

"The second thing, or was that it?" I ask.

"This Myles holding company. It seems the ghost of Edward James Myles, stabbing victim, has managed to file an annual reregistration for Myles Holding Limited for the last twenty-five years. I recall you saying that *The Press* were tipped off about Myles Holdings and a link to Putis, but that the tipster had died. Anyone inquired into that death?"

"Natural causes, heart attack. That's verified info."

He says, "I'm thinking Eddie's son, calling himself Oliver Collinge, might have kept the company name registered for Putis Insurance Consortium. But that might just be me."

"Not just you, mate. Oliver Collinge is not a registered taxpayer, despite what he's pulling in from EI."

"Got enough for an arrest, you reckon?"

"Stacking up. I'll see Coman this afternoon."

FRIDAY, 10 AUGUST 2012
13.40 HOURS

When I arrive at Coman's office he tells me he's got his formal performance appraisal this afternoon. He shakes his head. "Now they're getting us to do self-assessments."

"Appreciate you picking up my exhibits from court the other day, boss."

His lips purse, eyebrows knitted.

"Trix," I add. "The fraud trial exhibits the court pestered me about."

"More than two months since I attended court. Good place to avoid."

I pull the exhibits receipt from my shirt pocket and hand it to him.

He tilts his head back. "Who the hell's forging my signature?"

"My problem, boss, is the one person able to describe or identify who uplifted the firearm isn't available."

"Ballistics match?"

"We haven't found the gun. Yet."

He crosses his arms and frowns. "Why do you think it wasn't buried with Trix?"

"The answer is not comforting. Based on what I'm about to tell you, it may be used again."

"So, you're punting this up for me to deal with?"

"Boss, Trix's murder is a complication in the unsolved murder of Nick Jarvis, and you're already OC. But I believe that murder, and Dowling's death, are covering an organized crime ring headed by AC Troup, Gwen Sinclair and one of Troup's long-time informants, Oliver Collinge."

"Gwen Sinclair?"

"Earthquake Insure. The CEO's wife."

"I know who she is," he says impatience in the response. "She's a generous donor to the local rape crisis center.

"Can I ask how you know, boss? Her donor status is not part of her limited internet profile."

"Wife number two chaired the RCC board at the time. Her desire for secrecy is why you won't find anything about her. I guess she didn't want all and sundry coming with their hands out. Fuck knows where she acquired her wealth."

I outline the meeting with Gwen and her lawyer and Nichol's revelations.

Coman walks to the window, his mouth set tight. He gazes out as he speaks. "Let's accept, for the moment, there's no innocent explanation, or," he says, raising his voice, "the roles were in reverse—Troup giving DI Dowling a firearm. In addition to Gwen being an arch fraudster, you're saying our AC is a murderer or a party—Section 66. Yes?"

"I am. Why does he need knowledge about a firearm from a fraud trial two years ago, secured at the court ever since? That doesn't strike you as unlikely, boss?"

He returns to his desk, yanks out a drawer so hard it-plummets to the floor. The whiskey bottle bounces out and he grips it in both hands.

"The photo, boss, shows the man who's made false fraud accusations about a murdered officer, accusations he attributes to you, holding the gun, in all likelihood the weapon to kill Trix. There's no other reasonable explanation for all those circumstances."

He puts the bottle down. "Context. What is it? A photograph, a moment, a split-second in time? Might be a different firearm, for all you know."

"It maybe split-second but implicating you in the weapon takes more time. And who needs to do that?" I pause while his head is down. "There's more between Troup and Dowling."

He flops into his chair. "Oh, Jesus. What else?"

I tell him about Dowling's taped confession, and he stares at the doodling on his desk pad. When I finish, he says, "How long have you known that info?"

My heart and guts drop to the floor. August 3, the day before Coman came to my father's funeral service.

"A week today, boss."

"Jesus Christ. And you go and meet Kevin Yan on the sixth after I told you Troup knew Yan?"

"Yes, boss. But Troup was not properly on our radar."

"Still, you might've cost a young man his life."

I nod but I'm staring at my toes.

He says, "So, Dowling's and Gwen's stories dovetail."

"Although she says she didn't know Dowling."

He gives a disbelieving smirk.

"I agree. Dowling's helped establish a motive for his own murder."

"I'll need to see it—the video. No more holding out on me, son."

I pause. "Yes, boss."

"Well, where is it?"

"Secured at home, containing information personal and private to me." This feels like Groundhog Day.

He glowers, eyebrows join. "If you're involved in any criminality, you need to come clean. Now!"

"Nothing like that, boss. Personal matters and associated advice."

He points a stubby finger. "Well, get it in here tomorrow. Now, back to Troup. Nothing in the way of hard evidence against him. Right?"

"Nothing we know linking him to any crime scene, but we can prove he's an associate of Collinge, something he's lied about. We'll need access to his bank accounts. Gwen Sinclair will give evidence he confessed to killing Trix, plus we have the photo evidence. There's also the money trail between Troup and Dowling."

"No forensics," he says with scorn.

"We can't be surprised by that, boss. We need the homemade gun and a match of the bullets in the grave and the slug in Trix. We're waiting on prints on the bullets but I'm not hopeful."

"The weapon only takes you so far. You need the shooter and your only witness on that front, if you're correct, is criminally involved. Where do the DCC and her little protégé, Quentin Sinclair, come into this picture?"

"She's trying to save her career after EI's inevitable collapse. Troup's using her as a front to show we're helping EI in fraud prevention. Dowling asked me to take Jarvis to intercept Trix. And either he or Troup passed that intel to Collinge. They planned the hit. I don't know where the rot stops. But I believe Troup's between her and Collinge and he's kept her on a need-to-know basis. That way she wouldn't know about Trix. As for Sinclair? O'Brien says he's incompetent, something I doubt Gwen would disagree with. I don't believe he's involved in any crime. Too stupid."

I pause. It's obvious by his pained expression, this is all a bit difficult. I prefer not to mention Troup's attempted bribe of promotion for me and keep the discussion focused on evidence. But I've learned my lesson on holding out.

"I said before, boss, I believed implicating you was deliberate. AC Troup disclosed plans about you when we met with Minister O'Brien."

"What?"

"He's got you pegged for retirement in six months."

"News to me," he says, rubbing the back of his neck. "And he said this in front of O'Brien?"

I nod.

He hitches his pants. "Fuck him. The bastard. We'll see..."

A two-tap knock at the door stops us both. Coman scrambles to hide the bottle before Hockley strides in. "Been looking for you, Sergeant," she says, her face thunderous.

"What can I do for you, boss?"

"I have reason to believe you headed a covert operation into Fergus Dowling's death after I directed you not to waste scarce resources."

I glance at Coman, suspecting he's informed her, as per the "no surprises." rule. His mouth's open but his eyes tell me he's surprised.

"I doubt the inspector can help you any further on this matter," she says, acerbic. "Do you deny it?"

"I do deny it, boss. Not only did I not waste resources, I have clear evidence his death warrants investigation."

Ignoring me, she says, "Furthermore, you claimed I hold some secret video recording that you allege Dowling made before he died."

"I did not assert that statement as the truth, but to test the veracity of a witness. Boss."

"Well, I suggest you save those feeble explanations for your next internal inquiry. I also suspect you, or someone under your direction, of impersonating a staff member of Assistant Commissioner Troup and, in so doing, undermining my relationship with Quentin Sinclair." She pauses. "You are hereby suspended from duty forthwith." She holds out her hand. "Your warrant and access cards please, Sergeant. I'll escort you to your office to pick up any personal effects and out of the building. Clear?"

"Yes, boss."

She leads me to Coman's door. I glance back at the inspector and he mimes a phone call. I nod, hoping he's now in my camp but concerned he hasn't fessed up to giving me permission to search Dowling's property.

FRIDAY, 10 AUGUST 2012
14.12 HOURS

The squad room is quiet. I don't speak to anyone and all Hockley does is ask for my work phone.

I lie that I misplaced it and am using my personal phone. "I'll find and return it tomorrow, boss."

Despite spending a lot of time at work, I gather few personal possessions. I stuff hiking shoes, an assortment of business books on coaching and one on back, neck and shoulder exercises as well as my personal laptop into a couple of plastic bags. I sense Hockley's cold eyes boring into my back. I dump an old water bottle and two used paper coffee cups into the bin.

On the way out, Blain is texting. I'm tempted to call out, "See you later," but I don't want to create tension between him and Hockley. With most staff out on calls, no one else witnesses my walk of shame.

Outside the building I open an email from Cadaverman: "Fergus Dowling died in a hypoglycemic coma, the result of not accessing adequate glucose. In view of the restraint mark on his wrist, and the pill lodged in his throat, I don't believe this was a suicide. I'll support a finding of suspicious death."

Blain's text says, "Result on Gwen. Will call."

I deposit belongings in my car and head for the RE:Start Mall. Aimless, I find myself in Ballantynes department store, looking for distractions. Numbness arrives, the shock of not having a job to go to for the first time in my life. What's worse, is the thought I exposed Yan to a life-threatening injury from which he might still die. I should've told Coman about my intentions to interview him. Distrusting him has been hard-wired.

I call Griff. But after his recorded message, I can only say, "Hope your day is going well." I realize I've never left a caring message for someone before. Griff will guess something's up.

In a bookstore, I resist spending money and congratulate myself on adapting to a life without the police. No. Too soon. I re-enter the store and buy *The Rosie Project,* hoping to open a lighter side to my life.

I text Blain a reply. *Suspended. You were right—plot to impers Trp staffer & 4 porkies to GS about vid. Don't let H put you off. Keep going. I will. 4 Nick.*

His reply: *Nxt step?*

Need 2 think.

Time to go home, tell Eve, blast her gym equipment, and do something useful for me. But I lack the energy for a workout. I wonder what Coman will do, whether Hockley is bugging his office and phone instead of my phone and desk.

My mobile vibrates. "My lawyer doesn't know I'm calling you, Mr. Solomon."

"Gwen? How did you get this number?"

"Sergeant Blain. Listen, Marty's taken Quentin. And your sister."

"What do you mean taken?"

"Abducted, kidnapped, for Christ's sake."

"Eve? No. Not possible."

"He said he's got them. I believe him."

"Why? What's this about?"

"Marty needs an exit strategy."

"I'll call you straight back."

Fingers trembling, Eve's phone gives me the mechanical voice. This can't be right. Sweating, I try her number again. And again same result.

I call Gwen. "He said he's got *Eve?*"

She shrieks, "Yes. I told you."

"But she doesn't open the d… Where?"

"Lake Pearson."

An hour and forty minutes away. I might arrive in the day's last light.

I ask, "Where at Lake Pearson?"

"Marty's holiday house. I can guide you. Have you got the recording?"

I pause, hear her puffing. "Yes."

"We go to the lake. You, me, and no other cops. Right?"

"I'll call you back." She yells something as I lower the phone to disconnect the call and try Eve again. She never leaves the phone off. If it's charging, she leaves it switched on. Three attempts—three more failures. Each failure takes me to the voice message and eats valuable seconds before I can call again.

Gwen's right. She answers my call back in seconds. "Gwen, you and your colleagues don't control this situation and you don't give a rat's ass about Quentin Sinclair. Let's drop the pretense."

"So, you're willing to hand over your sister to the fate of

desperate men? My God, you're a bigger monster than the men you're after."

"Enough of the melodrama, Gwen. I accept Troup's corrupt, and he discussed murder to cover up his crimes, but Collinge is the real criminal here. The sooner you distance yourself from him, the easier your life will become. You lied to us in your lawyer's office, which means we can't use your photograph. But I believe his influence on you is powerful, your own life is at risk, as you said. Except it's not Troup who's threatening you. It's Collinge."

She starts to cry. "What the fuck am I supposed to do? I can't help your sister if you don't bring the bloody video."

She's right. Neither of us can. If I refuse to enter the obvious trap, I'm signing Eve's death warrant. "We'll go together. Is it Collinge or Troup I'm dealing with on this?"

She snuffles into the phone. "It's Oliver, but Troup's there as well. I'm heading to your work as we speak," she says.

"Meet me on the ramp, Northern entrance to the building."

FRIDAY, 10 AUGUST 2012
14.43 HOURS

Waiting for Gwen, I call Blain. "Did you give Gwen Sinclair my mobile number?"

"No way."

"Didn't think so. She called me," I say, walking at pace. "She said Eve's been abducted by Troup but admitted Collinge is the driving force. They want me and Gwen at Troup's place in Lake Pearson with the Dowling video."

"He's got your sister? Jesus. What do you need?"

"I'm still trying to figure that out. If I leave now, I should make it before sixteen thirty."

"Tracey's got intel on Gwen's case," he says. Don't go, boss. They'll kill…"

I cut him off. "Sorry, can't talk. Gwen's here. Call me in half an hour on my personal phone."

Close to panic, we both run to my car. I try Eve's number again. Nothing. In Darfield, I figure we're about halfway. My personal mobile rings. I curse and pull in at the side of the road.

"What's wrong?" Gwen asks.

"My personal phone. Not paired to the hands free."

I answer, keeping the phone close to my ear.

Blain says, concern in his tone, "Might just be me, but you're entering a trap."

"Appreciate the call."

"About Gwen," Blain says. "You ready for Tracey's result?"

"Cheers. You're a good listener."

A pause.

"What's that mean, Solly?"

"I wish others possessed your comms skill."

"Coded message?"

"Yes. You'll need to persevere a bit longer."

"I should stay on the line?"

"Yes."

"Roger. Can I carry on?"

"Indeed."

"As we suspected, Gwen was Wendy Myles-Milburn, and is Oliver Collinge's sister. Eddie Myles was stabbed at the Belfast freezing works. Fergus Dowling locked up the offender, one Owen Webb."

I catch Gwen looking at me and, despite my guts lurching at hearing my father's name and history, I try to present a calm face. "I understand."

Blain continues, "Gwen got into trouble up at Foxton, the reason she didn't return to Victoria Milburn. She gave Social Welfare her father's old contact details, which led to the Welfare placing her in a semi-secure facility."

"Dowling served in Foxton. Didn't he?" I ask.

He says, "Yeah, local sergeant before his stint at the Police College. Wendy, as she was called then, reported a case of being stalked. The old file says the stalker was unidentified but also, Dowling found intel Wendy was a low-level offender in an organized gang of burglary, also fencing the stolen goods.

He let her off with a warning and she withdrew the stalking complaint. Nothing else recorded. Martin Troup was a new inspector at the time. Dowling reported to him."

"I understand."

"Gotta say, smells fuckin' fishy to me. Coman's briefed," Blain says. "He ran some discreet inquiries for the commissioner after Dowling was pushed out of Foxton into the college job. But Dowling found out Coman was looking into him. Sealed it off somehow. I'd say with Troup's help."

"What happened to the complainant?"

"She got her commerce degree majoring in IT, buggered off overseas where she got her doctorate. All legit. So, with the tie to Collinge, and with Troup, I think we've got something."

"Understood." I fake a smile at Gwen, who's staring at me. "We'll talk again soon. Got another call coming through. And again, appreciate your patience."

I keep the line open, hoping Blain will capture every word until we run out of cell coverage. I guess a few minutes of transmission time is left. The question is whether he can build on my work with Coman, encourage the inspector to stick his neck out far enough and authorize our own air support.

On my work phone I get a call from a number I don't recognize. "Solomon," I answer, speaker phone on.

"I gotta admit you getting suspended as a way out of your life of lies wasn't on my radar."

"Sorry to deprive you of your fun, Collinge."

"Plenty of fun to come. I promise."

"What do you want?"

"Out of this little shit hole, with Dowling's vid in my pocket. I'm taking Troup's fancy new chopper and I want the freedom to fly unrestricted."

We both know he means out to sea where he'll be picked up. Driving or landing anywhere in this country is no escape. "What's Troup say about that?"

"Marty's always acted in his own best interests. So, to be clear, any fuckin' Rambo actions and your sister goes down with me. Right?"

My chest is heavy and in response I'm hunched over the wheel. "I need to speak to her."

He chuckles. "Who's got the power here, boy? Take a wild guess—fifty percent chance of getting it right."

"Let me talk to her, Collinge. If I don't, you get nothing."

He shouts away from the mouthpiece. "Say hello to your darling brother."

Given the opportunity, I'd relish the chance to put a bullet in this prick. I glance at my personal phone in my shirt pocket. Still transmitting. I refocus.

Eve's uncertain tone in the distance, "Solly?"

"You're on speaker," Collinge says.

"He hasn't hurt you?"

In between sobs, she says four words. "He—had—a—key."

Ken, the neighbor's burglary, two days ago. *He said nothing taken*. How long have these people been watching my house?

"It's okay, Eve. You'll be okay."

"Oh, such sweet reassurance," Collinge says. "Bring Dowling's tape. Arrive without it, your sister's dead. Someone runs interference for you, she's dead. And when I'm airborne, if another chopper comes anywhere near us, I give your sister a thrill and roll her out the fuckin' door. With me?"

"If Eve is not alive and well..."

Collinge ends the call.

FRIDAY, 10 AUGUST 2012
16.15 HOURS

I taste acid in my mouth. I stop chewing on my inner cheek, pull my shoulders back and flex my cold fingers a few times. Gwen stares at me but says nothing.

On a granite shingle road parallel to the lake, we take a left bend and cross a rickety bridge over an alpine stream. I push a button on my phone to open the home screen and get confirmation we're out of cellular range.

I say, "I'm guessing your detailed confession about the frauds is true."

Gwen nods.

"So, whose camp are you in, Gwen? Your lover's or your brother's?"

"I want my life back. I'm not in anyone's camp."

"Appears to me, Oliver's the priority."

"But I killed no one. I didn't want Nick Jarvis to die."

"Are you serious? You tried to kill us both."

"You don't understand. *I* didn't want it. Oliver was at the wheel. I had no intention of killing you. I aimed for your leg when the gun misfired."

"Nick's mother told us he had a confidential informant at EI. Are you saying there was no one other than Trix?"

"I heard water-cooler talk Trix was in a relationship with a cop. We had to know more details, the extent of ongoing contact. I told Jarvis I received a report of a female ex-cop on staff who knew him and we needed to talk."

"How did you get Nick to talk to you?"

"I said a staff member believed a claim from his mother's church didn't look right and I wanted to discuss the possibility someone may've been acting fraudulently without the knowledge of the church."

"Where and when did you meet?"

"I don't remember when. We met in my office and I remember he was concerned a colleague watched him enter the building. I assume, Vincent."

"What did he say?"

"We didn't get far. He said his ex called him one night, drunk, and accused him of making a false claim. He told me if anyone believed that they should take it up with you or Detective Inspector Dowling. He said he had a conflict of interest between the church's claim, which he helped his mother make and any potential investigation of that claim. But as he left, he said he would tell Dowling to expect my call."

"And you reported this conversation to Collinge and Troup?"

"Of course. But I don't know whether Jarvis reported his conversation with me back to Dowling. Troup suggested we hold tight. Trix was dead so couldn't harm us any further. Over the next few weeks, Oliver got more and more agitated and became convinced Jarvis would've told you."

I glance at her. "Can we go back a while? What happened to you after your father died, after you left the Milburns?"

"You mean, after your father killed mine?"

I rub my head. I'd carried this too long, worked too hard to keep the circumstances secret, the weight of it all, now heavy chains burrowing into skin, muscle, and bone.

I ask, "Do you know why that happened?"

"Because he hated my father's control."

"No, Gwen. Because your father raped me, and I told Owen."

"So, you're still holding on to that story?"

"When he raped me, Owen confronted him, said he was a sick bastard and needed help. Owen had no intention of pressing charges because he didn't want me going through what most complainants go through in sex cases. But Eddie went for him with the knife. Owen killed him in self-defense."

"Oliver said that story was a lie."

"Why would I lie about something I hid from everyone except my sister? My closest mates don't know. Why would I tell a lie like that, Gwen?"

She stares ahead, glancing at me twice, as she seems to be weighing it.

I say, "You never forget. Can't, even when you want to."

"I know. Better than most."

"Is that why you've been a patron of a rape crisis center?"

She nods. "Dowling."

"Are you saying Dowling raped you?"

Still staring straight ahead, she nods again.

"I'd like you to tell me, Gwen. Who knows, you might not have another chance to share it with someone who understands."

"Maybe," she says and presses her lips together. "Troup's as guilty as Dowling. He was the big boss looking after his men. I told Troup that Dowling raped me, but Troup covered it up."

Long moments of silence pass before she says, "It was a couple of weeks after I reported it, Troup told me Dowling was killed in an operation, some drugs thing. That he couldn't take my complaint further. I was only fifteen, for Christ's sake."

I ease off the gas. "How did Dowling make it happen?"

She stares through the windscreen. I notice the vehicle's lights are starting to catch the reflective strips on the verge marking the road ahead. "Someone in Foxton stalked me and I reported it to Dowling. But he found out I was hooked up with a bad crowd. One night," she says, sotto voce, "he followed me to my friend's place, waited in one of those old, unmarked cars, the front seats all joined up, same as in the back. You know the type?"

I nod.

"I walked past him, and he called my name. Said he wanted to update me on the stalker and get me to identify a guy who ran a motel out at Foxton Beach. He drove us to a motel. I was surprised we walked into a room without a key. It happened in that room."

"And after, he drove you back?"

"Like nothing ever happened. Like he pretended I wanted him to fuck me. When I found the courage to search out his boss and tell him what happened…" She stopped.

"Tell me the full story."

She shakes her head. "What's the point?"

I offer an understanding tone. "What happened to you was as huge in your life as it was in mine."

She gives a long sigh. "I made a statement. Troup made me

admit I was fencing stolen goods before he took my statement that Dowling raped me in a police car. I got the whole patter from Troup. Serious allegation, full inquiry, etcetera. All the bullshit. He promised to keep me fully informed. I heard nothing. My father taught us—you take backward steps in life; people stomp all over you. So, I didn't let it go. I couldn't."

"We must've been about the same age when we were raped. I'm so sorry it happened to you. A terrible thing. We, the police, should've made you safe."

She narrows her eyes. "And I believed Troup until thirty years later, when I helped the prison with bespoke software and Dowling showed up on a corruption investigation. I recognized him and told Oliver. At first, he didn't believe me."

"Did you speak to Dowling there?"

"He never flinched when he saw me. You know why?"

"I assume he didn't remember you."

"Because to Fergus bloody Dowling, I was only a bit of fifteen-year-old pussy, not his first, nor his last. Twenty years later, he didn't recognize the sophisticated and confident woman."

A rabbit runs out in front of the car headlights. I brake and Gwen lurches forward. I ask, "What happened after you told Oliver?"

"We planned for me to take an interest in Dowling, flatter him, flirt a bit. Have you any idea how hard it was to engage with my rapist, a monster, pretend I liked him? It was all I could do not to retch. So, I listened to his life story, heard about you, his dead wife, everything, all part of Oliver's plan. I got in Dowling's head, got him to fancy me and he did—big time."

"How could Oliver make you get close to Dowling? That's vile."

"Oliver's plan was to set Troup and Dowling up for a big fall. But I needed to prove to him that we were brother and sister like the old days, that we were close, a team again."

She sees me shaking my head and adds, "Oliver said I abandoned him. In a way it was true. We had a huge falling out after I left the Milburns. I was younger than him, but he leaned on me for emotional support. I felt guilty. I had a choice—redeem myself with Oliver, get revenge and get rich. Or protect myself from Dowling. I drew the line at sex. Not at any price."

"How did you keep Dowling off you?"

"When Oliver saw I was committed, we agreed when Dowling made the move, I would stall him until our first night on the QE11. He was smitten, very happy to comply. I knew Troup and he were both going to be at the EI function. I made Dowling agree not to have eye contact or give clues about our relationship."

I ask, "What about Quentin?"

"Like I said, I used him. He had no hint of my relationship with Troup. He was so preoccupied with all the adverse publicity about EI's performance. We were sleeping in separate rooms by the time of the EI function. That suited me fine."

Our climb up higher ground is steady and, even though it's not fully dark, the road signs advising caution are increasingly prominent in the car lights as we pass through trees either side of the road.

I say, "Dowling says he knew about you and Troup?"

She nods. 'The sick bastard said that was all part of his enjoyment."

"And the money. How did that work?"

"As soon as I got the identifying info Oliver needed, we put money in accounts we created in both their names—Dowling and Troup."

I say, "But with Troup's involvement in the Putis transfers, he had to know about the payments."

She smiles and shakes her head.

"What?" I ask.

"Of course. And how we hid the money. But they didn't know we put money in accounts we created for them without their knowledge. And we left the source of that money discoverable—straight from EI. When they had enough funds to get lengthy jail terms, stupid Trix and her greed ruined our plan."

"What exactly did she do and how did you find out?"

"Because Vincent was a cop, Troup installed a motion sensor camera over his desk. Perhaps he hoped to get something to hold over Vincent. I don't really know. The camera focused on Vincent's screen. That's how we know she was snooping into his work. Somehow she got his password because we saw her operating his computer."

I think about Trix stealing my password and planting a bug inside my phone.

"But she would write things on paper and take them away. Then we heard, well Marty did, that a woman calling herself Harriet rang Dowling and spoke about discovering fraudulent payments that benefitted cops or their families. Of course, Marty knew straight away. That was the name he got for her. She mentioned your rugby club and the church Jarvis's mother was associated with. And because Oliver brought her to EI, she went to him with what she knew. He pretended to take it seriously and said he would look into it. I don't know, but as far as we know Trix had no idea of the connection between

Dowling and Troup—probably thought she was safe calling Dowling as Harriet."

"I didn't know the Dowling-Troup connection myself until the EI function. I thought it was just a professional connection. So, after Trix told Oliver what she knew, he decided to take her out?"

"First, he tried to buy her off, offered her a piece of the pie. Up until then, Troup, Oliver and I had a third of the syphoned funds each, less what we were paying to Dowling, but they were one-off payments. So, we went to Trix and offered her twenty-five percent, basically an equal partner. But she wanted fifty percent. She signed her death warrant with that. Oliver fast-forwarded the plan to drop Dowling and Troup in the shit and get their help to dispose of her."

"And you showed Troup what you had against him—the traceable payments—and asked for an untraceable gun?"

"Exactly. Oliver told Troup his problems would disappear if he played ball. The photo's authentic. I took it to have something extra over them both. Call it insurance, something we know about." She reaches into the back of her waistband. "This is what you've been looking for. What Dowling got back from the court."

I glance down. "For Christ's sake. Be careful. If I go off the road here, we're both dead. Can you at least put it down by your feet?"

She complies and says, "When did you know?"

"I felt the explanation about how you came to take the picture and Trix's disappearance from work immediately after didn't hang together. But when I asked you whether you knew Dowling, I knew for sure. What I didn't know was why you were covering for Collinge."

As we come to a clearing, Gwen reaches down, picks up the gun and orders me to stop and get out of the car. I smell wood smoke in the cold air but see little in the gloom except the tall, dark pines hovering over us.

"The memory stick, lawyer's letter and Dowling's confession," I say. "They're in the trunk."

Her response gives me little hope. She raises the .45 to my stomach. "Turn around."

"If you want to finish the job, at least do it now, front on."

"I don't want to kill you. Just turn around and walk."

"Well, if you don't *want* to kill me, don't do it by accident. Put the bloody safety on."

She squints and complies. Remembering what the safety does to this gun, my hopes climb a notch.

FRIDAY, 10 AUGUST 2012
16.36 HOURS

The house is no holiday retreat for a rich, corrupt cop. The weatherboard structure tilts from problems with the foundations. Closer to the house, a porch light illuminates flaking paint from window sashes.

Gwen says, "This place belongs to your informant. I don't think Kevin will mind us using it. We anticipated your people would come after us. Marty's place is on the other side of the lake."

We walk past Collinge's Porsche and Troup's Lamborghini.

Inside the house, the floor is uneven and jagged cracks run through a wall to a support beam. Collinge stands behind Troup, who is bound hand and foot to a wooden chair in front of a cheap kitchen breakfast bar. Troup lifts his chin from his chest and gives me a look of resignation. A blood trail from a head wound flows down his left cheek and under his jaw.

"Where are Eve and Sinclair?" I ask.

Collinge, wearing gloves, grips a baseball bat in one hand and in his other takes the homemade gun with which he killed Trix. He instructs Gwen to tie me to another chair and jabs the gun at me to move.

Gwen fetches rope from the table, secures my arms behind me, and binds them to the back of my chair.

Collinge says, "Don't worry. Not long before you join them. I don't miss her fucking banshee wailing. An easy choice in the end, so thanks are unnecessary."

The energy drains from me like I'm a windup toy with a broken spring. I can't speak and I ache with immediate pain in my elbow and knee joints.

Gwen tightens my rope. I've missed the chance to charge at Collinge like a bull and tear at his carotid artery with my teeth—a suicide move, advancing my imminent death by minutes.

Collinge rips Troup's gag from his mouth. To Gwen, he says, "Switch on your phone's video and record him chest up from his right side. Make sure you don't get me or the gun in the video."

Troup flinches when Collinge pushes the gun barrel into his temple.

"We're going to record your confession, Troupie, old mate. You're going to answer true or false. Understand?"

Troup's chin trembles and he presses his elbows into his side, perhaps in a futile attempt to make himself less visible. I think about Eve. Maybe the functionary at Harewood Crematorium will burn us together.

"Start recording."

She raises her phone and puts up her thumb.

Collinge, voice loud, "You are Assistant Commissioner Martin Troup. True or false."

Troup mutters, "True."

"Speak up for the tape, please."

Troup repeats his answer.

Collinge puts a series of questions requiring yes and no answers about Foxton in 1992, the information Gwen shared in the car about Dowling. He asks, "And after you took her statement and promised an investigation, you visited Gwen at work. True?"

"True."

"You made no record of a complaint against Dowling. Did you?"

"True."

"When you told her Dowling died in a failed drugs operation, you lied?"

"True."

"Lies to a powerless girl and to close off further action. True?"

"True."

Collinge moves to the EI frauds. "The idea to rip off EI was yours. True or false?"

"Gwen's and mine, but you deserve some of the credit."

Collinge leads him through the details Gwen gave us in Latham's office. I twist my wrists around, try to find some space for my fingers to probe the rope.

Collinge asks her, "What else do we need?

"Trix's bail?" she asks.

Collinge says, "Rachel Trix. After she robbed Bank Secure, you told Dowling you wanted the court file, and you removed the details allowing police to oppose her bail. True or false?"

In Troup's wet eyes, I can't decide whether he wants me to speak or implores me to forgive him. He turns away from me when he says, "True."

"You realized when she robbed Bank Secure, she was a liability."

"True. But she was a liability before that."

"You wanted her out, so she could be silenced."

"True."

"You had Dowling obtain the forty-five firearm from the court. True?"

"I had no choice. Did I?"

Collinge shrugs. "At Dowling's West Melton property, he refused to confess to raping my sister in Foxton?"

"True."

"We left him unharmed to think about his situation, but he died due to diabetes complications."

"That's our speculation," Troup says. "We left him unable to reach insulin."

I shout, "The suicide note. Who typed it?"

"Shut your fuckin' mouth, sunshine. Your turn's coming."

Troup says, "Gwen typed it and Oliver phoned Yvonne Hockley, saying Dowling was an old drinking buddy…"

"Shut the fuck up, both of you." Collinge turns to Gwen. "I told you that note and text were stupid mistakes."

Gwen shrugs. "Bought us some time."

Collinge says, "Enough. Camera off. We can spare the world the rest. We're not fuckin' terrorists."

Troup whimpers and then turns it to a full moan. "Please," he begs. "No more. You're getting away. Gwen, if you surrender, we can ensure you'll be treated leniently."

Collinge laughs in mock derision. "You miserable, weak, dog. The SPCA wouldn't have you. I'm putting you down."

Gwen shouts, "No, Oliver. Wait. Please. We agreed. Only Trix and Jarvis. That and the money to send them away was all we ever needed. No more killing. I insist."

Blood floods Collinge's face and neck. He shouts. "Don't

be the weak bitch our mother was." He points the gun at her. "Shut up or you'll make me do something I might regret."

Collinge grabs Troup by the hair and pulls his head back. "Now, spit in the cunt's face," Collinge says. "Go on, a decent glob."

Gwen shuffles forward, moves her jaw, perhaps trying to muster saliva. She takes water from a bottle and then spits. Troup drops his chin so most of the spray goes into his hair.

Collinge grins, repositions himself to kneel in front of Troup and lifts his chin with the barrel. "Any last requests?"

For all his greed and corruption, I don't want Troup executed, his head turned to pulp as a bullet rips through skull and brain.

Collinge says, "This all ends in a tragic lovers' tiff, Marty. Some unlucky prick will discover your boy here shot you and topped himself."

When Troup cries, Collinge touches his own jeans. His penis is erect.

"Collinge," I say, shaking my head. "Once a victim, now with the power of a bully. Your schoolboy stiffy shows you enjoy tormenting people who can't defend themselves. So pitiful." I lean back in the chair.

White spittle dribbles from his mouth. He approaches and points the barrel at my forehead. "You miserable piece of shit," he yells. "You wanna go first? We can role reverse the murder suicide."

His engagement bolsters me. My back is straight. "You go one better than your father. Don't you? You take his need to control people to a new level. You need help, Oliver."

Gwen shrieks. "Please, don't goad him."

"Ha," he says. "The son of a murderer calling me and my

father out. Don't make me laugh." He glares at Gwen. "My dad never raped anyone."

He sounds like he doesn't believe his denial.

"If he didn't rape me," I say, "your dad would still be alive."

Troup's mouth is open, eyes wide.

Collinge glances at Gwen, back at me, momentarily unsettled. Gwen's arms droop by her sides, and a tear runs down her cheek.

"You think killing me evens the score," I say. "All my father wanted was justice, but yours wanted to make sure the story never came out. He had a reason. Didn't he, Oliver?"

He says, "Basic cop training: how to tell a bullshit story." He starts to shout again. "You're the one from poor stock. A father who couldn't hold a job, spent his life in prison. *True or false!*" he screams, spittle spraying me.

I say, "And when your mother found out Eddie raped you, she hanged herself for not protecting you."

Collinge's jaw moves but he's beyond words.

Gwen shouts, "We must go, Ollie. Please. Now. Leave them. You have the confession you want."

Collinge reaches toward me with his left hand, gun in his right. I turn my face, but he grabs my nose, pulls my head around, and pinches my nostrils to force my lips apart. He forces the barrel in my mouth, and a couple of teeth break. Blood gushes onto on my tastebuds. Collinge smiles before he says, "Say goodbye, pig."

He pulls the trigger.

The click of a misfire.

He says, "What the fuck?"

Collinge rips the gun from my mouth, cutting the inside

of my top lip. One of the bloodied teeth falls into my lap and blood drips down my chin.

"Leave it, Ollie," Gwen pleads. "Come on."

He tries to open the chamber with shaking hands. "Only a misfire. I can fix it."

"No, Oliver. We must leave. Now. There'll be a tracker on Solomon's car."

"Shut up. I'm telling you I'm fixing this."

Clumsy, hands shaking, he turns the gun, fiddles some more. "Kitchen knife," he says, and wrenches open a drawer. He drops the gun on the floor, retrieves and bangs it on the kitchen sideboard. His face is contorted.

"C'mon. Please," Gwen says.

Troup's surprise at my revelation is over. He is hunched, chin on his chest, weak in defeat.

"For fuck's sake," Collinge says. "Give up the whining. Will you? I'm getting there." He opens the bolt. "Done."

He returns with a rictus smile. "Open up, brown boy."

Collinge forces the barrel into my mouth again. "You should be a master at this," he says and slides the barrel back and forth three times. Gwen begs him to stop.

Collinge pulls the trigger. Nothing.

"What the fuck?" he says. He frowns, lifts the gun to his face, seems to study it.

A tremor vibrates under my feet and up the seat of my chair, but it's not fear. I no longer feel pain in my mouth or aches in my body. Perhaps it's no longer carrying the burden of secrecy. Perhaps it's the realization I won't benefit from any more misfires. I don't want to die, not like this, but I will die with dignity. The tremor intensifies. Troup shows no sign of recognizing anything. Collinge rocks from one foot to the other in apparent concentration.

A roar comes with the force of a 747 jet, all four engines on full power. So close, breath-sucking, instant terror signals to the brain. The floor moves up and down, rolls from side to side, and throws Gwen for a heavy fall. I spread my legs for stability, my groin strains in the effort but I can't stop from toppling to my right side. On my way down, the gun explodes over the roar of the quake, a spray of something warm hits my face. Collinge collapses nearby, and I realize it's his blood. Gwen screams.

I twist to see Troup. He is on the ground, still tied, but he half-smiles at me, perhaps hoping the quake that killed Collinge has saved him. A cabinet empties glassware into the kitchenette and cheap framed prints crash to the heavy oak table, which slides toward Troup's chair. It knocks him sideways about ninety degrees. Plaster falls from the ceiling in white sheets and covers my legs. I'm powerless to protect my head from anything heavy.

Still, the quake engines roar and Gwen continues to scream. Something causes my eyes to sting. Still tied, I bend forward, use a knee to wipe one eye. I yell, "Get under the table." She stops screaming, crawls, and makes it.

Curled up and on the floor, I'm tossed around like a skiff in a storm. I hear a creak before the tearing groan of timber. A beam crashes somewhere behind me. I twist again. A structural support beam lies across Troup's bloodied head. His eyes are open but I'm sure he's dead.

Gwen screams something, still incoherent.

The rolling slows, and I yell at her. "Gwen. Untie me, let's get outside." I repeat the words three times before she responds.

She fumbles with the ropes, sobbing an apology. At last, I'm free.

"Where's Eve's body?" I ask.

She runs from the house without a word. The ground settles and the Porsche's engine gives a throaty rev.

Then nothing—not a bird, no rustling of leaves, no movement of the wind.

Total silence.

I struggle to my feet wondering where to start the search.

In the distance I hear, "Please, help me. Please."

SATURDAY, 11 AUGUST 2012
11.32 HOURS

In hospital for overnight observations, my return home is deferred. Griff decides he is taking me to the dentist nearest my neighborhood. Although most of the swelling on the back of my head is gone, I feel its pressure when I lean back in the dentist's chair.

"There's bruising in the gums," she says. "You'll need three temporary crowns for those broken teeth, and I'll give you some amoxicillin to ward off any developing infection."

Griff's the only person in the waiting room when I come out. I give him my smile under repair. He whispers, "Much better, less cartoonish. But your house is a crime scene."

I say, "Our housekeeping is nowhere near that bad."

Outside, he says, "Your neighbor, Ken. The cops gave him the dog food in your house. He's looking after Pugwash until you return. He asked me who I was and what was going on?"

I touch the sore spot on my head. "What did you tell him?"

"I said I was a golfing friend and while you were at work, someone came in and took Eve away, which is why the police visited your place last night. I saw no sign of a break-in."

We sit inside Griff's car. I ask, "Did Ken notice anyone or anything suspicious?"

"Never mind about all that, Solly. How's Eve."

"No physical injuries. They checked her out and sent her to the mental hospital. Christ knows what sort of state she's going to be in."

"Might not be as bad as you think." He pats me on the leg, just as I did to Nick Jarvis, but I don't give Griff the concerned look Nick gave me. He says, "I'm sure the psychologists will try and use the fact she's been out of the house as something positive in Eve's recuperative therapy. By the way, one of the cops who attended Lake Pearson put your car back in your driveway."

"Thoughtful. Where are we going now?"

"My apartment. I made the Greek salad you like."

"I look forward to it. I've lived off adrenaline since yesterday morning."

In his apartment, Griff cooks lamb fillets, slices them, and puts the rested meat on the salad. He says, "For all our talk about communication, I don't want you to feel you must tell me what happened. I want us to enjoy our lunch. But I will say I was delighted to get a voicemail from you yesterday morning. And surprised."

"Hockley escorted me from the building before I left that message." I tell him why. "I'll be interviewed later this afternoon. They said if I'm up to it."

"Isn't it too soon? After what you've been through?"

"Thing is, we need to catch Gwen Sinclair."

"But if you're suspended… I thought you'd take a day or two to recover, emotionally as much as anything else. We could spend a bit more time together, prepare your veggie garden for spring planting."

"What about your cases?"

"My work takes second place to personal issues, or I can't be effective in the job. My docket's been dealt with by adjournments and reallocations to other judges."

"Well, I have a team to lead, but I can compromise."

Griff smiles and nods in agreement.

I add, "I'll do the equivalent of what the court has done for you to see that things are in order. I'll visit Eve, if they'll let me, and take what she'll need for a couple of days. I'll talk to people I need to talk to, and go and check out the house. If you'd like me to stay tonight, I will."

"Only if you want to," he says.

SUNDAY, 12 AUGUST 2012
08.48 HOURS

Yesterday, after lunch with Griff, I took essentials to a sedated Eve. Her bed is in a place once called Sunnyside Lunatic Asylum. Police colleagues have deferred my interview and Griff and I used the time to shop and cook meals I can freeze and later microwave. I decided the garden could wait. We took a long walk around the river and saw another two houses in the neighborhood demolished.

Today, as arranged, Blain lets me in at work and escorts me to our floor. My security card is still in Hockley's custody.

"I wish you'd take more time off, mate," he says, concern in his voice.

"Patched up and sent back to the front line. No malingering allowed."

"You believe the team can't cope without you?"

"Must finish that management course. I trust them to notice leadership in action. Something like that. Yes?" I pause for a second then give a small cough. "Listen, mate, I don't know how I've gotten through all..."

He holds up a hand. "No need to say anything."

"Yes. There is." I run a finger inside my collar. "You've given me more support than I… I'm trying to say, I owe you mate."

He nods and pats me on the back. "I'm sure I can come up with various ways for you to eke out the debt until you die. C'mon. The team wants to share some news with you."

On our floor, I'm greeted like a farmer throwing out feed. Even Vincent is smiling, perhaps a little naïve about his future in the police. "Appreciate the support," I say.

Tracey says, "Wendy Myles-Milburn will appear in court this afternoon, boss. Charges of murder, attempted murder, and obstructing justice."

"Superior work, Trace. Everyone. Someone take a coffee and cake order, my shout. Drinks tonight for those who can stay. I'll tell you the whole sorry saga."

I catch Blain's eye and point up. "Guess I gotta get this over."

"She's with Coman. Volunteered to stand down while the Prof Con artists start the witch hunt." He smiles. "Coman will be acting DCC."

I knock on Coman's door and enter. Hockley sits in the same place where she told me porkies about Jarvis and Dowling.

The big man radiates his presence, like he's been out on a long run. He exudes a new, rosy complexion and the creases in his suit are where they should be. A water bottle sits to the side of his desk. Hockley can't hide looking gaunt, or the deeper lines around puffy eyes.

"Good to see you back in one piece, Jonah," Coman says. "Congratulations on busting EI open. Terrific result."

I shoot Hockley a glance, her eyes dead in an expressionless face.

"Thanks, boss. But also, for getting Eve and me out and putting my car back in the driveway. Considerate."

"Vincent managed to do it without crashing. How's Eve doing?"

"Getting the right kind of therapy and meds. On the mend. Prognosis is positive."

"Perhaps the forced exit from the house might have a silver lining?"

"The therapists are working with that. But the PTSD will keep her agoraphobia company, so they'll be earning their money."

Hockley stands with my warrant and security card in her hand. She hands them to me. "These are yours. I'm sorry about the other day."

I think about asking which day of the many she's sorry for. "Tough situation when your direct report up is a greedy criminal, boss. You can't be expected to assume or distrust him on instinct."

"Thank you. That's gracious in the circumstances." She pinches the skin at her throat and her eyes flick around the room. "I need to leave the command to Mick and you. If you need any information, systems stuff, etcetera, call my PA. I've briefed her."

"Thanks, boss."

She leaves the office without glancing back and closes the door behind her.

Coman says, "She's on garden leave while Prof Con crawl over everything she's touched. Might be the police commissioner's sacrificial lamb now Troup's out of his reach."

"Blain tells me you went to the Deputy Commissioner after Hockley marched me out."

He gives a little shrug. "Given what you said, I needed to do something."

"You had my back, boss. Took quite a risk."

"Fuck, if we can't take care of our own, we're no use to anyone else."

"I won't forget your support."

Coman grins. "Well, doesn't stop me kicking your ass. Right?"

"No, boss."

"On the subject of change," he says, "I'm recommending your promotion to senior sergeant. When it comes through, I'll make you an acting inspector."

"Thanks, boss. But it's only ever been about Nick, and of course, EI's victims. And then Eve."

"Many affected by this clusterfuck. But with Dowling gone, the DCC on leave for an unknown duration, I'll need to spread the load. I'm not as young as I used to be."

Back at my desk, Blain fills me in on changes at EI. "Though nothing alters the fact the public swallow a daily shit sandwich as far as further delays in settling claims is concerned."

I say, "Explains why effigies of Sinclair are being burned in red zones."

He chuckles. "City's run out of straw. Media's reported that more than EI's new CEO, a bloke retired from one of their competitors. Coman knows him, same Rotary club. The guy started yesterday and Coman and I paid him a visit. He warned us we may never find out how much was stolen."

"What about the Putis accounts, following the money trail?"

"Years of work for some poor bastard. Sums routed all over the world. We'll get most of Troup's eighteen million dollars back—the tranche Collinge and Gwen paid into their secret accounts. Ditto Dowling, at four million."

I say, "I've been thinking about Nick's parents."

"Positive news there, too. Coman told the new CEO that Nick was instrumental in uncovering New Zealand's most sophisticated organized crime syndicate, but his parents continued to pay the price. He made a decision on their claim when we were with him."

"Real estate's too good for you, mate. You thought about social work?" I slap him on the shoulder. "I'll call on Alice later. Check how she's doing, tell her Nick was a top bloke."

"Oh, and before I forget," Blain says, "Yan pulled through. He didn't see who stabbed him. He's confirmed what Gwen said about the complaint against me."

"Some poetic justice all round."

He smiles. "A shitload of it. Pity the courts don't work like that."

"Trace seems okay?"

"She's told little Becky she won't be seeing her granddad again. But she's getting there." He frowns. "Sorry to raise this, but Coman told Trace about the video her father made. She wants to see it."

"He wants it too. Last I saw, Gwen had it. I'll have a word with Trace. I prefer his name is never uttered again." I walk toward Dowling's office and shake my head.

"What?" he says.

"I didn't sit in his office out of some sort of respect thing. Now I think it needs to be cleaned and exorcised. He was fastidious in keeping everything locked up. I can barely believe how stupid I've been."

FRIDAY, 22 FEBRUARY 2013
12.45 HOURS

On the second anniversary of the killer quake, Griff and I take the day off to play golf on the city's eastern links course. The surf sounds like the distant rumblings of many well-fed lions, and the salty air is a spiritual cleansing after Gwen's trial, which finished two days ago. Despite the forsaken look of the neighborhood, gutted by the rise of the sprawling suburban malls and finished off by the quakes, this is an agreeable place to be—especially on the beach, where we walked yesterday.

We both wear black lightweight Gortex jackets to battle a cool and stiff northeasterly. Trekking side by side up the low-cut fairway, he asks, "Are you disappointed the autopsy report for Fergus Dowling didn't go far enough to show an intent to kill?"

The question is a distraction to the game at hand. He could be up to his old tricks, like the unorthodox way he won the last match we played.

"No. We still charged her with impeding rescue, preventing Dowling from saving his own life. The voice analysis cleared her of planning to put Nick and me at the scene of Nick's death. In the absence of any forensics or a formal confession, we didn't have enough evidence to convict her of being involved in his murder or my attempted murder."

"And the frauds?"

"We're here for golf. Right?"

He feigns a teenage "whatever" shrug.

"She pleaded guilty to fraud. Because she was so effective in destroying records, we negotiated with Latham a single charge of one hundred million dollars representing all frauds."

The result of our tee shots reveals little distance between us, although Griff, closer to the pine trees, isn't as well placed for an approach to the par four green. These trees are in proximity to the meeting hall where Sinclair hosted his self-congratulatory party.

My second shot takes me to the edge of the eighteenth green, one fewer than Griff within three feet. I don't want to get too far ahead of myself, but lunch is here for the taking. We walk up the fairway together. "What's happening with Putis?" he asks.

"We're making an application to the court for seizure of all assets. We've got what went into Troup's and Dowling's accounts. Somehow, Tracey discovered funds laundered into a few swanky buildings in downtown Auckland. The entire company is predicated on the proceeds of crime. Premium payers, including my rugby club, might get some of their money returned."

Griff hits his third shot to leave a six-foot putt. If I chip close to the hole, I'll pressure him to make it. Griff asks, "What did you think of Gwen's seven-year prison sentence?"

"She was lucky. The death of her parents was life changing, the historic rape, both mitigated a longer term. And the lack of evidence of fraud was only overcome by her own admission."

He says, "I suspect Eve will be doing better now the trial's over?"

"She's more at ease in the house although still anxious when I leave. The latest prognosis is for a full recovery. No one can say how long."

At 12:51, the blast of a shotgun reverberates around the course. A chalkboard outside the club house warned us before we teed off. This was the exact time the quake began its terror that fateful day. We stand in silence, remembering the panic, the chaos, the desperate attempts of loved ones to make phone contact, the injured, the rescuers, the medics, the many selfless helpers, and heroes, the bereaved and the homeless—some in both states, the anguished, the depressed and the dead. I think about how the freakish force of nature delivered justice to a pitiful few who tried to profit from it, leaving so many others with an ongoing struggle for insurance justice.

Griff nods, business-like, and with a stern concentration, withdraws his putter and strides to the edge of the green. He waits for my third.

My chip leaves me a four-foot putt but Griff exudes calm. He's the better putter of the two of us and I don't help myself with a focus split between the game and the thousands of people still struggling to achieve their basic life needs. No doubt, Griff intends this.

It's been too long since he's cooked the post-golf lunch. Win or lose, I have a surprise for him. He fusses with his golf glove as he bends over his ball, faces the hole, and holds a putter up in front of him at ninety degrees to the manicured surface below. I don't understand what any golfer achieves by a technique more suited to discovering water.

When he settles himself for his putt, I say, "In."

He stands upright and frowns. "What?"

"In. The last time we played, you asked me, as I was about to hit my ball, whether I breathe in or out on my backswing. I never answered."

He resets himself over the ball then frowns in intense concentration. I wait for him to line up his putt. His normal practice is to sneak a look three times before making contact and sending the ball on its way.

When he's finishes his final peek at the hole, I say, "What about you?"

He cannons the face of the putter into the ball, and it races past the hole. "You prick," he says.

I laugh. "Happy for you to concede this hole, mate."

I win the match.

As we put away our clubs and golf shoes, I ask, "You're a man for home truths. Right?"

In an even tone, he says, "My advocacy to you on that front makes little difference."

"On the contrary, Judge. Those who live by the sword, often enough, die by the sword. A home truth worth knowing. Yes?"

He says, "I believe I'm cooking, Detective Senior Sergeant Solomon."

I nod at the clubhouse. "What say we pop in here. Not too public for you?"

He slips an arm around my shoulders and kisses me on the cheek.

"Steady on," I say. "Baby steps."

If you enjoyed this story, please tell others.
It's the best way to help authors have their work read.

To get a free short story about a serial killer in the Christchurch earthquakes, and to keep up to date with my writing news, adventures and new releases, check out and sign up for the McGinn Crime Ring newsletter at www.mcginncrime.com

ABOUT THE AUTHOR

During a lengthy career as a court registrar and manager in the New Zealand justice system, Mark McGinn had the privilege of assisting some of the finest lawyers and judges in action. Both that experience and his behavioral assessment work in staff recruitment and development have enriched and driven his writing of crime stories and thrillers. Mark is also a Story Grid Certified Editor specializing in Crime stories.

Made in the USA
Columbia, SC
23 August 2021

43217546R00231